THE MOTHE⸺

ᛏhe Epic Noɩ ⸻ᴢ

VOLUME FOUR

THE
FOOTSTEPS
OF FOREVER

1983 – 2005

THE MOTHERLAND SAGA

The Epic Novel of Turkey

VOLUME FOUR

THE
FOOTSTEPS
OF FOREVER
1983 – 2005

HUGO N. GERSTL

PANGÆA
PUBLISHING GROUP

THE FOOTSTEPS OF FOREVER: 1983 – 2005
Volume Four - The Motherland Saga
The Epic Novel of Turkey

Copyright © 2021 Hugo N. Gerstl
www.HugoGerstl.com
ISBN 978-1-950134-37-3
Pangæa Publishing Group
www.PangaeaPublishing.com

This book is a work of fiction. With the exception of certain anchors of fact, all of the characters in this book are the author's creation. As in all novels, much of what occurs in this book originated in the author's imagination. Any similarity to persons living or dead or to events claimed to have occurred are purely coincidental.

Editors: *Joyce Krieg, Paul Karrer, Katharine Ball, Donna Young. T.J. Moran, Dan Presser*

Cover image: *Istanbul twilight © Daniel Boiteau, Dreamstime.com*
Inside images: *Border © Antsvgdal, Dreamstime.com*

Cover design and typesetting by
DesignPeaks@gmail.com

For information contact:

PANGÆA PUBLISHING GROUP
25579 Carmel Knolls Drive
Carmel, CA 93923
Telephone: 831-624-3508/831-649-0668
Fax: 831-649-8007
Email: info@pangaeapublishing.com

To Dick & Claire Gorman
Herb & Sharon Chelner
Lisa & Richard Peaks
Metin & Nazan Gürgün
Joyce, Paul, Katharine, Donna, Terry, Dan

And always
FOR LORRAINE

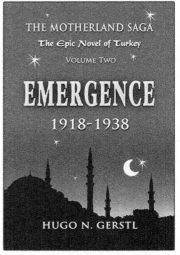
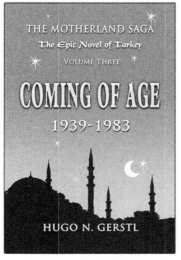
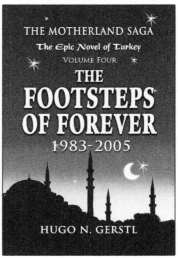

FOREWORD

This volume is the fourth book in **THE MOTHERLAND SAGA**. In **LEGACY**, the first volume, the reader is present as the Ottoman Empire continues to lose possession after possession and finally aligns itself with the German Central Powers against the Allies in World War I, irrevocably sounding the death knell for the five-hundred-year-old Islamic superpower. We start our journey in 1897, when **Turhan Türkoğlu**, born a lowly, illegitimate child in the southeastern part of his country, is four years old. Banished to Diyarbakir for his role in trying to save his first teacher, an Armenian, he swears he will get even with a corrupt system. He is rescued from a life of petty thievery by a worldly-wise butcher, and experiences his sexual awakening with the bored wife of an older merchant. Turhan's *inamorata* prevails upon **Ibrahim the Caravan Master**, Turhan's most important mentor, to take young Turhan with him on his journey across Anatolia to the Black Sea. When Ibrahim succumbs to a heart attack at the end of the journey, he surprisingly leaves Turhan with enough money for the boy to finish his schooling in Istanbul.

We meet **Abbas Hükümdar**, a severely abused child, saved from oblivion and poverty by a homosexual mentor. Abbas combines his ambiguous sexuality with a desire to cleanse his country of all foreign influences and a lust for power at any cost.

Halide Orhan, hunchbacked child of a Turkish-French misalliance, risks a harrowing journey across a Europe at war, determined to join her Turkish fiancé, Metin. They consummate their love on the evening she arrives at Gallipoli. After surviving Metin's death on the battlefield a day later and the collapse of the Ottoman Empire, Halide vows to honor Metin's memory by helping bring her adopted nation into the twentieth century.

In *EMERGENCE*, we meet Nadji Akdemir, descended from centuries-old military nobility, who rejects the defeatist Ottoman Empire and casts his lot with the new Nationalist Army as it fights the hated Greeks to preserve Turkey's independence — and its very existence. We experience the horror of war firsthand as Nadji learns that a dying Greek soldier, a husband, father, and teacher, whom he has killed to avoid being killed, was no less a human being than he. We suffer as Nadji suffers a near fatal, crippling injury in the hell that is war. Later, we celebrate his twin peaks of happiness as he starts his own rise up the military ladder and marries Ayşe, the stunningly beautiful daughter of a Turkish diplomat.

After Turkey has won its War of Independence, Mustafa Kemal, who adopts the name Kemal Atatürk and becomes the George Washington *and* Abraham Lincoln of his country, prevails upon the best and the brightest of the young, educated Turkish nation, including Turhan, Halide, and Nadji, to carry Turkey forward into the Twentieth Century. They are signally successful in their efforts during the period 1925-31.

In a preview of what is to come, Turhan is sent to Germany as Atatürk's eyes and ears, just as the Third Reich is beginning to show its terrible muscle. Banished from the Reich because of his independence of thought and expression, Turhan and his wife Sezer, an illiterate orphan who had been Halide's first village student, return to Turkey, where Turhan resumes his position as Turkey's most powerful radio personality and journalist, and Sezer resumes her work with Halide at the teachers' college Halide had founded in her father's memory. *EMERGENCE* concludes with the death of Turhan's wife and their expected first child in one of Turkey's periodic major earthquakes, which kills 40,000 people.

The third volume, *COMING OF AGE*, takes the reader through the Holocaust of World War II, Turhan's most profound heartbreak, and Turhan's rebirth through a trial which was to save the life of young **Kâzım Hükümdar**. We follow the lives and fortunes of Turhan, Halide, and Nadji through the Korean Conflict, the political upheavals of democratic Turkey, and through their monumental tragedies and triumphs, to the last quarter of the Twentieth Century. As *COMING*

OF AGE concludes, Turhan is, at 86, the last survivor of the three giants who populated the first three books in the series.

Now it is time for the torch to be passed once again. Of the four main characters in the earlier works, only two, Nadji Akdemir, and Abbas Hükümdar, have left progeny: Kâzim Hükümdar, who escaped his father's villainy to become a highly respected Judge, and brothers Omer and Yavuz Akdemir, who are proudly carrying on their family tradition, one an Air Force officer, the other an Army officer, as the story begins in 1983. Abdullah Heper, *Isharet's* "young" publisher, is soon to retire, and the last of the giants, Turhan Türkoğlu, is in his 87th year.

Originally, **THE MOTHERLAND SAGA** ended in 1983, and what came thereafter was a brief epilogue. However, the past thirty-eight years have witnessed unimaginable changes in the fabric of the people, the culture, and the politics of Turkey. The emerging history of this great and troubled land compelled the writing of this fourth volume, **THE FOOTSTEPS OF FOREVER.**

From 2005 to 2020, the events in Turkey have witnessed a sea change in the fortunes of this tortured land: a cataclysmic turn from the EU toward the East; a shift from a strategic alliance with Israel to enmity with the Jewish state; the emergence of a dictatorial one-man oligarchy, the likes of which have not been seen since the absolutist days of the Sultans; the demise of freedom of speech and freedom of the press; the destruction and virtual dismemberment of the military, which controlled Turkish democracy for nearly half a century; and what appears to be a complete reversal in Turkey's international alliances and its worldview. That part of the saga has yet to be written.

Finally, while it might be helpful to the reader to read **LEGACY,** **EMERGENCE,** and **COMING OF AGE** first, it is not really necessary, for you are traveling on a time train through the Twentieth and into the Twenty-First Century, and if you choose to get on the train in 1897 or today, your ultimate destination will be the same.

May you — and may Turkey — be blessed.

CHARACTERS
(IN ORDER OF APPEARANCE)

Lyuba Rabinovitz Kolchuk: Young Russian Jewess (22). She and her fiancé, Sergei Vonets, finally managed to secure exit visas from the Workers' Paradise, to go to Israel. Sergei leaves first. They plan to marry immediately when both reunite. Lyuba, who is pregnant with his child, learns that Sergei has been killed in a bus explosion orchestrated by Palestinian terrorists. Shortly after she arrives in Israel and gives birth to a son, the baby, **Yossi Vonets**, is kidnapped by Palestinians and secreted in Jabalia Palestinian refugee camp. She is a **major secondary character** in this novel.

Aviva Kohn (subsequently Aviva Baumueller): 23-year-old Israeli woman, the granddaughter of Zahavah ("Zari") ben David Kohn Barak.who was born in Turkey in 1900. greets Lyuba when the young Russian gets off the plane from the Soviet Union. **The primary female protagonist of this novel**.

Edwin "Jake" Baumueller IV: 29, wealthy, unattached scion of the New York *World* family, the grandson of Ed Baumueller II, who was an important character in *Emergence* and *Coming of Age*. Jake is **the primary male protagonist of this novel**.

Edwin "Ed" Baumueller, Jr.: Jake's 83-year-old grandfather and mentor, an important, positive influence on Jake.

Abdullah Heper: 65, soon-to-be retiring publisher and son of the founder of *Isharet*, the newspaper that gave Turhan his start just after World War I. Turhan became – and remained – *Isharet's* star for more than 65 years.

Turhan Türkoğlu: 86, the central character in *Legacy, Emergence,* and *Coming of Age.*

Sara Barak: 36, daughter of Zahavah and her second husband. Sara, **Aviva's aunt,** is an Israeli Lieutenant Colonel attached to the Turkish Air Force. She is a **major character in this novel**, the lover and subsequently the wife of Turkish Lieutenant Colonel **Omer Akdemir**, the oldest son of **General Nadji Akdemir**, one of the three major protagonists of *Emergence,* and *Coming of Age.*

Omer Akdemir: 37, Turkish Air Force Lieutenant Colonel. A **major character.**

Yavuz Akdemir: 35, Turkish Army Lieutenant Colonel. Younger son of General Nadji Akdemir and younger brother of Omer Akdemir. **A major character**.

Muren Kolchuk Yildiz: 18, Kurdish. He destroys a Turkish Air Force fighter jet, killing the pilot. His family is killed in a Turkish reprisal action. He is spirited away to Istanbul, where his momentary infatuation with **Aviva** will change his life. **A major character.**

Abdullah Öcalan: A real person, known as "Apo." Kurdish political leader, still active.

Abu Ammar (Yasser Arafat): A real person, Palestinian leader, now deceased.

Ajda Pekkan: A real person. Now 74 and still actively performing, she is Turkey's Barbra Streisand, an international superstar whose career began in the early 1960s. Despite her age, the "Diva" maintains her incredible beauty, even to this day. At the time we meet her, she is 37. Jake Baumueller is dazzled and smitten by her.

Melek Heper: Abdullah Heper's son and successor as editor-in-chief of *Isharet.*

Yitzhak Shamir: A real person. Prime Minister of Israel, 1983-84 and 1986-1992.

Zahavah Kohn Barak: 82, **Sara's** mother, **Aviva's** grandmother, and the *grand dame* of the family. An important secondary character in the first half of this novel.

John Hayden: 21-year-old U.S. Army private accused of a capital crime against the Turkish Republic while serving at the American radar station in Sinop. Northern Turkey.

Kâzim Hükümdar: Retired Justice of the Turkish Supreme Court, whose life was saved by Zahavah and Turhan in the 1940s and who later paid Turhan back in kind. A major character in both *Coming of Age* and this novel as well.

Avshalom bar Leoni: Israeli Intelligence agent masquerading as **Abu Moussa**, a Palestinian freedom fighter.

Şenol Demiroz: Planning Director for the Turkish Radio-Television Authority. A seminal figure in developing Aviva's transition from newspaper reporter to television personality.

Erol Gürgün: Manager of a small local TV station in Aksaray, Turkey – "in the middle of nowhere" – and Aviva's boss in her first job as a television personality.

Refik Arslan: (born Reuven Levi in Bulgaria). Turkey's most popular male television news anchor. When TRT feels it's time to try Aviva on a major nationwide TV station, she is paired with Arslan as his co-anchor.

Marco, Count Napolitano: An Italian count who's been disowned by his family. Attempts unsuccessfully to seduce Aviva, then exacts severe revenge. **Major antagonist.**

Lisa Lumet Erdbacher: Jake Baumuelle's fiancée, with whom he breaks up when he realizes that Aviva has always been the one he truly wants to marry. Lisa subsequently becomes Count Marco Napolitano's associate and second-in-command.

Detective (later retired Captain) Ahmet Mütlü: Investigates arson fire which destroyed Aviva's apartment and which he suspects was caused by Count Napolitano. He will assume a major secondary role later in this novel.

Hüsseyin Ovacık: Aviva's pilot flying over Mount Ararat for an international TV show. He suffers a fatal heart attack while they are flying near the fabled mountain.

Gençler Süyü: Aviva's cameraman who, along with Aviva and Jake, survives the crash of the aircraft.

Arov Nikssarian: An Armenian doctor.

Nadya Vartunian: His niece.

Narek Artakian: An Armenian Interior Ministry officer.

Frank O'Neil: An officer at the American consulate, Yerevan, Armenia.

Rosa Dudayev: A Georgian housekeeper at Itum-Shale revolutionary base, Chechnya and friend of Nadya Vartunian.

Terrance Moran: American burn surgeon flown to Ankara by the New York *World* to treat Jake Baumueller.

Richard Gorman: A junior diplomat at the American Embassy, Ankara, Turkey.

Colleen Miller: Pilot on the American "egg flight," Ankara-Israel-Armenia.

Simcha Bar Ilan: An operative from the Israeli consulate in Tbilisi, Georgian SSR.

Gyorgiy Raskov: A Georgian working at Itum-Shale camp as a guard, in love with Rosa.

Kari Akdemir: Yavuz Akdemir's daughter and headstrong eldest child, who is as beautiful as her grandmother Ayşe, a major character in *Emergence* and *Coming of Age*.

Kemal Araslı: a young political science professor, four years Kari Akdemir's senior and Kari's love interest.

Recep Tayyip Erdoğan: A real person. Mayor of Istanbul and Islamist politician who is destined to become the strongest and most influential political leader since Atatürk.

Nessim Akdemir: Yavuz Akdemir's second child and eldest son, an engineer who will be involved in a tragic star-crossed love affair with Talia Kalkan.

Gyula Ferenc: A Hungarian engineer working on the Atatürk Dam Project with Nessim. He befriends Nessim and tries to warn him about the relationship with Talia Kalkan.

Talia Kalkan: Daughter of Kurdish leader, deemed a terrorist organization by Turkey.

Arusha Kalkan: A Kurdish separatist leader, Talia Kalkan's father.

Hüseyin Kalkan: Talia's brother, who will act as mediator on Talia's behalf.

Semra Heper Osman: One of Abdullah Heper's two daughters and Melek Heper's two sisters. With Melek's sudden death, she owns a major stake (12½%) in *Isharet Communications*.

Lâle Heper Kemer, Semra's sister, who also owns 12 ½ share of *Isharet Communications*.

Ali Karaca: The Melek family's lawyer.

Edwin Baumueller V ("Eddie"): 13-year old son of Jacob and Aviva.

Deborah Baumueller ("Debbie"): 9 year-old daughter of Jacob and Aviva.

Yossi Vontz Kolchuk: Lyuba's son, now 20 and on active duty with the Israel Defense Forces.

Amir: 20, a Palestinian soldier.

Turkey

PART EIGHT:
THE CHANGING
OF THE GUARD
1983–1990

1

The El Al 747 lurched once as it hit clear air turbulence, then settled into the landing pattern as it approached Lod Airport. Lyuba Rabinovitz felt a rebellious kick from inside her as the plane's trajectory flattened out. She'd experienced nausea since the Israeli craft had taken off from Shermetyevo, Moscow's airport, several hours earlier, but she'd dealt with worse things in her twenty-two years.

The throng of Russians, dour and long-suffering émigrés, had believed it was just one more ghastly trick played by an angry Soviet god. They'd felt certain they'd get as far as the exit gate before an army of bureaucrats descended on them once again, politely but firmly telling them that this paper was not in order, that that exit visa didn't have the required number of stamps, that this document had been signed by an official who was no longer authorized. They were sure that the huge American-built plane with its bright blue-and-white color scheme and the oversized Star of David was another cruel hoax — undoubtedly like the Potemkin villages of eighty years ago. That the aircraft was nothing more than an intricately-constructed piece of aluminum put up for show.

But the bureaucrats hadn't descended. Three hundred Russian Jews had boarded the plane — it was a *real* plane after all — and now, after it had left Soviet airspace, crossed the Black Sea, and flown over the sere hills and steppes of the Turkish countryside, it had started descending. As the large jetliner left the southeastern tip of Cyprus behind, pandemonium erupted in the plane. The Russian Jews were coming to their new home, a place where Jews, *all* Jews, were welcomed with open hearts. *Eretz Israel.*

Lyuba Rabinovitz huddled miserably in her window seat, into the shell she'd erected to mask her fear and sadness. She and Sergei Vonets had been lovers in Leningrad, where he'd been a junior engineer and she'd been a student of foreign languages at the university. They'd hesitated to get married for fear it would interfere with their departure from the Soviet Socialist workers' paradise. So, it had been arranged that he'd leave for Israel first and she would follow as soon as she could. That had been six months ago. They'd known before he left that she was carrying his child. They'd be reunited in *Eretz Israel* in time to be married before the child was born, and it would truly be a rebirth for them.

For the first three months after he landed, Sergei had written her every week. The mail delivery being what it was in the Soviet Union, it would take several weeks for letters to arrive from Israel. Often letters written weeks apart had arrived at the same time. As Lyuba ticked off the days of the calendar, she knew it would only be a matter of time before she joined her man.

In July 1983, two months ago, her own exit visa had finally arrived. She'd immediately dispatched a celebratory letter to Sergei, who had secured a position as a hydrological engineer in Ashdod, Israel's southernmost city on the Mediterranean Coast. He'd written her saying he'd found an affordable apartment near the sea, twice as large as their place in Leningrad, and it would be perfect for the three of them.

A month passed without word from Sergei. This was so unlike him. If he had such a fine job and was starting his ascent up Israel's societal ladder, surely he would have telegraphed or even telephoned the university. Failing that, he would have contacted mutual relatives or acquaintances, if for no other reason than to tell her how excited he was. Maybe he was planning to surprise her by returning to the Soviet Union to gather her in his arms and fly with her to Israel.

The bitter, ugly truth had surfaced three weeks ago. Sergei had been one of twenty persons on an *Eged* bus in Ashdod when a young Palestinian suicide bomber had boarded it. A bomb had been secreted under his shirt. There had been no survivors.

Now Lyuba was descending to a future that was ambiguous at best. But even if Sergei was gone, there would be one to take his place, a part of him that, God willing, would carry Sergei's heritage into the time to come.

The woman's keening wail could be heard from one end of the huge refugee camp to the other. They had come to the camp several weeks ago, the armed ones, and they'd told her and her husband they would have to select one of her sons to sacrifice for the cause of Allah. She was forty years old. She scarcely remembered when she'd not lived in a tiny, barely-furnished tent, one of ten thousand that stood side by side throughout the camp. A single toilet served every twenty "residential units." Cold water washing facilities served every fifty. She, her husband, three sons and one daughter occupied the tent.

They were given no choice. She knew this "suggestion" was an order. If she disobeyed, all of her children would be slaughtered in the night. It was scant comfort to her to know that after the boy — he was only sixteen — boarded the bus in that area of Palestine now occupied by the Zionist devils and the deed was done, the family would receive twenty-five thousand American dollars — more money than they could hope to earn in a lifetime. She remembered back to the time she had borne Abu Yassir Beira in her twenty-fourth year, how she'd given him suck, and how voracious an eater he'd been. Growing up, he'd always been the leader of his comrades, a bright, happy, friendly child, and they'd had plans for him. Plans that did not include an early death.

Life was Allah's Will, but Allah was not always good and Allah was not always great, and wasn't it amazing that the armed ones, who'd elected themselves as Allah's chosen, never sent one of their own to die for the Grace of Allah? They always came to the camps. It didn't matter whether you tried to stay out of their path when they came. They knew. They always knew. And yesterday it had been Yassir's turn.

Lyuba was one of the last to disembark. The immigrants, most of whom wore clothing that might have been stylish a decade ago, were searched, poked, and prodded as vigorously and viciously as though they were enemy aliens. Security guards meticulously searched their pitifully small cardboard suitcases, for concealed weapons, contraband, or any other suspicious contents. Lyuba, who carried nothing except a couple of cheap dresses and three changes of underwear, was unconcerned. Her only valuables were on her person — a gold ring Sergei had given her a year ago, and her unborn child.

After the search, Lyuba dutifully followed the nearest cluster of her compatriots through a hall at the far end of the arrivals area to an adjacent building with a discreet sign bearing the words "Welcome Center" in many languages, one of which was Russian. Unlike the inspectors at airport customs, the hosts and hostesses, some thirty men and women of various ages, who greeted the new arrivals as they entered a softly-lit room, were warm and welcoming. Lyuba gratefully accepted a cup of hot, steaming tea from one of several samovars and plucked some sweet cookies from a nearby platter.

"*Shalom.* You must be Lyuba bat Jochanan," a female voice said in unaccented Russian. "I was so sorry to learn that your Sergei perished so needlessly."

Lyuba turned toward the voice and found herself looking into the frank, friendly, hazel-colored eyes of a young woman her own age. "I'm sorry, I don't know you," was the only thing she could think of to say.

"I wouldn't expect you to. I'm Aviva Kohn. A group of us from Tel Aviv University have spent the last six months welcoming Russian Jews to *Eretz Israel.* I recently graduated from journalism school."

"How did you know —?"

"It's our job to learn something about each new arrival. I met your Sergei when he first arrived. He told me it would only be a matter of months 'til you joined him. I spent a week with him while he was at the resettlement center, then he went south to Ashdod. I didn't hear from him again until …"

Lyuba started weeping, but she did not cry very long, since she'd spent the last month doing just that. Aviva reached over and held Lyuba's hand. "We're used to death and we're used to beginning again," Aviva said. "That's been the lot of our people for the past fifty years," she said.

"Do you think it's safe to get on the buses?" Lyuba asked, pointing at the first of the transports and remembering what had happed to Sergei.

"These buses, yes," Aviva said. "They've been completely searched by airport security. I'll ride on the bus with you if it makes you feel safer."

The two young women sat side by side toward the rear of the bus. "My grandmother actually came from Sinop, Turkey," Aviva said. "She was a famous lawyer there. She's eighty-two now and still as sharp as can be. A couple of years after my grandfather died of cancer, she met Aharon Barak, who was an early settler here. Grandma says they had a fairy-tale romance, from the day they met until he died eight years ago. He was with the underground and ferried more than a thousand Jews from Turkey to Israel. Listening to her talk, you'd think she was the kind of heroine you read about in novels. She said Aharon won out over two other would-be suitors, a famous Turkish journalist and a high-ranking military man."

Lyuba felt herself warming to this *sabra* who was so bright, so *alive*. "It wasn't easy being a Jew in the Soviet Union," she said. "It's interesting you should mention Turkey. My grandfather, Aleksandr Mishkin, was a border official in Batum, near the Turkish border. I heard he helped a Turkish colonel get his sons back when they'd been kidnapped by a turncoat Turkish minister, a fellow named Hükümdar. Grandfather rose quite high in the diplomatic corps before he died. Perhaps my being his relative helped me get out of the U.S.S.R. so many years later. Aviva, do you have a … husband or a special fellow or anything like that?" Lyuba asked, blushing.

"Not really. I'm not a virgin if that's what you're getting at, but there's no one special in my life right now."

"How do you think the Israelis will react to my … my condition … I mean, not being married and all …"

"We Israelis accept any Jew with happiness. We live on the edge of death every day, so we're not nearly as hypocritical about sex as many more 'advanced' countries. We feel that every child brings a blessing to the world."

"The last thing on my mind is another man, but —"

"Lyuba, half the men in Israel are in the army, and a large percentage of them die young. You've got lovely blonde hair and beautiful features. If we put some makeup on you, let your hair hang freely, and dress you in Israeli-style clothes, you'll have to beat the men off with a stick.

You'll be at the resettlement center for a week. Would you feel offended if I asked my grandma if you could stay with her for a little while?"

"Of course not, but —?"

"You'll see, you'll love her as much as I do."

❀❀❀

When Lyuba's time came, Aviva accompanied her to a small hospital outside Tel Aviv. Sergei Yosef Vonets, whom Lyuba immediately called Yossi, burst his way into the world with a hale and healthy set of lungs, a thatch of blond hair, and his father's deep blue eyes. On the third day after Yossi's birth, after Lyuba had nursed the baby, she fell into the deepest sleep she'd enjoyed in several months. Baby Yossi was taken to the nursery where the night nurse, a middle-aged Palestinian woman, took care of the fifteen newborns.

Just after midnight, the nurse heard a scratching sound coming from outside the nursery. As she opened the door to investigate, a shrouded figure suddenly lunged forward, stabbing her to death. Five of the infants, all boys, were taken from the nursery that night by the murderer and his three accomplices. One of them was Sergei Yosef Vonets.

❀❀❀

"Woman, cease your weeping," the armed man said. "I have just come from the rancid shit-town the Jews call Tel Aviv. Allah has replaced the son you lost." The Palestinian woman cowered before the man and renewed her wails. Her action was greeted by a sharp slap across her face. "I said shut up, you stupid cow. Allah has provided you with a son to replace your Yassir."

The Palestinian woman could hardly believe her eyes. This boy was a newborn who looked nothing like her Yassir, but he didn't look like an Israeli either. He had tufts of yellow hair and large blue eyes. He seemed so alert, so strong. Maybe he truly was her Yassir come back to life in another incarnation. Of course, she would have to find a wet nurse, but that would be easy, for the camp had several hundred young women available to fulfill that purpose.

Allah had taken a precious life, but through this new child, He had just shown He could give life back as well. "Allah is good and Allah is great and there is none like Allah, His Name be praised in heaven and on earth," she cried. "I will raise him as my own, my Yassir Beir and his name will be praised and feared throughout Palestine."

2

At five-foot-ten, Edwin J. Baumueller IV, "Jake" to his family and close friends, was not classically handsome. He had brown hair that had never lost its cowlick, and a "Jewish" nose, courtesy of his forebears. He kept himself in reasonably good physical and mental shape by regularly exercising both his body and his mind. He was the latest presumptive heir to the New York *World*, which his great grandfather had started over a hundred years earlier.

Disdaining the Orthodox *Ashkenazic* Jewish custom of not naming a child after a living relative, Avigdor Müller, the first in the line, had emigrated from Hamburg during the first large-scale wave of German Jews coming to America. Renaming himself Edwin Baumueller, he had helped found a Reform congregation and started a small neighborhood newspaper in the mid-nineteenth century. Now Temple Emanu-El and the New York *World* were among the largest and most prominent institutions in the United States.

Jake Baumueller was every Jewish mother's dream of a *khop,* a "catch," but so far Jake reveled in the freedom his bachelorhood gave him.

A decade ago, during his first year at Yale, he'd become seriously interested in the business aspect of pop-rock music, when a nineteen-year-old coed had inducted him into the joyous world of lovemaking to the accompaniment of Roberta Flack's "Killing Me Softy With His Song," and Stevie Wonder's "You Are the Sunshine of My Life."

23

Although the relationship had cooled after a few months, Jake's passion for the pop-rock scene had not. Between law school and Skull and Bones, he'd learned enough guitar to be a credible sideman. Six years earlier he'd bankrolled a struggling vocal group. When, a year later, they'd hit the charts and followed that with a smaller hit, he'd raked in some additional "play money," and been bitten still harder by the entertainment bug.

He wasn't the first publishing house scion to hit it big in pop music. Carly Simon had done the same thing a few years earlier. This past year had been a roller coaster ride. He'd wanted to put all of his winnings — half a million dollars from the record and the trust fund income he hadn't spent — into a new, untested venture. Jake had gotten a tremendous amount of emotional support from his favorite relative, his eighty-three-year-old grandfather, Edwin Baumueller, Jr., the *World's* publisher emeritus, and, in Jake's mind, his greatest mentor.

"Let me get this straight," the elder Baumueller had said. "You want to invest in something to do with cable television?"

"It's a form of cable TV, Pop-Pop," Jake had said, reverting to his nickname for his grandfather. "It's a new station that makes videos to go with songs. Some of the most *avant garde* and outrageous videos I've ever seen, but if it catches on …?"

"A new way of communicating, eh?"

"I guess."

"You think it's the wave of the future?"

"I do."

"Sounds like some people I once knew a long time ago, who were willing to mess with the old ways in the belief they could accomplish the impossible. How much are you thinking of investing?"

"Half a mil."

The old man whistled. "That could put quite a dent in your fortune."

"*My* fortune," Jake said. "Money I earned from the music business and money I didn't spend."

"Good point. I trust you've given in a lot of thought?"

"I have."

"Very well. On the off-chance you may be right, how would you feel if I matched your investment dollar for dollar?"

"You'd do that for me, Pop-Pop?"

"Hell, no!" the old man said. "For *me*. It's just that when a new company's getting started, you don't want to see everything collapse because it's undercapitalized. This way, both of us can hedge our bets."

September 18, 1983 was a beautiful, balmy day. The stifling heat and humidity of New York City's summer had given way to cooling breezes, with just enough light rain in the early morning hours to make Jake's Sunday morning habit a pleasure. For the past several months, Jake had walked every Sunday, regardless of the weather, from the New York *World* building on West 3rd Street between Seventh and Eighth Avenue, down to Battery Park at the southern tip of Manhattan. It was far less taxing than sweating in the health club three times a week, and, since he varied the route from time to time, it gave him plenty of opportunity to sweep the week's cobwebs from his mind.

He took the stairs two-at-a-time to the *World's* third floor gymnasium, grabbed a hot shower, donned his sweats, and was on the way out the door when he saw his grandfather at the far corner of the gym, steadily working the *World's* brand new Stairmaster, which had arrived only a week before. "Pop-pop? What the hell is an old geezer like you doing at the gym at nine on a Sunday morning?"

"I'll thank you to mind your manners and your breeding. Hopefully, I'll live to spend the five million I've made thanks to your harebrained music video investment idea and my soft-headed decision to ride that train with you."

"I guess it wasn't such a bad idea, after all," Jake said, grinning and handing his grandfather a towel. "I couldn't help but notice your second remark about breeding, Pop-Pop. Has mom gotten to you, too?"

"Hardly, but if you keep being a bachelor much longer, the tabloids will start wondering if you're really a *gay* bachelor."

"Not hardly," Jake said, laughing. "They've got me paired up with everyone from Cindy Crawford to Leona Helmsley. I keep my private life private, but I've got plenty on my plate."

"Including …?"

"Including."

"Want some company on your Sunday morning quarter-marathon?"

"Sure."

They crossed Fifth Avenue and headed west toward Broadway. When they reached the bottom of Times Square, they turned south. A few coffee shops were open, but most of New York City was closed. "Fifty cents for your thoughts," Grandpa Ed said as they passed 36th Street.

"Remember earlier this year when you told me you once knew some people in a faraway place, who were willing to mess with the old ways and believed they could accomplish the impossible?"

"I do. The last of them's still kicking at eighty-six." The old man's expression clouded over, as if he were in another world, another time. "I first met Turhan Türkoğlu more than fifty years ago, before the War. Talk about time flying."

"The guy whose picture's in your office?"

"The same," Ed Baumueller II said. "Hey, I just got an idea. How'd you like to do a stint at the *World's* Istanbul bureau for a couple of months?"

"To tell you the truth, Pop-Pop, Turkey's never been on my short list."

"You might want to put it there," Ed Junior said. "Helluva place. Mount Ararat, the Tigris and Euphrates Rivers, Istanbul, and a whole lot more. It's the only Muslim country in the world that has a strategic alliance with Israel."

"Turkey has an alliance with Israel?" Jake said. "Doesn't that piss off the other Arab countries?"

"Shows how much you know, Yale man," grandpa said. "Turkey's not an Arab country. The Turks look down on the Arabs as raghead goatherders and the Arabs look down on the Turks as stupid Mongols. No love lost there."

"Was your friend Turhan one of those people who believed he could accomplish the impossible?"

"He was and he did. Over and over and over again, from before Hitler's rise until most recently about three years ago. You know, Jake, I haven't seen Turhan Türkoğlu for almost four years. Who knows how long we've got left? Want to make an old guy very happy? Why don't the two of us fly over to Istanbul for a week or two? It'll give you a chance to see if Turkey's all that boring, and it'll give me a chance to see my old friend."

"Sounds like a plan," the younger Baumueller said.

NOVEMBER 1983
ISTANBUL, TURKEY

"Ed Baumueller's coming to Istanbul?" Abdullah Heper, now in his early sixties, seemed genuinely delighted at the prospect. Turhan Türkoğlu who, less than two months before, had been elected to the Turkish Hall of Immortals, sat sipping çay, Turkish tea, served in a tiny tulip glass, as he and Heper overlooked the Bosphorus. "How does it feel to be one of Turkey's only living 'immortals' with your bust housed in the National Museum and a huge pension each year until you croak?"

"Don't try to get me to say I appreciated the 'government's' efforts," Turhan grumbled. "But when I saw that Halide and Nadji had been elected — I don't think Ayşe knew he was even on the list — I figured that since the three of us started out together, we might as well remain together." He turned to the waiter who'd approached them. "Two more glasses of tea, please, and two plates of baklava." The waiter turned to fetch their order.

"That's what I've always loved best about you, your persnickety old curmudgeon. Always looking on the bright side of things. You know, a simple 'Fine, thank you,' would have been enough of an answer for me."

"Easy for you to say, my young friend. Sixty-five is it?"

"Not 'til December, but the trustees at *Isharet* have made it known they'd as soon have me become 'publisher emeritus' with a huge retirement package, just as I politely 'canned' you sixteen years ago."

"Trustees, my arse," Turhan growled. "You're Chairman of the Board, you own the paper, you could fire every one of the trustees, and you're trying to lay the blame for your retirement on them." Turhan pulled out a pack of *Yeni Harmans*, the cheap, smelly Turkish cigarettes he'd favored for more than seventy years, and offered one to his friend. Heper declined, and none too politely at that.

"You think they'll give you the same big party they gave me?" Turhan continued. "Demirel and Ecevit are still around, Allah-knows-how. So there's at least two who'll come to the gala, and if I'm still around …"

"You'll be around, my friend," Heper replied, "but you aren't even going to be invited unless you leave those shitty-smelling cigarettes at home. By the way, even though I'm willing to pay for the munificent repast we've just had, I find myself without money to leave a tip."

Turhan raised his eyes heavenward. "Why you cheap-ass young skinflint," he said. "You've probably got more money than Allah himself. But Turhan Türkoğlu, even at his advanced age, won't be supported by anyone." The ancient journalist reached into his pocket and extracted the smallest coin he could find. Slapping it ceremoniously into the publisher's hand, he said, "All right, Heper, don't ever say Turhan Türkoğlu didn't pay his way, even after you forced me to retire."

To Turhan's mild surprise, Abdullah Heper took the coin and wrote out a receipt.

"Received this first day of December, 1983 the sum of 100 TL
in full payment for Share Certificate Number 1 for
One (1) Share of Isharet Communications Common Stock.
s/Abdullah Heper, President."

"What's this?" Turhan asked. "Isn't it a little bit late to give me stock ownership rights in *Isharet*."

"Not really, old friend," Abdullah said. "I've decided to take the company public. We're issuing one hundred million shares, so I can't see where your one share would make any difference, but who knows? Someday it may be worth something. Besides, as the oldest living human being that had anything to do with the success of *Isharet*, isn't it only fitting that you have share certificate number one?" He handed Turhan a formally printed share certificate.

"Now, come on, you old arthritic. The three-block walk to *Isharet's* headquarters will do you good, and it'll give you a chance to fill me in on Ed Baumueller's upcoming visit."

As they left Taksim Square and headed down pedestrian-only Istiklal Caddesi, the heart of European Istanbul, their ears were assaulted by the cacophonous sound of Arabesque music, the shrill, modern "music of the common folk" that was now so popular in Turkey's largest metropolis.

"Ed's got to be close to your age," Heper remarked.

"A little younger and a lot wealthier," Turhan replied. "He told me he's bringing another Baumueller."

"His son?"

"Nope. His *grand*son, twenty-eight, never been to Turkey …"

They arrived at the *Isharet* building and took the lift up two floors to Heper's surprisingly spartan office. "You really think the generals will let Turkey have free elections?" Turhan asked, changing the subject.

"General Evren said the army was simply reacting to political anarchy and this was going to be a caretaker government only until democracy got back on its feet."

"Assuming they let the election take place, who do you pick to win?"

"Türgüt Özal's the best of the current bunch. Of course, there's the Welfare Party."

"Islamic extremists," Turhan muttered. "There's no way our military would let them hold office, but you know, I think the military might be making a long-term mistake by ignoring them. Ninety-eight out of every hundred Turks are villagers. They're the poorest and most reactionary element in the country."

"And the most fundamentally religious," Heper remarked.

"The very people the Welfare Party solicits," Turhan said. "The Party's banned for now. They'll make no inroads this year, but ten years from now it'll be 1993 and ten years after that who knows what the world will look like?" Turhan smiled sardonically and lit up another of his endless *Yeni Harman* cigarettes. "By that time, I'll be long in the ground, and if I'm not, I'll surely want to be there. How much influence do you think you'll have then?"

"About as much as I have now," the publisher grinned. "Not very much. Certainly not as much as the scantily-clad ladies who adorn the front pages of almost every daily in Turkey *including* Welfare's paper."

3

"Hey *Yarbay*, there's a familiar-looking Army officer in the outer office waiting to see you. Better not keep him waiting." Lieutenant Colonel Sara Barak, the Israeli intelligence officer assigned to Turkey's Second Tactical Air Force Headquarters, and who'd become Omer Akdemir's lover three months ago, came into his office bearing three cups of tea and an assortment of pastries. Sara was one year his junior, thirty-six. They were of equivalent rank in their respective services. Still, appearances had to be kept up, and they were circumspect in their romantic dealings.

This morning, Omer had become acutely aware that Sara's assignment to Turkey was half over. Five months from now she'd be back in Israel — not so far away in kilometers, but a world apart nonetheless. The realization had hit him just after she'd left his quarters in the early morning light. It was not a comforting thought. Still, it was hard to be unhappy in her presence. When she awoke, she opened her lovely brown eyes and her mouth almost simultaneously, invariably greeting the day with a smile. He was happier than he'd been since Cana had died four years before.

"*Three* cups of tea?"

"Well, I thought you might want to act like an officer *and* a gentleman," she said sassily. "As I said, the other *Yarbay* looks familiar and you might want to visit awhile."

"Looks familiar, eh?" Omer smiled.

"Well …" she said. "A little younger, maybe even a little handsomer …"

Omer very ungallantly folded his morning copy of *Isharet* and pretended to swat at her bottom. As he did so, his office door opened and he saw the *other* Lieutenant Colonel Akdemir, his younger brother.

"Yavuz!" he called out. "What in the world is my baby brother doing in this godforsaken hellhole?"

"Trying to make certain the senior surviving Colonel Akdemir doesn't embarrass a hundred years of military excellence," Yavuz said. "Or has it become the custom in the East to assault lovely allied officers? By the way, *Abi*," he grinned, using the Turkish slang for brother, "you can skip the introductions. Colonel Barak already made them. Are you aware that your, uh, relationship with the enticing Sara Barak might be somewhat incestuous?"

"What?" Omer was genuinely shocked. "What do you mean, Yavuz?"

"Many years ago, Uncle Turhan told me that before we were born, mom and dad were separated for awhile, and both dad and Turhan momentarily competed for the same woman, a Turkish lawyer named Zahavah Kohn, who'd been widowed. Unfortunately for both of the old guys, and *very* fortunately for us, because we wouldn't have been around had dad been successful, Zahavah had already fallen in love with an Israeli named Aharon Barak …"

"My parents," Sara finished the sentence. "My father died eight years ago, but *Ema*, my mother Zahavah, God bless her, is eighty-two and still as feisty as ever. She was forty-six when she had me."

"You never told me …?"

"I didn't think it was that important until this morning," Sara said. "Nor did I know that your brother knew about us, Omer."

"I wrote him …"

"Yavuz, what brings you to the great Southeast and the would-be capital of Kurdistan?"

"There've been reports of stepped-up activity among our separatist 'mountain Turks.' I don't mean the usual put-boulders-in-the-middle-of-the-road, stop travelers at midnight, and strip-them-down-to-nothing variety. I mean reports of arms shipments and serious terrorist activities."

"I'm not surprised," Sara said. "The Kurds have always looked at this area as the nation of Kurdistan, and to them Diyarbakir is Kurdistan's heart."

"That's why I've been sent here," Yavuz said. "The Kurds have organized a Kurdistan Workers' Party in defiance of our government, and Turkey believes that showing up with a few 'uniforms' will underscore the message that such activity is not allowed."

"Welcome to the Middle East," Omer said sardonically.

They sat around a low coffee table in Omer's office, drinking tea and enjoying pastries in comfortable silence, broken only when Omer asked his younger brother, "How long since you've been to Diyarbakir?"

"1960, when we came here with our parents," Yavuz responded. "Does that count?"

"Not really," Omer said. "When does the conference start?"

"Two days from now."

"That doesn't give you much time to sightsee, but you really don't need more than one day for the city. Sara, would you like to come along?"

"I'd love to, but I've got a full calendar today. You brothers probably have a lot of catching up to do, and I'd just be in the way. Maybe next time. I'll make your excuses for you at the staff meeting, Colonel," she said, addressing Omer. "You two have a good time."

❊❊❊

It took the brothers less than a day to see Diyarbakir, the ancient city on the banks of the Tigris River, but Yavuz was fascinated by the place. The city, surrounded by huge black basalt walls that had been built during Roman days and reconstructed during the Middle Ages, seemed a combination of medieval Europe and the Biblical Holy Land, filled with Turks, Kurds, Arabs, Armenians, and oil speculators and businessmen from a dozen assorted nations.

"Is Diyarbakir really that dangerous?" Yavuz asked.

"No one goes out after three in the afternoon. Except for Second TAF, the American radar station, and the oil boom several kilometers south of here, the area's economically depressed."

"Are you going to marry Sara?"

"That's what I like best about you, little brother. So diplomatic and circuitous."

"You carry the Akdemir tradition of stiff upper lip, hide-your-feelings, and silence very well."

"I've got a four-year-old son to think of, Yavuz."

"Yes? Halil's never known his mother and he's gone from one nanny to the next whenever you change assignments. Does Sara have any children?"

"No. She had a very short marriage when she was twenty, a year's relationship later, and nothing since."

"And she pays her own way?"

"That's one of many problems. She's been completely independent most of her life. She's Jewish to the core and a *Sabra*."

"With a Turkish mother."

"Well, there is that."

They rounded a corner and Yavuz exclaimed, "What in the devil is that? A minaret on stilts?"

Omer laughed. "That's just what it is. The Kasim Padishah Mosque's tower is built on four tiny pillars, each about six feet high. It's a tourist attraction, the four-legged minaret."

"At least it's different. I thought I'd never see anything except families washing carpets and drying fruits and vegetables, and sheep shit on the rooftops. How strictly does Sara practice her Judaism?"

"Hardly at all."

"So she's about as Jewish as you are Muslim."

"Just about."

"From the way you talk, you and Sara have spoken of many things besides military intelligence."

"We have."

"And?"

"Nothing definite."

"A little advice from a younger brother?"

"Go ahead."

"She's not going to be in Turkey forever. You're thirty-seven. She's thirty-six. You're not kids anymore. I trust you've slept together?"

Omer remained silent.

"That pretty well answers that question," Yavuz said. "If you truly feel what I think you do for one another, both of you are wasting a lot of time and I think it's pretty silly when you don't know how much time you has. At this rate, she'll be gone before either of you really have a chance to realize the happiness you could be enjoying every day of your lives."

"You make it sound so simple."

"And it can be, older brother. Wasn't it Uncle Turhan who said, 'Don't be afraid to dare the impossible, you just might achieve it?'"

✸✿✸

Muren Kolchuk would be eighteen next week, and if he succeeded, he would be inducted into the Kurdistan Peoples' Party. He'd dreamt of this night since he was twelve. For the past five years, he'd attended Young Patriots meetings. A year ago, they'd let him attend meetings of a different sort, gatherings where he learned there truly was only one way his proud, oppressed people could fulfill their God-given right to a land of their own.

The local branch of the PKK, the Kurdistan Workers' Party, was not an organized army. At most, it boasted three or four thousand members, and like the early Communist Party, on which it was fashioned, it functioned in small cells of two or three people whom you trusted without ever learning their names. Muren soon learned that the unit included not only Kurds, but also a few Russian advisers, some Arabs, and even, it was rumored, one or two members of Israel's legendary *Mossad*, although the latter did not make sense to Muren.

If he failed tonight … but it had never entered his mind that he *could* fail. That was simply not an option.

Eight months ago, he'd taken a menial job with the contractor who ran the commissary at Diyarbakir Air Base. Muren was a diligent worker who never shirked working extra hours. He made certain that he was always clean about his person and courteous to everyone. It soon became apparent to his supervisors that Muren Kolchuk was as dependable a young man as they'd ever employed, and he was given periodic raises of pay well ahead of his peers.

Evenings, he met secretly with PKK operatives and learned everything there was to know about the installation of plastique explosives.

That night, he remained on duty after the commissary had closed. He'd told his supervisor he needed to spend an extra hour inventorying non-perishable food items. He would work late out of loyalty to his employer, and it would not be necessary to pay him. After the supervisor left, Muren found himself a quiet place among sacks of rice in the warehouse, and slept for several hours. At two the next morning, he drove a small commissary truck into one of the maintenance hangars, where he met with a man of sixty.

"Is this the plane?" No names were exchanged.

"Yes."

An hour later, Muren asked, "Would you like to inspect it?"

"No. I'm sure they trained you very well," the older man said, closing the cowling.

"Are you sure no one suspects?"

"I'm certain. I've been a line mechanic for thirty years."

"What if the pilot inspects the aircraft?"

"If you've done your job right, he'll find nothing. The plastique looks like any of five thousand almost identical wires. The explosive is slaved to the altimeter. It will go off the moment the aircraft passes through eight thousand feet."

"Good," Muren said, noticing how clammy his hands felt. He drove the truck back to the warehouse, returned to the rice sacks, and fell asleep once again.

Four hours later, the pilot and his line crew performed a thorough preflight inspection of the American-built Lockheed F-104G Starfighter. Everything functioned normally. The pilot, a young Lieutenant of *Pars* Squadron, looked at his watch. Seven-thirty. A clear, cool, wonderful morning for a flight. He would take his supersonic interceptor up to twenty thousand feet, streak across the steppe to Erhac at the speed of sound, then return to Diyarbakir in time for an early lunch.

At quarter to eight, the silver bird trundled slowly down the taxiway, turned, and shot into the sky. Four minutes after takeoff, there was a sound like distant cannon as the aircraft exploded in an angry ball of orange and black smoke.

At a remote end of the Air Base, Muren Kolchuk, who'd awakened half an hour before, looked up as pieces of the wreckage drifted down. He smiled and clapped his hands together silently.

4

Turkish retaliation was swift and brutal. By the evening following the Starfighter's explosion, the Kurdish Peoples Liberation Coalition headquarters was a bombed-out memory. The six-foot deep crater that remained after the annihilation of the two-story wooden building was filled in with bleach and lime. Turkish police summarily shot, then decapitated, sixty leaders of the local Kurdish Party, including Muren's father and his older brother. The police jammed the severed heads of their victims atop poled spikes. The headless bodies were draped unceremoniously over a hastily-built series of wooden sawhorses, where myriad flies finished the job the Turks had started. The law enforcement officials took another fifty of the younger men into police headquarters, where they were tied and the bottoms of their feet were beaten viciously for hours. Muren Kolchuk was not one of them. By dawn of the following day, he'd been spirited off to Lebanon's Bekaa Valley, where he was introduced to a twenty-five-year-old Iraqi named Banr al Sidi, and to an older man who looked like a Turkish peasant, thirty-five-year-old Abdullah Öcalan, whom Muren's rescuers respectfully called *Apo* — Uncle.

Now, a week later, they were seated around a campfire. The mustachioed *Apo's* face was inscrutable. "The time is coming, my friends. The PKK will launch the armed struggle for a Kurdish state within three months. The evil Empire is becoming more desperate, as you've seen in the last few days."

"But *Apo*," Muren addressed the leader, "Our local party had four thousand members and they were crushed like a bug. How can we hope to compete with their numbers, their modern weapons?"

"Because we have a greater power on our side — the power to dream of freedom, the power to last several lifetimes if it comes to that, to insure a Kurdish nation, one allied with our International Socialist brothers in the Soviet Union, Cuba, and China. We Kurds may seem like few, but our allies swell that number to two *billion*. How can the puny Turkish Fascist state and the American cowboys," he spat the words out in disgust, "hope to stem the growing world tide?"

Muren was deeply moved by the master's words. Later that night, he approached Banr al Sidi. "Banr, how long have you been with *Apo*?"

"Nearly eight years, why?"

"You were the same age then that I am now."

"Yes. Trust me, Muren, the Apo speaks the absolute truth. I've seen him survive at least four assassination attempts by the Turkish overlords. He has as many lives as a cat. Each time he suffers a reversal, he comes back stronger."

"But thousands could die if he has his way."

"He expects that. Even if a hundred thousand people die in a single year, our movement cannot be stopped."

"You believe in him, then?"

"With my life."

They walked over to a nearby tent, where they helped themselves to hot tea and cold lamb left over from the evening meal. "Do you think there's room in his organization for me?"

"Absolutely. The Kurdish Peoples' Party is the largest Kurdish organization. We have fifty thousand members and another five million supporters throughout Kurdistan. If you remain close to the head of the PKK, you can only succeed. Öcalan is fiercely protective of those loyal to him, and they share his wealth and his glory. We're caught between Turkey and the Zionist State, but we have friends in the area as well."

The quiet darkness of the night was broken by four pairs of headlights as a series of American-built Jeeps pulled up to Öcalan's compound. Two blindfolded, shackled, uniformed men were roughly jerked from the rear door of one of the vehicles. Muren watched as they were frogmarched into Öcalan's tent. Less than ten minutes later, Banr al Sidi and Muren were summoned to the large tent.

When they stepped into the capacious Hereke-carpeted tent, they saw Öcalan standing next to a much shorter, pockmarked man who wore a *keffiyeh*, a shawl-like covering, and a brown military uniform. The Apo nodded at the young men.

"Banr, Muren," Öcalan addressed them. "I would like you to meet Kurdistan's great friend, Abu Ammar, who has come to Lebanon to help his cause and our own."

The short man bowed and greeted al Sidi and Muren with great courtesy and a deceptively soft voice. Muren stared speechless at the man whose face he'd seen numerous times on television and plastered on the front page of newspapers throughout Kurdistan and the Arab states. "That's not the man's name," Muren whispered to Banr al Sidi. "That's – "

"Ssh!" Banr said quickly, putting his hand on Muren's to divert attention. "He's Abu Ammar as far as we're concerned."

Öcalan continued, as though he'd not even heard the two young men. "Our beloved Abu Ammar, who regularly lives in his own homeland, the Greater Palestinian state, is here not only to vex the Israelis, but also to test the mettle of his Kurdish allies."

At that moment, two burly guards forced the blindfolded, uniformed men forward. "As you can see, these are two Turkish officers. Muren, we learned earlier today that the larger one on the left killed your older brother in Diyarbakir. Banr, the other fellow, a captain, was instrumental in last week's raid on Mosul. Do you fellows prefer the gun or the blade?"

Each opted for the sword. Without a word, each of the young warriors calmly severed the necks of their captives, then cut out the hearts of the slain Turkish soldiers, and presented them to the two leaders. Öcalan looked with pride at Banr al Sidi, his loyal student, and with particular pleasure at Muren Kolchuk, who was not even eighteen. "What did I tell you, Abu?"

"You were right, *Apo*. They're equal to my own best forces. Might it not be appropriate for their own safety that these two marvelous freedom fighters serve on detached duty in Palestine until the heat cools down?"

"Al Sidi has been with me for eight years. He's an Iraqi, so he can fit in anywhere in the Arab world. Kolchuk is one of our own. Where best to hide a star than among its own brothers?"

SOUTHEASTERN TURKEY – THE SYRIAN BORDER

As Arafat had predicted, the kidnapping and murder of the two Turkish officers whipped the Turks into an even greater frenzy. Another hundred Kurds, men, women, and children, were gunned down in broad daylight in Diyarbakir's streets. The police, assisted by army and air force "volunteers," searched the home of every known Kurdish inhabitant of the city. If any arms or ammunition were found, they were confiscated and the head of the household was arrested and languished in one of the area's fetid Turkish jails. But the Kurds gave as well as they got. For every dozen Kurds killed, a dozen Turks, mostly civilians, were annihilated. Ultimately, the area's military commandant imposed martial law and the provincial governor declared a thirty-day curfew from one hour before sundown to one hour after sunup.

The conference between the Turkish and Kurdish leadership was abruptly canceled and Yavuz Akdemir returned to Ankara. The Turkish Air Force Base at Diyarbakir became a closed military fortress. The troubles had begun in earnest.

Next day, Banr al Sidi and Yasser Arafat left the Bekaa Valley compound. Three days later, Öcalan summoned Muren to his tent.

"Sir?" the younger man said politely, nodding his head in deference to the leader.

"Muren," the Kurdish leader said, "I invited you here to wish you a happy birthday."

"I'm shocked you would know that, *Apo*," Muren remarked in delighted surprise.

"Don't be. It's my job to know everything that goes on in our movement."

"I noticed that Banr is no longer with us," Muren said. "He was your loyal lieutenant for a long time."

"Eight years."

"*Apo*, could I ask you something?"

"Speak."

"The other night you said, 'Hide a star among its own brothers' What did you mean by that?"

"Muren, if we were to send you south, both the Israelis and the Arab Palestinians would know you were not an Arab. You are more valuable to our movement if you remain closer to home."

"So you don't trust Abu Ammar?"

"No further than I can see him. Frankly, I can't stomach anyone who loves to play with young boys. That may be the Arab way, but … Don't look so shocked, my young friend. It's an open secret throughout the Arab world that the Palestinian leader has certain, er, eccentricities. Why do you think not one Arab state is willing to send even one soldier to help their Palestinian brothers?"

"But 'hiding me among the stars?'"

"Muren, you finished first in your class in the *gymnasium* and distinguished yourself in the local branch of the Kurdish People's Party. You've shown mastery of explosives and a willingness to kill without question. Such a man clearly has a future in the PKK, but you need seasoning. Other than Diyarbakir and now this hideout, have you traveled much?"

"No."

"I thought not. Turkey's not *an* enemy, it's *the* enemy. How do you expect to undermine it if you've only seen one pinprick on the map? Cigarette?"

"Thank you, no."

"Good. It's a nasty habit. Best avoid it if you can. The PKK is by no means poverty-stricken. Have you ever thought about a university education?"

Muren Kolchuk sucked in his breath sharply. He could hardly believe what he was hearing. He had never dared dream he might attend university. Kurds simply did not have the financial means to do that.

"But I'm talking in riddles," Öcalan continued. "Do you know why they call Kurds 'Mountain Turks?'"

"Because we're indistinguishable from Turks except for our dress?"

"Exactly. Dress you up in city clothing and you look like any one of ten million *Istanbulus*. That's what I mean by 'hide a star among its own brothers.' You'd be one of several million *Turkish* faces. Even though you think of yourself as high on a Turkish list of 'terrorists' in Diyarbakir, I doubt if anyone outside that "metropolis" has any idea who you are. Istanbul is so large the police simply can't control the whole city."

Muren shuffled back and forth nervously.

"It won't be necessary to change your first name. There are several million 'Murens' throughout Turkey. But we should change your last name for your own safety and, for now, anonymity. Kolchuk sounds Kurdish. Why take a chance? Our movement's future is made up of bright young men like you, so why not give you an appropriate name? Muren *Yildiz*, Muren the Star. What do you think?"

Muren's face brightened as he rolled the name around on his tongue. It sounded dazzling.

"Many major world leaders adopted names other than their own. Dzhugashvili became *Stalin*, Josip Broz became *Tito*, even the Turkish devil, Mustafa Kemal, called himself *Atatürk*, not to mention our recent guest."

"I don't know what to say."

"Perhaps this may help you." Öcalan walked over to a bureau and extracted a thick plastic envelope. He placed it on the table in front of Muren and nodded to the younger man to look inside.

When he saw what was there, the young Kurd gasped. The first document was a very real-looking Turkish identity card, with his own picture, the name Muren Yildiz, and an Istanbul address. The second was a birth certificate showing that Muren Yildiz had been born October 18, 1965 in Niğde, well west of Kurdistan, in the conservative heart of Turkey. The certificate was signed by the prefect of Niğde and properly stamped. The third item in the packet, a batch of papers, truly stunned him. There was a letter of admission signed by the Deputy Associate Dean of Istanbul University School of Engineering, a student identity card, a list of classes in which Muren Yildiz was enrolled, and various student passes. Muren rubbed his fingers over the documents, searching for some sign of forgery.

"They're all genuine," Öcalan said. "We have bureaucrats in place all over Turkey. If you're going to be a future leader in our movement, it is imperative that you be educated. If you have any trouble at all in the university, all you need do is seek an appointment with the Deputy Associate Dean who signed your letter of admission. He's one of ours."

"How long have you planned this, *Apo?*"

"We've been watching you for the past year. The 'test' you were given for admission to your local party was much more significant than you imagined."

Muren looked through the rest of the contents of the plastic envelope. They included a key and a bankbook.

"No one says you have to live like a beggar, although you shouldn't look too prosperous. The key fits a flat in the student quarter of Stamboul, between the Süleimaniye Mosque and the University. It's not fancy, but it's clean and well-furnished. The bankbook will identify you to the local branch of *İş Bankası* and will authorize sufficient, if not generous, funds for your needs."

"How can I possibly thank you enough, *Apo*?"

"By succeeding."

5

"*Mazel Tov*, Yitzhak! The estimable Mister Shamir has gone from being a terrorist to becoming the Prime Minister of Israel, and I expect you to do something about this outrage!"

"But Zari," the exasperated Israeli leader said into the phone. "Arafat and his thugs do these kinds of things every month. The babies are either killed outright or they're raised as Palestinians. We've only got so many agents in Gaza and the West Bank. Why would Zahavah Barak come out of a well-earned retirement to pursue this particular kidnapping?"

"The mother, Lyuba Rabinovitz, is my granddaughter Aviva's friend and a Soviet émigré. Aviva's taken the girl under her wing. She lived with us for a while after she immigrated. Her fiancé, Sergei Vonets, was killed in the bus attack four months ago in Ashdod."

"I remember the incident. Zari," Yitzhak Shamir said, lighting a cigarette, "we've got six million pathetic stories in *Eretz Israel*. How old is the mother?"

"Twenty-two, not much more than a child herself."

"Can you give me any other information about the little one? Any distinguishing characteristics?"

"In an infant? Hardly. He has blond hair, if that's any help."

"Most likely the Palestinians will cut it off, if they haven't killed him. They're not partial to blond hair. I'll have one of our operatives come by your house. When's a good time?"

❧❧❧

"Do you hold out much hope, Grandma?" The two young women and the elderly advocate sat around Zahavah's coffee table, sharing tea and slices of honey cake.

"Probably not. But we Israelis have learned never to give up hope. It may take a year, it may take ten, but if Yossi's alive, we'll find a way to get him back."

In the two months since Yossi's abduction, Lyuba had started to cobble her life back together. Grandma Zari had been a surrogate mother to the Russian girl. Zari, who seemed to know every Israeli of consequence in the land, had found Lyuba a job as a secretary with Israel Air Industries. Shortly thereafter, Aviva and Lyuba had found a flat to share in Tel Aviv. Aviva was pleasantly surprised to find that, if anything, she'd underestimated how attractive her friend was, once she'd decided to adapt to Israeli styles.

"But grandma," Aviva said. "You weren't born an Israeli. You were a Turk for the first forty-seven years of your life."

"That may be true, little girl," her grandmother said mock-sternly. "But I've been an Israeli citizen since Israel's independence and I married Aharon, God rest his soul. So I'm as much an Israeli as you are, my dear. Speaking of Turks," Zahavah continued, "how did you like having Melek Heper here for the week?"

"Nice man," Aviva said, noncommittally. "Of course he's a little old ..."

"Thirty-three is not that old," her grandmother remarked tartly.

"Oh, Grandma, you sound like a Jewish mother! Besides, I've heard he's got a lady friend in Istanbul."

"Surely he has friends," Zahavah persisted.

"Could be. I'm more interested that his father's the publisher of Turkey's largest newspaper."

Isharet, Zari said. "My God, my friend Turhan Türkoğlu worked for that paper for more than fifty years. He must be in his mid-eighties!"

"Turkey's one of the few places in the Middle East where Israelis are welcome, Grandma. I've never been out of the country. I'm due for my annual two-week vacation at the end of the month. Suppose I were to telephone Melek and find out if your friend Turhan's still alive. The three of us could go jaunting off to Istanbul for a week."

"I'd love to go," Lyuba said, "but I'd best stay here, in case they find my son."

DECEMBER 1983

ISTANBUL

"Istanbul, crossroads of the world and crossroads of three generations," Abdullah Heper crowed. "Here it is, mid-December, twenty degrees Celsius, and we're getting lots of company this evening. You're obviously thrilled, my friend. I haven't seen you so spiffed up in years, not even for the *Immortals* ceremony."

They were seated at the wood-and-brass bar of Istanbul's wonderful dowager queen of hotels, the *Pera Palas*, which had been built ninety years before. Turhan's mind momentarily rolled back fifty-one years, to an uncomfortable night when he and his wife Sezer had been afforded a suite at this very hotel — the night they had argued over Turhan's posting to Nazi Germany. Then his mind went back even further, to 1912 and a beautiful young Jewish girl.

"Zahavah ben David," Turhan sighed. "She's single once again. You can never tell …"

"She's twice a widow and eighty-two."

"That's not so old."

"Besides, you're supposed to spend at least as much time with Ed Baumueller who, just in case you've forgotten, has been one of your closest friends for fifty years."

"What a glorious time to be alive, Abdullah!" Turhan said. "The military actually let the elections go forward, Türgüt Özal's the new Prime Minister, and I get to see Zari and Ed. I tell you, I feel like a young buck of seventy again!"

"I'm sure it's going to be just as wonderful for them. Your lawyer friend may feel outnumbered by the press corps, though. Baumueller's still a powerhouse at the New York *World*, Zahavah's granddaughter is a budding journalist, Ed Baumueller IV has four generations of newspaper blood in his veins, and there's you and me."

Turhan glanced at his watch. "It's almost noon."

"You really are nervous, aren't you? We've got several hours yet. The Baumuellers are coming in from Frankfurt at five-thirty on Pan Am. The *schedule* says El Al five-eighty-one from *Lod* Airport is due into Atatürk International at seven-fifty, which means it'll arrive any time between four in the afternoon and midnight. The Israelis are fanatics about security and you never know what time the scheduled flight will leave."

"They'll be here ten days and we can't spend every moment in deep discussion. What's going on in town?"

"Your 'old girlfriend' Ajda Pekkan is doing her *Superstar '83* program at İnönü Stadium next Tuesday and Wednesday night. The tickets have been sold out for a month, but between us we ought to be able to find *something*."

"Ajda," Turhan mused. "She was at my retirement party in sixty-eight, fifteen years ago, just after she had her first hit record. Now they're calling her the 'Barbra Streisand of Turkey,' She's sure come a long way."

"Very talented lady. You can always do the regular tourist stuff. Don't forget, it's the first time the young people have been here. Zahavah's as familiar with Istanbul as you are."

"It's been thirty-five years since she's been here. There've been a lot of changes since nineteen forty-eight, but Istanbul's still the most cosmopolitan city in Turkey."

"Changing subjects, what do you think about the Kurdish troubles in Diyarbakir?" the publisher asked.

"Turkey's lived with that kind of trouble for more years than I've been alive. As long as the Kurds are out in southeast Anatolia, it's fine. Diyarbakir's nine hundred miles away."

The Pan Am 727 was half an hour late landing at Atatürk International Airport. The Baumuellers were among the first off the plane. Turhan,

Abdullah, and Abdullah's son Melek had been driven to the airport in two chauffered *Isharet* staff cars. Abdullah had made arrangements to speed the Baumuellers through customs and Turhan had brought the equivalent of two thousand American dollars in Turkish lira, so that neither the Baumuellers nor Zahavah Barak and her granddaughter would have to waste time changing money at the airport bank.

After great bear hugs between the two ancient friends, the five of them were walking toward the airport's coffee shop when an amplified voice announced the arrival of El Al Flight 581 from Tel Aviv.

"Perfect timing," Melek Heper said. "Almost an hour early." He and Jake Baumueller paired off together, while the three older men walked ahead.

"Shouldn't we wait for the Israeli ladies to deplane and then go into the city for a real dinner?" Abdullah asked.

"Sounds wonderful to me," Edwin Baumueller II said. "Last time I was in Istanbul, Adnan Menderes was still in power. Is the old *Sarniç* Restaurant still in business?"

"It is, and it's going stronger than ever, probably because of its 'unique' location. The old Roman cistern's quite a popular tourist spot," Abdullah said.

They turned and retraced their steps to the international arrivals hall. Israeli security was much stricter than Pan American security. It took forty minutes before Zahavah Barak and her granddaughter Aviva emerged from customs. To Turhan, Zahavah looked at least twenty years younger than her age.

"Allah, Zari, you're more beautiful than ever," he said.

Her eyes were bright as she grasped both his hands warmly. "Oh, Turhan, it's so good to see you. So much blood has passed under the bridge. Aviva," she said, turning to her granddaughter. "This is Turhan Türkoğlu, my great friend, and truly one of Turkey's living legends."

"I'm charmed," Turhan said, squeezing Aviva's hand.

Meanwhile, conversation between Melek and Jake Baumueller had ceased. Jake looked with frank admiration at Aviva, only a few inches shorter than he, with brown hair and hazel-colored eyes. The businesslike traveling outfit she wore did nothing to hide her natural curves.

"Hi, Melek," she said in English. "Who's your good-looking friend?" Jake felt a flush rising in his neck at her directness.

"Jake Baumueller. Jake, this is Aviva Kohn."

"Your grandmother's last name is Barak and your last name is Kohn. That means you must be married," Jake stumbled.

"Not hardly," Aviva rejoined. "My father was Granny Zari's son from her *first* marriage. Aunt Sara's the only child from her second."

"I'm … I'm glad to hear that," he said.

Aviva, who was quite used to young men openly flirting with her, smiled coquettishly at him. At that moment, Abdullah Heper called out, "All right, if we're going to do anything of value tonight, we've got to get organized. I suggest that Zahavah, Turhan, and Ed ride in one car. Aviva, Melek, Jake, and I will ride in the second car. It's obvious Turhan and Zahavah will need a chaperone, and so will the young people. Let's go to the Cistern Restaurant while they're still serving dinner."

Over a superb meal, the four old friends relived times well prior to the birth of the youngest generation, while Melek listened avidly to Aviva and Jake comparing the social mores, pop culture, and the differences between life in Israel and America.

It wasn't long before the three young people found common interest in journalism. Talk turned to the differences and similarities between *Isharet* and the *New York World*. The two men were deeply engaged in their comparisons, while Aviva looked around the large room, "people watching." In a far corner, she noticed an olive-skinned, quite handsome young man, wiping down the tables as patrons left, and setting up those same tables for the next groups of diners. When he looked her way and caught her eye, he smiled uncertainly.

Their group remained at the restaurant for another forty minutes. By that time, it was close to ten. Abdullah Heper suggested they check into their hotels in Taksim and get a good night's rest. While they were on their way out of the restaurant, the young man who'd been cleaning the tables came forward to hold the door for them. Unseen by the others, he casually slipped a note into Aviva's hand.

Later that night, after returning to his apartment from work, Muren Yildiz felt a mixture of excitement and fear. The young woman he'd seen in the restaurant had been striking. He couldn't really explain his fascination, but it was wildly different than he had ever felt before. It was as though there were magnets drawing him and the woman closer. He didn't even know her nationality or anything else about her. It had been only a single look, and that across a large, busy room, but it had been enough.

She hadn't looked Turkish. He guessed she might be conversant with the only other language he knew, English, which he'd studied since elementary school. In any event, he'd risked everything and written her the note in simple English. He had passed her the note in a moment of insane bravado, not knowing what effect it might have.

It was not until she was ensconced in her hotel room much later than night, that Aviva removed the note from her coat pocket and read the imperfect English. "You are very beautiful. I would very much honored be to see you again. Muren Yildiz, University of Istanbul, Department of Engineering, 15/3 442 Sokak, Istanbul."

Istanbul

6

The following morning, Aviva said, "Grandma, we've got ten days in Istanbul. I don't want to interfere with your visit with Turhan, Mr. Baumueller, and Mr. Heper. If it's all right with you, I'd just like to prowl the city on my own today."

Zahavah, who'd been wondering what she'd do to relieve her granddaughter of boredom and still have time to spend visiting with her friends, thought about Aviva's proposal for a moment. "That's not a bad idea," she said, "but I'd feel better if you had a chaperone. Turkish men believe a young woman alone on the street is an open invitation and I'd worry for your safety."

"You're probably right. Suppose you drop me off at the University. That's probably the one place in the city where I'd feel safe, since there are bound to be lots of young women my age in the area."

"You're sure you don't want me to get Melek Heper or that other young man to go with you? The way young Jake Baumueller was looking at you last night … "

"Perhaps tomorrow, but I'd really like one day to see Istanbul for myself. The University's near Kapalı Çarşı, the covered bazaar, isn't it?"

"Closer to Süleimaniye Mosque, which is something you really should see. All the tourists want to see Aya Sofia and Sultanahmet, the 'Blue' Mosque, but Süleimaniye's so much nicer.. I swear, you young people today are so independent. Maybe it's the times we live in, but everything seems to be moving so much faster these days."

"That's the Israeli way, Grandma."

"Maybe. But I tell you what. It's been so long since I've seen the Süleimanye, I'll take you there myself, then we can go our separate ways and meet back here in time for dinner."

As they walked purposefully through a rabbit warren of small, crowded alleys below the great mosque, Aviva noted that the streets bore numbers rather than names. She'd made sure to put the note Muren Yildiz had left her in her coat pocket, and knew exactly why she'd told her grandmother she wanted to explore Istanbul alone today. She felt a tingle of excitement as they crossed 442 Sokak and started their climb to the mosque.

The view from Süleimaniye was magnificent. The mosque was situated at the summit of Stamboul's highest hill. From there, the two women could see out over the Golden Horn to "European" Istanbul, Pera. Unlike the crowds she had seen out front of the Sultanahmet Mosque, the Süleimaniye was a quiet, deeply spiritual place. The sarcophagus housing Süleyman, whom Western Europeans continued to call "the Magnificent," and his wife, the "foreigner" Roxelana, was simple and dignified.

Promptly at ten-thirty, when they were in sight of the university, Zahavah announced, "Well, my dear, you wanted to have the city to yourself, and now it will be yours. I'm going to leave you here and catch the bus back to Taksim. You're sure you know how to get back?"

"I do, Grandma," she said, hugging the older woman. "If need be, I can ask one of the girls at the university."

Hardly had her grandmother left, than Aviva sensed a presence just behind her. "How long have you been following me?" she asked.

"Since you crossed 442 Sokak, half a block from my flat."

"You're pretty sure of yourself, aren't you?"

"Not really. I think you must have felt it, too, or you wouldn't have come. You've been walking a long time. Would you like some tea?"

"That sounds wonderful. You look younger in the daylight than you did last night."

"And you are even more beautiful in the morning sun," he said. "I don't even know your name, only that your face was before my eyes and in my dreams all night."

"I'm Aviva Kohn. This is my first time in Istanbul. I'll be here for ten days."

Muren guided her to the campus cafeteria. "Apple tea or plain tea?" he asked.

"Apple, please."

She found an empty table with two chairs and he returned shortly, bearing two glasses of apple tea and four pieces of *lokum*, Turkish delight candy. Aviva felt a pleasant buzz when he sat down across from her.

"How old are you, Muren?"

"Eighteen."

"I'm twenty-three. Does it disturb you that you're sitting with an 'older woman' and a foreigner at that?"

"Not if it doesn't bother you," he replied.

"Are you from Istanbul?" she asked.

"No. From the East. Diyarbakir."

"My Aunt Sara is assigned to the Air Base there as a visiting officer."

The young man stiffened for a moment, then relaxed. "With the Second Turkish Air Force?"

"That's right. Have you been there?"

"I used to work there, just before I entered the university."

"Do you have family there?"

He hesitated, then looked at the ground. "They were killed."

"I'm so sorry. Was it in an accident?"

"Not really," he said. "My family is Kurdish."

"Oh." She didn't know what else to say. She'd read about the festering troubles between the Turks and the Kurds in southeastern Turkey, but she had no idea of the magnitude of the problem.

"Would you like to walk through the neighborhood where I live?" he asked. "If it's your first time in Istanbul, you may as well see places tourists normally don't see, and if you are with a man, it will be much safer."

They walked for the next hour, around the university campus, back toward Süleimaniye Mosque, then down the hill toward where her grandmother had said she could catch the bus for Taksim Square. They talked of many things. Muren told her that the Kurds were outcasts in their own land, much like the Israelis were a pariah to the Arab states around them, and how wonderful it would be if the Israelis and the Kurds allied themselves against common foes. She seemed interested in everything he had to say.

As they stood in a side street near the bus stop, she said, "Well, Muren, it's time for me to get back to the other side of the Golden Horn. You've given me a wonderful introduction to the city. I hope we'll see one another again."

He looked at his watch. "It's not even one o'clock. Can't you stay for even a little while longer?"

She took his hand in hers and gave it a squeeze, smiling at him. "I really must go," she said.

"Would you … would you at least let me kiss you?"

"Well …" she said. "I see no harm in that."

She waited for what she anticipated would be a brotherly kiss on the cheek, but he surprised her by kissing her full on the mouth. "Poor boy," she thought. "Probably a case of puppy love. I'll give it five seconds." She counted mentally to three and inexplicably, she found herself kissing him back. Aviva felt Muren's hardness against her, and smiled inwardly. He was so young, so inexperienced.

Just before she stepped over the precipice, she regained control of her spiraling emotions. "Why don't we walk for a while longer?"

"But —?" he started to protest.

"Muren," she said. "I know exactly what you want, and I can't say I don't want it, too, but … we've only just met. …"

"I —?"

"Ssh," she said, putting two fingers to his lips. "Let's just be friends for now and see where it leads."

⚜

"Ed, you chose this time to came to Istanbul for a reason," *Isharet's* publisher said.

"That's true, Abdullah. Word on the street's that you're thinking of taking *Isharet* public and retiring."

"I'm not surprised you'd know about that. You have any interest in playing in my sandbox?"

"Can't say I don't. Now that I'm out of the day-to-day rat race, I've got some 'play money' and I'm still in the poker game of life. What're you selling and what are you offering?"

"*Isharet's* initial public offering is 100 million shares. I plan to hold back twenty -five percent in trust for my four kids so the family will never have to worry about losing contact. I'll be offering the rest at 263 lira per share."

"About a dollar a share at today's official exchange rate."

"Mmm-hmm."

"And yes, now that you're walking over to the liquor cabinet, I will have a shot of Johnnie Walker Blue label, not that horsepiss firewater you make over here." Baumueller continued, "*Isharet's* the *New York World* of Turkey. Do you see an upside?"

"I won't try to bullshit you, since you know this business better than I do."

"I'm not looking for the *World* to invest, Abdullah. This is entirely my personal game."

"O.K, here's my pitch. I'd like to entrust whatever it takes to keep control to someone I trust without question. That means you if you're interested."

"I appreciate that, Abdullah. I would have expected nothing less from you. What are you looking to sell privately?"

"Anther twenty percent."

"Dollars or lira?"

"Whatever you feel comfortable with, Ed."

"You and I both know the lira's history against the dollar. I seem to remember when your great and good government wanted a loan from me. The lira wasn't worth shit then and it's falling faster than a rock now. I'll give you twenty million U.S. dollars now if you promise to put it in an account at Chase Manhattan Bank so whoever's in power won't be able to grab it."

"That's 300 Turkish lira a share. Awfully generous of you, my friend."

"Generous my ass," Baumueller said, lifting his shot glass to toast his Turkish partner. "I expect to make ten times that from my investment if I'm still alive, and if I'm not, Baumueller IV will be one rich kid." He reached into his briefcase and extracted a checkbook. "To whom do I make it out?"

"Isharet Communications," Heper said gratefully.

When Ed Baumueller signed the check with a flourish, the Turkish publisher handed him a receipt:

"Received this third day of December,
1983 the sum of Twenty Million U.S. Dollars
in full payment for Share Certificate Number 2 for
Twenty million (20,000,000) Shares
of Isharet Communications Common Stock.
s/Abdullah Heper, President."

Looking at the receipt, Baumueller said, "I see you've already issued share certificate number one to yourself."

"Not so."

"Then who?"

"Who do you think got share number one? I'll give you a hint. It was for *one share*."

"The curmudgeon who calls himself the Conscience of the Nation?"

"Uh huh."

✿

At quarter to four, Muren and Aviva returned to the nearby bus stop, arm in arm. As the bus to Taksim Square approached, Muren tried to kiss her passionately. Aviva kissed him on the cheek and squeezed his hand. Unknown to her, a pair of eyes were watching as she left the area. Jake Baumueller, whom Zahavah had asked to make sure her granddaughter was safe, shrugged ruefully. He walked in the opposite direction from Aviva, toward a different part of Stamboul, to catch a different bus to the same destination as the Israeli girl.

✿

"Well, granddaughter, I'm sure you couldn't have seen everything there was to see in Istanbul in one day."

"You're right," Aviva said, smiling serenely. "I certainly saw enough to keep me busy most of the afternoon. This is a huge city and I feel rather sticky after my day's activities. Have we got an hour so I can just soak in a hot bath before we go to dinner?"

"Of course, dear. You can't believe what an interesting day I've had with my old friend. We'll trade stories later this evening. Did you, by any chance, run into Jake Baumueller?"

"No, Grandma, why do you ask?"

"Shortly after I got back to *Isharet's* office, Ed Baumueller told me Jake wanted to visit an old friend of his who's teaching at a private school near Istanbul University this year. I thought the two of you might have crossed paths while you were there."

7

The following Saturday morning, Sara Barak awoke with even more than her usual good humor, opened the bedroom window blinds to let in the bright sunlight, and stretched sensuously as she came back to bed and rubbed against her man. "Well, Colonel," she said, "I've got a little news that might affect us."

"*Might* affect us?" Omer said, opening his eyes. He was more convinced than ever that Yavuz had been right: this would be the perfect woman with whom to share his life and he'd be a fool to let her go.

"'Might' depends on which option you take," she said.

"Meaning?"

"You can either make an honest woman of me and give Halil a little brother or sister in the process, or you can let me go back to Israel and —"

The magnitude of what she was saying hit him like a shock wave. "You mean …?"

"Uh-huh. *Hamile.* Oh, Omer!" she said, throwing her arms around him.

"Well, that certainly makes my decision easier. All I've been thinking about for the past week is how to ask you to marry me. You certainly know how to bring things to a head."

"Are you upset?" she asked, nuzzling him.

"Of course not! But we have to make arrangements, and it could be awkward."

"Why?"

"You're a career officer, I'm a career officer. The only problem is, we're career officers in the military of two different countries."

"Thank God or Praise Allah the countries are allies," she said.

After celebratory lovemaking, as she was frying French toast for him, Sara said, "I really have thought about the problems, Omer. What's happened to us is pretty common in the Israeli army. My mother's still a powerful force in Israel. She was a member of the *Knesset* back in the sixties and she's kept solid friendships. She was worried I'd be single forever."

"But you've been married."

"When I was twenty-one, and then only for six months. We were children and we'd been boyfriend and girlfriend since the first year of high school. We'd gone about as far as we could go, and it was get married or break up. Thank goodness I never got pregnant. And now I am — and I'm still not married. You're sure you want a wicked woman like me?"

"I couldn't be more certain. You were starting to talk about your mother …"

"Who *might* have been *your* mother if she hadn't fallen in love with my father first. It's amazing how far a little influence goes in Israel. Mama's also kept her Turkish connections, Omer. I wouldn't put it past her to arrange for me to be more-or-less permanently stationed in Turkey. Or, for that matter, from time to time you could be detached for duty in Israel with the Embassy."

"It sounds so easy when you say it, Sara, but I come from four generations of military officers. As goes the military, so goes Turkey, and if I want to carve my own niche, I need to stay in Turkey."

She ladled three pieces of French toast for him and two for her onto their plates, poured each of them a glass of tea, and sat down across from him at the small table.

"I'm not saying you'd be away from Turkey for long periods, but I recall your father was in the States on a diplomatic mission for General Evren, and that didn't hurt his career one bit."

"He was retired at the time."

"A retired three-star general."

"Well, there is that. What about our religious beliefs, Sara? I wouldn't expect you to give up Judaism, but what would your mother say about you marrying non-Jew, a *sheygetz*?"

"She'd probably say, '*Mazel tov.*' She's about as religious as I am."

"That simple?"

"Yes."

"And our child?"

"Why don't we see what happens when it happens? Now, then, you're convinced you want to marry me?"

"Absolutely."

"I trust your brother Yavuz would be your best man."

"Who else?"

"I've got a young niece, Aviva, who'd be my maid of honor. It needn't be a large wedding. I don't care if it's just us and our immediate families. And since my fiancé is Turkish … Wait a minute, you haven't even asked me to marry you. How can I be so bold as to call you my fiancé?"

At that, Lieutenant Colonel Omer Akdemir got down on his knee and held her hand in his. "Sara Barak, I am formally asking. Would you do me the greatest honor in the world and marry me?"

"Depends," she snapped, coolly. "Before or after the little one is born?"

❖

A few days later, Sara approached Omer and said, "Darling, I hate to leave the arrangements up to you, but with things heating up in Lebanon, my commanding general has requested that I return to Tel Aviv. I'm sure it won't be longer than two weeks at most."

"Couldn't you put it off, Sara? What could be more important than our wedding?"

"Absolutely nothing," she said, kissing him lightly. "But, as you said, you're career military, I'm career military, and I haven't resigned or been discharged yet. Who knows? Maybe General Lior will announce that I've been promoted to full colonel."

❖

December 29, 1983
Tel Aviv, Israel

"Sara, I couldn't be more thrilled for you!" Major General Tomi Lior said, embracing her. "I think your idea of remaining in the service on detached duty in Turkey couldn't be a better one! Turkey's our only Muslim ally in the area, and it's one of the two greatest powers in the Middle East. The closer we stay to them, the better for us. When's the wedding?"

"February 1, 1984 in the Christian calendar," she said. "A little more than a month from now. Will you come, Tomi?"

"I wouldn't miss it, my dear," he said. "After all, you are like a daughter to me."

"Is that why you recalled me to Israel?" she asked.

"No. I've got a rather sensitive assignment for you in the Bekaa Valley."

"Lebanon? Why me?" Sara asked, looking at the large map behind Lior's desk.

"Because we need to mollify our American friends."

"And one lieutenant colonel can do that?"

"If it's a woman, yes. For some reason, the Americans love to see Israeli women involved in leadership positions. For years, their popular press has emphasized how in Israel men and women are equal in everything. Do I have to tell you how much they loved Golda Meir? Or, to be perfectly blunt, how they love your mother? Being Zahavah Barak's daughter carries weight with the Americans."

"Why not fly me to Washington?" she said. "Or have me meet them in Turkey?"

"Because we have a large, internationally unpopular presence in Lebanon at the moment. We need something that will convince our allies they have a *strong* friend in Israel, and our politicians think they have a way to do it."

General Lior shifted verbal gears. "It's a beautiful day in Tel Aviv. Let's get out of this stuffy office and walk by the seashore." Sara caught his drift immediately.

They walked ten minutes to Tel Aviv's mile-long boardwalk along the Mediterranean. The temperature was in the mild mid-sixties.

Numerous modern high-rise buildings on the land side of the beach shielded the area from the noise of the inner city.

"The Bekaa Valley is not the center of active hostilities," Lior said. "The American leaders have set up their camp near Baalbek. Caspar Weinberger, the U.S. Secretary of Defense, is a great world traveler. He's using his position not only to bolster his reputation, but also to satisfy his urge to travel. He's coming to Lebanon next week on one of those 'show the flag' trips the Americans do so well. Our intelligence says he would react well to a relatively spectacular 'gift' from us. I'd like you to be part of it."

"Tomi, you'd hardly expect me to …"

"Of course not, woman!" he said, blushing furiously. "It's much more serious than that. No American has ever seen Dimona."

Sara gasped involuntarily. "Very few Israelis have seen it."

"And with good reason. As far as the world is concerned, it doesn't exist. It's nothing but a small outpost in the southern Negev. The government thinks it's time we shared its existence with the Americans, but only at the highest, most secret level. Secretary Weinberger's no dummy. He's a graduate of Harvard Law School and has President Reagan's full attention."

"Am I to understand you want me to meet with Secretary Weinberger in the Bekaa Valley and from there escort him to the nuclear reactor at Dimona?"

"Sara, no one ever said you were a dummy either."

JANUARY 4, 1984
BEKAA VALLEY, LEBANON

"Beirut is gorgeous!" Sara exclaimed.

"It is, Colonel Barak. Before the war, *Al Hamra* was said to be the most stylish boulevard in the entire Middle East. The country was the one place where Christians and Muslims co-existed peacefully together, as long as Lebanon wasn't the toy of larger, more powerful nations. One year Lebanon had a Christian President and a Muslim Prime Minister. The next year it was reversed."

"What a shame it had to come apart, Captain Gali," Sara said to her young escort officer. "How far is it to Baalbek?"

"Fifty-one miles. We climb into the hills east of the city, then down into the Bekaa Valley."

Gali drove an older model, unmarked Mercedes 220 sedan bearing Lebanese license plates. "No sense in making ourselves too conspicuous."

"Is there any chance we could visit the Cedars?" she asked.

"I wouldn't advise it. Our forces are nowhere near that far north."

"How far is 'not far,' Captain?"

"Less than eighty miles. Khalil Gibran country, Colonel."

They drove north from Deir al Ahmar. The road snaked up the bare eastern slope of Mount Lebanon, presenting marvelous views at every turn. Villages of red-tile-roofed houses perched atop hills or clung precariously to the mountainsides. Sara admired the olive groves, vineyards, lush valleys and mountain peaks at every turn. As they climbed ever higher, they looked down the other side into a gigantic bowl where a ski resort lay before them. Snow had not yet closed the route for the winter, and the mid-afternoon sun gave the entire area a golden glow. Five miles outside Bscharré, they were flagged down by two men standing beside a Lebanese constabulary automobile.

"Your papers, please?" a man of thirty-five asked. He was of medium height with dark bushy hair and moustache, and a gap between his two front teeth.

"Anything wrong, officer?"

"No. It's just that we've heard there are terrorists southwest of here, and we want make certain to preserve security in our quadrant."

"Of course," said Captain Gali, extracting his identity cards and the car's registration.

The official gave the papers a studied glance, then looked at Gali to make sure the photograph matched the identity card. "Everything seems to be in order, Captain," he said. "You may proceed."

"Is this the right road to the Cedars?" Gali asked.

"Yes, but there's a much shorter way. You passed the cutoff about a mile back. If you'll step outside for a moment, I can point it out to you."

Gali opened the door and got out of the car, shivering in the bracing mountain air.

"Something wrong, Captain?" the man asked.

"No, it's just that …" He did not finish the sentence before the second man, younger and burlier than the first, stepped up behind the Israeli officer and clubbed him unconscious with the butt of a rifle.

Sara forced herself to remain calm as the two men approached her. "Gentlemen, I don't know who you are or where you're from, but the American armed forces are expecting me at Baalbek this afternoon, and if I'm not there on time, they'll send out a search party."

"Colonel Barak, you're rather a long way from Baalbek," the unformed "policeman" said. "Mister Weinberger, will just have to wait a while, won't he?"

"You seem to know who I am and where I'm going, which is rather more than I can say. Are you PLO?"

"Hardly. Excuse my poor manners, Colonel. I'm Deputy Foreign Minister to Abdullah Öcalan. For the time being, consider yourself a guest of the Republic of Kurdistan."

8

EASTERN LEBANON

"So, Mister Öcalan," Sara said calmly. "The Kurds have now moved their operations to Lebanon?"

They were seated in a comfortable room in front of a roaring fireplace, in an Alpine-style cabin. "Some would call my people 'Mountain Turks.'"

"Your people blew up the F-104 at Diyarbakir Air Base."

"And the Turks, of which your boyfriend Colonel Akdemir is a senior officer, retaliated rather brutally, wouldn't you say?"

"I would hardly call him my boyfriend," Sara remarked.

"Pardon me, your fiancé. I congratulate you. Actually, we've found Akdemir a decent chap. Pity he's a Turk."

"And you aren't?"

"Absolutely not!" he barked, rising and angrily pushing another log into the fire. "My people are fighting for their freedom, just like the Armenians, the Greeks, and so many others who've been oppressed for centuries by the Evil Ottoman Empire." He softened. "Sometimes unfortunate events like the bombing of the aircraft do occur. They don't help either side."

"How long do you intend to keep me here, Mister Öcalan?"

"You may call me *Apo* if you wish. That's what most of my friends call me."

"Is that what your prisoners call you?" Sara said, surprised that she was neither frightened nor angry. More curious than anything.

"I'd hardly call you a prisoner," Öcalan said. "There are no jail cells. You'll be treated with all the respect to which a field officer is entitled, and you're free to leave any time you want."

She laughed without humor. "Exactly how far do you think I'd get, Mister Öcalan? We're two-thirds of the way up Mount Lebanon, the place gets down into the low twenties at night, and it's obvious I'm a member of an unwanted alien military force in this country."

"You have a point there, Colonel."

"What will happen to Captain Gali? Do you intend to kill him?"

"Why should I?" Öcalan seemed surprised. "He's not an enemy combatant, and we don't need to cause an unpleasant international incident. I'm sure he simply woke up with a headache half an hour after we left for this house. The keys are still in his car, only his passenger is missing. If you still want to see the Cedar Grove, we can drive you there tomorrow morning."

At that moment, an old woman entered bearing *mezes*, the ubiquitous appetizers of the Middle East, and lamb stew. She set two places for them at a cedar table. Öcalan bade Sara join him. As they ate their evening meal, Öcalan said, "You're not afraid of me?"

"Should I be?"

"No. I mean you no harm."

"Then why did you kidnap me?"

"Rather a harsh accusation, wouldn't you say?"

"Rather a harsh way to invite a lady to your home."

"Touché," the mustachioed man said, smiling. "It would have been rather stupid of me to walk into Headquarters Second Turkish Air Force and ask to speak to the Israeli Intelligence Officer. My name and my face are well-known to the Turks. There's quite a price on my head."

"You're right," Sara said. "But I still don't understand why you'd seek me out."

"Many reasons," Öcalan said. "Your mother is a highly-placed Turkish native who made *aliyah* to Israel and married a *Sabra*. Your own reputation is impeccable. You seem to have made no real enemies, and your General Lior thinks enough of you to send you as an emissary to the American Secretary of Defense, Mister Weinberger. The Kurds are not at war with Israel. Indeed, we see the Israelis as oppressed people, much like ourselves."

"Yet you profess friendship with the Palestinians."

"The enemy of my enemy is my friend," he said, smiling sardonically. "I don't trust *Abu Ammar* and his Palestinian cutthroats any more than you do. At this moment, we find his PLO convenient."

"Is that how you've learned what you know about me?"

"Miss Barak, we Kurds are neither as bumbling nor as stupid as we might appear to outsiders. Certainly not as bumbling and stupid as the Palestinians. Tea, baklava?"

"Yes, thank you. Why did you kidnap — invite me — to your lair?"

"To enlist your aid. Don't look at me like that, Colonel Barak, I'm not asking you to act outside your country's own best interests. I simply ask that you act as an intermediary to let your commanders know we mean *Eretz Israel* no harm, and there might be common ground for discussions about mutual cooperation regarding shared interests."

"Playing both sides against the middle?"

"No. You're not the first Israeli we've spoken to. You're an intelligence officer and an intelligent woman, Miss Barak. You know as well as I that the business of *business* transcends the rhetoric of politics. You're aware where most of Israel's oil comes from?"

"Of course. Iran."

"No one talks to anyone else in the region, yet everyone talks to everyone else, if you gather where I am going with this conversation."

"The Kurds speak with the Turks?"

"Occasionally. Mostly indirectly."

"Through the good offices of …?"

"The Moroccan Embassy."

"You know I'm engaged to a Turkish officer. What makes you think I won't go directly to him with whatever you tell me?"

Öcalan smiled, and his peasant features took on a sharp, lupine look. "Colonel Barak, that's exactly what I'm planning on." He walked over to a nearby desk and picked up three sheets of paper with identical writing, an original and two photocopies. "The original is for the Israeli commandant in Lebanon. I flatter myself to assume if I give you a copy for yourself, it will end up in Colonel Akdemir's hands."

"And the third?"

"You intend to meet with Secretary Weinberger. Tomorrow morning, one of our drivers will take you to Bscharré, where you'll be met by an Israeli sergeant, a friend of the Kurdish people, who will drive you to your meeting. General Lior wanted you to share certain matters with Secretary Weinberger to enhance Israel's relations with America. I suggest that if a copy of this note somehow finds its way into his hands…"

"What if I choose not to go along with your request, Mister Öcalan?"

The Kurdish leader chuckled mirthlessly. "That is entirely up to you, Miss Barak. You won't be killed, you won't be touched in any way. Everything will be exactly as it was. By the way, I learned a few days ago that your niece, Aviva, may be romantically involved with the young Kurd who blew up the fighter aircraft in Diyarbakir. You might tell her to be more careful about the company she keeps."

9

Heper was right on two counts. Ajda Pekkan's *Superstar '83* program at Inönü Stadium had been sold out for more than a month. And he was able to obtain four tickets to the Wednesday night concert. He presented the tickets to Turhan and Zahavah.

"I was certain the two young people would hit it off," he said, using American slang. "They have so much in common. But it seems each of them had something else to do during the time they've been here. Turhan, you were with Ajda at the very beginning of her career, and you know how far she's come since then. Zari, I'm sure you'd like to spend most of your last couple of days with Turhan. Maybe if we convinced the kids to go to the concert with you? Rock concerts seem to be a magnet for young people …"

Jake was eager to explore the Turkish music scene, so he readily assented. Aviva begged off, claiming she'd just like to walk up and down Istiklal Caddesi. Melek Heper was unable to go that evening, so it ended up that Turhan, Zahavah, Jake, and his grandfather, Ed Baumueller, took a taxi to Inönü Stadium. Jake was slightly disappointed that Aviva did not come along. She was an attractive girl. In other circumstances …

The seats were excellent — fourth row center — and Jake found the warm-up band certainly up to the standards he was used to in New York. The laser beams converged at center stage and focused on an astonishingly striking woman in a skintight, gold lamé outfit. Her strong, husky voice, accompanied by a large orchestra, belted out her opening song, Billy Joel's *I Love You Just the Way You Are,* his first gold record, that Jake recognized from eight years before.

As she launched into the bridge, Jake Baumueller was so jolted by the woman's rendition of the Billy Joel hit that, ignoring his companions and the fact that he was in a stadium with fifteen thousand other people, he robustly sang the refrain in harmony with the singer, oblivious to anyone else in the arena.

The rest of the evening spun by in a whirl. Jake Baumueller, who'd never been interested in anything beyond the next day, found himself mesmerized, unable to take his eyes off the diva.

"You can wake up now. It's intermission," his grandfather said, shaking him out of his reverie.

"How long has it been?"

"Hour-and-a-half. This lady gives a pretty good show."

"A *pretty* good show?" Jake was flabbergasted. "It's the greatest show I've ever seen. How can I meet her?"

"Fight your way through thousands eager to meet the goddess," Turhan remarked. "You know, she kissed me once — more than fifteen years ago it was, at my retirement party. I wonder if she'd even remember me. She was a pretty little girl then."

"How old do you think she is?" Zahavah asked.

"Thirty-seven," Turhan said.

"Not that much older than me," Jake murmured. "I'll be twenty-nine in two months. If I could only meet her, talk to her. She'd be dynamite in the U.S."

"Calm down," Ed Baumueller chimed in. "First, she's an international superstar already. More important, we're leaving for home in two days, and even you can't act that fast, *conquistador.*"

"I don't really need to leave that soon. The *World* has a bureau here. Mister Heper would certainly make sure I was all right, and Manhattan can do without me for a while. I'm sure we could extend the return date on my ticket."

"Must you leave Istanbul so soon, darling?" he asked as they gazed over the hill on which the Süleimaniye mosque sat in silent grandeur toward the Golden Horn.

"As sweet as this has been, Muren, I must be getting back to Jerusalem."

"Why?" he asked, petulantly. "Would my begging make you stay?"

"Truthfully, dear, it wouldn't, although I do find Istanbul to be a fascinating place, and by that I don't only mean your attentiveness. I'm Israeli and Jewish and you're a Kurd and a Muslim. "Walk me to the bus stop?"

"You seem to take this whole thing so lightly."

"Hey, my friend, what do you expect?" she said, lifting herself up on tiptoes and kissing his forehead. "There's no question we're attracted to each other, but can you imagine what kind of future we'd have?"

"We could always go to a country where it wouldn't matter — Argentina, Canada?"

"I don't know about you, but I've got family, you're fighting for a cause you believe in, and I have no particular desire to start a new life in a place I know nothing about. I've seen what that's done to my friend Lyuba, and she emigrated from a land where she wasn't welcome to a place she wanted to call home."

"Doesn't it matter that I love you?" the Kurdish boy continued.

"Yes, it does," she said, holding both his hands in hers and looking him in the eye. "It matters a great deal to me, and in another time, another place, perhaps another life, it could have gone much farther."

"Is this goodbye, Aviva?" he asked miserably.

"I don't know," she replied. "I do know we'll always be friends and I hope we'll always be there for one another."

They walked down the hill in an uncomfortable silence, he more so than she. *Men*, she thought to herself. *They always seem to go overboard.* Truth to tell, she was tiring of his intensity, his all-too-serious *seriousness* for one so young, and she was certainly not ready to settle down.

"Aviva, I've got a lovely surprise for you," Grandma Zari said as the girl came into their hotel room. "Mister Heper told me he'd love to have you stay on for a couple of months. He's even willing to pay you enough to avoid starving," she chuckled. "What do you say to that offer?"

Aviva was assailed with a plethora of thoughts, none of them unpleasant.

"My dear old Turhan will certainly show you the ropes — no one knows this town better than he does. and Heper's a nice man. Jake Baumueller will be doing an internship with the New York *World's* Istanbul bureau. That means you'll even have someone close to your own age to keep you company. What do you say, Aviva?"

"Why not?" Zahavah's vivacious granddaughter said. "There are worse things to do."

10

Caspar Weinberger, and his escort officer, Sara Barak had arrived in the southern Negev town of Dimona the night before. Thankfully, it was mid-January and the weather was dry and balmy.

"My God, Golda wasn't bluffing after all when she told Kissinger that Israel was prepared to take the most drastic steps if we didn't stop the 1973 war," Weinberger said,

They were walking through the complex that housed the nine giant buildings — *machons* — of the ultra-secret nuclear facility. Machon 1 was the reactor building that was identifiable by its sixty-foot silver dome. Machon 2 was a nondescript, two-story windowless building, eighty feet wide and two hundred feet long.

As they entered, Sara read from a booklet she'd been given by her Military Intelligence superior. "The above-ground structure houses an air filtration plant, some offices, storage space, and a worker's canteen. Elevators transport people to the six underground levels, extending eighty feet below the surface."

"What goes on in that area?" Weinberger asked.

"It's pretty much a secret, even from me," she replied. They spent the next hour walking through the huge building. Secretary Weinberger tactfully refrained from taking any notes.

When they were outside, Sara continued her brief talk about the rest of the buildings. "Machon 3 is a chemical plant that produces lithium-6 deuteride, processes natural uranium, and fabricates reactor fuel rods. Machon 4 is a waste treatment plant for the radioactive effluent from the plutonium extraction process of Machon 2. Machon 5 coats the uranium fuel rods with aluminum. Machon 6 provides power and other services for Dimona."

The next building was marked with the number 8.

"No Machon 7?" the American Secretary of Defense asked."

"Not to my knowledge, Mister Secretary," Sara said. "Machon 8 contains a laboratory for testing and process development. Machon 9 houses a laser isotope enrichment plant for enriching uranium, and Machon 10 produces depleted uranium metal for anti-armor ammunition use."

As they walked back toward the entrance to the huge complex, Caspar Weinberger said, "I appreciate your government allowing me to see this incredible facility. When was it built?"

"Back in the nineteen-fifties, when relations were much better between France and Israel."

Abruptly, he changed the subject. "Is your government aware of Mr. Öcalan's note?"

"They are."

"And that you shared the note with me?"

"My Commanding Officer told me to use my own discretion. He also said that since America's our strongest ally we'd be silly not to share everything."

"Might I ask your personal reaction, Sara? Off the record, of course."

"Not really, Cap," she said, easily adapting to the use of his first name. "He's putting forth the same case for his people that the Palestinians are trying to do vis-à-vis Israel. All they want is their historic homeland. They need any help they can get from larger, established nations. I see this from a doubly prejudiced viewpoint."

"You say 'doubly prejudiced'?" the American Secretary of Defense said.

"I do. I'm engaged to a Turkish Air Force officer, his brother's a Turkish Army Officer, and my mother is a native-born Turk who never renounced her citizenship."

"But Öcalan doesn't say the Kurds want the whole of Turkey."

"Have you ever seen their map of Kurdistan?"

"Yes. They claim about one-eighth of Turkey's land area, plus some pretty substantial parts of Syria, Iraq, Iran, and even Lebanon. It would be a fairly large state. It's kind of like the West Bank, though. What they're looking for is a slice of inhospitable land."

"Maybe, but that 'slice of inhospitable land' controls both the Tigris and Euphrates Rivers. The key to the whole puzzle is that a Kurdistani Turkey would control all the oil in the country and would have the ability to shut off water from the Tigris and Euphrates before it ever reached Iran or Iraq. Think of the international crisis that might come about from that."

"Good point."

"Another critical point is that to understand how unimaginable to Turkey losing an eighth of its land to the Kurds would be, you have to understand Turkish history."

"Meaning?"

"Five hundred years ago, the Mediterranean was a Turkish lake. Turkey owned most of the Middle East and extended into Europe as far as the gates of Vienna. Even though the Ottoman Empire was called 'the Sick Man of Europe' for more than two hundred years thereafter, it managed to hold on to a great deal of real estate until the end of World War One, when the big powers tried to carve what was left into almost nothing. The Turks laid almost every life they had on the line. When you ask them to give away so much as a square *inch* of land today, the Turks immediately hark back to those terrible days. Not to mention that they've been the diplomatic 'punching bags,' to use an American term, for every Armenian, Greek, and Kurd in the world."

Weinberger took a folded copy of the note from his pocket. "Öcalan says the Kurds and the Israelis have a natural affinity for one another as oppressed peoples."

"Mister Öcalan may feel that way. That's his right. I don't question that the Jews have always been an oppressed people. But we have long memories, and it's hard to forget that in 1492, at the height of the Spanish Inquisition, the Ottoman Sultan sent ships to pick us up. The Jews and the Turks have an historical friendship, that goes back almost five hundred years. We'd be foolish to give that friendship up."

Caspar Weinberger raised his hands, palms up, in a conciliatory manner, then changed the subject. "The Israelis deny they've ever developed nuclear weapons capabilities."

"Yes?" Sara smiled.

There was silence as Weinberger smiled back. "And?"

Sara laughed outright. "Mister Secretary, Cap, we can play the game of one-word questions into eternity. We both know what you're getting at. What do you want me to say? You can see for yourself what we have here."

"You are one sharp woman," he replied. "I can't see a thing except shipments of materials that I know are not used for the desalination of water. Two hundred?"

"Probably more."

"Small ones?"

"Tactical devices, not strategic. The Arab world knows they can use all the rhetoric they want, but they also know that the pit bull is a rather small dog."

"Touché again, Sara. Is there a restaurant nearby? I've had nothing but *shwarma* and *falafel* since I've been in this part of the world. Surely they've got better fare?"

ISTANBUL

"Turhan Türkoğlu? Of course I remember you. How could I possibly forget the first love of my life? I still remember your retirement party."

"You truly get lovelier each year, more popular, and, I'm sure, wealthier. Your hair used to be a chestnut brown. It's a bit lighter now."

"At least I'm not blonde," she laughed. "Although that, too, may come in time. Enough flattery, Turhan, I've never known you to call without a purpose."

"All right, you've got me dead to rights. I've got a young man who told me his life is at an end if he doesn't get to meet you."

"Spare me the indignity," she said, sighing theatrically, "even though it so happens I'm not married this week. Has Turhan Türkoğlu taken to hustling sweet young girls like me at his, er, advanced age?"

"Silence, woman!" he said gruffly, his voiced edged with humor. "You might even want to meet *this* young man. Aside from being bright, likable and American, he could probably afford to take even the great Ajda Pekkan to a feast she'd enjoy — anywhere in the world. And by that, I mean <u>world</u> as in *New York World*. Do I make my meaning clear?"

"Edwin Baumueller's son?"

"Edwin Baumueller's *grandson*."

"Allah! How old would he be? Twelve? Thirteen?"

"Twenty-nine next month."

The line was silent for a moment. "About two or three years younger than me?"

"Eight or nine years younger, Ajda. He simply wants to meet you, interview you for the *New York World*. He's with their Istanbul bureau for the next half year or so. Ed just left Istanbul, by the way. Looks great for an octogenarian, but then again, so do I."

"I've got to be in Paris next week, but I can squeeze in an hour or two before I leave. Where would this interview take place?"

"Belgrade Palas. We might as well keep things completely proper. And Ajda?"

"Yes?"

"Çok teşekkür ederim. Many, many thanks from an old man."

"Oh, Turhan, you'll never be old. *Inshallah*, you'll live forever."

"From your mouth the God's ear. Uh-oh. Young Abdullah's just come into the office. Probably going to ask me to pay for this phone call."

✿❁✿

On January 27, 1984, the day before the scheduled interview at Belgrade Palas, Turhan Türkoğlu, who'd survived a life-threatening stroke and numerous imprisonments, who'd smoked the strongest, cheapest cigarettes in the world for more than sixty-five years; who'd played poker with Kemal Atatürk and been thrown out of Hitler's Reich by the German government; who'd been "the Voice of Turkey" and later "the Conscience of a Nation," was walking on the sidewalk adjacent to Nasrettin Bulvari when a car driven by a seventeen-year-old boy with a learner's permit, going forty miles an hour, spun out of control, climbed the sidewalk, and ran into five pedestrians. One of them was Turhan. Less than two months short of his eighty-seventh birthday, this living immortal, truly the last of the giants, was instantly killed.

11

The funeral had been very simple, but over a thousand people had braved Istanbul's rain to attend. Afterward, Abdullah Heper had opened up Belgrade Palas for the promised celebration of Turhan's life to one hundred of Turhan's closest associates and friends.

"He didn't want a fancy funeral. He wanted the last memory people had of him to be a celebration of his life," said Heper, Turhan's close friend and long-time editor. "If he'd known how I cried when I gave his eulogy, I don't know what he would have thought."

"He'd probably have said something like, 'Stop spending *Isharet's* money on paper tissues. We've got a newspaper to run, and every sheet of that stuff you use will only increase the cost of newsprint.'"

"I'm sure he would have said that, Mister Prime Minister," Heper said, shaking Türgüt Özal's hand. "You're fortunate you've not been in office long enough to catch the pointed end of one of his barbs."

"Was he still writing for you?"

"Once a month or so. He always thought *Isharet* was doing *him* a favor to let him write. It was actually the other way around. He was as sharp as a razor to the very end."

Ajda Pekkan had postponed her trip to Paris. The demurely dressed diva stood off in a corner of the library, looking out the window at the contrast between the gray, rainy sky and the green of the Palas's mature trees and gardens. Like so many entertainment celebrities, once the distance between star and audience had been stripped away, she was a painfully shy woman, who used her stardom or canned phrases to maintain the distance between herself and other human beings.

"It's beautiful, isn't it? Almost as beautiful as you, Miss Pekkan." He spoke in French, having learned this was her second tongue, and one she preferred to English.

She turned to find herself looking into the frankly admiring — and admiringly frank — look of a clean-cut young man in a Savile Row suit who did not seem overwhelmed to be in her presence. "Thank you," she said. "I understand we were supposed to have met in the next few days. You're Mister Baumueller, are you not?"

"The fourth person in my family to bear that name. However, there are only three Edwin Baumuellers presently living." He smiled candidly and, she found, disarmingly. "Mister Joel would have enjoyed your opening number the other night. That's his real name, by the way."

"You know him?" she asked, her eyebrows rising.

"We did a few sessions together. He still enjoys playing sideman on other artists' sessions. We met after I'd done some work with the Village People on *Y.M.C.A.*"

"You've done recordings?" she asked, impressed.

"Mostly financed some, played guitar on a few."

"What's he like, Billy Joel?"

"He's very determined that his way is the right way. He's thirty-four and Jewish, although he doesn't practice the religion."

"And you, Mister Baumueller?"

"Why don't you call me Jake? Everyone else does. To answer your question, I'm Jewish to a degree. We attend Temple Emanu-El in New York on the High Holy Days, simply because my parents expect our family to be seen in the world's largest synagogue, Miss Pekkan."

"Turnabout's fair play, Jake. Why don't you call me Ayşe if you prefer? That's my given name. Turhan told me you're working at the *World's* Istanbul bureau for six months."

"Only because I wanted to meet you." Unlike most American men she'd met, who tended to shift their eyes when looking at a woman, he did not avert her gaze. "Would you like me to get you a plate of *mezerler*? I noticed that when you came in, you walked straight to the most inconspicuous place on the ground floor of this house, and you've kept to your own ever since. Surely you must be a little hungry?"

"I'm famished," she said, smiling dazzlingly. "I neglected to have breakfast this morning."

When he returned to the library with the plate of hors d'oeuvres, he found her sitting in one of the two comfortable rocking chairs in the room. "Don't get up," he said. "I didn't know if you wanted anything to drink, so I took it upon myself to bring some *elma çay*."

"Apple tea. Thank you, Mister Baumueller — Jake. Turhan told me you wanted to interview me?"

"Actually, I wanted to *meet* you. I couldn't think of a more natural way — well, let's be honest, a more forced way — to meet you. I researched and got the basic facts of your life down, long before today. I was surprised at how much Turhan Türkoğlu was able to add to my information. He was one of your admirers for more than a decade."

"He is — was — a sweet man. But for him, I probably wouldn't have agreed to meet with you. He didn't tell me you were involved in the entertainment industry."

"He didn't know. Have you ever been to New York, Ayşe?"

"No. I find the idea a bit frightening."

"And you're not put off by Paris?"

"Ah, no," she sighed. "What a wonderful, romantic city. Have you been there, Jake?"

"Five times," he said. "It's a magnet for Americans, even though we're fond of saying how rude Parisians are."

"I would hardly call them rude," she replied. "They know they're the custodians of the greatest city in the world and they simply act the part so well."

"New York's a bit like that," Jake said. "It's a lot of bluster and it can be intimidating, but I often wonder if I'd really be happy anywhere else. Perhaps someday you'll allow me to escort you there?"

She looked levelly at him. "Is that the way you approach every woman, Jake?"

"No, Miss Pekkan," he said formally. "Only the truly beautiful ones."

Aviva Kohn, eager to absorb everything, was slowly and, she thought, unobtrusively, inspecting the large, imposing mansion that had housed so much Turkish history and so many memories — Halide Orhan's old study, where she'd conceived the idea of the Yucel Orhan Teachers' College; a charred wall on the second floor, a grim reminder of the days when, as a Miracle House, Belgrade Palas had housed three hundred fifty Jewish refugees fleeing the nightmare of Hitler's holocaust; a door that was, even now, locked and bore a tiny placard with one word, "Rachela."

In a tiny bedroom toward the rear of the house, Aviva found a carefully preserved sepia photo of a slender, handsome, moustachioed young man in an ancient military uniform. Grandma Zari had long ago told her of the love story between Halide and Metin Ermenek which, even now, choked her up and caused her involuntarily to put her hand to her mouth and gasp. She recalled how the tiny, hunchbacked, French-born Halide, then only seventeen, had traveled all the way to Anatolia on an ancient steamer and, by escaping her chaperone and disguising herself as a Turkish soldier, had found her way to the battlefield of Gallipoli and her lover's arms. How Halide and Metin had made love just once, and how he'd been fatally wounded in battle the next day. How Halide had stayed on as a nurse at the front, to become the Angel of Gallipoli, and, during the next fifty years, the Angel of Turkey.

The ancient story came to life for Aviva as she faced that faded photograph. Suddenly, she started weeping. As her sobs wound down, she felt comforting hands gently rubbing and patting her upper back. "Grandma?" she queried in a little girl voice.

"Yes, child," Zahavah said gently. "Sometimes the dam needs to break to let the excess pressure out." She held her granddaughter to her until the crying stopped.

"Oh, Grandma, I feel like such a fool."

"Your young man at the university?"

Aviva stifled a gasp. "You know?"

"I have since the day after you first became involved."

"You didn't say anything."

"Should I have?"

"How did you find out?"

"Does it really matter? Does your generation think it invented infatuation?"

"Grandma!" Aviva had never heard the old woman talk this way.

"You've been sitting here and crying for the last fifteen minutes over something you perceive as so heroic you could never hope to match it. What do you think propelled Halide Orhan and Metin Ermenek toward one another? Do you really believe it was such magnanimous, high ideals that caused her to come to Turkey? My girl, Halide's noble ambition was nothing more than to get to her man and do what people have been doing since the first caveman stripped off the first cave woman's fur outfit. And stop looking so shocked, my dear. I'm eighty-two and I can damn well say what I please. Or do you think I wasn't young once, and filled with the same sap as you?"

Aviva rose, walked over to the bedroom window, and looked at the large trees that covered the property.

"Those huge trees were tiny saplings once, and in their own way they were motivated in the same way as human beings," her grandmother said. "All of us are links in an eternal chain, each connected with one another."

"What connection could I possibly have to Halide Orhan?" Aviva asked. "I never met her. I was ten years old when she died."

"I first met Turhan Türkoğlu when I was twelve and he was fifteen. The way I met him was that *his* link to the past, a caravan master named Ibrahim who'd known *my* father, suffered a fatal heart attack the day I met him. You met Turhan at the end of his life, and only for a very few days, but, whether you know it or not, he is as much *your* link to the past as I am. And your link to Halide Orhan and Metin Ermenek."

"How can you say that?"

"Halide and Turhan were the closest of lifelong friends. At the end, she left him Belgrade Palas in her will. After her death, Turhan brought Halide's life mementos back to Belgrade Palas from Kuşadası. He arranged all her belongings as she'd had them when she lived here. Do you know how Turhan and Halide met?"

"Uh-uh."

"Turhan was a medical orderly at Gallipoli the day after Halide and Metin came together, the day Metin Ermenek was right in the path of the grenade. Turhan was the one who brought Metin in to the field dispensary and who, knowing he could face a court-martial if he was caught, stole morphine from the company hospital to relieve Metin's pain while he lay dying. Turhan spent endless hours sitting with Halide, and brought her back to life when she felt she had nothing left to live for. And you, my darling girl, are now a part of the endless chain. So is everyone whose path you cross in life. So, my Aviva, it's time to stop feeling sorry for yourself and time to start thinking about the value of every *today*, and not about your wasted *yesterdays*."

"What do you suggest, Grandma?"

"Keep an eye on young Baumueller. There's a lot more to him than meets the eye. He's got much more character than even he believes he has. You never know what might happen. Oh, and one more thing?"

"Yes?"

"*He's* pretty infatuated with that famous singer downstairs, who's much too old and, I fear, much too experienced for him. I've no idea where that relationship will lead, but you might be in a much worse place than Istanbul if *his* life starts to fall apart and you're there to pick up the pieces."

12

"Now that we're legally married, it's high time my *Pasha* chose a place to take his soon-to-be-*bulging* bride on a honeymoon," Sara said, mussing his hair in their now-matrimonial bed.

"Turkey or Israel, Sara? Either is fine as long as you're there with me."

"Turkey's more practical," she said. "You're due to be transferred to LandSoutheast next month and General Lior used his influence to get me assigned to Çiğli Air Base, outside of Izmir, so we'll be under the same roof for at least the next year."

"I've got thirty days' accrued leave. Why do you say Turkey's more practical?"

"How much time does the Turkish Air Force give you to report to your new assignment?"

"Twenty days."

"I get three weeks to report to Çiğli. That means we could fly to Ankara and drop Halil off with your brother Yavuz and his wife. From there, we could take the Izmir Express overnight to the coast, celebrate our honeymoon in style, and then report to our new assignments without taking one day's leave."

"So, you've made all the decisions already. Do I get a say in anything?"

"Oh, yes, my Colonel. I'm not beyond *that* kind of activity yet."

"My God, darling, I've never seen anything like this in my life, not even in the Holy Land!"

"It's been a place of a legend in our family for sixty years," he said, smiling enigmatically.

"The night your mother hypnotized your *baba*?" Sara said. At his quizzical stare, she responded, "Another family secret? Yavuz showed me some photographs of your mother as a young woman. I've never seen anyone as stunning."

"Did he tell you it happened *twice*?"

"Uh-huh, but don't get your hopes up, *Yarbay*. In my present condition, I don't expect to go traipsing around Ephesus in the nude, either in daylight or at night. I wonder how much it's changed since they were last here."

"Hard to tell," he said, as they looked down from the upper reaches of the enormous twenty-five thousand-seat outdoor theater. The blue, nearly cloudless sky and the bright sunshine made it hard to believe it was February.

"That long street seems to lead to nowhere," Sara said, pointing to a wide, white thoroughfare that headed into a green field in the distance, then suddenly quit.

"Harbor Street," Omer said. "It used to be the main commercial boulevard to the port. Ephesus was the third largest city in the Roman Empire. It had about three hundred thousand people at the time of Jesus. That field in the distance used to be one of safest bays in the Aegean."

When they had carefully picked their way down to the orchestra section of the massive theater, Omer pointed out that since the theater was set against a hill, the acoustics were such that you could drop a coin on the stage and it could be heard clearly as far as the upper seats, more than a hundred yards away.

As they headed toward the center of Ephesus. Sara suddenly exclaimed, "Omer! You've simply *got* to take my photograph over there!" She pointed toward a low, U-shaped structure, housing about a hundred open toilets, none of which was separated by any type of enclosure. In the center of the structure, Sara pointed out a raised proscenium. Before he could stop her, Sara handed him her camera and seated herself on one of the toilets. "Come on, take my picture," she said. "The folks at home will never believe this."

"I've got a better idea," he said, laughing. He handed the camera to a passerby. After a few moments of conversation, he sat down immediately adjacent to his wife, while the obliging tourist photographed both of them.

"I think I can piece together what this was all about," Sara said, "but why the raised stage in the center?"

"The city's businessmen came here each morning at about the same time to do what nature intended. The running water underneath kept the place clean and relatively odor-free. Since these men *paid* to do what they did here, they expected to be entertained. They had lecturers, poets, even musicians performing each morning, and ... don't look at me like that. It was a regular job, like any other ..."

"Uh-huh," Sara said. "What do you do for a living, daddy? Where do you work, papa?" The newlyweds broke into a fit of giggles.

Immediately across the street from the public toilets, they came to an impressive two-story marble building. "The Library of Celsus," Omer pointed out. "One of the three largest in the ancient world. Only the one at Alexandria held more volumes." After three hours enjoying the magic that was Ephesus, they returned to their hotel in nearby Kusadasi for a well-needed nap.

FEBRUARY 1984
ISTANBUL

February 2, 1984. By prearrangement, Muren and Abdullah Öcalan met at the home of a successful lawyer in the fashionable Şişli district of Istanbul. "You've done very well so far," the Apo said. "Your professors tell me that in the last month you've really buckled down."

"Thank you, Sir," Muren mumbled, his eyes downcast. "I've been working awfully hard since December."

"First heartbreak, eh?" Öcalan said, smiling knowingly.

"You knew?"

"Oh, yes. Miss Kohn's an attractive young lady. We don't view Israel as our enemy. Indeed, I had the opportunity to meet with the girl's aunt, an Israeli Lieutenant Colonel, last November. We had a very constructive exchange of ideas. It's time you had a little holiday. February in Istanbul can be rather dreary."

"You have something in mind, *Apo?*"

"I do. Colonel Barak — she's now Colonel Akdemir — is on honeymoon with her new husband, the former Executive Officer at Diyarbakir Air Base. I'd like you to pass her a personal note of thanks from me."

"How would I go about doing that without being caught, *Apo?*"

"Easily. They're on the way down the Aegean. We've made arrangements for you to fly to Antalya, where one of our operatives will drive you to the small town of Kaş. Their boat captain, another one of our agents, will direct them to a wonderful fish restaurant on the quay. You'll be arranging their table that night. You'll simply leave this envelope under Madame Akdemir's place setting."

KAŞ, AT THE SOUTHWEST CORNER OF TURKEY

The "operative" who picked Muren up was an attractive female student his own age, who seemed much more interested in Turkish pop than politics. On the fifty-kilometer trip to Kaş, she didn't once mention the Kurdish cause.

"Did you know, the new Prime Minister's wife is a Kurd?" he asked, trying to gauge the extent of her commitment to the cause.

"No." She seemed unconcerned. "Have you heard the latest album by Edip Akbayram? He's still working with Dostlar, but that band's not nearly as popular as Dadaslar or Mogollar. I was really upset that Sertab Erener didn't win at Eurovision last year. She really had the best song. Maybe it's because she's Turkish."

As the girl droned on and on, it dawned on Murten that she considered herself part of the Turkish culture, and felt personally insulted when she perceived that a Turkish singer had been slighted.

He had always viewed every Turk as evil, simply because he was a Turk, and every Kurd as noble and good, simply because he was a Kurd. He'd done as he'd been told, without question, because it was for the cause, but he'd never once stopped to think that the pilot who'd been killed when the F-104 exploded was someone's brother, son, husband, or father. And the Turkish officer he'd killed in Lebanon? Surely that officer had not set out in life with the avowed aim of personally hurting a Kurdish teenager, whom he didn't even know existed. What it really came down to was that there were good people and bad people everywhere, and for the most part, the only lives that really mattered to them were their own and the lives of those close to them. Muren felt an unpleasant sensation as the cold edge of guilt stabbed at his innards. He had always thought of himself as one of the good ones. But he'd killed two people without any real provocation.

❈❈❈

The boat rounded a peninsula and entered a gorgeous crescent-shaped bay. Here, the water was almost the color of rich, red wine, although it was still remarkably clear. Behind the bay, high, pine-clad mountains descended almost to the water itself. There was a large, wooded island in the middle of the bay. Sara noticed the largest flag she'd ever seen — a *Greek* banner — hanging desultorily from a pole on the highest point of the island. She glanced questioningly at her husband.

"It's exactly what you think you see," Omer said. "*Kastelhorizo*. We Turks call it *Meis*. The southeasternmost point in Greece. There are no 'official' dealings between Kastelhorizo and Kaş, but there are supply boats and tour boats going out every day and coming back every evening."

❈❈❈

Once his driver had dropped him off, Muren spent the next several hours walking in the hills above Kaş. His mind was in turmoil, as he thought about how many people had died needlessly. He did not feel that Öcalan was a bad man. To the contrary, he was a very dedicated one, but he, himself, had told Muren that the Israelis were not the enemy.

He was a Kurd. Not so anyone would notice the difference between Muren and any Turk, and no one would be able to pick him out of a crowd of students at Istanbul University as being any different from them. But was he really any different? Once again, questions he'd never thought to ask assailed him. It hadn't mattered to Aviva and it hadn't mattered to Muren that she was an Israeli.

As the hours passed, the tentacles binding his mind started to unravel. He made up his mind what he must do that evening.

The young man who'd been filling their water glasses, refilling their bread tray, and delivering *mezerler* to them all evening held out Sara's chair as she finished her meal. "Excuse me," he said. "Would it offend you if I asked if we could speak for a few moments?"

Sara and Omer looked at the young man, then at one another, uncomprehendingly.

"I assure you, Colonel and Madame Akdemir," he continued, calmly observing the startled looks on their faces, "it would be best for the three of us if we did."

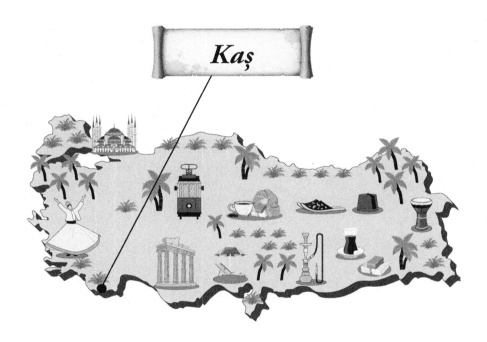

Kaş

13

The three of them were seated at a small table on the deck of the Akdemirs' chartered boat, which was floating serenely, just offshore. The lights had been doused and there was no one else on board.

"Let me understand what you're saying," Omer said coldly, but quietly. "You planted an explosive in the fighter plane at Diyarkabir, you admit to killing a Turkish officer in Lebanon, and you're asking *me* to grant you clemency?"

"Yes, sir."

"You understand I could be court-martialed for going along with what you're proposing?"

"Yes, sir."

"And even if the Turkish government somehow decided to spare your life, you could rot in prison until you were more than fifty years old? Not to mention you'd be the target of every Kurd-hating Turk in the country?"

"I'm aware of that, Colonel. The Kurds who worked at Second Turkish Air Force said you were a good man, so I used this opportunity to throw myself on your mercy. If I'm mistaken, the sea wall is only fifty meters away. I can jump over the side and be gone from your life in an instant. On the other hand, you're larger and stronger than I am, and for all I know, you have a gun, so you're free to take me prisoner."

Omer paused. His late father had often told him that when a dog or a wolf bares his throat to his adversary, that adversary takes it as a sign of submission and refrains from killing. Now, this boy was doing that very thing.

"You lost family after the Diyarbakir incident?" Omer asked.

"I did, Colonel. My father, both my brothers, two uncles, and ..." he choked on the next words, "my mother and my younger sister."

Omer Akdemir winced inwardly. He'd heard of Turkish "cleansing" before, but the victims had been nameless, faceless enemies. "How old were you at the time?"

"Seventeen."

"And the Lebanese incident?"

"I was taken to Lebanon to save my life. I was told that those Turkish officers had killed my family."

"You met Abdullah Öcalan there?" Sara asked.

"Yes, Colonel," he answered, "and Abu Ammar as well."

"Arafat," she said, responding to her husband's questioning look. "Would you like a cigarette, Muren?"

"No, thank you, Madame ... Colonel ...?" the Kurd said, momentarily confused and not knowing quite how to address her, since each of them seemed to be questioning him. "I don't smoke."

"What did Ammar want?"

"To cement relations between the PLO and the PKK."

"What was Öcalan's response?"

"He was very cordial to Ammar's face. He dispatched Banr al Sidi, an Iraqi whom I met in the camp, to Palestine to work with Ammar."

"You said 'to his face,'" Omer said.

"Yes, Colonel. I think Öcalan was quite disgusted with Arafat as a man, and the only reason he cooperated with the PLO was that it was one of the few movements in the Middle East that gave any credence to our cause."

"The enemy of my enemy is my friend," Sara remarked.

"Why did you blow up the plane?"

"It was a test of my loyalty to the cause, Colonel Akdemir."

"You didn't think you were killing another human being?"

"Not at that time, Colonel. But there's been so much killing on both sides, and ... and things have happened in my life during the past year. Not all of them turned out as I thought — and sometimes hoped they would. Then I started to believe that the lines between good and evil often blur."

Omer Akdemir looked directly at the young man, neither accepting nor condemning his words.

"Tell me, Colonel, was he ... was he married? A ... a father?"

"No. He was a bachelor second lieutenant, not much older than you."

The three of them sat quietly for a few moments, the lights of town twinkling a stone's throw away. Sara brought three bottles of spring water from a cooler on deck, passed one bottle to each of the men, and unscrewed the top from her own.

"Did you tell any of this to Aviva?" Sara asked. Muren abruptly sucked in his breath. "Your friend the *Apo* told me about your relationship the day we met," she continued. "You needn't worry, I never discussed anything about it with my niece. She's an adult. What she does is her own business."

"No," Muren said, recovering himself. "We never discussed anything except that I was a Kurdish student."

"I'm sure you discussed other things as well," Sara said, smiling enigmatically.

"Must we discuss that now? I love ... loved her very much."

"Then you still consider her a friend?"

"Much more than that," he said forcefully. "I'd do anything for her. If only ..."

"If only ..." Sara repeated. "The two saddest words in any language. So it hasn't gone as well as you'd hoped?"

He shrugged. "She's, uh, older than I am."

Omer chuckled appreciatively, the first time he'd shown any warmth. "That's never stopped a man and a woman before," he said.

"Darling," Sara said to her husband. "You could get into all kinds of trouble if our Kurdish friend disclosed everything to *you* and you didn't tell your superiors. But the note from his leader was addressed to *me*. Perhaps Muren meant to talk to *me* and not to you."

"What are you saying, Sara?"

"In the ancient Hebrew liturgy it's said that 'He who takes a life, it is as if he had destroyed the entire universe.' But it also goes on, 'He who saves a life, it is as if he had saved the entire universe.'"

Omer scratched his head. "You're talking in riddles, Sara."

In response, Sara looked directly at both men. "Muren, you say there exists good relations between the PKK and the PLO?"

"On the face of it."

"And the PKK has a plant within the PLO?"

A sudden small wave lifted the boat a foot, not enough to jar any of them, but it momentarily interrupted their conversation.

Taking a deep breath, Muren replied, "Banr al Sidi."

"How close is he to the PLO leadership?"

"It's hard to say."

"Do you think Mister Öcalan would allow you to visit al Sidi in Palestine?"

"Why?" Muren asked.

"I'm sure when Arafat was in Lebanon he mentioned the Palestinian refugee camps?"

"He said if anything could convince the world of the justice of the Palestinian cause, it was those camps. Thousands of innocent people caged like animals in barbed-wire enclosures."

"Did you believe him?"

"Yes."

"Even though you'd never seen the camps?"

"That's true."

"And the *Apo*? What does he think?"

"He's never been to Israel, or to Palestine."

"Why not?"

"He's told me he doesn't trust Ammar any farther than he can see him, and he believes Ammar would use such a visit by the *Apo* to promote his own aims. He also worries he wouldn't be entirely safe there."

"But Öcalan sent one of his own to Palestine."

"Al Sidi is not high up in the organization."

"And you?" Sara probed.

"Even lower."

"He trusts you, though?"

"I believe so."

"Al Sidi's an Iraqi. You're a Kurd."

"True."

"So, if you asked the *Apo* to allow you to visit Palestine, he'd probably say yes?"

"What reason would I have to go to Palestine?"

"To see for yourself whether or not the stories of the refugee camps are true."

"To what end?"

Sara stood for a moment and descended into the galley of the pleasure boat. Shortly afterward, she returned with a tray bearing three tulip glasses of *Elma Cay*, the ubiquitous Turkish apple tea. She offered one to each of the men and took one for herself. They spent the next few minutes staring over the water to the flickering lights of town. At the end of that time, Sara said, "Excuse us a few moments, would you, Muren? You need not leave the boat and don't worry that someone will apprehend you. I'd like to speak to my husband alone for a few moments."

When they returned to the deck of the boat, Muren was nervously pacing from prow to stern. He looked up as they approached.

"Muren," Colonel Omer Akdemir said. "As my wife told you, I cannot be party to what I don't know. I'm going onshore for a little while. You may or may not be here when I return, but I think the Israeli Colonel Akdemir, would like a few words with you alone."

With that, Omer lowered a small rubber raft to the water, climbed into it, and silently rowed his way to shore.

"When you did what you did, quite a few people suffered. Yet if you do what I ask, you might even save a larger universe than you destroyed."

"How could I hope to get away with it?"

"You're a friend of the PLO authorities. You'd be in the company of trusted higher-ups, with a *carte de passage* from Abu Ammar himself. No Israeli could ever have such open access to the camps."

"And you think the baby is in one of the camps?"

"If they haven't killed him. They may have used the child as a replacement for one of their teenage suicide bombers. In that way, they manage to keep the mothers complacent, saying it's Allah's will."

"How would I be able to identify him?"

"Mostly by using your ears and your intellect. Although he was born with light-colored hair, that is not a badge of honor in the Palestinian culture, so they've either shaved his head or darkened what hair he has. He was with his mother for only three days, but they say there's a very powerful life-force between a mother and her child."

"Even if the baby is alive, how can I possibly expect to get him out of the camp without anyone finding out?"

"That, Muren, will call for some very creative thinking. Oh, and one more thing."

"Yes?"

"It might interest you to know that the baby's mother is Aviva's closest friend."

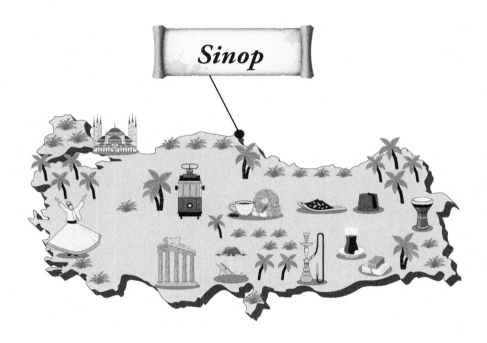

14

Sinop, March 5, 1984
Dear Donnie,

Hey, little brother, Happy B'day! I've been on The Hill for ten months now. Two more and I'm outta' this place — and it won't be a moment too soon! I'm counting the days. I've been half drunk since I first arrived here, since drinking's about all there is to do in this place. Remember how mama came down on me when I first got here and I sent her a postcard from Sinop? She said, "That's got to be one gorgeous place. I can't see why you're complaining." After I sent her the same postcard for thirty days in a row, she finally got the picture.

Det-4 sits up on a hill, the highest point on a peninsula, surrounded by the Black Sea. On one side it's so windy and rough you'd swear the waves will climb up the hill or the wind will blow you off the hill. On the other side, the water is so calm you can walk out a hundred yards or more and pick up old pieces of mosaics just lying in the water, Of course, if the Turkish government ever finds out you're takin' any of their precious shit, you are screwed and tattooed.

That's been a big problem here. You might find some local street artist to tattoo you, but you sure as hell aren't gonna' get screwed! Don't even think of tryin' to get any. The Turks are damned protective

of their women. The Turkish cops found one of our guys talking —
talking — to some young chick down in the city about six months
ago, and he was outta' here that night. They'd have liked to kill him
— after they'd cut his balls off. All of us get certificates of membership
in the Sexless Society of Sinop when we first get here.

"Uncle Sugar" tries his damnedest to keep us from killing one
another or killing our friendly neighborhood Turks. There's all the
food you'd ever want, and you can get Johnny Walker Black for
fifteen cents a throw at the Enlisted Men's Club.

One day last summer, we were buzzed by a black jet that flew
right over the hill and then back again. That sucker was so low I
could see the hammer and sickle on the fuselage. That made it real
clear just how close we are to the Commies.

Hey, Bro', two of my buddies just knocked on my door. They've got
a sackload of Turkish vodka one of 'em brought in the laundry bags,
and we are gonna' tie on the biggest bender of the year. So I'll post this
letter in the APO mailbox, and it'll soon be one day less in hell. Take
care m'man! John

ISTANBUL – *ISHARET'S* OFFICES
A WEEK LATER

"Aviva, are you ready for your first out-of-town assignment?"

"What do you mean, Mister Heper?"

"We've got a touchy situation. I'll need some objective reporting, and it will be better if my reporter is not a Turk. I don't want anyone from *Isharet's* Samsun bureau on the scene. Those people have to live in that city. I've asked Jake Baumueller to accompany you."

"Mister Heper, doesn't that sound a little bit contrived?"

"No, Miss Kohn, it does not, and if you aren't interested in going to your grandmother's home town of Sinop —"

"Sinop? Nothing ever happens there."

"I think you'll change your mind when you hear about this."

At that moment, the door to Abdullah Heper's office opened and Jake Baumueller burst in without knocking. "You wanted to see me, Mister Heper?"

"I do. Jake, you're working the *World's* Istanbul bureau?"

"For the next year in any event." He smiled an easy, casual smile which Aviva found charming.

"It seems one of your countrymen has been a bad boy. I'd like you to accompany Aviva to Sinop to find out what it's all about."

ISHARET'S ISTANBUL OFFICE
THE NEXT DAY

"Jesus H. Christ! That's got international repercussions that could shake the whole alliance!" Jake Baumueller exclaimed. "Some twenty-year-old American GI stationed at Sinop got drunk out of his mind, lowered the Turkish flag from the flagpole at the post, cut out the star and crescent, and then ran the flag back up the pole?"

"That's right. Defacing the Turkish flag is one of the only capital offenses under Turkish law."

"Were there witnesses?" Aviva asked.

"Two Turkish guards at the base and a dishwasher who was on her way home at the time. Detachment 4 has been under a state of siege since it happened, twelve hours ago. Over five thousand of Sinop's citizens are standing outside the gate. No one's going in, no one's coming out. They are deadly quiet, no demonstrations, no shouting. That's the scariest part of all."

"Why us?" Aviva asked. "You've got seasoned reporters, *Turkish* reporters, who understand the people and the culture. Have you ever thought we might be a bit inexperienced to handle something this big?"

The publisher smiled enigmatically. "More than sixty years ago, a young, wet-behind-the-ears fellow said the same thing to my father. Dad sent him to cover a story that changed the course of Turkish history. Looking back, I'd say it was a pretty good decision to take a chance on Turhan Türkoğlu, wouldn't you?"

"How would you expect us to get in?" Jake persisted.

"The American ambassador received clearance from the Turkish government to allow you to fly direct to the Hill by Turkish Army helicopter," Heper responded. "It's very touchy. The Americans aren't allowing any Turks except employees onto the American base, for obvious reasons. Aviva, you're an Israeli, even if you're on *Isharet's* staff. Jake, you represent the largest American newspaper. Your family's well-connected to the Washington power base. They're already hollering in the U.S. about what's going on."

"Are you sure we should be the ones to go?" Jake asked.

"Yes. This story's the biggest one all year. The Turks and the Americans have entirely different ideas on how they want the news presented. If Turkey's largest daily newspaper is represented and if the New York *World*, the most prestigious American newspaper, has a reporter on the scene, no one can say the reports were fabricated."

"But if Jake and I disagree?" Aviva said.

"Then you disagree. All I care about is that you get to the bottom of the story."

MARCH 1984 – THE NEXT DAY
U.S. ARMY, DETACHMENT 4
SINOP, NORTHEASTERN TURKEY

Jake and Aviva boarded a UH-1 Bell Iroquois helicopter with no identifying marks. "One of our gifts to the Turkish government," the American colonel said. "We're replacing the Huey with the new UH-60 Blackhawks, and we're hoping to sell off some of these older birds to the Turkish Army. This ship was part of the price we paid to allow us to fly directly onto Det-4 and bypass the town."

The helicopter lifted over the sere hills surrounding Ankara, then headed northeast. An hour later, the dun-colored steppe gave way to green, forested mountains. Aviva involuntarily put her hand to her mouth and gazed at the ground in amazement. "I've always thought the Turkish countryside was a never-ending brown, wrinkled mass of earth," she shouted, trying to make her voice heard over the *wop-wop-wop* of the 'copter's blades.

"Most people would agree with you," the colonel replied, "but from Sinop east to the Georgian border, the Black Sea region's completely different from the rest of the country. We'll fly to the Bafra Peninsula, then come in over the sea from the northeast, so we don't have to overfly the town."

The Huey landed. Aviva, Jake, and the colonel were greeted by Major Gene Daniels, the post commander. As they exited the helicopter and removed their foam earplugs, Jake looked out from the facility to the town below.

"Quite a view, Major," he shouted over the din of the Huey's engines.

"It is," Daniels replied, his tone equally strident. "Let's get on over to my office, where we can talk in normal voices." Once in the commandant's office, an orderly brought in tea and cakes. The four of them sat at a rectangular table, covered with a large relief model of the Sinop Peninsula and the station.

After perfunctory greetings and introductions, Jake got down to business. "Major, I'd like to get some background on Det-4 before I get into the incident and the players."

"All right, Mister Baumueller, here's the short version. Det-4's built on a seven hundred-foot high hill at the edge of the peninsula. The officers call it 'Diogenes Station.' Everyone up here calls it 'The Hill.' Until twenty years ago, the only ways to get here from Ankara was a fourteen-hour trip in the back of a two-and-a-half-ton truck, in a cramped, overloaded Turkish bus through the mountains, or, if you were stationed at Det 4 or visiting the post, via *Eshek Ekspress,* a six-seater aircraft attached to our station."

"What's the mission of this installation, Major?" Jake continued.

"Sinop's the northernmost point in Turkey and the closest to the Soviet Union. Det-4's America's forward listening post for catching all kinds of information on Soviet military units, the Soviet space program, and their ICBM sites."

"Sounds exciting," Aviva said.

Major Daniels cocked his head and smiled. "Critical to our country's security, yes. Exciting? I don't think anyone up here would describe it quite that way. Hours and hours of boredom, for a few seconds of what might be, but usually isn't, flash information. We were the first to know about a lot of Soviet activities. Remember the U-2 spy plane incident?"

"Francis Gary Powers," Aviva said. "That was more than twenty years ago."

"Powers and his U-2 were based at Incirlik, down in southern Turkey. We felt a good deal of the heat up here. The Soviet Union demanded that Det-4 be shut down. It wasn't, but it was touch and go. Finally, they came to an agreement that Soviet missiles would be removed from Cuba in return for the removal of Jupiter missiles from Turkey."

"I didn't know that," Jake said.

"Neither did I at the time," the major said. "You're what, late twenties?"

"Twenty-eight."

"I'm thirty-four. We were both kids when it happened. The United States never admitted it even had Jupiter missiles on Turkish soil."

15

"I'd hardly call him threatening," Aviva said to Jake and Master Sergeant Callaghan, shortly after they'd left the stockade area where they'd been introduced to John Hayden. "Five-eight, one hundred thirty pounds. The guy looks and smells as if he hadn't showered or shaved in a long time."

"He's scared shitless," the sergeant remarked. "I'd be, too, if I were in his position. Twenty-year-old kid, fresh off an Iowa farm, and he could be facing the death penalty."

"He wouldn't even talk to us," Aviva remarked. "except to grunt a few words."

"His lawyer told him not to talk to anybody."

"They've got a lawyer for him?"

"Two. One Air Force JAG type and one big-shot Turkish lawyer the embassy hired. Miss, I notice you speak with an accent. Are you originally from the States?"

"No, Sergeant. I'm Israeli."

"No kidding. Hey, you guys really kicked butt in sixty-seven and seventy-three. I'm from Mobile, Alabama. One of our city councilmen's Jewish, Jacob Levy. Do you know him?"

"I'm afraid not, Sergeant. I've never been to the States."

"Man, Miss, you sure know the lingo. Can you speak Turkish, too?"
"Uh-huh."

"My mama always said Jews are the smartest people in the world, especially when it comes to money."

"Has Private Hayden spoken with you, Sergeant?" Jake asked.

"Interesting you'd call him 'Private.' Most Americans think the only American servicemen stationed in Turkey are USAF, but Det-4's an army outpost. And yes, I knew him a little bit from before. Everyone knows everybody else on this post. There's only a couple hundred of us up here on the hill. He's talked to me and to a couple of his buddies on post, but that's about it."

"Assuming he *did* do it, do you have any idea why"

The Sergeant went over to an aluminum coffee maker and poured some of the hot liquid into a well-used, chipped cup. He filled two clean styrofoam cups and offered one each to the two visitors, which they gratefully accepted.

"For one thing, the kid was bombed out of his mind and probably doesn't even remember what he was doing. That's not uncommon up here. These young kids are full of piss and vinegar, no women at all, eight hours of the most boring work you can imagine, and absolutely no place to go. It's the end of the earth and the Army is one gigantic tit — excuse me, Miss — dispensing cheap booze. What else have they got?"

"But cutting out the star and crescent?" Aviva asked.

"Hey, when these guys get high, they do the most reckless thing they can do after drinking. They bet on anything, 'cause they don't have anything else to spend their money on. Some of the stuff gets pretty gross, Miss."

"Sergeant Callaghan, I'm here to get the full details. You don't need to sugar coat anything because I'm a woman. If you'd like, I'd be happy to leave you two alone."

"Well, uh … You promise you won't be offended?"

"That's what I just said, Sergeant."

"Being from the South …"

"Yes, sir, I understand. Mobile, Alabama, where Jacob Levy's a city councilman."

That broke the tension and the guard laughed heartily. "All right, Miss. You asked for it. One of the things these boys do when they get good and drunk, they have a pissing contest — for real. They start out right at the edge of the hill. Then, while they're doin' it, they each back up a few steps at a time. The winner's the guy who can still shoot over the cliff when he's farthest from it."

"Lovely," Jake Baumueller remarked.

"You're saying he pulled the flag down, did what he did, and sent the defaced flag back up on a bet? Who was with him at the time?"

"Nobody'll say."

At that moment, Major Daniels entered the prison area. "How's the prisoner, Sergeant?"

"Same old same old," Callaghan replied. "Is there any way we can get 'im outta' here, Major? Them Turks outside the gate are likely to batter it down come nighttime, and then there'll be hell to pay, and not only for Hayden."

"I wish we could, Reuben," Daniels said.

"Where's he supposed to be tried?" Jake asked.

"Samsun, if we can get him there in one piece."

"Do you think he can get a fair trial there?"

"Nope. Folks are pretty conservative around here. Samsun's where Atatürk landed when he declared the Turkish Republic."

"Why can't we just spirit him out of the country?"

"Wouldn't work. The Turks would go crazy and the whole American presence here would be in jeopardy. It's one thing when our soldiers try to talk to one of their women. It's something else to cut the star and crescent out of their flag."

"I almost feel sorry for him," Aviva said.

"It's bad judgment, all right," Major Daniels replied. "You don't want to see someone branded for life because of something he did at twenty. On the other hand, we've got three thousand American troops in Turkey. One stupid kid goes on a bender and puts it all on the line."

"What do his lawyers say?" Aviva persisted.

"The JAG guy can't say anything. He's a junior captain sent up here on TDY from Ankara who's got absolutely no standing with the Turks. Under the NATO Status of Forces Agreement, Turkey's got jurisdiction, even if this is an American station. The important man is the Turkish lawyer. He told me the best shot is if they can work out some agreement to send Private Hayden to a place like Afyon, as far away as possible, for trial, have the kid plead guilty, and hopefully get him out in about five years. Of course, five years in a Turkish prison …"

"But our government has always taken care of its own," Jake started to say.

"Not so, Mister Baumueller," the major replied. "Our government has always taken care of its own *interests*, and maintaining good relations with our ally is very high up on America's scale of interests at the moment."

✽✾✽

"My grandmother was born and grew up here," Aviva said.

"The countryside around town is quite attractive, but I wouldn't advise going there now," Major Daniels said. They had just finished eating a meal of American steak, broccoli, and country-fried potatoes, followed by apple pie a-lá-mode and Turkish tea. "When you went by the perimeter fence, did you see that crowd?"

"They looked pretty sullen," Jake said.

"They assemble in four-hour shifts," Major Daniels said. "I suppose if you really wanted to go into town that bad, I could have our Turkish liaison call the mayor's office in the morning and see what can be done. You'll have a Turkish driver, but otherwise you're on your own. Sinop's off-limits to the troops."

"I could carry a weapon …" Jake began.

"Don't even think of such a thing," the major said. "That's all they'd need to start a riot. Miss Kohn's not an American and she works for Turkey's largest newspaper."

"Yes, but I wouldn't dream of letting her go without me."

"To protect me? How chivalrous of you, Mister Baumueller," Aviva said archly.

Jake blushed. "I didn't mean that at all."

"Then what did you mean?" she asked, smiling at his discomfort.

"Well, uh, that is …" he stammered.

"Or are you afraid I'll get more of a story than you?"

Major Daniels watched the exchange with amusement. "I suppose there's no harm in Mister Baumueller asking the mayor for the community's side of the story. After all, even in Sinop they've heard of the New York *World*."

✽✾✽

Downtown Sinop

Two days later, a Turkish Army car called for Aviva and Jake at the post's far gate. There were no Americans at the gate, only Turkish soldiers from the garrison at Samsun. No one molested the car on its drive down the hill, although many in the crowd lining Sinop's main street glared with unmasked hostility at the two foreigners in the back seat of the automobile.

The mayor, fiftyish, with thin hair, a thick belly, and a neatly-trimmed moustache, was extraordinarily courteous. The American journalist and his Israeli counterpart noticed another person in the room, a tall, impeccably groomed older man, whose thick head of steel-gray hair and startlingly bright blue eyes gave him an aura of profound dignity.

"Good afternoon," the mayor began. "Before we begin, I'd like to introduce you to a very special gentleman who's been sent here from Ankara." The man stood and bowed. Aviva could not help but note how strikingly handsome he looked.

"I don't believe these young people have met me, Mister Mayor," the man said, nodding at Jake and Aviva, "but I am very well acquainted with their families, especially with Miss Kohn's grandmother. Permit me to introduce myself. I am Kâzım Hükümdar."

Aviva's hand flew to her mouth. "You are …? My God!" She was momentarily at a loss for words. "Excuse my rudeness," she said. "My grandmother told me you were the most courageous boy … man … she ever met."

"Oh, she did, did she?" The man pushed his perfectly coiffed hair back from his forehead with three fingers of his right hand. His white-toothed smile was dazzling. "Well, good for her. I can say the feeling is more than mutual," he continued smoothly. "You know the story, then."

"I do, Kâzım Bey Effendim," she said. "You are a legend in our family. One day, might we perhaps talk?"

"Of course," said Hükümdar. "But for now, we have serious business to attend to — a very difficult and sensitive business, and I would like your input, off the record of course, as much as I am sure you'd like mine."

"Mister Justice Hükümdar, the Presiding Justice of the Court of Cassation in Ankara, has been designated by the Ministry of Justice to act as mediator," the mayor said. "When the ministry learned we'd be meeting today, they arranged to fly Justice Hükümdar to Sinop for an exchange of ideas."

For the next hour, the conversation was candid and productive. The mayor expressed his citizens' dual concerns: first, of course, that there had been a gross insult to the Turkish nation, and second, and more directly relevant, Sinop's residents were deeply humiliated because such an outrage had happened here.

"I understand that," Jake said. "What we need to do is find a way to assuage their feelings and their pride, and yet let them know that Americans aren't all bad people."

"Precisely," the Justice said. "If there was some way we could get the young man to make a public apology, a public show of humiliation…"

"That would immediately result in his being declared guilty, something his lawyer might not tolerate. I don't know that any judge in Sinop, given the citizens' present state of mind, would be able to impose anything short of the death penalty," Baumueller said.

"But he is guilty," the mayor rejoined. "There are three Turkish witnesses, and no American serviceman dares come forward as a witness in Mister Hayden's behalf. We need a face-saving device."

"I have an idea," Aviva said. "First, I must ask to what extent Private Hayden could be protected from harm if we were somehow able to convince him to make this public apology?"

"Military guards," Hükümdar said.

"But all it would take would be one man with a gun in the middle of the crowd."

"A published writing would not be acceptable," the mayor said, "because the people would simply say the Americans had drafted it, and they were not allowed to see Mister Hayden face to face."

"Suppose the following," Justice Hükümdar suggested. "We announce that Private Hayden would publicly address anyone who wanted to hear his apology on the parade ground of Detachment 4 itself? There would be a maximum of five hundred people allowed on the post at a time, and everyone who came onto the grounds would have to come through a single gate where he or she would be checked for weapons. For those who did not want to subject themselves to such a search, the Turkish military could set up a series of loudspeakers up and down the road into town, and the confession and apology would be broadcast to anyone who wanted to listen."

The two Turkish dignitaries mulled over Hükümdar's suggestion.

"But there would still have to be a trial," the mayor said.

"I agree," said the justice. "But I have an idea how that could be handled."

"How?" Baumueller asked.

"Perhaps if I were present at each of Private Hayden's confessions. I would follow his words by telling the crowd who I am, announcing that Sinop's embarrassment was assuaged, and affirming that Sinop could stand as a beacon for all that is honorable about the Republic of Turkey. However, the Ministry of Justice felt that the town had suffered enough, and so the best thing would be to have Hayden tried and sentenced in a place where the citizens of Sinop would never have to hear his name again."

"A place like Afyon?" Jake said.

"Something like that," the justice replied. "Of course, what we've said here today remains in this room and goes no farther."

Four nights later, when Private Hayden had been whisked out of Sinop by an armored Turkish military vehicle, Aviva and Baumueller asked Major Daniels if it would be safe for them to see Sinop. "After all, this is our last night here," Jake said, "and with everything happening so fast, we never got a chance to see the town."

"I see no reason why you shouldn't," he said. "Justice Hükümdar's solution seems to have cooled the situation down."

After taking a cab down to the thin neck of the peninsula, Aviva and Jake got out and walked along the quay, then strolled along the town's main street, where they browsed in several shops. Aviva pulled Jake into one of them, where she pointed out a miniature pair of wooden clog shoes with delicate silver filigree work. Before she could so much as utter a protest, Jake had purchased two pairs for her. She smiled and squeezed his hand thankfully. Farther down the street, Jake stopped at a small artist's studio, where he was fascinated by framed wood burnings. The artist had scraped local pinewood, then burned and etched images of traditional Turkish farmers, fishermen, hooded women, and other characters, onto the wood. He purchased one of the framed works for himself and one for Aviva.

"I wish we could find the house where grandma grew up," she said. "But in all the rush to get here, I didn't have time to even find out the address, let alone if it's still here."

"Major Daniels told me that one of the places we shouldn't miss is Mosaic Beach, that quiet, protected area we saw from the top of the hill. Shall we go there, Aviva?"

"Sure."

The late afternoon sun was descending in a fiery red ball.

"Oh, look!" Aviva said, delightedly. "There's a mosaic in the water. Do you think they'd really mind if we — ?"

"We'd better not," Jake said uncertainly. "I think we've had enough of violating the locals' habits in the past few days."

"I'll say you have," a voice behind them suddenly snarled.

Turning quickly, they beheld three local men in their early twenties, shorter than Jake but muscularly built. "You think your 'bought' judge's words made everything better?" the first man taunted.

"I'll handle this," Jake said softly to Aviva. "We mean you no harm," he said. "Besides, the lady is not American, she's Israeli."

"Is-ra-ey-li?" the second man said. "Even worse, those people think they own the world," he said, advancing on Aviva. He bumped her rudely and shoved her to the ground.

Reacting immediately, Jake lunged toward Aviva's attacker, but the assailant's two accomplices quickly grabbed each of his arms and pulled him back. Jake struggled valiantly, but he was held fast. The men, who were much heavier than he, reeked of garlic and sweat.

"Shall I soften her up?" the first man brayed to his fellows.

"Why not? You'll get to be first."

Jake watched, horrified, as the man reached back to punch Aviva's jaw with the heel of his palm. With a strength he didn't know he possessed, Jake broke loose from his captors and cried out in rage. Before he could reach Aviva, one of the two men who'd been holding him punched him in the kidney with the force of a jackhammer. Jake collapsed, his pain so great he could hardly think.

As he looked up, he heard a surprised grunt. The man who'd been about to attack Aviva doubled over and sank to the ground, clutching the area below his midsection. The man who'd floored Jake turned toward Aviva. In a split second, Aviva, brandishing the plastic bag containing the filigreed miniature clogs, slammed the bag at the man's head and followed with a solid blow to his groin. The third man, abandoning his mates, ran down the beach and into town.

Aviva rushed to where Jake was lying. "Are you all right?" she asked.

"Uh … I think so. I was just surprised, that's all. Aren't you glad I was there to protect you?" He grinned. "Or, maybe it was the other way around."

As they walked back toward town, Aviva said, "I suppose I should be a proper lady and thank you for *trying* to protect my honor." Jake, embarrassed, said nothing. "I don't want you to feel that bad," she said. "You can even treat me to dinner."

"Do you mind if I ask — ?"

"Not at all," she said. *"Krav Maga.* "Israeli form of hand-to-hand combat."

16

Half-an-hour later, Jake and Aviva were seated in a small *lokanta*, which boasted four tables, on Sinop's main street. True to custom, they'd gone toward the kitchen and pointed to what looked and smelled delectable.

"What I truly like about this country is that you can go into the meanest looking little place, go back to the kitchen, point out what you want, and know it's going to be delicious," Jake said, dipping a chunk of bread into the hearty lamb, potato and carrot stew.

"They come by it naturally," Aviva replied. "I've heard that Turkish cooking is one of the three great world cuisines. I understand your friend Ajda Pekkan is in Paris doing a series of concerts this month."

"More like an acquaintance," Jake said good-naturedly. "Nothing ever really got off the ground between us. The headline in the tabloids could read, 'Twenty-eight-year-old man has case of unrequited puppy love for superdiva.'" He chuckled. "No secret I was infatuated with her. How are things going with you and your Kurdish friend?"

Aviva smiled. How odd, she thought. Here we are talking about relationships with other people and neither of us feels the least bit embarrassed. "Grandma Zari told me you knew all about Muren."

"Knew?"

"*Knew.* Past tense. I'm sure Muren didn't want it that way. He was so intense. But after a while, the relationship just wound down. About that time, Abdullah Heper offered me an internship at *Isharet*. I've thrown myself into my work."

A waiter carrying a number of small tulip glasses on a large metal tray stopped at their table, gave each of them a fresh glass of tea, and continued on to the next table.

"So here we are, two unattached foreigners in a very large country, and Heper just happens to push us out to the Black Sea town of Sinop, which just so happens to be the town where your grandmother was born. Foxy old devil, wouldn't you say?"

"I said the same thing when he proposed this trip," Aviva said, unconsciously stroking the back of her head to make sure her dark tresses were in place. "But it *was* a pretty exciting story, and I can't say I didn't enjoy sharing the time with you."

Jake noticed, not for the first time, how attractive this very candid young woman was. "Would you like some dessert?" he asked.

"You're as Jewish as I am, Jake Baumueller," she said, laughing. "Have you ever known a Jewish girl anywhere who did not have a 'sweet tooth?' But I certainly don't see anything resembling dessert in this restaurant."

"You wouldn't find anything even if you searched this place from top to bottom," he said. "Turks have separate places for 'real food' and for pastries. I noticed a great looking *pasthane* about two blocks down the street."

"Sounds wonderful," she said.

He paid their bill, which was shockingly small, left a generous tip, and they departed the tiny restaurant. A brisk breeze blew in from the sea. Aviva, wearing a light sweater, shivered involuntarily. Jake wordlessly removed his own jacket and placed it over her shoulders.

Over more tea and an assortment of delicious pastries, the ubiquitous *baklava* and *tel kadayif*, their animated conversation continued. "So, you've never had a serious involvement?" she asked.

"Do you count four months when you're twenty-one as serious?"

"Did you?"

"At the time, yes. Natalie turned me on to the pop music scene … and other things."

"I'll bet it was mostly the 'other things' that meant more at the time," she said.

"Are all Israelis as direct as you?" he asked.

"When it comes to things so natural, yes. That probably sounds quite forward to you, but I've heard that Americans cover their feelings as if anything having to do with sex is automatically bad or must be hidden. Jake, I don't pretend to be an innocent. I think honesty is a lot more important than appearances and if people don't communicate openly with one another, how will they ever know what the other one means?"

"Point taken," he said. "To change the subject, but for the accent, your English is every bit as good as mine, and I noticed you rattled off Turkish like a native as well."

"That's not really such a big deal. Israel is very small, not especially populous, and very isolated. We learn English, French, German, and Arabic at the same time we learn Hebrew because we have to speak to others in the world." She glanced at her wristwatch. "My God, it's nine o'clock already," she said. "Major Daniels wanted us back at Diogenes Station by eight. He must be frantic by now."

As if to underscore her words, a Chevrolet from the post drove slowly up and down Cumhüriyet Caddesi, its driver looking through the windows of any business that was still open. Jake rose and flagged the driver down.

"Any problems?" he asked, as they drove back up the hill.

"Nothing we couldn't handle," Aviva said quickly, glancing meaningfully at Jake. "What time are we supposed to fly out tomorrow, Sergeant?"

"Ten-thirty. You folks been to the capital before?"

"No," Jake said.

"You ever been to Pittsburgh, sir?" the driver said.

"A couple of times."

"One's just about as charming as the other," he said. "Of course, Atatürk's Mausoleum and the new Hall of the Immortals are worth seeing. And the Hittite Museum, if you're into that kind of stuff."

"My time's pretty much my own," Jake said to Aviva. "Has Heper given you any word as to when he wants you back?"

"Not really. I think he's pretty happy with what he's gotten. I should telephone him, though, and let him know I'd like to see Ankara and also that I've got my protector with me."

17

APRIL 1984
ANKARA, TURKEY

"This place is much more impressive than I thought it would be," Aviva said, as they walked down the wide, quarter-mile-long sandstone causeway, flanked by carved stone lions. "It's obviously the face Turkey wants the world to see."

"Atatürk's Mausoleum on one side, the Hall of the Immortals on the other," Jake responded. "And to think we really got to meet one of the immortals —"

"Two," she replied. Even though I never met Halide Orhan, I felt like I knew her the day we went to Turhan's memorial at Belgrade Palas and Grandma Zari told me all about her life."

"It's a bit sad," he said as they gazed at the stark square travertine and marble edifice which housed Kemal Atatürk's final resting place. "Their memories are fading into the history books, like everyone else who's lived before us. Do you ever imagine what their lives must have been like? Their *lives* ..." he continued. "Not the layers of legends and rumors and stories."

"That's a sobering thought," Aviva replied. "We're so busy living our own lives that it's hard to think about anyone else's life, particularly when they're no longer with us."

After they'd spent ten minutes inside the *Anıt Kabir* walking around the former leader's sarcophagus, they crossed the ceremonial ground turned toward the recently completed Hall of the Immortals. Jake raised a cupped hand to the side of his face to block the stiff breeze that had come up.

"When they died, the whole universe ended for them," he said.

"That makes logical sense, now that you put it that way. From inside my head, everything else as *outside*." Once they were inside the building, she continued, "There are about fifty people in my line of sight, each of them thinking their own thoughts. I'll bet I don't matter any more to any one of them than they do to me."

"You think Private Hayden will ever think of us?" Jake asked.

"Probably not. People don't feel comfortable reliving bad memories."

An hour later, they retraced their steps down the Road of the Lions, where they entered a waiting taxi. Jake directed the driver to go to the top of Çankaya hill, the highest point in the city. The view from here was impressive: a city of two million set in a bowl, crawling up the sides of the surrounding hills.

"How could our driver in Sinop have thought Ankara was similar to Pittsburgh?" Aviva said.

"Have you been to Pittsburgh?"

"No."

"Maybe he hadn't been to Pittsburgh either. Every place in the world has its own charm. You just have to know where to find it."

"You sound as though you actually liked Pittsburgh."

"I did," Jake said. "I had a friend there, who showed me around. Do you have your walking shoes on?"

"Uh-huh. Why?"

"I thought we'd walk over to the Pink House. It's about half a mile from here according to the guidebook."

"The Pink House?"

"The Presidential Palace. Atatürk was its first inhabitant. It's got a lot of relics from his time."

By the time they got back to the center of town, it was late afternoon. Abdullah Heper had recommended they stay at the Kent Hotel, no longer the fanciest place in Ankara, but clean, comfortable, and well-priced. After a nap in their respective rooms, Jake and Aviva strolled south on Atatürk Bulvari, Ankara's main thoroughfare, until they reached Kızılay Square and the multistory Gima Department Store. Afterward, they entered a new pedestrian-only outdoor mall for dinner, where they enjoyed flaky white fish baked on its own tile, and light Turkish wine.

"Have you lived in New York most of your life, Jake?"

"Pretty much. I still consider anything west of the Mississippi River as 'the frontier.' California's 'the left coast,' and 'the South' means Palm Beach, Fort Lauderdale, and the Keys."

"What a huge country," Aviva sighed. "To me, 'The South' means Eilat, a three-hour drive from Jerusalem. There are places in Israel where it takes less than an hour to drive from one side of the country to the other. Have you been there?"

"Once, six years ago, for ten days. I know what you mean. That was more than enough time to see everything there was to see and go over to Petra to boot."

After dinner, they resumed their companionable stroll up Atatürk Bulvari talking about anything and everything, from books they'd read to their mutual interest in journalism, to Paul McCartney and Michael Jackson's number one hit, *Say Say Say*.

18

A week after their return to the old Ottoman capital Abdullah Heper called Aviva and Jake into his office where they saw a contraption that resembled a small black-and-white television set with a typewriter keyboard attached.

"Your grandpa just sent this gadget over," Heper said, addressing Jake. "He thought the two of you had done so well with the Sinop story that you'd probably want to try your hands at researching and writing a feature article on this machine."

"An Apple Macintosh personal computer," Aviva said. "They're betting they can compete with IBM."

"You already know about it?" the publisher said, surprised.

"I haven't seen one in person, but my techie cousin in Tel Aviv wrote me about it just after it came out three months ago."

"Techie?"

"Uh-huh, Mister Heper," Jake responded. "Someone who's a computer technology groupie. The word's been around since the sixties, but it only came into common use a couple of years ago."

"Sound's like Ed had the right idea to put you two into harness again."

Aviva and Jake found it easy to work together. Each genuinely liked and respected one another and they found that their writing styles merged comfortably with one another. If Jake expressed particular interest in one aspect of the story, Aviva's "take" complemented and supplemented his. In a week, they'd completed a well-written story which appeared under their joint byline in the *World* and in *Isharet*.

It was their third "choose-it-yourself" assignment that cemented their professional success.

Most days found them sharing lunch adjacent to the seventy-two year-old Galata Bridge, the floating emblem of the City that spanned the Golden Horn. Every day from sunup to sundown, sinewy men in small outboard-motor-driven boats fished the waters of the Bosphorus. When they'd amassed a sufficient cargo, they'd light charcoal-fired braziers in the front of the boat and head for Eminönü landing, where they'd place the sizzling filets into a half-loaf of broad-grained Turkish bread and hand them out to hordes waiting at the dock. A massive sandwich with the freshest fish available anywhere sold for less than a dollar, and nearby street-merchants supplemented this magnificent meal by selling ears of roasted corn and cups of freshly-squeezed orange juice.

"Istanbulus are so familiar with this lunch that they take it for granted," Jake said.

"Are you thinking what I'm thinking?" he writing partner asked.

"Why not?"

❀❀❀

Three weeks later, Jake and Aviva learned that their article "Under the Boardwalk – Turkish Style" had been selected for publication in Travel + Leisure Magazine, that they'd be paid a handsome stipend, which, of course, they would share with *Isharet*, and that their writing would expose them to nearly five million people worldwide.

❀❀❀

Early May in Istanbul is especially lovely. The freezing winter temperatures are long gone and the sultry summers along the Bosphorus haven't set in yet. On a slow Wednesday news morning when there was nothing better to do, Aviva telephoned Jake from her *Isharet* office.

"Hey, partner," she started. "Want to get out of the hustle and bustle of the big city and chase down our next big story?

"Are you calling to tell me we'll be flying to the South Pacific? The Seychelles? The Caribbean?"

"You wish!" she rejoined. "How about an intercontinental boat ride to a different place for lunch?"

"The Turistic Ferry?"

"You have anything better to do today?"

"I'll have to check my calendar, friend."

"What if I said I'd treat? And bring your bathing suit in case we decide to go up to the Black Sea afterward."

"Sounds like a plan."

Promptly at 10:30 that morning, they boarded one of the Turistic Ferrys which regularly plied the Bosphorus from the Galata Bridge to Sarıyer, a tourist-destination fishing village twenty miles and a world away from Istanbul. For five dollars, each of them enjoyed the ever-changing scenery as the ship ambled from the European to the Asiatic side of the Bosphorus and back again, as it zigzagged its way north, passing under the Bosphorus Bridge, which, a dozen years ago, had erased the physical divide between Europe and Asia. From Sarıyer, they could see the twin pillars marking the northern terminus of the Bosphorus and the entryway to the Black Sea.

Aviva wore a sleeveless summery blouse and short skirt. It was hard to ignore the longing looks she'd generated from men — and the frankly envious looks she'd received from women — all morning. As soon as they disembarked from the ferry, Jake and Aviva walked a hundred yards along the waterfront to the commercial reason for Sarıyer's existence, a long string of fish market-restaurants.

They'd passed four or five of these establishments, when Aviva said, "This looks as good as any since I'm treating —"

"O.K. by me," her companion said, whereupon they went inside the large fish market across the coast road from the restaurant.

Aviva selected *palamut,* bonito, and Jake pointed to *lüfer,* the bluefish which was commonly caught in the Bosphorus. Each of their choices was displayed on a bed of chipped ice, with a price tag stuck in the ice beside it — the cost of the fish when it was cooked and served with rice, salad, *ekmek* — the ubiquitous freshly-baked hot Turkish bread — and carafe of white wine.

They ate their lunch in an open, covered area on the water, from which they threw chunks of bread into the Bosphorus and watched as the living inhabitants of that body of water greedily snapped at food to which they'd become accustomed.

After lunch, they walked inland to the center of town where they stood in a queue waiting to board a *dolmush*, the ubiquitous shared taxi, for the thirty-minute ride to Kilyos, Istanbul's northernmost suburb at the southwestern terminus of the Black Sea.

Fortunately for Jake and Aviva, the summertime crowds from the city had not yet overwhelmed the beaches and the afternoon was deliciously warm with only the slightest breeze blowing off the water.

"Did you remember to bring your swimsuit?" Aviva chided him.

"Yep. You?"

"Of course.'

Ten minutes later, he waited on the sand outside one of the myriad hotels. During the past month, Jake had viewed the Israeli girl as a pretty, talented writing associate, but no bells and whistles had gone off in his head. That all changed when Aviva emerged from the changing room, wearing a one-piece bathing suit. By any measure, she was stunning.

They spent the next few hours immersing themselves in the cool Black Sea waters, sunning on the warm sand, and engaging in a pick-up game of volleyball with several other young people who'd come to Kilyos.

By five-thirty that afternoon, they'd had their fill of the northern suburb. After they'd returned to Sarıyer, Jake said, "I feel flush this afternoon. I've been treated to a luxury cruise, a wonderful lunch, and an afternoon at the area's finest beach. What say you let me pay for dinner at the Büyük Tarabya, about halfway to the City?"

"Trying to one-up me, my friend? The Büyük's the *crème-de-la-crème*."

"Used to be," he said. "It's now more of a *grande dame*, aging but still elegant."

An hour later, they sat on the balcony overlooking the Bosphorus amid a spacious, tree-lined park. As the sun set, Aviva and Jake toasted the day, the sunset, the evening, and their successful partnership, with Turkey's exquisite *Kavaklidere* white wine and an elegant dinner of roast lamb and spring vegetables. Later that evening, they strolled arm in arm along the waterfront.

"Too late to go back now," Aviva said. "You were generous enough to pay for dinner. I'm willing to pay for my room here if you're willing to spring for yours."

Jake yawned, relaxed from this wonderful day. "I'm willing if you are. I have no problem spending the night with the loveliest girl in Turkey, even though I won't be spending the *night* with her."

"Flatterer," she said, but gazed at him levelly, not for a moment averting eye contact.

"I'm sure it's not the first time you've been told you're a beautiful woman, Aviva," he said. "I just thought I'd be up front about it."

By ten o'clock, neither Jake nor Aviva was that tired, so they sat in the hotel's lounge on the mezzanine floor for the next half hour making small talk. At quarter of eleven, Aviva stood, stretched, and said, "Jake Baumueller, thank you for today. You are truly a gentleman and a gentle man. Tomorrow afternoon, it's back to the big city. I'm glad you'll be there with me."

"I fully agree, Miss Kohn," he said, bowing gallantly.

Her room was on the third floor, his was on the fourth. She gave him a peck on the cheek as she exited the elevator.

As Jake was showering, he found himself whistling and thinking happy thoughts. My God, I've been in Turkey nearly five months. What must have been going through my mind that I didn't notice her? It's just that it seemed like such a set-up from the beginning. Ah, well, there's still half a year to go in Istanbul. Who knows?

He was just toweling himself dry when he heard a sharp knock at his door. Who could it be at this hour? He threw on a thick, white 'Turkish towel' bathrobe, called out, "Just a moment," in English, and headed for the door.

When he opened it, he was pleasantly surprised to see Aviva standing there, half a foot shorter than he was, in a similar white bathrobe, her dark hair falling in waves to her shoulders.

"Jake," she said. "I wanted to ask you one last thing before I went to sleep."

"What's that?"

"Back at the restaurant, you told me you thought I was one of the most beautiful women in the world."

"I did, because you are."

"That's always nice for a woman to hear, but how could you have known that?"

"Because my eyes saw what they saw and they told me the truth."

"Can I come in for a moment?"

"Sure," he said, a bit uncertainly.

She entered and closed the door behind them. "How can you say how beautiful you thought I was when you've seen so little of me?"

"What do you mean?"

In answer, she opened her bathrobe. She wore nothing underneath. Jake gasped. "Aviva …?"

"Sshh," she said, playfully, putting her fingers to his lips. "You can think of better things to do than talk," she said.

He could. And they did.

19

"Its Arabic name is *Gazat Hashem*, after the Prophet's great-grandfather who's buried here. How come I didn't hear you were coming?" Al Sidi asked Muren, as they walked toward the Al Omari Mosque.

"Öcalan wanted this to be a very secret trip. He felt that if Arafat knew I was coming, he'd have put on a big show. He told me you were the only one I could trust."

"Did he mention anything about when I should return to Kurdistan?"

"Why do you ask?"

"Let's go back to my flat and we can talk," al Sidi said. No sooner they got there, al Sidi drew the blinds. "Muren, this place is a pestilential hellhole. I don't believe Arafat wants peace — not with the Israelis, not with the Kurds, not even with his Arab brothers. The more he can keep things unsettled, the better it is for Yasser Arafat."

"Is this the same Banr al Sidi who wanted so badly to go off with Abu Ammar only a few months ago?"

"It was Öcalan's idea that I go. He's aware of how disgusted I've become with these 'ragheads.'"

"What do you mean, Banr?"

"Are you aware that the Israelis are our friends, too?"

"No," Muren said.

"The Israelis can't appear to violate their great friendship with Turkey, but they're helping us gain a viable Kurdistan in northwestern Iraq. There are over a hundred very well-placed Israelis in Mosul province, which is a lot more than I can say for the Palestinians, who seem to be full of a lot of empty talk."

"How do you know this?"

"I'm Iraqi, Muren. My family's lived in Mosul for more than two hundred years. We're in touch. Besides, the Palestinians play a rather dirty game."

"What do you mean?"

"You know about the suicide bombings?"

"I've heard about 'patriotic' bombings for the greater glory of Allah."

"Yes, well, the leadership will tell the poor idiots anything they want to hear. What they don't tell the world is that they replace the 'soldiers' they've 'lost' with kidnapped Israeli babies, whom they raise in the camps as Palestinians."

Muren sat silent for a few moments. Al Sidi brought two cups of Arabic coffee and set them down on the low table in front of them.

"Does Öcalan know of such things?"

"I doubt it," al Sidi said.

"How did you find out?"

"The 'underground telegraph.' It's hard to keep a secret in the camps. Every young Palestinian buck thinks he needs to brag to the world about what he's done."

"That sounds like something the *Apo* should know. Is there any way I could get into one of the camps?"

"Not legally."

"But you know someone?"

"One of the section commanders."

"How hard would it be to get in?"

"Five U.S. dollars," al Sidi said sardonically.

"This is Abu Moussa," al Sidi said.

"*Salaam Aleikum,*" Muren said respectfully.

"*Aleikum salaam,*" Moussa replied. "Why do you want to see the camps?"

"Mister al Sidi has already told you I was sent by *Apo* Abdullah Öcalan?"

"He has."

"I understand the camps are overcrowded, a disgrace to all Palestine."

"The work of the Israelis," Moussa said, spitting contemptuously.

"My commandant might be interested in recruiting some young men to serve as warriors in the Kurdish liberation army."

"I see." Moussa nodded at al Sidi, who passed the obligatory five-dollar bill to him.

"When should I return Abu?" al Sidi asked.

Moussa glanced at Muren, who replied, "You needn't trouble yourself to return. When I'm finished, I can find my way back."

Banr al Sidi took his leave, heading back into Gaza City, while Abu Moussa led Muren into the largest of the camps.

❈❈❈

"He's an Israeli spy," the largest of the three toughs, who had grabbed al Sidi as he entered his flat, growled. He'd forced the Iraqi's arm into a hammerlock, and now he pushed it up, toward al Sidi's shoulder blade. The pain was excruciating.

"He's not," al Sidi wheezed. "He's a Kurd."

"Liar!" the man continued, edging al Sidi's arm further upward. "He landed at Ben Gurion Airport, met with two Israelis, and crossed the border under armed Israeli guard."

"I know no such thing!" al Sidi cried. "Ask Abu Ammar himself. They met in Lebanon with Abdullah Öcalan last fall."

"Let him sit down," a second, smaller man said. "Listen, Mister al Sidi," he continued. "Let us speak as reasonable men. You know who this man was?"

"By sight," al Sidi said, trembling.

"His name?"

"Muren Yildiz," al Sidi said, almost automatically.

"Good. At least that's the truth, although one never knows if that's his real name. Now, listen carefully, Mister al Sidi. We know you're no friend of the Iraqi regime. Arafat doesn't trust you any more than we do."

"We?"

"KGB. We've kept watch on your family long enough to know they're separatists." He took out a grainy black-and-white photograph and shoved it across the table. "Your parents. The photo was taken last month in Mosul. They look quite happy, don't they? I'm sure you would agree you'd like them to stay happy — and alive."

"What do you want?" al Sidi croaked.

"Very simple. Your friend Muren is presently inside Jabalia Camp. We watched you take him there and we watched him go in with one of the section leaders. You know, of course, that's entirely illegal." Al Sidi continued to sit silently. "We believe he intends to assist the Israelis in some way. We want it arranged that he does not leave the camp alive."

"He reports directly to Abdullah Öcalan."

"Öcalan's a man of the world. He knows such things happen."

"But he's — " al Sidi stopped himself in mid-sentence.

"Your friend?" the small man said. The ash on his cigarette had now grown to where it was quite noticeable. The man flicked the ash so it landed on the carpet, then ground it under the sole of his shoe to ensure it did not ignite. "The choice is yours, Mister al Sidi. Who's more important, your friend or your parents?" Ah, I see by your face you've answered already."

"How will I know where to find him?"

"It's a large camp, but it's not *that* large, and you're a resourceful man."

❋

"Abu Moussa, I've heard that your — our — brothers are able to replace fallen warriors with new ones?"

"Indeed," Moussa said smugly. "It's quite easy. The Israelis are so lazy they rely on the nearest 'under class,' the Palestinians, to do their menial work for them. The orderlies in Israeli hospitals, the janitors, those who empty out the chamber pots, all Palestinians. They know when the best times are, when the mothers are asleep … As I said, it's very simple, and the mothers in Jabalia camp are so thankful."

"Have you ever been involved in any such operation?" Muren asked, offering his host a pack of cigarettes.

"Oh, yes," Moussa said proudly. "I've done my two."

"Two?"

"The Israelis are lazy, but they are clever. No doubt my photograph is in some intelligence basement, even as we speak. They've put hidden electronic eyes in every hospital, and they keep changing the locations of these cameras. So, anyone given the honor of liberating Israeli babies is only asked to do it twice. Then we disappear back into the camps. To the Israelis, we camp inmates have no identity. To them, one of us looks like any other."

Muren glanced about his sorrowful surroundings. A once-white horse, its ribs poking through a flyblown coat, limped along the potholed tar street, dragging a platform of rotted wood atop two creaking wheels. Six young boys crowded onto the makeshift cart. A clean-shaven man of twenty, wearing gold-tinted sunglasses and a faux leather jacket, twisted the fuel release on a Chinese-built motor scooter, and was rewarded by a loud backfire, but little motion. He glared at a middle-aged woman in a shapeless dark-red woolen outfit, wearing a long white headscarf, who'd jumped to avoid being hit when the younger man had tried to accelerate.

The sweet, acrid odor of uncollected garbage and smell of dog feces that had festered on what passed for a sidewalk nauseated him. He struggled to find a space wide enough for him to walk between the never-ending crush of unwashed humanity. One hundred thousand people crammed into one-half a square mile. Welcome to Jabalia.

Still, the Kurd felt his excitement growing. When he'd landed at Ben Gurion, he'd been given a photo of Yossi Vonets. The photo was more than half a year old, and to Muren all babies looked alike. But Moussa's words had stirred him, and he vowed to look much more carefully when the opportunity presented. Perhaps he could draw this braggart out a little more.

"Moussa, how long has it been since you were involved in your last operation?"

"Five months ago. We took five of them, all boys, none more than a few days old. I remember one in particular because he had yellow hair. That's very strange for an Israeli, and it would have made him easy for the Israelis to spot, which is why the mother keeps his head shaved."

"Have you seen him lately?"

"Of course. He lives in my sector. I can point him out to you, if you'd like."

"No, that's all right," Muren said, his tone deliberately flat.

"I thought you were eager to see the camp," Moussa said, his own voice betraying slightly wounded pride.

"Well … if you're sure it's all right."

"Of course, follow me."

"Wait. Abu Moussa?"

"Yes?"

"You've been so hospitable to me I feel my friend must have underpaid you."

"No, no, it's my pleasure," Moussa said, his eyes alight with ill-masked greed.

"I insist," Muren said, pulling out an American twenty-dollar bill. "You have family. I'm appalled by the manner in which our poor brothers are treated. Perhaps you might use some of the money to buy that small child a treat," he continued, as a dark-haired, elfin girl of six walked by them.

Abu Moussa pocketed the money in a casual manner, and continued walking down a row of tents. Halfway down the row, he stopped. "Beira?" he called out. A woman who looked at least fifty slunk out of the tent, holding a baby in her arms.

"Abu Moussa," she intoned deferentially.

"This man is Muren Yildiz," Moussa said. "He wanted to see your Yassir Beir. Ah, I see his hair is growing out a bit. Isn't it time to cut it back?" he chided.

"Yes, Abu Moussa," the woman said. "I'll attend to it first thing tomorrow morning."

Muren tried to slow the pounding of his own heart. There was no question this baby was Yossi Vonets.

20

Moussa insisted that Muren have dinner with him. The Palestinian lived alone in a small tent, and the meal was a very poor one, but Muren pretended to enjoy the mashed chickpeas and flat bread his host offered. It was just after sunset, when they'd finished the meal, that Moussa said, "Mister Yildiz, all outsiders must be out of the camp before dark. I've got to report to the camp commandant. I'll return in ten minutes and escort you out."

"That's fine with me," Muren said. "Is there a place I might relieve myself?"

"Seven tents down on your left," he said, pointing. "I'll meet you outside the stalls as soon as I'm finished with the commandant.

"Muren! Muren Yildiz!" Moussa's voice echoed throughout his sector. The Kurd was nowhere to be found. Moussa immediately advised the camp commandant that his guest was missing. Within an hour, every tent and latrine in the camp had been searched. The guards had even made a cursory inspection of the two garbage dumps at the far end, but the smell emanating from the pits was so horrendous they assured themselves no one would hide there.

Frustrated, Moussa was about to return to his own tent in disgrace, when a young man who might have been Moussa's brother approached him. "Are you looking for someone about our age, light-skinned, a little taller than we are?"

"Yes."

"A little over an hour ago, just after twilight fell, a man fitting that description walked out the south gate, headed toward Gaza City."

Moussa reported back to the camp commandant that his alarm had been premature, and that his guest had indeed left the compound.

❀❀❀

Midnight. The camp slept. There was no need to post a sentry. What would anyone want to take from the camp? Why would anyone in his right mind want to enter the camp at night?

Muren had found a plastic tarpaulin just before he arrived at the camp's cesspit. The stench was overpowering, but the tarp cover had made it bearable The most difficult part was when he'd had to relieve himself. He hadn't exactly lied to Moussa, but he hadn't gone to the latrine as he'd said he intended. He'd gone straight to the dump, and straight under a mound of garbage. After two hours, he felt his bladder would burst if he didn't void himself. Slowly, he had crawled out from under the effluent. By that time, it was totally dark, and he heard no sound nor saw any movement. Still, to make sure he'd not been detected, he returned to the pit and buried himself under the garbage for another hour.

Muren used stealth and darkness as camouflage as he moved from tent to tent. He'd stopped at the closest latrine and doused himself with as much water as the rusty pipe would disgorge, hoping to rid himself of as much as the dump's stink as he could. He had memorized how to backtrack to Moussa's sector. Once there, he was able to find the row of tents where Yossi Vonets undoubtedly lay sleeping.

It took him the better part of an hour to traverse the camp, cautiously moving from shadow to shadow, then remaining in each pool of darkness for several moments, looking in every direction to make sure he'd not been seen or followed. He'd come to the tent next to the one where the baby slept when he heard a slight rustling. Ever wary, he backed into a patch of darkness.

Suddenly, he bumped into something soft and giving — and very human. Muren stifled a scream, then turned. "Banr?" he whispered. "What are you doing here?"

"I might ask the same of you," the Iraqi answered in as soft a whisper.

"I must get into that tent," Muren said softly. "There's a kidnapped Israeli child in there."

Without a pause, al Sidi said, "The tents have doors, but the doors don't have locks."

"I thought as much," Muren whispered.

"I'll go first," al Sidi said. "That'll create enough of a distraction. Follow me in and …"

"Good," Muren said. "How did you know …?"

"We'll talk about it later."

The family — husband, wife, and two grown daughters — could not have been more surprised or shocked when a sick man lurched into their tent. They started beating the intruder about the head and shoulders with what little furniture they had. The baby had awakened and was lustily crying when Muren grabbed him and quickly ran out the door of the tent. The tiny child, feeling only a rocking motion, quickly returned to sleep. Muren raced down to the end of the row, then turned right, heading for the nearest gate.

He'd covered less than a hundred feet when he heard a sharp, peremptory voice and turned to see himself facing a snub-nosed pistol. "Stop right there, Mister Kurd." A small man waved the gun in his direction. "We'll relieve you of your burden." A larger man came out of the shadows and grabbed the bundle Muren was carrying. "All right Kurd," the man said, pointing the gun at Muren. "Why don't we simply go back to the garbage pit as quietly as we came? From dust we cme and to dust we return." He laughed nastily.

Muren was terrified, but he tried to keep his voice calm. "What about the baby?"

"He'll be returned to his mother, none the worse for wear."

"My friend Banr al Sidi's close by."

"Yes, and a very good friend he turned out to be. He's the one who led us to you."

"He what?" Muren couldn't believe his ears. "He's part of the Kurdish movement. He'd never betray me."

"I'm afraid that's where you're wrong. Isn't that so, Mister al Sidi?" nasal voice said as they rounded a corner.

"I couldn't help it, Muren," al Sidi said miserably. "These bastards have my family up in Mosul. They said if I didn't help them, they'd kill my parents."

"And you believed them?" Muren said acidly.

"What choice did I have? They showed me pictures …"

"So, what happens now?"

The larger of the two men, the one carrying Yossi Vonets, said, "Two dead men in the garbage pit won't alter the smell much."

"But you promised …" al Sidi barked angrily.

"We promised your *parents* would remain happy. We didn't say anything about you, swine!" the small man growled. "Now shut up, both of you. Not another word or you'll be dead within a hundred yards."

"I think not," a soft voice said from the darkness.

The assailants turned rapidly. Four quick, silenced shots, two from each gun held by almost identical young men, cut them down in an instant.

"Moussa?" al Sidi said, as he gazed incredulously at the two dead men.

"Let's just say there *was* an Abu Moussa until four days ago. A substitution was made."

"But how? Who?"

"Later," the man said. "I have a key to the gate. We must get out of this place as soon as possible. The less said until we're safely inside Israel, the better."

LATER THAT NIGHT
SDEROT GEVIM, ISRAEL

"So you're not really Abu Moussa?"

"Hardly."

"But you look exactly like him," a bewildered al Sidi said.

"Didn't 'Moussa' tell you the 'stupid Israelis' had electronic eye cameras everywhere?" the man asked. "And didn't he also tell you, Muren Effendim, that once they disappeared back into the camps we'd never find them because they all look alike?"

"That's true."

"It doesn't quite work that way. Being as Semitic a people as the Palestinians, the right haircut, contact lenses, and tanning solutions, dialect lessons … well, let's simply say that Abu Moussa's mother, had she still been alive, would not have been able to tell the difference."

"You are?"

"Avshalom bar Leoni, Israeli Intelligence," he said. Nodding at the other man, he said, "This is my partner, Yoel Naftali, Israeli External Security. For your own safety, that's all you need to know, Two Toyota Corollas will stop at the coffee shop across the street in half an hour. Turning to Banr al Sidi, he said, "One of them will take you directly to Ben Gurion airport. From there, you'll fly to Lefkosia, then Mosul. Your entire family is perfectly safe."

"And me?" Muren asked.

"The second car will take you into Jerusalem, where I think you're going to make one very lovely young immigrant an incredibly happy woman."

21

A week later, they met in Zahavah Barak's apartment. The elderly advocate, after serving them tea and scones, absented herself to an adjacent kitchen, leaving the young people alone.

"You're Lyuba Rabinovitz?" Muren said. He felt like he'd been hit on the head with a mallet. Lyuba looked her best that day. To Muren Kolchuk she was the most beautiful apparition he'd ever seen.

"Da, yes, *evet*," she replied, giving the affirmative in Russian, English, and Turkish. "Is something wrong *Gospodin* Kolchuk?"

"No, uh, yes, uh … how does it feel to have Yossi home?"

They spoke clumsily, without guile, not knowing how to deal with an event larger in their lives than they knew how to handle.

"I … I don't know. Sergei was killed, then Yossi disappeared … I can't remember what it was like to feel alive. I think I'll have to learn again. I have so much to thank you for, Gospodin … may I call you Muren?"

"Of course."

"That's such a beautiful name. Not at all like Russian names. My manners must seem dreadful to you. I really don't know what to say. Aviva wrote me about you," she blurted out.

Muren blushed furiously. He hadn't thought about Aviva since he'd gotten off the plane at Ben Gurion. Now, thinking back, he felt guilty. Aviva was a lovely woman, but how could she possibly compare to this one?

"Did she tell you nothing ever happened between us?"

"She did." Lyuba smiled, and it lit up his heart. "She's my closest friend."

"It was her decision," he said.

"Were you crushed?" she asked, gently.

"At the moment it happened, it felt like a huge hole in the earth had opened up and swallowed me. Worse, even, than the garbage pit in Gaza."

She laughed, then turned more serious. "If anything, it felt worse than that when first my Sergei, then Yossi, was taken from me. Now, I have to figure out how to become a mother. I've never really had that experience. I've got a job and other responsibilities."

"A man friend?" Muren said uncertainly.

"No, that's never entered my mind."

He breathed a sigh of relief. "Would you feel it very forward of me if I offered to take care of the … of Yossi while you're at work? To make sure he's safe?"

The look she gave him at that moment was one that would have melted a mountain of ice. It was grateful, but it was so much more than that. And Muren was not a mountain of ice. He was a man, a very warm man who, at that moment, could think of nothing but the incredible brightness that enveloped him.

"Lyuba, I'd … I'd like to be your friend … I'd …."

"I'd like that, Muren Kolchuk. I think I'd like that very much."

Jerusalem, September 1984
Dear Aviva,

I don't quite know how to begin this letter. I suppose I should say "Thank you, thank you, thank you," a million times, but it probably wouldn't be enough. I know you and Muren were seeing each other this time last year. That doesn't bother me and it doesn't bother him, any more than when he asks me about my time with Sergei. What was, was, and neither of us can turn back the hands of time.

Would we have fallen in love if those two experiences had not happened? It's hard to say. You once told me to trust in God's wisdom, and at that time I paid it lip service to make you feel you'd helped me. But I really didn't trust in God's mercy. How wrong I was!

The day after we met, he appeared at my flat promptly at 7:30 in the morning, just as I was preparing to take Yossi over to Grandma Zari's. He acted like a little boy or a puppy. He looked so proud of himself. I think I fell in love with him at that moment, at least a little bit. "Muren Kolchuk, reporting for duty," he said, and, would you believe it, he actually bowed from the waist. Does that sound silly? Maybe it was, but it was so endearing to me.

After that, he came every day at 7:30 and left at 4:30 for the next few months. I had no idea how he managed to keep body and soul together until Grandma Zari told me he worked two jobs at night. He was a waiter at the Yemenite Step, and when the restaurant closed for the evening, he worked until midnight as a security guard in Ben Yehuda Street. One day, I came home at two in the afternoon and found the two of them sleeping in the living room. Muren had brought Yossi's crib into the room, and he was lying on the floor next to it. That made me start crying. I went into the bedroom, so as not to disturb them.

Twice a week, there was a small vase filled with flowers waiting for me when I got home. One night, I opened up the refrigerator to get some milk for Yossi and there were two stuffed toy bears there, a mama bear and a little baby bear. Oh, Aviva, this probably sounds so silly to you, but it wasn't to me.

The only chance we really had to talk during the first months was during Shabbat, when Israel is closed down. As time went on, we found more and more time to talk. Muren convinced me to take an extension course at the university. He told me he'd enrolled three weeks after he'd started babysitting Yossi. He said Yossi slept a good part of the day and they'd arranged their schedules to suit one another. Can you believe that statement?

Little Yossi is not so little anymore. Ten kilos! He eats anything that doesn't bite back! He and Muren get along so well that I often feel I'm intruding on their friendship. And there are times I catch the older one watching me, just looking at me, and it's so clear that he's blindly in love.

And yet, he has never even touched me except for an occasional shy kiss. I feel that if I were to initiate anything, I'd scare him off. He acts like he's afraid that if he tries something, I'll break.

Last night, Muren asked me to marry him. It took me about a second-and-a-half to say yes! He's just turned twenty and I'm an old woman of twenty-four, but it seems so <u>right</u>. We agreed to ask you to be the maid of honor and to ask Omer Akdemir to be the best man. Since neither of us has any family, and since we couldn't find a rabbi to marry us, we decided we'd fly to Cyprus for a small wedding in January ... Love you, my dearest friend, Lyuba

✿✿✿

Istanbul, October 1, 1984
Dear Lyuba,

Mazel tov! If there ever was a match made in heaven, it's you and Muren.

Jake is leaving Turkey at the end of this month. I'm only now realizing how much I'll miss the guy. I'd thought ... but who knows what the future holds?

Abdullah Heper's turning sixty-seven next month. He'll be turning control over to his son Melek, who I think will be a great successor to his father. He's got some really good ideas.

Yes, I'll be dancing at your wedding! I know it's an old cliché, but wild horses couldn't keep me from coming! Of course, with Jake gone and no one on the horizon, I'll probably be the "old maid" of honor, but I promise I won't try to steal your bridegroom from you, not that I think I'd even be in the running. As for having a family, don't worry, we'll be your family. The Akdemir brothers have five children. Kari already babysits little Nadji when she's in Izmir and she's a born mama hen. Having Yossi around will only make her happier.

I've decided to sign on for another year in Turkey. Don't get me wrong, I was born and bred in Israel, and I'll always be Israeli, but there's something about this land that makes me feel as much at home as Israel. I had such a strange feeling when I was in Sinop for those few days, kind of like I could have stepped back in time and been Grandma Zari when she was a young girl.

Enough of me, girl. I've got a wedding to attend in two months and I want to look smashing!   Love, Aviva

22

When Abdullah Heper asked Aviva to interview Şenol Demiroz in Ankara, she had mixed feelings, not so much about the subject of her assignment but rather that the capital had been the place where she and Jake had become more than just friends. He had left Turkey seven months ago. Although they'd continued to correspond and telephone one another at least once a week, it wasn't the same. She missed him. Much more often than she'd thought she would. And when she flew back to Istanbul after Lyuba's and Muren's wedding, she felt an emptiness. *Let's face it, girl, being alone means being lonely. And maybe he was Mister Right.*

Still, a trip to the capital was better than spending evenings moping around her apartment. Aviva gathered as much information on Demiroz as she could find. Thirty-five, not much older than Jake, and a rising star in the firmament of TRT, the Turkish Radio-Television authority. There was only one national channel in Turkey and TRT controlled it. Like Aviva, Şenol Demiroz had started out as a journalist. Nine years ago, he'd taken a job as Broadcast Planning Manager of TRT and it was rumored that he would one day succeed Şaban Karataş as General Manager, the top authority of the government television and radio monopoly.

When Aviva approached the address she'd been given, 47 Midhat Pasha Caddesi, she was surprised and the dowdiness of the structure. She was looking at the address card she'd been given to make sure this was the right place, when she was hailed by a pudgy, urbane-looking man, a younger, mustachioed version of Prime Minister Turgut Özal.

"Miss Kohn?" he said, his voice exuding warmth. He approached her and shook her hand, simultaneously saying, "If you're looking for Şenol Demiroz you've just found him."

"Good morning, Şenol Bey. I thought —"

"We'd meet in more impressive-looking splendor?"

"Well …?"

"Ordinarily we might have done so, but I wanted to give you a special treat. Meeting the 'big shot' manager at the place where it all began."

"TRT 1, Studio A?"

"Correct. To impress you even less, it's in the basement."

Minutes later, he led her to a spartan, unprepossessing office, where each of them sat on green plastic chairs across from one another at a small round table. A secretary brought in a stainless steel teapot, two cups and saucers, and a large platter of pastries, then left the room.

Aviva, very much aware of the value of Demiroz's time, kept the small talk to a minimum. "I prefer to get right to the points we need to cover, Şenol Bey. You're an important man and a busy one. The last thing you need is someone wasting half a day of your time."

"That's very courteous of you, Miss Kohn —"

"Aviva."

The older man lifted his eyebrows appreciatively. Aviva found herself very much at ease with the TRT director, and for the next hour, they exchanged their views on subjects well beyond what she'd anticipated they'd talk about.

"If you'll excuse my saying so, Şenol," she said, dropping the honorific in favor of the far friendlier, more informal means of address, "I almost get the feeling we were interviewing one another instead of my seeking information from you."

"Very perceptive, Aviva," the TRT man said. "You obviously did your homework before you came today. Might I ask what you know about Turkish television?"

In response, she rattled off sufficient information about the history and development of the medium to demonstrate that she had more than a cursory knowledge. "My turn?" she asked, smiling.

"Go ahead."

"I've heard that private commercial stations may be allowed to telecast into Turkey within the near future. Would you like to talk about these plans … off the record, of course."

"What you've heard is true, Aviva. TRT has operated the only legal television station in Turkey since 1968. Recently, at least two 'pirate' stations and one legitimate applicant for a license, Magic Box, have been broadcasting into Turkey from Germany. We can't stop satellites beaming signals in from space."

"Unlike the old pirate radio stations that broadcast into Britain from offshore in the sixties."

"Correct. We can't shoot down TelSat. So our government has decided to start its own experimental private station, *2 Kanal*, to gauge the public's reaction and refine our policies."

The Director of TRT continued. "For the past six months, we've been negotiating to form a partnership with a consortium headed up by *Isharet*. We've studied the American television model in great detail." He picked up the half-full teapot and refilled their respective cups. "Although Turkey has always been a male-dominated society — and notwithstanding Atatürk's reforms it still is — our studies have shown that we might do well to follow America's lead in putting female personalities on the air."

"Babara Walters, Andrea Mitchell, Deborah Norville?" Aviva said.

"You're familiar with them?"

"Surely you're not suggesting …?"

"As a matter of fact, I am, Aviva. All three of them, as well as many of the current younger group of women come from news backgrounds. That's only natural, since journalists are interested in everything and can think on their feet."

Aviva said nothing, but stared at the TRT man, stunned.

"When the floodgates open and Turkey is forced to allow private stations to broadcast into the country, there's no question they'll pay higher wages and attract the best talent money can buy. Not only will that put the government at a decided disadvantage, but bureaucracy being what it is, TRT will probably hire four new employees for every one we now have, to fill the gap. And believe me when I say they'll be useless but well-connected drudges with all the personality and talent of trained monkeys."

"But you've only met me once," Aviva said uncertainly.

"Yes, but we've done as much homework on you as I'm sure you did on me before you came here this morning."

"You'll have to give me time to think about this," she said, recovering from her initial shock. From everything I've heard about the industry, things don't happen overnight. It can take years of work …"

"In ordinary times, you'd be lucky to be an on-mic personality at a second-tier station in ten years. But these are not ordinary times."

"Can you give me time to consult with Abdullah Heper?"

"Whatever time you need, provided it's no more than a week."

"Abdullah, what the —?"

"Something amiss, Aviva?"

"You've known all along," she said, her voice rising but by no means angry.

"I wasn't exactly surprised, if that's what you mean."

"Does Jake know about this?"

"I have no idea, and that's the truth. Ed Baumueller knows, of course, since he's heavily invested in *Isharet* Communications."

"Don't get me wrong, Abdullah. I can't say I'm not flattered by Şenol's offer … I trust it's legitimate?"

"It is."

"But there is the little matter of my full-time job at *Isharet*. I'd like to keep a roof over my head and food in my tummy while each of us considers how this will impact us."

"Not a problem," Abdullah Heper said. "*Isharet* stands to make a substantial profit if the TRT-*Isharet* gamble pays off. It won't break us to keep you on payroll and actually working a news beat while you're interning."

"What's the next step?" she asked.

"If you're interested, we'll meet with Şenol Demiroz in Ankara next Monday."

"Gentlemen, has it ever occurred to you that people will say I got this job because I've got the right connections rather than talent? Or even worse …?"

"That's a valid question," the TRT director said. "On the one hand, what we're proposing is not fair to anyone else who'd apply. You'll step to the front of the line into a situation where, if you succeed, an awful lot of jealous and powerful people will believe, to put it bluntly, that you slept your way to the top."

"That wouldn't be true you and you know it!" she exclaimed, turning to face her mentor.

"Doesn't matter what's true and what's made-up, Aviva," Abdullah Heper replied. "People always love a scandal as long as it's *someone else's scandal.* You've got to decide pretty damn quickly if can take the heat that goes with what could happen if you win the lottery."

"On the other hand, there's no guarantee you'll even win the smallest prize in any lottery," Demiroz continued smoothly. "Your opening salary will be about the same as a low-level secretary. You won't be given anything on a silver platter and you're going to have to work your ass off to prove you're good enough to make it in one of the most cutthroat jobs in any industry. If you think you're going to be rich and famous next week, or even next year, you'd better wake up from that dream right now."

"Meaning?"

"You've got at least six months, maybe a year of learning the ropes on some station no one's ever heard of in some Sheep's Ass, Turkey backwater place. You fail there, you might, and I say *might,* get one more chance *somewhere* where you'll make *half* of what a streetsweeper makes."

"Sounds lovely," Aviva replied, the smallest hint of sarcasm in her voice.

"It's entirely up to you," Demiroz said mildly. "Everything in this world is risk-reward."

"What's the next step, gentlemen?"

"Does that mean —?"

"Mister Heper, what would Turhan Türkoğlu have done?"

"Exactly what you're going to do, my dear," he said, standing up and hugging her.

July 1, 1985 – Aksaray, Turkey
Dear Lyuba,

You read the return address right. Aksaray, population one jackass, four pine cones, and an apple, smack dab in the middle of Nowhere, Turkey. Well, maybe a few more people than that. Once upon a time, it was an important stopover on the Silk Road … but that once upon a time was a long, long time ago. Although this city of 50,000 sits in the middle of a rich agricultural area and there's more to see than you can imagine, Aksaray has never attracted many tourists.

I've been working my new job for two weeks. If I ever thought being in the entertainment business would be glamorous, I was given *a dose of reality my first week here. We're a small local station hooked in to nationwide TRT. We have no independent programming. Erol Gürgün, the station manager, is sixty or so, a down-in-the mouth character with <u>no</u> character. He realizes he's not going any higher in the food chain. That leaves the only other two employees Mustafa Aydin, a Niğde University student who's our part-time cameraman, and me. to pretty much do what we want — which is not much of anything. I replaced a fiftyish woman who gave her notice two weeks before I arrived. My "training," consists of listening to Erol's "war stories" and advice that he's repeated at least thirty times since I've been here.*

I get here at six each morning. empty the ash tray and the trash can, mop the floor once a week, and have hot tea ready for Erol. When he gets in at six-thirty, he brings the early — and only — edition of Kayseri Gündem from the largest city in the area, eighty miles to the east. That gives me less than half an hour to skim the paper, memorize the local news and weather, say good morning to Mustafa, and be ready to go on the air at seven for my two minutes of fame. Studio 1-A, my Queendom, is a bare room about eight feet square. Two minutes. I don't even have time to identify myself. So far as I know, no one even knows my name. I repeat my two-minute anonymous performance at noon and again at six in the evening, and <u>that's it</u>, except for opening the few pieces of mail we get each day, usually advertisements or bills, occasionally a check or two. The most exciting thing I seem to do all day is watch the grass grow outside our tiny office building. I can't just continue this way. I've got to do <u>something</u>. Enough of my bitching.

My love to you, Muren & Yossi. – Aviva

❦

Three weeks later, bored and frustrated, Aviva told Mustafa about her idea. He eagerly approved but said he was low man on the totem pole and had no authority to make any decision. When she brought her idea up to the Erol Gürgün, the station manager said, "Why bother? It's been that way for ten years. There's no need to rock the boat, our jobs are secure and I've only got to stick it out two more years."

"Would you feel offended if I contacted two people I know in Istanbul and Ankara?"

"You can contact Turgut Özal as far as I'm concerned. Ankara pays your salary and they're the ones that sent you here. I must say, you make a better cup of tea than my last seceetary."

She telephoned Istanbul the following week.

"Abdullah, we're the only TV station within a hundred-mile radius, but less than ten percent of the population watches us except between eight and ten at night. Every time I bring it up, Mister Gürgün just shrugs it off."

"You feel you're on a treadmill to nowhere?"

"Pretty much. I have an idea I'd like to run an idea by you and see if you can get Mister Demiroz to give me a half-hour time slot between one and two in the afternoon. If you give me the green light, you'll have to give Mustafa some extra hours."

❊

September 1985 – Aksaray, Central Turkey

Mustafa's university classes let out at two o'clock each weekday. For the next three weeks, Aviva and Mustafa spent the time from three to five scouring Aksaray and speaking with people neither of them had ever met. A surprising number of those they spoke with agreed to participate. When they said yes, Mustafa's camera started rolling.

At 1:00 p.m. on Monday, September 2, 1985, the few people who were watching TRT's Aksaray station suddenly came awake as the camera focused on a pert, attractive young woman who, up til now, had delivered regional news and weather for two minutes at six in the morning, noon, and six in the evening.

"Good afternoon, my friends! I'm Aviva. Time to spotlight our wonderful community: every day a new and wonderful surprise. Interviews with ordinary people and extraordinary people. Football games between our local high schools. The *Hasandağı Middle School* marching band, graduations, parades, festivals, and so much more! Welcome to *The Heartbeat of Aksaray*!" ...

❊

A month later, Aviva was summoned to TRT-Ankara. When she arrived at Şenol Demiroz's office, the director greeted her warmly and bade her sit down across from him. Without preamble he advised her that the ratings at her station in Aksaray had risen by five percent.

"But I thought I was doing so well," she said, disheartened. "From the number of telephone calls the station received and even the newspaper coverage …"

"Aviva," he said gently. "Aksaray doesn't watch much television in the afternoon or at all. You're ninety miles *east* of Konya and the same distance *west* of Kayseri, in the very heart of the most conservative area in the country. The last place in Turkey to adapt to anything new. The *imam* trumps the television ten times out of ten."

"But this is 1985 —"

"In Ankara, most of the time. In Istanbul about two-thirds of the time. In the east, they'd prefer if it were 1485."

"So, I'm a failure?" she said miserably. "And I gave it everything I had."

Demiroz stood, walked around the table and patted her paternally on the arm. "I'd hardly call a fifty percent rise in your audience a failure," he said. "Besides, that's not why I wanted you to come to Ankara."

"So I've still got a job?"

"Of course," he said. "In fact, if you're interested, I can offer you a lateral transfer position coming available in two months. We'll need a night-time sports announcer. You'd get three minutes at 11:20 p.m. and you'd get to do the weather at seven and nine on weekend mornings. They'd identify you by name. No increase in pay, but the surroundings would be considerably more congenial."

"A second chance?"

"Call it what you will. I'll keep it open for a week while you decide."

"Where is it?"

"Izmir."

"I'll give you my answer right now. How soon can I pack?"

23

Şenol Demiroz had telephoned her from Istanbul "We launch 2 *Kanal* on September 15th. Management has spent a good deal of time studying your progression and we believe you'd make a good fit. We'd appreciate it if you could come to our Istanbul studios for a screen test before any final decision is made. Would next week be alright?"

Aviva could hardly contain her excitement. During the time she'd spent in Turkey's third largest market, she had expanded her presence on TRT's outlet, first to features reporter, then to late night local news co-anchor, and finally to her present spot as morning co-host on *Günaydın Izmir.* She's supplemented her modest income by writing feature articles for *Isharet's* Izmir bureau and making personal appearances at shopping center openings, sports events, and even high school classes. She could not deny she'd been bitten hard by the broadcast industry bug.

Now, the TRT director himself had insinuated that it was time for her to *really* move up. His words "a good addition" would most likely mean starting at the bottom once again, but the difference was it would be an entry level position at the *national* level.

"Of course, Şenol Bey," she replied, trying to keep her voice natural, hoping he could not near the thumping of her heart over the telephone.

When she arrived at TRT's Istanbul headquarters the following Tuesday, she was met at the front desk by Abdullah Heper, Şenol Demiroz, and a strikingly handsome man who looked vaguely familiar.

"Good morning, Aviva," Demiroz said. "We've brought someone to share your screen test with you. This is —"

Suddenly it dawned on her who the third man was. "Refik Arslan!" she exclaimed, struggling to keep from openly gushing. "You're … you're the most famous newscaster in Turkey!"

His dazzling smile, electric blue eyes, and perfect white teeth made him appear even more handsome than he was on the six o'clock news. "I'm delighted to meet you Aviva *hanım* he replied," shaking her hand with a firm, collegial grip.

"As I told you a year ago," Demiroz continued, "when *2 Kanal* opens we'll need to have every big gun we can muster. Refik has agreed to move to the new channel. Your screen test will consist of three five-minute segments. First, you stand alone and welcome viewers to *Turkiye Today*, our morning show. Second, you deliver a weather forecast. Finally you interview Refik Arslan. These will all be unscripted, so you're on your own."

Less than an hour later, Aviva emerged from the studio, which was as far removed from the cubicle in Aksaray as Istanbul was different from the small farm town. "Well?" she asked nervously.

Demiroz was noncommittal. "We'll have some people take a look and call you back in, in a day or two.

❊❊❊

"A brilliant choice," the station manager said. "A woman every Turkish male can dream about and every Turkish woman can hope to emulate."

"What about the accent?" Demiroz asked. "It's not native Turkish."

"I don't see that as a problem," Solmaz Akpolat, a short, squat sixty-year-old woman said. The assembly listened to her with particular interest, since she'd directed nearly every program since the inception of the Turkish television industry, "Her accent is not recognizable as any specific Middle Eastern nationality. Not to mention that her three years in the country has 'Turkified' her speech."

Turning to Refik Arslan, she quipped, "I seem to remember a young Jewish lad from Plovdiv, Bulgaria, Reuven Levi, whose accent was a little shaky at first." She winked broadly as Turkey's leading anchor blushed.

"So it's unanimous?" Demiroz asked, setting down his cup of tea. There was no dissent.

"Will you still be my boss, Melek?" Aviva asked.

"Nominally, although you'll have voice coaches, hair stylists, makeup artists and script editors."

"So I'm being marketed as a product."

"Uh-huh. From now 'til *2 Kanal* opens, you'll work harder than you've ever worked in your life. Intense off-air training critiqued by some of the top professionals in the industry. After the station goes on the air, we'll slip you in for a few 'color' segments, interviews and such. If your ratings increase …"

DECEMBER 1986

Within a month of her small interludes between "hard" news stories, people were starting to ask, "Who is that girl?" The evening news ratings seemed to "spike" whenever the audience knew she was going to host a segment.

TRT soon experimented with allowing Aviva to choose some of her own material. After all, she had started out as a print journalist and had an eye for the kind of stories that would entice viewers. TRT / *Isharet* announced that as of February 1, 1987, Aviva would join Refik Arslan as co-anchor on the nightly news.

The only downside was that Aviva had no social life outside the station. She was expected to be everywhere the station wanted her to be, when it wanted her to be there. The daily newspapers, including the ever-growing number of tabloids, began to write speculative stories. This created a further social vacuum for Aviva. She was portrayed as every Turkish man's unattainable dream, but Turkish males, often so forward when it came to foreign women, did not want to risk approaching Aviva, only to be rebuffed.

Nor was she attracted to anyone inside her social ambit, not even Refik Arslan, who was happily married and the father of three. More and more, she found herself missing Jake Baumueller. He had not been the least bit intimidated or put off by her, and had treated her in all ways as his intellectual and emotional equal. Most charming of all, he'd turned out to be a surprisingly old-time romantic.

How odd that he had not written to her since she'd started her astonishing rise to television anchor, although she knew he was interested in things Turkish. How could he *not* have known, for God's sake? The New York *World* maintained an important bureau in Istanbul. The fact that he had not attempted to communicate with her was even more disappointing because he had promised …

As days, then weeks passed, Aviva created in her own mind a combination of the Jake she had known and the Jake she believed he could be. She missed him. Slowly, the shock of not hearing from him turned to anger, then to resignation.

On December 28, 1986, she received her answer.

She'd made certain always to read the Sunday edition of the New York *World*, if for no other reason than to keep up on what was going on in places beyond Turkey. It was nine in the morning and Aviva had just poured herself a cup of tea. Her fourth floor flat overlooking the Bosphorus was sumptuous and quite large by Turkish standards. Today, a cold, gray pallor held Istanbul in its grip. There were even a few ice floes coming down from the Black Sea.

She had just sat down at her dining room table and turned to the society section of the *World* when she read the banner headline: "*WORLD SCION TO WED BRYN MAWR SOCIALITE*," and immediately under that, in smaller letters, *Edwin Baumueller IV, New York's Most Eligible Bachelor, To Tie Knot in June.*"

She forced herself to read the next paragraph.

"*Mr. & Mrs. Edwin Baumueller III and Warren Erdbacher and Dorothy Erdbacher-Lane have announced the engagement of their children, Edwin 'Jake' Baumueller IV and Lisa Lumet Erdbacher. The bride-to-be, a cum laude graduate of Bryn Mawr College, is presently an editor with Doubleday Books in New York, where she serves under Nan A. Talese. Her fiancé is well-known in New York circles. As heir to the New York World's publisher, he presently serves as City Manager for the paper.*"

She was wistful and regretful as the impact of what she'd read sank in. The next morning, she picked up the telephone placed an international call to a number in Jerusalem.

DECEMBER 29, 1986 – ISTANBUL-JERUSALEM

"All right then, I'll put it another way. Do you see yourself living with him for the rest of your life, having children with him, or are you one of those modern career women who don't want to think of those 'old fashioned' thing?" Zahavah continued.

"That's what I love best about you, Grandma. You're so gentle and diplomatic," Aviva said, smiling for the first time all day.

"Look, Aviva, from what the newspaper said the wedding is taking place six months from now. Do you want to fight for this man or not? You're going to have to make your own decision, although you made that decision the minute you saw the article."

"I've got commitments …"

"Horse manure! Do you or don't you love him? I've been a successful lawyer, a successful politician, and I've been married twice, happily both times. I can tell you right now, my girl, that all the stardom in the world won't keep your bed warm at night And if you think there's anything that can come close to the intimacy a man and a woman can share, you simply don't have your head screwed on straight."

"Grandma …?"

"And don't start that whiny little girl voice with me, Aviva Kohn. You're made of better stuff than that."

"Do you have any ideas?"

"I may or I may not. That's up to me. The answer to the bigger question is up to you."

FEBRUARY 1987 JERUSALEM – NEW YORK CITY

"Ed? It's Zahavah Kohn-Barak. Yes, *that* Zahavah bat David Kohn-Barak. What? I can't hear you. Put the damned mouthpiece closer to your mouth."

"Zari," the old man said, a wide grin on his face. "My God, it's been more than two years! Would you believe it we're still standing up and sucking air? How're things in Israel?"

"How should they be? They're bad and they're getting worse. They're *always* bad and they're *always* getting worse. If only we Israelis could *afford* to live the way we *do* live, *oy*, we would live the life of Rothschild!"

"You're calling to tell me old jokes?"

"No, Ed. Aviva read the article about Jake planning to get married."

"Uh-oh, I knew you wouldn't be calling all the way from Israel to discuss the weather."

"What do you know about the girl?"

"Smart, wealthy, socially plugged-in."

"Does he love her?"

"Who's to say what love is?"

"Ed, between you on the one hand and my granddaughter on the other, I'm hearing enough fertilizer to make the land of Israel truly a land of milk and honey. Bumper crops."

"My personal feeling?"

"Uh-huh."

"Bad choice. They'll look beautiful in the magazines, they'll have the requisite two-point-three children, that'll be all the loving he'll ever get, they'll go on separate vacations, and he'll be miserable the rest of his life."

"So why is he doing it?"

"Duty."

"Is this coming from you?"

"No, from his father and mother. She's a 'nice' girl, cool and so blonde she could pass for a *shiksa* anywhere. And I can guarantee you they'll never speak a less-than-genteel word between them."

"Did he say anything about Aviva when he came back?"

"He was nuts about her! And with me he didn't talk 'polite society,' he talked about what he felt."

"Would it surprise you to know she feels the same way?"

"Not at all, but you know the old saw. It's 'Absence makes the heart grow fonder' for awhile, then it's 'Out of sight, out of mind.'"

"She's getting to be a famous TV star in Turkey, did you know that?"

"Hell, yes! I've got a fairly big stake in the partnership that owns the station."

"He hasn't written to her in nearly a year."

"Like all other friends — or, in their case, more than friends — if you don't write for a couple of days, you feel guilty and put it off for a couple of weeks. If you put it off for a couple of weeks, you feel even guiltier, and so it goes until a year has gone by."

"And you get engaged to someone else?"

"Zari, if there's any way I could bring him together with Aviva … heck, it's almost as if Turhan and you and I brought them together …"

"Ed, do you have any connections with any American television companies?"

"As a matter of fact, I still have a great relationship with the PBS affiliate in New York, since we've sponsored so many of their programs. They owe me a favor or two. Why do you ask?"

"Listen., Ed, here's my idea …"

When he heard it, the old man chuckled appreciatively. "Zari, you are still arguably the brightest woman I've ever met."

"So, what else is new?"

24

"Have you heard of PBS, Aviva?"

"No, Melek, I can't say I have," she responded to Abdullah's son, now *Isharet's* publisher.

"It's a huge American television consortium. They operate three-hundred-fifty stations and they've had some amazing successes. Have you ever heard of *Sesame Street?*"

"Who hasn't?" she replied. "Big Bird, Ernie, Bert, Kermit, Miss Piggy …"

"Not to forget the Cookie Monster. That was PBS's first big show and it put them on the map as a major player."

"What does that have to do with me?"

"PBS's largest single source of funds approached TRT-*Isharet* about doing a series of travel programs on Turkey. They even have a name for the series, *Rondo a la Turca*, based on a melody originally written by Mozart."

"Sounds like a magnificent opportunity for TRT-Isharet."

"And a better opportunity for Aviva."

"What do you mean?"

"The pilot will be a 1½-hour travelogue focusing on Istanbul. It'll be a high-budget program, which they'll use in their fundraising efforts. The producers want someone who speaks fluent English, but with a European accent. They've spent the last few weeks looking at film clips, sorting through over a hundred potential candidates. It seems they settled on you. One thing led to another, and they contacted me to offer you a screen test."

Aviva felt a flush creeping up her neck. Although she wasn't the type to tremble with excitement, her hands began to flutter nervously as she asked a few questions about the production. Finally, she asked, "Is there any payment attached to this?"

"Eighty-five thousand U.S. dollars plus a percentage of royalties if the program plays more than three times in any given market."

"Eighty-five *thousand* … *dollars*?" She was stunned. "That's nearly twice as much as I make in a year. When would they expect me to make this screen test?"

"Day after tomorrow."

NEW YORK CITY – MARCH 1987

"Yes, yes, yes!" the producer exclaimed after he'd seen Aviva's rushes. "She's absolutely perfect!" Principal photography of *Rondo a la Turca — The Rhapsody of Istanbul*, began on March 20, 1987.

25

APRIL 1987 – NEW YORK CITY

"Jake, I've just received a rush from PBS on a project they'd like the *World* to review. Since I've got the whole afternoon full, could you do the old man a favor and give me your unbiased opinion? If it's too much to ask, I can have one of our junior staffers do the review."

Jake sighed theatrically. "I suppose I can spare the *World* a couple of hours."

As the room darkened and the fifty-five inch screen lit up, a tall African-American woman began, "You're about to see a wonderful new program made possible by your generosity. If you're willing to pledge one hundred-fifty dollars, *less than fifty cents a day,* WNET, Channel Twelve will send you, as our gift to you, a videotape of this wonderful travelogue we're about to see. It's called *Rondo a la Turca — The Rhapsody of Istanbul,* and I think when you see it, you'll feel like getting on a magic carpet and flying over there tomorrow morning."

Jake cocked his head. It had been more than eighteen months since he'd been in Turkey. He thought back to Aviva and their last time together. Of all the programs in the world he did *not* want to watch this afternoon, of all the people he did *not* want to think about this afternoon …

The music started, the saccharin-sweet *Samanyoğlu,* which had been popular in Turkey fifteen years ago, and which Turks still occasionally hummed in the street when he'd been there. The camera swept in on

Istanbul. After a minute, it panned in on a solitary figure, a woman in a form-fitting light blue sweater and darker skirt. Closer and closer the camera came. Jake was reminded of the opening scene in *The Sound Of Music,* but as the camera drew closer it wasn't Julie Andrews. It was a much younger woman. There was something familiar in the way she stood … her left arm on her hip, her right arm describing an arc over the city. *My God, it can't be …*

"Hello and *Hoş Geldeniz*," the woman said, in slightly accented English. "My name is Aviva, and I'd like to welcome you to my country. My Turkey."

The camera followed Aviva into a narrow street filled with tiny shops. The street's potholes were filled with water from an earlier shower. A 1956 Chevrolet that had been converted into a *dolmuş* — the shared taxi so common throughout the Middle East — was still sleeping. As Aviva admired the ancient car, a barrel-chested man of fifty emerged from a nearby building.

"Gün aydin, Effendim. Eyn güzel araba! What a beautiful car!" she exclaimed.

"You are American?" the man asked, raising an eyebrow.

"No, but I have a special friend in America."

Jake sat up with a start.

"I have a friend who lives in Pittes-burg Pencil-ven-ya. You maybe know him?"

"My friend told me he visited Pittsburgh once. He lives in New York."

Jake felt a painfully strong yearning.

"Is O.K., *yok problem*," the man said, cheerily combining Turkish and English in a single phrase. "You come into my house now, have tea, we talk."

As the travelogue continued, Jake rubbed the sides of his temples. His head ached from the emotions coursing through him.

During the next forty minutes, Aviva introduced viewers to the sights and sounds of the two-thousand-year-old metropolis, Jake tried with increasing difficulty to focus on her words. He watched with agitation as Aviva entered Kapalı Çarşı, the covered Grand Bazaar, as he thought back to the times they'd wandered through these same passages together. He felt the warmth of her lips on his, the soft contours of her exquisite body. When she approached a certain small shop, Jake Baumueller felt an involuntary shiver.

"The one man in the bazaar whom I do not bargain with is Murat Bilir, an extraordinary gentleman who was referred to me nearly three years ago. Murat has been written up in the *New York World*."

The camera panned in on a forty-five-year-old man of medium height and build, with thinning dark brown hair and a neatly-trimmed mustache. His shop was tiny, eight feet by eight feet, and crammed floor-to-ceiling with copper and brass pieces. Two other people were already inside, filling the shop to overflowing. Murat's brown eyes took on a distinct sparkle. "Ah, Istanbul's sweetheart! I watch you on the news every evening. I remember you were writing for *Isharet* when you were here with that nice young American. Whatever happened to him?"

"He went back to America to work in his family's business." Jake Baumueller scarcely heard the remainder of the program. His mind was now firmly made up, and as difficult as it was going to be, he knew what he was going to do.

❦

A mile away, in the penthouse suite of the Waldorf-Astoria Hotel, another pair of eyes had been watching the entire program. Marco, Count Napolitano, a splendidly dressed, supremely elegant man of who'd come here for a brief holiday after sailing from Cape Cod to New York harbor, gazed in undisguised rapture at the woman on the television screen.

"Ah, *bellissima*," he sighed to himself. "I must have that one at any cost." He punched a button on the telephone adjacent to his chair. "Concierge? Please book me on the next available flight to Istanbul. First class, of course. Can you have the limousine waiting for me within the hour? *Mille grazie*."

❦

APRIL 1987 – ISTANBUL

That afternoon, when she returned to the 2 *Kanal* studios, Aviva's dressing room was filled floor-to-ceiling with orchids. No one at *2 Kanal* admitted to sending her such an incredible array of flowers. She was preparing to telephone some of her Istanbul acquaintances who might have a clue, when she saw a small handwritten note on a creamy white vellum card on her desk.

"*Signorina*, it would be my great privilege to host you for dinner after your early show this evening. My chauffeur will call for you at seven tonight and I will have you back in time for your late-night show. *Ciao*. Marco, Count Napolitano."

NEW YORK CITY – THE SAME DAY

"Lisa, I'm just not ready to get married," Jake said. "I wanted to tell you this face to face, rather than by telephone or messenger or note."

The tall, willowy blonde woman looked calmly at Jake. "I suppose I should call you the rottenest bastard who ever lived, give you the requisite slap in the face and walk out with my head held high," she replied.

"You could, and I'd accept that."

"How should we break it to our parents?

"Directly," he replied. "There's no question I'll reimburse your parents for the expenses they've put out so far."

"That could be over a hundred thousand dollars."

"I assumed it would be something like that. I'd like you to keep the ring as a gift," he said. "It's a beautiful stone and you're a beautiful person, Lisa."

"It did come together awfully quickly, didn't it?" she said, smiling ruefully.

"Maybe too quickly," he agreed.

"What will you do now?"

"Leave the country for a while, until things cool off and the tabloids have lost interest. What about you, Lisa?"

"I haven't given it any thought at all. After all," she said, an edge of bitterness in her voice, "this conversation was not exactly what I'd expected."

ISTANBUL – EARLY EVENING

That afternoon, Aviva's initial amazement at the invitation and the roomful of flowers gave way to her news reporter's investigative instinct, and she spent the next two hours conducting research into the background of her admirer. When she saw the pearl grey Rolls Royce arrive at the front door of the *Isharet* building, she left word with the security guard to invite Count Napolitano to come upstairs to the conference room, implying that she would need half-an-hour to finish preparations for her 11:00 p.m. telecast.

When he arrived at *Isharet's* third-floor offices, Napolitano was immediately escorted into a large, plush conference room. No sooner had he entered the room than Aviva came in through the opposite door. "Signor Napolitano, thank you so much for accommodating my work schedule. I thought we'd have a little before-dinner chat, if you don't mind."

"Of course not, but please you must call me Marco."

She seated herself across the table from him.

"Marco, then. You claim to have no hidden agenda?"

"Honestly?"

"Of course."

"When a man sees a beautiful woman from five thousand miles away, he would be insane not to have a, as you say, hidden agenda. I'm sure you deduced that."

"A deduction or a seduction," she said lightly. "Are you married, Signor ... Marco?"

"At the moment, no, my dear."

"Pity. A handsome, urbane man like you, wealthy and titled, running loose in a world full of willing women."

"You're not married and never have been, but you've undoubtedly have had ... liaisons? I'd say we're evenly matched."

"I see you've done your research," Aviva said evenly. "Should I be angry or simply disgusted?"

"Hardly. One doesn't pursue the most beautiful woman in Turkey without such preliminary efforts."

"And yet, you expect me to know nothing about you?"

"Signorina, I am, after all, the man, the initiator of such … adventures."

Aviva sighed. "I suppose you're right, Count Marco Napolitano, thrice married, four children, the eldest of whom is six years my junior. Fifteen years ago, you were implicated in, I believe they call it the 'White slave trade,' arranging for the transfer of young women out of the Moldavian S.S.R. You were arrested five years ago on a charge of smuggling arms into South Africa. No need to turn pale, Signor Napolitano. Nowadays, as you say, men and women like to know something about those with whom they may associate."

"I see you are more attuned than I would have thought," he replied stiffly. "Still, our respective pasts make it more, umm, challenging."

"Meaning?"

"You're an Israeli masquerading as a Turk. Your grandmother, a former Turk turned Israeli, has been active in assisting a known Kurdish terrorist, Muren Kolchuk. How would it look if Istanbulus learned their darling is not the person they believe her to be. I think your American sponsors on PBS would not look kindly on controversy, particularly from one who looks so angelic on the American television."

Aviva faced Napolitano calmly across the conference table. "So you are proposing an affair in exchange for any protection from disclosure you could offer?"

"That, *bellissima*, is an unfortunately harsh way of putting it. You think only of the stick and choose to ignore the carrot."

"Meaning?"

"As you are undoubtedly aware, I am a wealthy man. You would live like a princess, better than a princess. Whatever embellishments you want would be yours to command, travel to extraordinary places, furs and jewelry such as a princess never dreamed of, a lifestyle second to none in the world …"

"For as long as you took pleasure in me. Then, what?"

"Ah, *carissima*, you choose to look on the downside. Why must there be a season or a term for happiness? We shall make each and every day our own lifetime."

"*Our* own lifetime?" she replied, archly. "But *you* would be fully in control of how long that would be."

"You don't understand, Signorina."

"I understand quite well. How many times have you played this little game before, Marco?"

"*Cara mia*, knowledgeable adults need not discuss such things."

"You're absolutely right, Marco," Aviva said, lifting the intercom phone. "Now, if you'll excuse me, I must regretfully request that security escort you out of the building. I have a news broadcast in a little over three hours, and I mustn't be ill-prepared. *Ciao*," she said, standing up abruptly exiting the door by which she had entered.

After she watched the Rolls Royce depart, Aviva telephoned Melek and Abdullah at their homes and disclosed the evening's events to them. "Melek," she said. "I fear I have made a dangerous enemy. I haven't even had a chance to telephone Grandma Zari yet, but events have moved more quickly than we could have imagined."

When she disclosed her plan, Abdullah remarked, "Aviva Kohn, the spirit of Turhan Türkoğlu is alive and well inside you. He would have been so proud. We'll have the story ready to go in *Isharet's* morning edition."

Melek seconded his father's feelings. "Regardless of the outcome, we'll deal with it appropriately," he said.

Aviva also advised Refik Arslan about what she was going to do. He shrugged his shoulders. "You're more courageous than I would be in the circumstances," he said. "Do you want me to tell the world …?"

"No, my friend," she said. "One of us is enough, and tonight's my night."

"Good evening, my friends," Aviva began calmly. "Our lead story tonight is a worldwide exclusive, a very personal worldwide exclusive about yours truly, whose real name, by the way, is Aviva Kohn. It's not every day that a newscaster makes news herself, but in this instance I think you, my viewers and my friends, are entitled to know the complete truth about me before you read it in the tabloids or before you hear gossip, that may well be a lie …"

26

"Well, Miss Kohn, it seems as if you were your own best public relations expert!" Melek Heper crowed two days layer. "Ninety-three percent of the responding public is in your corner. 2 *Kanal* has been deluged with telephone calls and letters. It doesn't take a blind man to see the favorable pickets, mostly from women, by the way — outside of 2 *Kanal* and *Isharet*. Some of my friendly competitors at the tabloids have called me to shout 'Foul!' and others to congratulate *Isharet* on its scoop."

"And PBS?"

"They're ecstatic. You're more in demand now than ever. We've gotten requests from the BBC, *Deutsche Welle,* and big stations throughout Europe to run 'A Day in the Life of …' programs with you."

"I don't pretend to false modesty," Aviva said, "but the more I'm known, the more vulnerable I become. I received a call from Ajda Pekkan the day after the broadcast. She and I met and had a long heart-to-heart talk about many things. The need for privacy was one of them."

"And the other things?" Abdullah piped up. He had entered the room in the middle of their conversation.

"Privacy things," she reiterated. "Some of them *very* private."

"Sorry to intrude, Aviva. I suppose you wouldn't be interested in a message I received via fax from the States this morning."

"If it's about the continuing PBS program …?"

"No, it's not. Never mind, it can wait."

"Does it concern me?" she asked, focusing directly on the older man.

"It might. Sorry to interrupt. I'll leave the two of you to your publicity coup."

Less than five minutes later, Aviva was in Abdullah's office. "All right, Mister Heper, may I please see the fax?"

Abdullah reached into the top drawer of his desk, extracted the dark, coated piece of fax-roll paper, which smelled vaguely of ink and ammonia, and handed it to her.

"Dear Abdullah,

"I don't know if you've heard the news yet, but Jake and Lisa decided to call it quits a month before the wedding. He acted kind of funny after he saw it the rush of Aviva's program. Maybe he just missed Turkey (ha-ha!). He was generous enough to reimburse her parents for what they'd put out, and it was a good slug of money, but it was a drop in the bucket, and he'll probably end up writing it off as an income tax deduction. Hard to keep up with the tax laws these days.

"Jake told me about the breakup two nights ago. He said he wanted to get out of the country for a couple of months until the heat died down. He didn't tell me where he was going and I knew better than to ask him, but I wouldn't be too surprised if a visitor shows up on your doorstep.

"Oh, how's Aviva, by the way? I saw her when the PBS program came out. She looked and sounded pretty good. Cheers, Ed."

Aviva Kohn, international television star, turned white, then red, and left Abdullah Heper's office without uttering a word. He could hear her shout, "Yes!" all the way down the hall.

Shortly after two in the morning, Aviva awoke groggily to the acrid smell of smoke coming from outside her door and the loud *whoo-eee, whoo-eee, whoo-ee* of sirens. The first meaningful noise came from a bullhorn in the street below. "Attention! Your attention please! All people living in 5 Gün Doğuşu Sokak do not, repeat, *do not* attempt to open your front door. This is not a false alarm! Please leave your apartment from your balcony and climb down the fire escape as far as you can. Please do so now!"

Aviva threw a bathrobe on top of her pajamas and pulled on a pair of boot-style slippers. Trying not to panic, she grabbed the only thing at hand, a five-by-seven-inch framed photograph of Jake, taken the day they'd gone for a sail on the Sea of Marmara, and exited onto her balcony. As she looked, first toward one end of the building, then the other, she saw that the apartment house was engulfed in flames. She could feel heat emanating from the wind churned up by the fire. Water from firehoses steadily pelted the area of the building. Her neighbors were descending the fire escape ladders in various stages of panic.

As she looked back into her apartment, the ceiling sprinklers started inundating her bedroom. She could see flames licking at the underside of her bedroom door. It suddenly struck her how close she'd come to being trapped in the flat. Less than a minute after she'd started descending, a piece of the balcony railing in the apartment above her tore loose, and came crashing down to her own balcony, bounced, and continued its fiery journey to the ground. *Thank God my own balcony stood firm and undoubtedly saved my life.*

She'd just about reached the second-floor balcony when it wrenched loose from its moorings, and swung like a door, held only by two large bolts. There was no way it would have taken her weight. She looked down and saw four firemen with a huge net standing in the street immediately below.

Putting the photograph in a pocket of her bathrobe, she hesitated an instant, before jumping twenty feet into the net. She felt her back spasm as she hit the net, but otherwise she was all of a piece. As she was pulled from the net, a pair of little girls, one of three and the other about six, bounced into the net. No sooner did the firemen grab them, she looked back toward the inferno that was her apartment building. She heard screams of frightened inhabitants and saw that three sides of the building were now engulfed in flames. It was only a matter of time before the entire building collapsed.

Aviva licked her teeth, trying to get rid of sleep-soured breath, at the same time smoothing down her hair to try to give it some shape. She returned to the net, helping the firemen as they moved others off the net. "Press," she said. "*Isharet*. Can I help?"

"Yes, ma'am," the nearest fireman said. "Please give these people wraps to put on over their nightclothes," he said, pointing to a pile of coats that had been stacked nearby.

As Aviva glanced back toward the building, the once modern and luxurious structure collapsed in its death throes. Another large fire engine, its siren blaring, came careening down the street. The firefighters had now given up hope of saving the apartment house and were concentrating on laying a water screen around the dying building to protect neighboring residences.

Aviva approached an older man who seemed to be in charge. She started to explain who she was. He put out his hand to stop her. "I know who you are, Miss, you're that television lady."

She noticed the epaulets on his shoulders. "Do you have any idea what caused the fire?"

"We won't know for a day or two. It could be arson-related."

"Why do you say that?"

In response, he pointed to the six-foot high walls surrounding the derelict building and its neighbors. As Aviva neared them, she saw spray- painted in red, yellow, and black, "Die, Jew!" "Fucking Jew bitch, go back where you belong!" "Don't fuck with Turkey, bitch!" and "Back where you belong, Israeli Jezebel!"

Aviva felt sick with horror and fear at the loathsome display.

"The arson division of the Istanbul police has already been notified," he continued.

A slender man of thirty, a few inches shorter than Aviva, approached her. "Miss Kohn, I'm Detective Sergeant Mütlü. Obviously, I'm embarrassed by this incident."

"You know my name?"

"Of course. We know the identity of everyone who lives in your apartment block. You're the most high-profile resident, although I'm pleased you've managed to preserve your privacy and security. You would be an ideal target for a kidnapper. It's also apparent that even if you're not the only Jewish resident in the immediate neighborhood, your disclosure of three nights ago would create what the Americans call a 'feeding frenzy' for those in our society who've abandoned the age-old tradition of Turkish hospitality."

"Do I have reason to fear for my life, Sergeant?"

"I'd be lying if I said no, Miss Kohn. Even your apartment house security was not able to protect against this," he said, sweeping his hand toward the still-burning building. "Did you suffer much loss, Miss Kohn?"

"Nothing that can't be replaced," she said, thinking of the photograph in her bathrobe pocket. For some reason, she was grateful she had rescued that particular memento. "Everything that was destroyed was insured."

"Do you have a place where you can stay?"

Aviva thought for a moment. "Thank you, I do, Lieutenant. I'll take a hotel room for a few days. Afterward, I have a number of available options."

"While this appears on its face to be a hate crime, your average hoodlum would have had problems executing this arson so perfectly. Do you know of anyone who would wish you specific harm, Miss Kohn? By that, I don't mean someone who doesn't like your newscast," he said. "I mean someone with whom you might have had a disagreement? A jilted lover perhaps?"

"Well ...," Aviva said. "There was a small rather unsavory incident involving an Italian man a few nights ago..."

MAY 1, 1987 – ISTANBUL

Aviva was at Yeşilköy-Atatürk International Airport at eight in the morning in the event the THY Flight from New York arrived earlier than its scheduled 9:55 a.m. time slot. Due to a delay in getting out of JFK, the Turkish Airlines Airbus did not actually land until 11:45 a.m. By that time, she had been nervously pacing for nearly four hours. He was the first one off the plane and she felt faint when she saw him.

His first words were, "Darling,. I can't apologize enough for the things that have happened, and I won't try. Let's just say ..."

But she wasn't listening. Aviva, the woman men all over Turkey coveted, had leaped into Jake's arms, almost knocking him to the ground.

"Hey, careful with the merchandise," he said, nuzzling her hair, drinking in its aroma, feeling her warmth. "And this is Turkey. What would your adoring fans say about such a public display of affection?"

"Oh, shut up," she said, kissing him all over his face, oblivious to the astonished looks they were getting from all quarters.

"Wait," he said, pulling away. "Don't you want to hear about …?"

"Not until after we've gone to …" She stopped in mid-sentence. "My God, Jake, I forgot. I don't *have* an apartment anymore."

"So that's it," Aviva said. "I've received offers of a new apartment, a house of my own, marriage, of course, but mostly expressions of shock and sadness, begging me not to think Turks are that way. I've spent the last couple of broadcasts telling them I fully understand and that I deeply appreciate their love and concern."

"Do you have any thoughts who might have been behind it?"

"Detective Mütlü doesn't believe it was a random act. He told me it was too perfectly executed and asked if I knew anyone who'd wish me specific harm. The only one I could think of was an allegedly wealthy Italian count, Marco Napolitano, who propositioned me amid enough orchids to fill every florist's shop in Istanbul."

"Marco Napolitano?" Jake asked.

"Mmm-hmm," Aviva replied. "I was able to find a rather unsavory background in the couple of hours before he arrived to pick me up for dinner. When I invited him into *Isharet's* conference room for a 'pre-dinner chat" he played a nasty game of carrot and stick with me. Life as a princess versus disclosure of any embarrassing little secrets he thought I might have."

"And your response was to hand him his walking papers and go on television with a tell-all confession."

"Correct."

"You think Count Napolitano might have been behind the fire?"

"I know in my heart he was," Aviva replied. "Lieutenant Mütlü sent me a copy of a note he found among the ruins of my apartment building." She handed Jake an unsigned single sheet of paper around the table. It read, "Ciao Carrissima! A shame you did not take advantage of my offer to give you an even warmer time."

❁❁❁

Over the next year, Jake's relationship with Aviva steadily progressed toward the goal they both wanted. On Sunday, May 8, 1988, the following article appeared at the top of page E3 of the *New York World*:

> *"The Baumueller family announces with great joy that Edwin 'Jake' Baumueller IV, heir to the New York World's publisher, and Aviva Kohn, of Jerusalem, Israel and Istanbul, Turkey, will be married on December 12, 1988 at the Neve Shalom Synagogue in Istanbul, Turkey. The bride-to-be is a noted television personality and news anchor, whose PBS travelogues to Turkey have garnered her acclaim in the United States and throughout Europe. At 28, she also serves as Assistant Vice President of International relations for Isharet Media Group, publisher of Turkey's largest newspaper and owner of a substantial stake in 2 Kanal, the most successful quasi-independent television station in Turkey. Mr. Baumueller, 33, is Associate Publisher of the World."*

❁❁❁

In October, Edwin Baumueller II, the last of the 'giants,' save for Grandma Zahavah, passed away peacefully in his sleep.

27

MAY 1989 – NEW YORK CITY

"What do you mean a 'working honeymoon?'" Aviva asked.

"There's a sudden interest in the Near East, my love," Jake replied. "The *New York World,* CBS, and PBS plan on producing a joint special and they want you to do a human-interest tour of the area."

❁❁❁

"I don't know why people say New York is intolerable in the summer," Aviva said, as the *World's* limousine glided to a stop outside the Pierre Hotel. "It's two in the afternoon and it can't be more than seventy-three degrees Fahrenheit."

"I wouldn't call May 'summer in the city,'" Jake replied. "If you were to come back next month, you'd see why New Yorkers complain."

"I've lived in Jerusalem, Tel Aviv, and Istanbul, so it would take a lot to convince me about miserable summer weather. My God, I've never seen a city like New York! How many rolls of pictures did I take when we walked down Broadway last night?"

He grinned. "One that I can recall, plus another roll in Central Park this morning, and I don't know how many when you were down in Greenwich Village. Of course, you were so busy listening to the Sony Walkman, you wouldn't have known."

"What time is the meeting?" she asked.

"Three o'clock. They've arranged for a conference room right in our hotel."

❧❧❧

That afternoon, Jake introduced Aviva to two senior New York *World* executives, and the Vice President of CBS news. Aviva already knew Randall Baynes and Doris Pakula from PBS.

"Ladies and gentlemen," CBS began, "the focus of today's meeting will be why Eastern Turkey is going to be so high on the nation's agenda in the next couple of years, and why we should make contingency plans, even now, to be there. The current administration believes the Soviet Union will collapse within the next year or two."

"But Gorbachev seems very much in control. *Glasnost* and *perestroika* have become household words here as well as the U.S.S.R. Are we being misled?" Pakula asked.

"No, Doris," the CBS man responded. "But we've started putting two and two together. Our correspondents have sent us some rather disturbing intelligence reports. Afghanistan has been the Soviet Union's Vietnam. It's one of the world's worst-kept secrets that we've been arming the Taliban, which seems to be our best hope of combating Communism in that part of the world, just as our government was rooting for Iraq to win its war with Iran.

"Russia's grain crop has failed for the sixth straight year. There are rumblings that fourteen member states of the Soviet Union might like to go it alone, without the Great Russian Bear to 'protect' them."

"Excuse me, folks," Aviva said. "But how do I fit into this?"

"That's the easiest part, Mrs. Baumueller," the CBS man said. "The Turkish government trusts you because you represent a very *establishment* newspaper and a very *establishment* national TV station. Americans and Europeans trust you because they've seen you on PBS."

"We'd fly you from Istanbul to Van, have you shoot the area around the lake, then get you to Doğubayazit," Doris Pakula said,

"In the shadow of Mount Ararat," Aviva mused.

"More than in the shadow, Aviva," Randall Baynes said.

"You want me to climb Mount Ararat?' she asked, wide-eyed.

"Not exactly. You'll get photo footage from the comfort of an aircraft."

"What's the timetable?" Jake asked.

"We'll start June 15," the CBS vice president said. "Aviva and Jake, you'll be our *public* stalking horses. Everyone will know you're coming and the publicity spotlight will be on Aviva, which will allow our correspondents to go quietly into different areas. After the camera crew gets enough footage of Aviva, they'll disperse to other areas. You'd be surprised at how unobtrusive our equipment has become."

"How long will we be there?" Aviva asked.

"Less than two months. You'll be back on 2 *Kanal* by August 15 at the latest."

As Jake and Aviva returned to their suite she remarked, "This sounds more like military operation than a TV program."

"That may be closer to the truth than you think."

That evening, the senior and junior Baumuellers enjoyed an informal barbecue at the Baumueller mansion on Long Island. Edwin III had served time in Turkey as an Air Force captain, and while he'd never enjoyed the love affair with that country that *his* father had, he'd kept up on the news coming from the *World's* Istanbul bureau.

Later that night, as Jake and Aviva snuggled into bed, Aviva asked, "How do you think it went with your parents?"

"Why is it every one of my wives asks me that very same question?"

In response she smacked his head with a pillow, then tickled him until he fell off the bed. "Can't you ever be serious?"

"Okay, okay, how does this sound? My mom asked me how long we'd wait before we gave her a grandchild."

"I see. And you told her …?"

"I told her we'd be starting the process tonight."

Mount Ararat

28

DOĞUBAYAZIT, EASTERN TURKEY

"Oh, my God!" Aviva exclaimed as she gazed at Mount Ararat, history's most famous mountain, for the first time. "How far away is it?"

"About a hundred miles," Jake replied. "We'll hit 'Dog Biscuit' in about an hour."

"Dog Biscuit?"

"The hippies who trekked from Istanbul to Katmandu during the early sixties called it that. Doğubayazit's the closest town to Ararat and the last substantial Turkish town before the Iranian frontier. We'll spend the next couple of days getting used to the altitude before we hike up to the first station."

Although it was the summer tourist season, there were only twenty guests at the hotel. There was a prominent display about former American astronaut Jim Irwin in the lobby. After he'd walked on the moon, he spent time exploring Mount Ararat in search of the legendary ruins of Noah's ark. The photo, like the lobby of the hotel, had seen better days, but their room was clean and comfortable.

Aviva awoke shortly after midnight and looked out toward the huge mountain. Moments later, Jake was standing behind her, his arms encircling her waist. The sky was clear and star-studded. "This reminds me of the night I climbed Mount Sinai," she said, sighing. "It's so perfect."

NEXT MORNING – LITTLE ARARAT

The wind whipped around them, at times pushing her scarf into her face and at other times almost blowing it off her neck. She was standing above the clouds in a world of white, despite the warm midsummer's day three thousand feet below.

"I'm speaking to you from the summit of *Küçük Ağrı Dağı, Little* Ararat," she said into the shielded microphone. "It's still more than four thousand feet to the top of Turkey's highest mountain. From here on up, it's covered in snow year 'round. The Kurds refer to it as the 'Mountain of Evil,' but the Armenians call it 'Mother of the Earth.' The Turkish name means 'Mountain of Pain,' and, of course, the Bible refers to it as *Ararat*, where Noah's ark supposedly landed after the great flood."

Their camera operator, Gençler Süyü, aimed his equipment toward the top of Great Ararat. "It takes four days to climb the mountain and at least one more day to descend from the summit to the second overnight camp," she continued. "Don't try it without a guide and don't try it without oxygen and warm, protective clothing. In a few moments, we'll see the mountain from an aircraft flying at twenty thousand feet. This is Aviva Baumueller broadcasting from Little Ararat on the Turkish-Iranian-Armenian border."

❊❊❊

"A few moments" was actually two days later. Aviva, Jake, and their cameraman met their pilot, Hüsseyin Ovacık, at a small airstrip south of Doğubayazit. Ovacık, a barrel-chested, middle-aged Turk, was busily checking out their aircraft, a DeHavilland Beaver, when they arrived shortly after 8:00 a.m. The high-winged single-engine plane looked like a very big brother to the old Piper Cubs.

"This plane seems pretty small to be flying over such a huge mountain," Aviva said uncertainly.

"Not to worry," the pilot said. "I've flown it for almost twenty years and been around Büyük Ağrı at least thirty times a year. It has never given me one minute's trouble.."

"How high will we be flying?" Jake asked.

"Twenty thousand feet, three thousand feet higher than the summit. But we won't fly over the mountain. It is safest to stay at least ten miles away from the peak and fly all around it. We have permission to fly over Iranian airspace, but I try to stay on the Turkish side of the mountain. As soon as we get to twelve thousand, five hundred feet, there is oxygen for everyone. It's required by international law. We'd best start early, before the wind picks up and clouds cover the top of the mountain."

They found the aircraft roomier than they'd expected. The pilot sat in the front left seat. Jake sat next to him. Aviva and Süyü, the cameraman, sat in the next row of seats, leaving two vacant seats behind them.

"It's a good idea to wear earplugs," the pilot said, handing three plastic packets around. "The Beaver is a noisy plane."

"It's a good thing I'm not broadcasting from the plane," Aviva said. "We'll patch in the audio when we get down."

Moments later, the bird took off. The airstrip was less than three thousand feet long, but the Beaver required only a third of that distance before it leapt into the air. Aviva's initial exhilaration gave way to surprise at how slowly the plane appeared to be flying. She pressed the intercom button on her headset and asked the pilot, "Are you sure we're going fast enough to stay up?"

"Oh, yes," he said. "We're traveling about one hundred ten miles an hour."

"It seems like we're sitting still."

"That's because we're flying higher than the surrounding land. Everything looks much smaller and it feels like we're going slower." When he reached twenty thousand feet, the pilot leveled the plane and headed toward Ararat.

As he neared the mountain, Jake looked anxious. "I thought you said we were going to stay at least ten miles away from Mount Ararat."

"We are still twenty miles from there," the pilot replied. He pressed the radio communications switch and continued in English. "Kars Tower, Beaver three-two-eight-one-seven, seventeen west of Ağrı Dağ, request permission to overfly Iğdir, then southeast."

"Eight-one-seven. Surface winds three-zero-zero at two-zero knots. TAF Hercules reported strong updrafts and downdrafts southeast of Iğdir, advise caution."

The three passengers were concentrating on the stunning vista below and to their right. Aviva pointed out the massive summit and the cameraman alternated between shots of her expressive features and the view from the plane. Suddenly, there was a brief coughing noise and the passengers could feel a slight jerking motion.

"What's that?" Jake asked. "Is that normal?"

"No, it isn't," the pilot said, his voice betraying slight concern. "It could be a number of things, most likely water in the fuel."

He pushed in one of the knobs on the console. The engine coughed, backfired once again, then smoothed out.

"Just as I suspected," Ovacık said. "Water must have thinned out the fuel getting to the engine. I pushed in the knob to your left, the manual choke, to enrich the fuel mixture and it seems to have worked out fine. I am concerned, though. I'm certain I topped off the aircraft with fuel before we left and the gauge show's we're nearly empty. That's never happened before."

The aircraft, its engine now running steadily, seemed to hang in the air. After what seemed like an hour, but was only twenty minutes according to Jake's watch, the sturdy craft passed over a featureless town and turned gently to the right. Another quarter hour and they seemed much closer to Mount Ararat.

Without warning, the aircraft started descending rapidly and seemed much nearer to the ground than Jake felt was safe. He poked the pilot on the right shoulder to gain his attention.

"Downdraft," the pilot said. "There should be an updraft within a minute and we'll be climbing even faster than we're going down."

"I don't know …" Jake began, then stopped in mid-sentence as the plane suddenly climbed steeply. He was just starting to relax when the aircraft went into a steep descent once again, followed immediately by a spate of turbulence that shook the craft like a giant hand.

He looked over at the pilot, who'd suddenly gone white. "*Kalp*!" he gasped. "My heart! *Allahhhh*!" The pilot let go of the wheel and doubled up in pain. Moments later, he'd ceased his breathing and gone blue.

Aviva screamed once, then gasped, then went silent.

Jake had no time to look back at his wife, nor at the cameraman. Although he had completed ground school and had twenty hours of flight time out of Teterboro Airport, twelve miles from midtown Manhattan, he'd had no mountain flying experience. Trying desperately not to panic, he remembered the international emergency radio frequency, which had been drummed into him both in ground school and during his first three hours in the cockpit of a Cessna 172, and dialed 121.5 KHz. He pressed the radio communications button, as he'd seen his flight instructor do back in New Jersey, and shouted into the microphone, "*Mayday! Mayday! Mayday!*

Less than ten seconds later, he received a response, thank God in English. "Aircraft calling Mayday, this is Erzurum Center, please identify yourself and your location."

"DeHavilland Beaver … we're very near Mount Ararat … I can't tell the altitude, it keeps going up and down rapidly."

"Beaver, are you a pilot?"

"Sort of …" Jake said. "Ground school plus twenty hours of flight training in America."

"Where is your captain? Put your captain on the radio, please."

The plane gave a sudden lurch upward and Jake's hands tightened on the wheel. "The captain had a heart attack. I don't know if he's alive."

"Beaver, do you have a transponder? Look in the center of the panel. You should see a tiny yellow bulb with a switch next to it. Is it blinking?"

"I see the bulb, but it is not blinking."

"All right. Beaver, listen to me and please follow my instructions. First thing, flip the small switch up." Jake did, and was encouraged as the small yellow light started blinking.

"I have you on my radar, Beaver. You are eight miles north-northeast of Büyük Ağrı. Look up at your compass. It's at the very top of the instrument panel, in the center of your windshield. What do the numbers read?"

"They're whirling around, but they seem to center on one hundred fifty."

"All right, Beaver, make an *immediate* left turn. *Gently* push in the left-side foot pedal and turn the wheel *gently* to the left. Keep doing that until I say stop."

"Y … yes, sir," Jake said. Despite the terror of the moment, Jake was not thinking of the danger. He was concentrating on the controller's words, silently blessing the disembodied voice. "The plane's still going up and down and rocking pretty hard."

"That's all right, Beaver. You're not in danger. Just concentrate on turning slowly to the left. My radar shows you turning north, away from Büyük Ağrı. What does the compass show?"

"Thirty."

"Good. Keep turning left until you hit three hundred. How's the turbulence?"

"A bit better."

"The pilot?"

"Not good."

"Any other souls on board?"

"Two. Where are we now?"

"On your present course, thirty miles south of Yerevan, Armenia. We'd like to keep you in Turkish airspace and get you as close to Kars as possible."

The ride had just smoothed out and Jake was starting to breathe regularly when the engine coughed and started to sputter. The engine caught, then faltered, caught, faltered again, and quit. Instinctively, he called out *"Mayday!"* again.

"Beaver, Erzurum Center still with you and you're heading's fine."

"Th … that's not the problem, Sir. We've lost power. We're going down."

"Beaver, did this happen before?"

"Yes, sir. About an hour ago the engine seemed to be backfiring. The pilot said it was water in the fuel. When he pushed the choke, it smoothed out. But now it's stopped running altogether."

"Can you try to turn on the ignition? It's the key to your left."

Jake tried the key a few times with no result. He immediately reported the controller and so advised him. The entire interchange took only a few seconds, and the controller's voice came back on immediately.

"All right, Beaver, listen carefully. What is your altitude?"

"Twelve thousand and falling rapidly."

Aviva had started screaming again and the cameraman, Gençler Süyü, was close to retching. With great effort, Jake forced himself to shut out the frightening sounds coming from behind him and concentrated on the disembodied voice coming from the console.

"Don't worry, you'll be fine," the voice continued calmly. "Push the wheel forward very slightly, to keep your airspeed up. Do not, repeat, *do not* turn the plane in any way. Look down and around the countryside for the most level piece of land you can see."

By that time, the two passengers had regained some semblance of control and were looking as well. The country was rolling and mountainous, but there appeared to be a long, flat valley between higher land. Aviva tapped Jake on the shoulder and pointed to the valley.

"Erzurum Center, I see a valley slightly to my right."

"Good. Aim for that valley. What is your airspeed? That's the round indicator that should be right in front of you."

"One hundred thirty."

"Perfect. Keep that speed up and point the nose of your aircraft down a little more. What's your altitude?"

"Ten thousand."

"Good. Do you have any power?"

"No."

"All right. I'd like you to avoid any turns because my radar shows high mountains on either side of you. The elevation of the land is fifty-two hundred feet. Do you have flaps?"

"I don't know."

"Look to your left, about the center of the plane. You should see something that looks like an emergency brake on a car."

"I see it."

"Lift up on the lever."

He did. The airspeed quickly dropped to ninety miles per hour. "Uh-oh. My airspeed has gone way down."

"That's all right, Beaver. Point the nose farther down." Jake did. "When your airspeed shows one hundred, leave the plane in exactly that position and push the *right* foot pedal gently."

Jake noticed that his hands, which had been squeezing hard on the wheel, had started to tremble. The controller's voice jarred him. "Beaver, my radar will lose you at six thousand feet. When you get to that altitude, start to flare for landing."

"Flare?"

"Pull the nose back up as high as you can."

"But we'll crash!"

"You'll probably have a hard landing, but you'll survive. The plane won't stall until you're going about sixty miles an hour. If you're within seventy-five feet of the ground by that time, you'll be just fine."

"Stay with me as long as you can, Erzurum. Just in case."

"Will do, Beaver, but you're off my radar now."

The plane settled down gently. A few moments later, Jake felt a sharp bump as the aircraft hit the ground, then relief flooded through him as the plane started to slow down and level off.

Suddenly, Aviva screamed, "Jake! Look out! There's a boulder up ahead!" The Beaver's nose was high, and Jake couldn't see the huge monolith directly ahead of the plane. The aircraft crashed into the huge rock at forty miles per hour.

29

"We don't know anything for certain, and the reports are very sketchy," Melek Heper told Lieutenant Colonel Omer Akdemir. They were speaking on a secure line between Çiğli Air Base and *Isharet's* Istanbul offices. "All we know for sure is that the plane took off from Doğubayazit at eight this morning and was supposed to be back three hours later. The pilot did not file a flight plan."

"It's now two o'clock," Omer replied. "They could have stopped for lunch."

"We've checked all the nearby airports, Ağrı, Van, Kars. Nothing. The Beaver carries four hours' worth of fuel. Unless they strayed into Georgia, Armenia, or Iran, someone should have heard from them by now."

"We've got bases throughout eastern Turkey," Omer said. "I'll check if they've heard anything." Ten minutes later, he was back on the line. "Erzurum Center reports that at 10:10 this morning they received a Mayday from a single engine Beaver, less than ten miles north of Mount Ararat. The pilot had a heart attack and whoever called in had very little experience. The controller said the guy handled himself very well. They steered him away from the mountain, but then the plane lost power. The controller lost radar contact ten miles southwest of Yerevan, Armenia. The pilot seemed to have found a valley where he could bring the bird down safely. There were four people on board. Erzurum's taped the whole conversation."

"It's a good bet it's them," Melek said. "Jake, Aviva, and the cameraman were supposed to go up this morning. Can you tell me anything about the plane, Omer?"

"The Beaver's a Canadian-built workhorse. Ugly as a rock and flies at about the same speed. Allah forbid, if they did crash, that's about the safest plane in the world in which to do it. Turkish Air Force has triangulated an area within forty miles of where the plane was last seen on radar. They've got two Beavers based at Kars and one at Erzurum. They'll send them up within the hour. Civilian ground personnel from four different stations have launched a search, and a military contingent from Kars is enroute to the area now. If they haven't found them by tonight, I'll fly East to try to help."

NO MAN'S LAND
SOMEWHERE NEAR THE ARMENIAN – TURKISH BORDER

The three survivors took stock of their situation.

Jake's right knee and wrist had apparently hit the control panel of the aircraft when it struck the boulder. When Aviva and their cameraman tried to help him out of the plane, his face turned a sickly shade of white and there was a sheen of perspiration on his forehead. By the time they were able to extract him from the craft, his knee had swollen significantly and become an angry black and blue.

As gently as she could, Aviva palpated Jake's leg from lower calf to upper thigh. "I've had only limited medical training from my time in the Israeli Defense Forces, As far as I can tell, blood has probably seeped into the joint, but thank God nothing seems to be broken. Your right wrist feels like it's badly sprained."

"How about you two?"

"We're bruised and shaken up, but none the worse for wear," their cameraman, Gençler Süyü, said. "As I feared, Ovacık's heart attack was fatal."

As Aviva and Süyü walked around the aircraft, the front end was a mangled mess. All attempts Jake made to raise anyone on the radio were met with silence.

Within an hour of their landing, Aviva and Süyü had fashioned a splint for Jake's leg out of some aluminum that had torn loose from the plane's exterior. Since they'd anticipated only a short trip, there was only an emergency kit on board. After a brief exploratory trip to a small rise above where they'd come to rest, Süyü reported, "Nothing but barren wasteland as far as I can see. We may as well be on Mars."

"No telephone lines or other signs of habitation?" Jake asked.

"Nothing. Not even a stream. Fortunately, I've got a three-liter bottle of water in my camera pack. I always carry a bottle of Advil with me, 'cause my back is not in that great a shape, and I saw an emergency first aid kit next to my seat before we took off. Otherwise, we'd really be in trouble."

"And you don't think we're in trouble now?" Aviva asked, arching her eyebrows. The three of them sat in a patch of shade created by the plane's shadow. Süyü poured four Advil tablets out of is bottle while they were splinting his leg. It was the best they could do for his pain.

"There's an entire TV crew back in Doğubayazit that knows we took off this morning at eight," Jake said. "It's now eight hours later, and there's been no word from us. Erzurum Center caught our Mayday signal and had us on radar until ten minutes before we landed. I wouldn't be surprised if someone's looking for us right now. Every survival handbook I've ever read says we should stay put right where we are, so we're a stationary target. We'll need less water that way. If necessary, we can survive a couple of days without food."

"What if we're attacked?" Aviva asked.

"What's for anyone to steal?" Jake said. "A TV camera, for which they'd have no use, a smashed-up plane …"

"A rather famous woman," Süyü replied. "On the other hand, she's *your* woman, and in this part of the world a man's honor would be questioned if he so much as looked at another man's woman. No matter who we're dealing with, hospitality to the guest and aid for someone in distress are the first rules of behavior in every society in the Middle East."

The pilot had been wearing a red shirt. They removed the garment from the corpse. After they'd carried his remains to a piece of scrub and covered the body as best they could, they fashioned a makeshift flag, which they strapped to the top of the aircraft. By sunset, they'd neither seen nor heard any sign of anyone.

When darkness was upon the land and wolves started howling in the distance, the three survivors climbed back into the aircraft for the night. They'd carefully marshaled their supply of water, so that half of it was left. Although Jake was experiencing some pain, Aviva had given him four more Ibuprofen. Just before returning to the plane, each took a turn privately relieving themselves, so that they need not leave the craft until daylight.

During the moonless night, the wolves' baying became louder. Each of the survivors slept restlessly, a couple of hours at a time. Just before dawn, the wolves' howling ceased altogether. It was then that Aviva said, "I can't hold it in any longer. Would you gentlemen turn your heads if I go outside and squat?"

"It's only half an hour until daylight," Jake said. "Can't you pee in a cup or a plastic bag?"

"You don't understand," she said.

"Let me come with you, then. You can never tell what might be around."

"Okay, but let me go first. You'll have trouble getting down."

She had just descended to the ground, squatted, and relieved herself when she heard a low growl. Turning, she saw a single gray wolf, its teeth bared. Aviva gasped and quickly started back up the stairs. The wolf snarled and leapt, barely nicking the skin above her boot with his teeth. Acting from pure instinct, Aviva lashed out at the beast. Her boot caught the animal squarely on its muzzle. With a scream and a whine of agony, the maddened canine turned in continuous circles, its mouth a mixture of blood and foaming saliva, then slunk away into the rocks.

Back in the plane, Aviva looked at her leg. There was a tiny droplet of saliva around the cut. "Oh, God, no!" she said. "Please don't let it be what I think it is."

30

CIĞLI AIR BASE – THE FOLLOWING DAY

Omer Akdemir telephoned Sara the following afternoon and reported that although land and air forces had scoured the entire area from Kars southeast to Doğubayazit and all along the Armenian border, they'd found no sign of the plane or what they'd hoped would be survivors. "The one quadrant we couldn't explore was the Armenian SSR," he said.

"Can't you communicate with the Armenians and tell them this is an emergency?" she shouted into the phone.

"They'd pay no attention to any request we'd make."

"Not even humanitarian aid?"

"Not even."

"But Jake's American and Aviva's Israeli."

"Not to the Armenians. I'm sure they've seen her on Turkish television, and the Americans are still the enemy as far as the Soviet Union is concerned."

"Is there absolutely nothing we can do?" Sara said, her voice rising in despair.

"I wouldn't say 'absolutely nothing.' There are back channel means of communicating with both the Armenians and Kurds in the area. We've been doing just that for the past twelve hours. There's no report yet."

SAME DAY — SITE OF THE CRASH

"How's your leg feel?" Jake asked. It was sundown. None of them had seen any sign of human existence all day.

"It started itching like mad a couple of hours ago. I noticed a bit of swelling, and there seem to be red streaks moving up my leg. I have no idea what that means and I don't want to even think about what it *might* mean."

"You haven't touched any water all day. You're sure you're not thirsty?"

"Not at all. Funny, I haven't been hungry all day either."

"The wound seems to be closing all right."

"How's *your* knee?"

"Very painful, but I can barely get about on it."

A few moments later, Süyü returned from guard duty. His look was serious and concerned. "No sign of life?" Jake asked.

"No humans," he said. "But I found the remains of last night's wolf."

"The remains?" Aviva asked.

"Yes. From its looks, the animal was ill even before it bit you. The dog sickness," the Turk replied. "Now we really have no time to lose."

Jake felt queasy, but he pulled himself together, realizing his wife's life was at stake. "Süyü, we've got about an hour before it gets dark. I'll toss anything that can possibly burn out of the plane. Our only hope is to build as big a fire as we can and pray that someone sees it."

THAT EVENING — A FEW MILES TO THE EAST

Efrem Hartunian, eleven, had come home with an excellent school report card earlier that week. His father had decided to give the boy a special treat.

"Two of my friends and I are going to countryside west of the capital tonight. How'd you like to go with us?"

"Amateur astronomer stuff, Papa?" Efrem asked.

"Uh-huh."

"How late do you plan to stay out there, Papa?"

"Late."

"Past my bedtime?" the boy asked eagerly.

"Very much so. But your report card tells me your taking responsibility like a young man and that means you've earned some grown-up privileges."

Efrem's face reddened as he preened with pride.

Now it was several hours later. Once the excitement of being outdoors well after his normal bedtime had worn off, Efrem became more interested in the sounds of night on the steppe and the sights of the seemingly endless horizon than on what the grown-ups were doing. He had very good eyesight. As Efrem scanned the distant horizon, he thought he saw a very dim, flickering light on the horizon to the south.

"Papa," he called softly. "I think there's a fire over there." He pointed to a spot in the far distance.

"Efrem, we're busy setting up the telescopes. It's probably just a reflection off a rock. Come over here. I think you'll love this view of Saturn. You can see the rings and even one of its moons."

"But, Papa …?"

"Efrem, it's nothing," his father said in a tone that brooked no argument. "Besides, we need you over here to help steady the large telescope.

THE CRASH SITE — LATER THAT NIGHT

"Jake," Aviva called. "Can you make the fire any larger?"

"I don't think so. We've got one more piece of dry wood and a canvas bag. Süyü?"

"There's nothing anywhere near here. I could siphon a few cups of fuel from the wing tank, but trying to throw that on the fire could cause the whole plane to explode."

"We've got to do something," Aviva said, through gritted teeth. "I refuse to sit helplessly and die in this land. Wait a minute. Did you say the plane could explode? Is there some way we can move far enough away from the plane so if it did explode —?"

"We couldn't move that far away before it got really dangerous."

"Could we hook something resembling a fuse up to the aircraft's wings?" Aviva asked. "Süyü, do we have any rope or rags in the plane? What about the film in the cans?"

"I have some extra cans of 35-millimeter nitrate film," the Turk said. "Highly flammable. I'll look through the plane and see if there's anything else we can use."

NEAR OKTEMBERIAN, ARMENIA

"What did you think of Saturn's rings, Efrem?" his father asked. "Fabulous, yes?"

"Very interesting, Papa," the boy said dutifully. He looked out toward where he'd seen what he thought was the fire. It had died down to the point where he could no longer see it. Perhaps Papa had been right after all.

"I found a dozen rags and a thirty-foot coil of rope," Süyü said.

"Good," Aviva replied. "Can you siphon enough fuel so that if we set the rope on fire it can burn all the way to the fuel tanks?"

"I don't know," the Turk said uncertainly. "If we set the plane ablaze we'll have absolutely nothing left. Not even a place to take cover if the wolves return. Shouldn't we wait until daylight, when I can scavenge more wood? Maybe a search party will find us."

"Süyü Bey," Jake said softly but decisively. "Whatever is in my wife's leg is starting to work its way through her system. We can't wait until tomorrow. If we aren't rescued tonight, there may not even *be* a tomorrow. I say we blow up the plane. If you're not willing to set it afire, I'll do it myself."

Fifteen minutes later, the rope, the rags, and a spool of film had been thoroughly soaked with aircraft fuel. The smell of the gasoline sickened Aviva, even from the small hill, fifty yards away. Jake had managed to limp to her side. The Turk, still close to the aircraft, worked carefully.

He touched the rope to the fire. Within a few moments, it started to burn.

Efrem had started to doze near the van. His father came over and put his arm around the boy. "We'll be done in another quarter hour, son. Do you need a wrap?"

"Please. Do you mind if I nap for a while?"

"Not at all. I'll get you a blanket in the van."

The flame had made it halfway from the end of the rope to the fuselage when the fire went out. "Damn!" Jake swore softly. Without waiting for anyone else, he hobbled as swiftly as he could toward the plane.

The Turk grabbed at Jake, trying to stop him. "It's no use, *Abi.*"

"It's my wife!" Jake roared. With that, he lunged at Süyü. The Turk lost his footing and fell back. Jake scurried toward the dying fire before Süyü could stop him. He was able to seize a burning faggot. Ignoring the heat from the wood and the pain radiating from his knee, Jake limped toward the plane. When he'd gotten to within ten feet of the aircraft, he held the burning faggot of wood against the rags and the rope until both had ignited once again. He screamed with pain as a shot of flame singed his hair and his leg buckled out from under him.

The fuel-soaked rope seemed to fight the fire for an instant, and appeared as though it would go out. But then a stray spark caught the next rag, and then the next. The fire picked up momentum as it neared the wing. If only it kept up this momentum, it would be ten seconds at most before —

Using his arms and his one useful leg, Jake dragged himself toward a nearby rise. It was only thirty feet from the plane, but it was his only hope. The fire inched closer to the aircraft. Closer, closer …"

"Father!" Efrem shouted suddenly. "There it is again! Over there! Look! I swear by the Holy Jesus there's something over there!"

One of the amateur astronomers confirmed Efrem's sighting. "It *is* something," he said. He lifted a pair of binoculars to his eyes. "It's a fire all right. Maybe an explosion," he said. "Can anyone train the telescope in that direction?"

Shortly afterward, Efrem's father sucked in his breath. "If I didn't know better, I'd say it's an aircraft, it's on fire and … My God! It just exploded! Start the van," he shouted. "I don't know how far away it is, but there could be people there!"

The explosion ripped the plane to pieces. Superheated shards shot out in every direction. Jake Baumueller was too close to be spared the onslaught. A small piece of the fuselage skinned the top of his forehead. As he reached up and felt a pool of warm liquid, a second, larger piece sliced through his left arm.

YEREVAN, SOVIET ARMENIA

Aviva had fallen asleep. The Turkish cameraman huddled, shivering miserably, in the back of the van, dreading what he would have to tell Aviva when she regained consciousness.

The interior of the van, crammed as it was, stank of unwashed bodies and human fear. At two in the morning the van reached the highway. Forty-five minutes later, they arrived at the Clinical Hospital of Yerevan State Medical University.

It took less than five minutes for Süyü to tell the duty physician, Arov Nikssarian, what had happened. Nikssarian lost no time in weighing the patient and injecting Aviva with human rabies immune globulin into and around the site of the bite. Even in Aviva's semiconscious state, the doctor used a numbing anaesthetic to decrease the pain.

"Is it …?" the cameraman asked.

"Thank goodness, no," the doctor said. Although from what you told me, it could well have been rabies, the young woman was very lucky. Most likely, she cut herself on a piece of dirty metal. Do you, by any chance, know if her leg started swelling up earlier this evening?"

"Yes," Süyü said. "She complained about red streaks moving up the leg."

"That's consistent with my preliminary diagnosis. Streptococcal. The streaks started moving up the leg as the infection spread."

"So, we don't have to worry about her dying?"

"We don't. but my concern is gangrene and the possible loss of her leg. She contracted a high fever, which dehydrated her. Thankfully you got her here in time. We'll treat her with fluids and antibiotics, and cleanse the wound. She should be as good as new in a day or two."

"Praise Allah," Süyü said.

"I'm more concerned about you, my friend," the doctor replied. I suggest you find a way to get out of Armenia any way you can, as soon as possible," he continued. Pulling a wad of Armenian currency from his pocket, he handed it to the cameraman, scribbled a name and a telephone number on a slip of paper, and gave this to Süyü as well. "Call this number as soon as you leave the hospital. He'll be able to help you."

At that moment the Turk looked distraught. "Is something wrong, *Bey Effendim*?"

"Yes, doctor. How can we tell the lady that her husband …?"

"Her husband?"

"Yes. When the fire went out, he ran to within ten feet of the plane and re-lit it…"

31

THE CRASH SITE. NEXT DAY.

Morning. Jake Baumueller was alive. Barely. He lapsed into and out of consciousness. The blood on his forehead had congealed quickly, cauterized by a shard that had fallen from the dying aircraft. His left arm, between the shoulder and the elbow, was sliced all the way down to the bone. The muscle tissue hung to his torso by a thin thread of ligament. Jake's periods of unconsciousness afforded his only relief from the merciless pain.

He'd had neither food nor water for twenty-four hours. The blazing midday sun gave way to a wind that fanned sand and dust into his wounds and into his lungs. He did not have the strength to resist the inevitable. Images wafted through his mind, images of Istanbul and of Aviva, the way she'd appeared on television when he'd watched the rush of her travelogue. Periodically, the images were washed in a red halo. He could not move, could not even raise his head. It was becoming colder. He shivered involuntarily. It would only be a matter of time, an hour or two at most...

Urdu Kamlican, fifteen, and his younger brother Ulgan, Kurdish villagers from Mahmutbey in the border country between Iğdir and Oktemberian, had heard about a downed aircraft when they listened to the afternoon news on Radio Yerevan. Believing there might be some salvageable material left in the plane, they had ridden their ponies to the approximate area where they thought the craft might be. As Urdu climbed a rise to try and spot the destroyed airplane, he came upon the still, nearly lifeless form of Jake Baumueller by sheer accident.

"Is he dead?" Ulgan asked, gazing at the charred, fragmented body.

"I think so," Urdu replied. He stepped gingerly toward the body and shoved gently at it with the toe of his shoe. At that moment, a soft sigh escaped Jake's lips. Both boys jumped back as if they'd been stung by a wasp.

"He's alive!" the younger boy exclaimed. "What should we do, older brother?"

"First, we must give him a little water." The young man went to his pony, extracted a water pouch, and took off his shirt. He poured a few drops of water onto the shirt and gently rubbed the wet cloth over Jake's mouth and face. Jake moaned. Urdu poured more water onto the shirt, and squeezed his shirt until the liquid found its way into Jake's mouth. He continued doing this until he'd exhausted half the water in the pouch, then poured a little more into the shirt and covered Jake's face with it.

Searching the area around the aircraft, the brothers found a small, flat, segment of the wing, two feet wide and six feet long, which was thin enough for them to drag toward their ponies, but sturdy enough to bear Jake's weight.

Urdu and Ulgan fashioned a primitive travois, which they connected by rope to the saddle on one of the ponies. Moving the nearly lifeless Jake onto the makeshift sledge was more challenging, but they were able to do it slowly and gently. Taking two lengths of rope from the other pony's saddlebag, they secured Jake's body by a cross-tie system. There was no way they could stop all of the bouncing and roughness of the ride back to the village, but in Jake's mostly unconscious state, he had no idea that the boys had saved his life.

KARS, NORTHEASTERN TURKEY

"Still nothing," Omer reported to his wife over the land line to Izmir. It was seven at night, and he'd been without sleep for thirty-six hours. His stomach was rebelling and he could hardly keep his eyes open. "If I don't hear something in the next couple of hours, I'll catch some sleep. My adjutant will call you if anything develops, Sara."

His frustration grew with every minute. Colonel Akdemir could not believe that three hundred troops, who had scoured the entire area, had come up with nothing. It was not their fault, of course. But still —. His reverie was interrupted by a buzz on the intercom in his office. "Yes?" he snapped.

"Colonel Akdemir, there's a telephone call from a man who says he's the *muhtar* of a small Kurdish village, Mahmutbey on the Armenian frontier..."

32

Within three hours after the call, the MedEvac helicopter from Kars had picked Jake up and flown him to Atatürk University Medical Center, where he was treated by a general surgeon. Two days later, he was evacuated by helicopter to the Numune Burn Center in Ankara, where he was immediately transferred to the intensive care unit. By week's end, Jake had returned to consciousness, although his right leg and his both arms were in full-length casts. He'd been diagnosed with severe third degree burns over thirty-five percent of his body and was listed in critical condition.

The following morning, Colonel Omer Akdemir packed his carry-on bag and was waiting to be picked up by the military vehicle to Kars-Harakani Airport, which had opened less than a year before. When he heard a knock on the office door, he picked up his bag and prepared to leave. Just as he had gotten to the door, the post adjutant entered with a slight, nondescript man of early middle age wearing black trousers, a plaid shirt, and an Aegean fisherman's hat.

"Good morning, Colonel Akdemir," the man said without preamble. "My name is Gençler Süyü …"

"So, they're both alive," Omer exclaimed gratefully. "You say Aviva's in hospital at Yerevan State Medical University in Armenia?"

"Yes. I don't know about her husband …" Süyü said uncertainly.

"He was found by two boys outside Mahmutbey on the Turkish-Armenian frontier," Akdemir replied. We ferried him to Numune Burn Center yesterday."

ANKARA, TURKEY

At the beginning of the second week, Doctor Terrance Moran, whom the New York *World* had flown from Hadassah Hospital near Jerusalem to Ankara, spoke seriously with his American patient. "Obviously, you're very lucky to be alive. I'd be less than honest if I didn't tell you that during the next months, they'll come times when you'll wish you weren't."

"I don't feel any pain right now," Jake said.

"That's because you've got so much morphine pumped into you," Moran replied. "Your leg seems to be healing just fine. Your left arm is something else again. The cut was so deep I fear it will be useless for a long time. Whether or not you ever get the feeling back will be up to you and God."

"I hadn't planned on being a concert pianist," Jake said, trying to lighten the atmosphere.

"Actually, Mister Baumueller, I'm more concerned about your face, your arms, and your upper torso. Severe third-degree burns like yours almost always leave extensive scars because the burns are so deep. We may need to do several skin graft operations."

"Will I … look different?" Jake said, uncertainly.

"Yes. At first, what you see will frighten you. Eventually we'll be able to restore most of your physical appearance to what it was, but you'll never be one hundred percent, and you certainly won't be asked to star as the leading man in any American movies."

"What about my wife?" Jake asked.

"Alive and, as far as we can make out, doing well. There's one problem, though."

"What's that?

"She's recovering in the hospital … in Yerevan, Armenia."

33

By week's end, Doctor Nikssarian greeted Aviva with an engaging smile. "Well, Mrs. Baumueller, it appears you're out of danger. All the vital signs are excellent. Thank God, the medication seems not to have affected the little one."

"What do you mean the little one?" she said dully.

"I mean that, God willing, in seven months you'll be the mother of a healthy baby."

"History repeating itself," Aviva said, with no apparent change of emotion.

"What do you mean?"

"My closest girlfriend, Lyuba Kolchuk became pregnant just before her … her fiancé, was killed. At least I can say I was married."

"Young lady, you still are married."

"What do you mean?" Aviva perked up, the scantest flicker of hope in her eyes.

"Your Turkish cameraman managed to smuggle a note to a friend of mine. Your husband survived the crash. Mister Baumueller's now in Numune Burn Center in Ankara, probably the best place in the Middle East other than Israel for that kind of thing."

Aviva's color returned to her face, a beam that was almost magical and added beauty to her features. It was only a moment before the beam lost its wattage. "He's in the burn center? It's been two-and-a-half weeks since the crash. Do you know anything about his condition?"

"Unfortunately, no," Nikssarian said gently. "Other than the note I received four days ago, there's been no word."

"How soon can I get out of here and back to Turkey?"

"Ah, that may be a bit of a problem, Mrs. Baumueller."

"How so?"

"Politics too often interfere with human lives. You're married to an American citizen, which gives you citizenship both as an American and as an Israeli. Israel and Armenia have cordial relations, but neither maintains an embassy in the other country. The Israeli Chargé d'Affaires is based in Tbilisi in the Georgian SSR. He visits Yerevan twice a month, but he's not due back for another ten days. The American consulate is here at sufferance."

"Why can't I simply go to the American consulate and leave this country?"

"It's not that easy, Mrs. Baumueller. You're not an anonymous Israeli or American. Your newscasts filter into Armenia from Kars every evening. Even though our government officially frowns on anyone watching programs from outside the Socialist workers' paradise, you seem to have achieved an icon status, especially among our younger generation."

"That should make it even easier for me to get back to Turkey," Aviva said. "I have … oh, damn! I *had* a press pass, but it's back in Doğubayezit."

"It wouldn't help you if you did. I very much doubt if the Armenian S.S.R. would even look at it, let alone honor it. Yerevan and Ankara have no diplomatic relations. Without Aviva on the air, her bad influence will be gone. The Armenian authorities undoubtedly feel the longer they can keep you here, the better."

Aviva pondered what the Armenian doctor was saying. "Why are you telling me these things, Doctor Nikssarian? Couldn't you get you into trouble?"

"I'm outside of the political stream. While this hospital is by no means immune from KGB scrutiny, I've said nothing to betray any state secrets."

"So, you're under orders to keep me here?" she asked.

"Not even that. The normal rabies treatment, and no one but me knows you weren't infected, is twenty-eight days. The authorities may suspect, but they haven't bothered us yet."

"Yet?"

"I received a call from KGB last week and dutifully reported that Mrs. Edwin Baumueller, the wife of an American newspaper publisher, was in hospital here. They put two and two together — the KGB is by no means stupid, despite how they're demonized in the Western press — and found out your more notorious identity. That large bouquet of flowers on the nightstand beside you came from them."

Ignoring the flowers, she asked, "Have their agents visited my room?"

"Undoubtedly," Nikssarian said. "There are moles in every major facility in the capital. Most likely a nurse or an orderly, it could be another doctor or part of the housekeeping staff."

"Is there no way I can escape their protective custody?"

"I'm afraid not," the Armenian doctor said. However, when he said it, Aviva noticed he had unobtrusively winked.

Doctor Nikssarian returned close to eleven that night, accompanied by a short, burly orderly who was wearing a surgical mask and pushing a small gurney. Aviva came awake instantly. Doctor Nikssarian closed the door behind him. "I'm sorry to have returned so late, but it's necessary to perform surgery," he said. "It's just a small procedure really, but it's critical to your recovery that it be done immediately. We should not wait until morning."

Aviva looked up, startled, and started to protest when the doctor put his fingers to his lips. The orderly unobtrusively pressed a piece of paper into Aviva's hand. Written in English were the words, "No surgery. Room bugged. Must talk privately."

Aviva, whose physical strength had returned a week ago, moved herself from the bed to the gurney. Once in the small, dimly-lit operating theater, the doctor spoke quietly. "The smaller operating rooms are not subject to surveillance. I'm sorry if we startled you, but we had no other way to do this. I have a small favor to ask."

Aviva nodded for the physician to continue.

"My niece Nadya is a graduate student at the State University. The authorities claim she's been involved in the recent anti-Soviet rallies.

Our Soviet brothers are very sensitive to this sort of thing. They want to make examples."

"And Nadya is an example?" Aviva asked.

"Three of her closest friends were detained last night. They haven't been heard from since then. The KGB always comes at about three in the morning, when they're least expected and their targets are at their most vulnerable."

"Couldn't Nadya simply disappear on her own?"

"Too late for that. The KGB has been keeping a careful watch on her. They know Nadya's one of the local leaders of the Armenian Nationalist Patriotic Front."

"You said you had a small favor to ask?" Aviva said.

"I can probably hide Nadya here for twenty-four hours at most. The American consulate is twenty minutes' ride from here. Do you have an American passport?"

Aviva looked down at the floor. "No, Doctor Nikssarian. Jake and I didn't even think of it. I assumed an Israeli passport was sufficient, but we didn't even take that with us, since we had no intention of leaving Turkey. Do the Americans know I'm here?"

"Of course. There are one or two American agents in this hospital even as we speak. At 4:30 tomorrow morning, a Bulgar Renault will appear at the hospital entrance. Just after it leaves, an ambulance will arrive to deliver you to the American Consulate. You'll be accompanied by a hospital orderly ..."

"Nadya," Aviva said.

"Correct. Once inside the consulate, she'll ask for political asylum, and I thought ...?"

"Of course, I'll sponsor her application. I don't see any risk for me, but what risk will there be for you and your family?"

"I will publicly disavow my niece's defection. Her mother will express shock and outrage. Her father's in the northwest, managing a mine in Gyumri on an extended assignment, so he won't know about this."

"But the KGB must know she's disguised herself and come to the hospital."

"As far as they know, she had dinner with her mother earlier in the evening, then adjourned to her own bedroom at ten o'clock. This orderly," he said, pointing toward the burly person accompanying him, "has been on duty since five this afternoon. But I've forgotten my manners. I'd like you to meet my niece, Nadya Vartunian."

With that, the 'orderly' peeled off several layers of towels and gowns to reveal a tiny, dark-haired young woman who could not have been more than twenty-three, nor weighed more than a hundred pounds.

"Good evening, Mrs. Baumueller," she said in lightly-accented English. "I've watched you on *2 Kanal* for the past year. I adore your show"

"Thank you, Nadya," Aviva replied. "Have you ever been outside Armenia?"

"No, but my family lived in a small village in southeastern Turkey for hundreds of years. When I was very young, my great, great grandfather told me life was horrible for an Armenian in Turkey. His older brother, Shadran Vartunian, was killed by Turkish troops. What was left of the family fled to Yerevan. A family legend says a ten-year-old Turkish boy was the only one in the entire village who tried to help the Armenians. The Turks probably killed him, but we still pray for Turhan's soul every night."

"Is there some way *I* could call the duty officer at the consulate?"

Doctor Nikssarian smiled and handed Aviva a small slip of paper on which there were some handwritten figures. "Wait at least half an hour before you call. The KGB will probably monitor the switchboard, but it's hardly likely they'll act before daylight."

Forty-five minutes later, Aviva rang the night operator at University Hospital. She was pleasant enough, altrhough her tone brooked no room for argument. "This is Aviva Baumueller in Room 317. I have just received word that my husband, who was with me when our airplane crashed, has survived and is in Ankara. Please call 572727 immediately."

"But Madame, it is nearly one o'clock in the morning," the operator said.

"I know. Do I need to speak with your supervisor?"

"No, madame. It's a local number. I'll put the call through."

It took four rings until a sleepy duty officer answered the phone. Aviva was all busines. "Good evening, Mister Ambassador," she said, elevating him several ranks. "I apologize for waking you up at this ungodly hour. This is Aviva Baumueller. My husband is Edwin

Baumueller IV of the New York *World*. I have an urgent problem. I'd really appreciate if you could give me some assistance..."

The telephone operator, following specific instructions from the political commissar's representative, patched Aviva's call through to local KGB headquarters, which unobtrusively recorded the call.

❈❈❈

At two-thirty a.m., Aviva came instantly awake when she heard a slight rustling noise in her room. She felt a momentary edge of panic when a heavyset middle-aged woman carrying a cheap cardboard suitcase approach her bed. The woman put two fingers to her lips.

"Don't talk," she said in a quiet voice. "You must leave the hospital immediately, right now." She handed Aviva a pair of baggy pants, a nondescript top, a scarf, flat-heeled shoes, and a thin jacket. "The suitcase has a change of clothing, some money, and an address."

Answering Aviv's frankly questioning stare, the woman continued, "KGB intercepted your phone call. We tapped their interception. They'll be here within the next half hour."

"We?"

"Friends. No time to waste. Half a block from here there's an abandoned store. Stay hidden in the back until sunup."

Now fully alert, Aviva turned suspicious. "How can I trust your word? I don't even know you..."

The woman abruptly switched from English to perfect Hebrew. "You don't, Sister. It's your choice whether to trust me or not. Your decision, Zahavah Barak's granddaughter."

❈❈❈

Within fifteen minutes, Aviva left the hospital through a single narrow door at the rear of the building. She had barely made it to the storefront when she heard the loud whoo-ee, whoo-ee, whoo-ee of multiple sirens and saw a cordon of police vehicles, red lights flashing as they raced up her street and pulled up to the front of the hospital.

❈❈❈

Within a week, Aviva had been shunted from one student room to another all over the city, never staying more than twelve hours in any given locale. She'd met with several young people in the underground movement, one of whom, the grandson of Soviet-Armenian filmmaker, Sergei Parajanov, eagerly agreed to help her make a series of short feature films to be sent all over the country and beyond Armenia's borders.

For the next few days, the two of them produced programs highlighting the aftermath of the crash, Aviva's inability to secure any assistance from either the local government or the American consulate and her need to return to Turkey immediately to be with her seriously injured husband. Knowing exactly what would appeal to every segment of the population, but primarily to women, Aviva emphasized that she desperately wanted him to know that she was carrying their first child. Recklessly oblivious to the effect her broadcasts would have on the Soviet Armenian authorities, she finished six broadcasts before her new friends warned her that the KGB was searching entire neighborhoods where she'd been spotted.

"There are less than five thousand Jews left in Armenia," Gideon Varzhapetyan said as he greeted Aviva in his Kentron District apartment. The tall, fortyish man continued, while he puffed contentedly at a meerschaum pipe, "There used to be more than twice that number, but since the troubles with Azerbaijan started, half have left for Israel and more emigrate every day."

"When did you learn I was in the hospital?"

"The day after you got there. Doctor Nikssarian sent your cameraman, Mister Şüyü to one of our people, who helped get him out of Armenia."

"So, you could get me back to Turkey?" Aviva asked hopefully.

"Much harder now than it was then. There's a tremendous amount of heat surrounding your sudden disappearance and outright fury after your telecasts became the most popular item to hit the *samizdat*, the underground circuit. Doctor Nikssarian and his niece were picked up for questioning less than twenty minutes after you left the hospital.

The interior ministry agents were less than pleased when they searched every room and closet in the building and couldn't find you."

"But could it be done?

"Anything *can* be done," Varzhapetyan replied. "But ..."

"I'm willing to take that chance. My husband's alive. I must go to him any way I can."

Midnight. The undulating fields, newly shorn of their wheat, were dark except for the muted shine of a half-moon and a dim pool of light surrounding the closed border crossing.

"I see no problem crossing the frontier anywhere for miles," Aviva said. "No border guards, not a sound except for the crickets chirping ..."

"Don't let appearances fool you," her guide said. "Almost invisible, electrified barbed-wire fences cover almost every step from border post to border post. Isolated land mines where there might be holes in the fences. Your only hope is to walk through the crossing station which looks like it's closed down for the night, but you never can tell."

As they approached the frontier post, Aviva's guide said, "I'll leave you here. Much better chance of a woman alone and on foot making it across."

Aviva turned to thank him, but he had disappeared into the night. The only vehicle in sight, a several-years-old Bulgar Renault, half-covered by a tarpaulin, looked like it hadn't moved in a decade.

Walking carefully around the faintly flickering light outside the small building, Aviva hardly noticed the slight scratch of a door being slowly opened. Suddenly, she found herself pinned in the glare of a powerful spotlight aimed at precisely where she stood. An officious-looking, bemedaled man addressed her in fluent English. "Good evening, Mrs. Baumueller." He extracted a card case which identified him as Narek Artakian, Captain, Interior Ministry, Armenian Soviet Socialist Republic. "If you will please join me in the office, I believe we have much to talk about."

34

THE ARMENIAN-TURKISH FRONTIER

They sat across from one another in the ten-foot by ten-foot room.

"I, sir, am an American citizen. I demand to see my Consul-general," Aviva said, her tone distinctly bolder than she felt.

"You can, and will, see him eventually, Mrs. Baumueller," Artakian remarked equably. "As for you being an American citizen, your status is rather ambiguous, isn't it? Our dossier lists you as an Israeli citizen, in the employ of the Turkish media."

"Is it supposed to frighten me that you know who I am? You are obviously aware I am married to an American citizen and thus claim American citizenship. I will say absolutely nothing until I have seen the United States representative."

"That is fine with me, Mrs. Baumueller. But I fear that may take some time. I would like to play you something on this tape recorder."

Aviva listened in shock, then in mounting horror as she heard her own voice. "Good evening, Mister Ambassador. I apologize for waking you up at this ungodly hour. This is Aviva Baumueller. My husband is Edwin Baumueller IV of the New York *World*. I have an urgent problem, and I'd really appreciate it if you could give me some assistance ..."

Aviva remained silent as the captain turned off the tape. In answer to her questioning look, he said, "The telephone operator at the hospital had strict instructions to patch any outgoing call into the KGB. Five-seven-two-seven-two-seven is the American consul-general's private number. So, it seems we have a Turkish resident coming across the border into Armenia, aiding and abetting an Armenian dissident attempting to commit treason, and conspiring to commit a treasonous escape to an unfriendly foreign state, not to mention engaging in underground propaganda which has inflamed a goodly section of our population. As I said, Mrs. Baumueller, it seems as though you've got a lot to answer for."

During the next half-hour Artakian brought Aviva up to date on what had happened during the three weeks she'd gone missing. "Nadya Vartunian and her uncle, Doctor Nikssarian, were summarily tried and sentenced to three years' imprisonment. Before Doctor Nikssarian was whisked away to Yevtushenko State Prison, he managed to smuggle out news of your escape to the United States consulate and the visiting Israeli Chargé d'Affairs, who passed the word along to Turkish authorities in Ankara." In this manner, Jake, still in the early stages of convalescence at Numune Burn Center, learned that his wife had survived.

"So now that you've arrested me, I trust I'm to be tried, convicted, and hanged?" Aviva said caustically. Surprisingly, she felt resignation rather than fear.

Captain Artakian, who'd been standing and pacing the small room since they'd entered, asked, "May I sit?"

"Do I have a choice?"

"Of course, but as long as there are just the two of us in this room and you no doubt know whose word will be accepted by the authorities, I'd like to speak candidly, as you media folks say, 'Off the record.'"

"I'm listening."

"Mrs. Baumueller, I am a senior public servant, and I have been such for nearly thirty years. One does not survive in the current regime without being a pragmatist." She noticed that, although accented, his English was perfect. "Don't get me wrong, I am in all ways loyal to my country and I would never do anything to betray my country's best interests."

"But?"

"Ah, you Israelis are so direct," Captain Artakian said, smiling. "I've heard that whenever someone says the word 'but' you don't listen to anything that went before, only those that follow."

"True."

"Our Soviet government, the beloved organ of the people, may continue in power for the next hundred years. Or it may not." Aviva looked at him wordlessly. "How much international news have you heard?"

"Hardly any."

"Two months ago, our overlords in Moscow granted economic independence to the Baltic States. Two million Lithuanians, Latvians and Estonians joined hands in a human chain, stretching nearly four hundred miles from Vilnius to Tallinn, to protest the fiftieth anniversary of the Molotov-Ribbentrop pact."

"So, the American media's intuition was correct," she said softly.

"I beg your pardon?"

"Contrary to what your government believes, Captain Artakian, I was never sent into Armenia to spy. The plane in which I was flying crashed in Armenian territory by sheer accident. Prior to that, I had been advised while I was still in America that the Soviet regime was by no means as unified and secure as Premier Gorbachev had led us to believe."

Artakian rose to his feet and walked around the room. "Last month, twelve thousand East Germans crossed to the West across Hungary's open border with East Germany." Aviva remained silent. "There are massive shortages of just about everything we need in Armenia. The malcontents are beginning to outnumber the duly constituted legal authority."

Aviva nodded.

"I am a loyal Armenian public servant. I emphasize the word *Armenian*. While I am loyal to the *Armenian* cause, I have a wife and three nearly grown children. My first loyalty is to them. You are a very public figure, Mrs. Baumueller. It never hurts to maintain friendships on both sides of the fence. Do you understand what I am saying?"

"Of course," she replied.

"There's an old motorcar outside that looks like it hasn't been driven in years. I ask that you accompany me while we travel back to Yerevan. Please remember there are those among us who are truly *Armenian* patriots."

The Bulgar Renault arrived at a driveway beyond which there was an electric gate. Captain Artakian pushed a set of numbers in a box mounted by its side. The gate swung slowly open. Moments later, Aviva was discharged at the front door of the American Diplomatic Mission. Captain Artakian nodded a curt dismissal and the car drove away.

35

THE UNITED STATES MISSION — AN HOUR LATER

Shortly after she'd entered the building, a nondescript middle-age man in a western cut gray suit, his hair clipped close to his head, introduced himself as Frank O'Neil, United States Secret Service.

"You are not officially here, Mrs. Baumueller," he said. "My instructions are to get you to Erebuni Airport. The authorities monitor every flight into and out of Zvartnots. Erebuni is Yerevan's domestic airport. It's hardly used at all." He pointed to a pile of peasant clothes and heavy shoes, and handed her a small, cheap cardboard suitcase similar to the one she'd been handed when she left University Hospital. "You're the same height, but your build is slighter than one of our young housekeepers," he said. "Those are her clothes. At some distance you'll be able to pass for her. First thing, you should put on the scarf. It's the best we can do on such short notice."

Within the hour, Aviva and O'Neil walked out the rear door of the consulate, where they were met by a dark blue Chevrolet sedan. "You think the authorities won't track an obviously American automobile?" she asked.

"I'm sure they will, Mrs. Baumueller. Even if we were driving a local car, our friends keep track of every movement into and out of the diplomatic mission. What we're doing will seem anything but suspicious. One of our housekeepers leaves the building every day at noon to pick up her daughter from daycare. She and her husband live near Sheram Street. We drop her off downtown at Andravar Street, where she catches the shared taxi. The housekeeper gets off at the Sheram Street station, the third stop. You'll stay on the shared taxi 'til its last stop, Erebuni Airport. Once you're there, there'll be further arrangements."

"What if I'm spotted?" Aviva asked.

"No problem," O'Neil said, as the chauffeur-driven Chevrolet turned into traffic. "There'll be someone in the shared taxi the whole way to make sure you get safely to where you're going."

"How will I recognize him?"

"You won't. In fact, you won't know if it's a 'him' or a 'her' until the last stop. Then you'll receive further instructions."

Although Aviva was nervous when she left the Chevy, she knew that sometimes the best way to be inconspicuous is often to be in the very middle of everything. She recalled reading, when she was much younger, that many Jews had survived in Germany during the second World War simply by remaining in Berlin where they'd lived all their lives. She'd been waiting at the taxi stop less than three minutes when a brown-and-white van bearing a large number one on its front window pulled up. She joined the ten other people crammed into the van, and paid her fare with a 100-dram coin.

During the trip, Aviva sat silently in the van, gazing out the window. The day was bright and sunny. She could see snow-topped Mount Ararat in the distance. Turkey was there, and so was Jake. Her heart raced as she thought about him. If only he could see her now. She felt the growing life inside her and smiled. Soon she would be with him.

At Erebuni Airport, the five people remaining in the van clambered out. Just as she was about to exit, an older woman who'd been sitting in front of her signaled for Aviva to follow. Aviva looked around. There was no one else who'd even taken notice of her. "Are you …?"

"*Da*," the woman answered. "Follow, please."

When they'd walked fifty feet from the shared taxi stop, an older model brown car of indeterminate make pulled up. "Madame Baumueller?" its driver, a young man, asked.

"Yes."

"Please get in. We're going to Armavir Airfield."

"Armavir?" Aviva said, her suspicion rising. "But I was told Erebuni."

"Too public," the man replied equably. "No one checks Armavir. It's very small and no scheduled airlines fly in there. Much easier to get you out of Armenia."

Last night, Aviva had faced arrest and imprisonment on the Armenian-Turkish frontier. Earlier this morning, she been whisked to what passed for American soil, where she'd remained for less than an hour. She'd been given ambiguous instructions. So far, she'd not been apprehended. There had indeed been representatives, just as Frank O'Neil had said there'd be. Yet her feeling of suspicion did not abate. She got in, and the sedan pulled away from the curb.

By the time they reached Armavir, it was late afternoon. The field looked almost abandoned. The terminal building was a squat, boxy one-story affair. There were three older model Cessnas and an ancient DC-3 sitting silently on the tarmac. As Aviva entered the building, she saw a large map of the surrounding area, encased in glass. Turkey was so close — she estimated twelve miles away — that she could probably walk to the border in four hours. Once there, she would immediately identify herself … But then, reality dawned on her. She had no identification papers of any kind.

"It's all right," her driver said in unaccented American English. "The plane will be here momentarily. You'll be out of Armenia within a couple of hours. Would you like some tea?"

"Yes, please," she said.

The young man went over to a kiosk attended by an old woman. Aviva watched as the woman filled a half-cracked cup with tea from a samovar. As the man walked back toward her, Aviva's attention was momentarily diverted as a small, unmarked jet aircraft touched down and braked to a stop at the far end of the runway. She turned and saw the man nodding. "There's your plane," he said, looking at his wristwatch. "A few minutes early. It'll get you out of this country sooner. I brought you a sugar cookie as well as tea. You must be famished. The plane will fuel up and the crew will take some time before they come to get you."

Aviva reached for the tea thankfully. It would be the first nourishment she'd had since this morning. She wolfed the delicious cookie down. She glanced over at the wall clock. Five minutes past four. Her eyes felt heavy, undoubtedly from knowing her ordeal was nearly over. Tonight, she'd be with Jake in Ankara.

"How long will it be until the crew is ready?" She realized she didn't even know the young man's name.

"Thirty minutes."

LATER

When she awoke, she was in a single bed, covered by a thin blanket, in a small room. As her eyes accommodated to the dark, she made out the only furniture in the room, the cot, a small table, and a lamp. When she turned on the light switch, she saw a framed print on the wall to her right, which contained Arabic writing. From her experience as an investigative reporter, she knew Arabic had been abandoned in Turkey for at least sixty-five years. More awake now, she felt her bladder would explode if she didn't go to the bathroom soon.

She swung her legs off the cot, stood up, and went toward the door. Odd. The door was locked from the outside. She banged softly, then more insistently. Moments later, she heard a key being inserted and tumblers moving as the key turned. The door opened, and a woman perhaps half a dozen years her junior said, "Ah, you are awake, Mrs. Baumueller. If you need to use the facilities, the loo is just down the hall."

"Thank you, Miss …?"

"Dudayev, Rosa Dudayev," the woman said, smiling.

After she returned from the toilet, Aviva saw that the young woman was still waiting by the door to her room.

"Rosa Dudayev?" Aviva said. "Would you mind telling me just where I am?"

The young woman had just started to answer when an impeccably dressed silver-haired man pushed his way through the door. Aviva felt a sudden chill as she recognized him, but she forced herself to remain calm.

"Why, Count Napolitano, how strange to see you. I'm sure the authorities would be most interested in speaking with you."

"You flatter yourself, Mrs. Baumueller," Napolitano replied archly. "Rather portlier than I remember."

"Thank you for your gentlemanly remarks, Marco. You seem annoyed that someone beat you into my bed?"

In response, he slapped her hard across the face. "I don't need to hear such garbage from you!"

Instinctively, Aviva responded with an equally vicious *krav maga* chop to Napolitano's neck. The man reeled back in shocked surprise.

He was just about to punch her with his closed fist, when he caught control of himself and said in a much courtlier tone, "You are in a most inappropriate position to spread vitriol my dear, particularly since you are my guest."

"And just how long do you think you'll be able to keep me as your 'guest?'" Aviva rejoined. "Don't kid yourself. It's obvious we're not in Turkey and you've added drugging and kidnapping me to your long list of good deeds, Marco. But you'd better believe you'll have to kill me before you try to rape me, and if you so much as turn your back on me for five seconds, you'll be dead before you get within two feet of my baby. Jake's baby, by the way."

She noticed for the first time that Rosa Dudayev had absented herself from the room as soon as Marco Napolitano had entered.

"I suggest, *Mrs. Baumueller*, that henceforth you'd best be a bit more respectful of me. We may be together longer than you think."

"Not that I think you're capable of giving me an honest answer, Marco, but would you mind telling me exactly where I am?"

"Of course, my dear. Welcome to Itum-Shale, a hundred miles south of Groszny, in the Freedom-loving Islamic Republic of Chechnya."

36

Jake Baumueller was perspiring as he stepped off the Stairmaster. Wiping his forehead with the clean white towel, he thought, *that darned doctor had been spot on.* Four weeks and a lot of pain, but he now noticed the gain more and more. Glancing in the hospital exercise room's mirror, he was gratified to see that he looked nowhere near the gargoyle he'd first seen when they'd brought him to the burn center.

As he left the gym, Doctor Moran signaled him.

"Yes, Terry?" he said.

"You're hot stuff. Some guy from the Embassy's waiting in the visitor's lounge to talk to you." The doctor pointed down the hall. "Third door to the right."

Ten minutes later, Jake stood up, the look on his face one of anger and impatience.

"What exactly do you mean, 'missing?'" Jake demanded of the young attaché who'd brought him this information. "American citizens simply don't vanish into thin air."

"Mister Baumueller, all I know is what I've just told you. Captain Artakian got her to the consulate. Frank O'Neil arranged for her to get to Erebuni, where an American Embassy 727 aircraft was sitting on the tarmac waiting for her arrival. She never showed up. The woman who'd been detailed to watch over her mistakenly believed a man in a brown sedan was the agent with whom she was supposed to connect. The last she saw, Aviva Baumueller drove away with the man."

"She's my wife, for God's sake!" Jake exploded. "American security couldn't do better than that to protect her?"

The attaché shrugged helplessly. "Look, Mister Baumueller, I'm sorry ..."

"Sorry's a damned weak word!" Jake exclaimed. Quickly he quieted down, somewhat embarrassed. *This man's a junior attaché. What could he have done?* "Listen, Mister —?"

"Dick Gorman. I understand your frustration, Mister Baumueller."

"I didn't mean to unload on you, Dick. None of this is your doing. Please understand I don't hold you responsible."

"No apologies necessary," Gorman commented.

"Dick, is there any way you can get me out of this hospital? As in *today*?"

"You're a free American citizen. Why don't you just leave?"

"The docs don't want to release me yet."

Gorman shrugged. "The truth is, as far as anyone knows, your wife's not in Armenia anymore."

"What if I were to go into Armenia?"

"I wouldn't advise it, sir."

"Is there any way the consulate could get me into Yerevan quietly, so I might talk to Frank O'Neil or somebody who might know something?"

"The Soviet Union is starting to crack apart."

"What does that have to do with finding my wife?"

"We're advising everybody to stay as far away as possible from any breakaway republic. Armenia's as high up on that list as you can go."

"I don't give a rat's ass about putting myself in danger. Three months ago, I was given up for dead. If our government wants to keep American citizens out of harm's way, that's their problem. If our government can't find my wife, that's *my* problem. Can you find any way to get me into Armenia?"

"Pardon me for saying so, Mister Baumueller, but you don't look like you're in any condition to rescue anyone. Let's go down to the cafeteria," Gorman said quietly.

Once they were seated at a table, sipping coffee, the young envoy continued, "There is one way, but it's got to be hush-hush."

"I'm listening."

"Israel, which is friendly with both Armenia and Turkey, has the largest egg production plant in the Middle East..."

Jake took a bite of his day-old croissant. "I'm listening."

"There's a semi-secret flight called 'the egg flight' twice a week. An old, slow 'Israeli Defense Force' C-54, actually operated by the U.S. Air Force, leaves Ankara at 10:00 p.m. and lands at Ben Gurion Airport just after midnight. It loads up on chickens and eggs as well as diplomatic messages and occasional 'Israeli' personnel, then flies from Tel Aviv to Yerevan, leaves Yerevan about 4:30 in the morning and flies back to Ankara, landing here at 9:30 a.m."

"Seems rather circuitous to me," Jake said. "I'm not interested in the details or the 'why.' I'd just like to know if you can get me on that flight."

"I can. A friend of mine's an Air Force captain who flies the route. I understand they keep the doors between the cockpit and the rest of the plane shut pretty tight, because it smells like a flying chicken coop. If there's an extra passenger or two on board, no one at Yerevan wants to wake up to check them out at four in the morning…"

During the next two days, Jake and Dick Gorman spent hours going over the plan they had worked out. Jake studied exactly which shared taxi ran from the airport to downtown, the closest street to the American Consulate, where Captain Artakian's precinct headquarters were located, the restaurant frequented by Frank O'Neil, and the date and time Dick Gorman had arranged for Jake to meet him there.

Baumueller had been provided with a current Canadian passport and visa identifying him as Carl Bayard Johnston, businessman, one thousand Soviet rubles, a return ticket from Yerevan to Moscow and then on to Toronto enclosed in an Air Canada envelope, a document proving he had reservations at the Razdan Hotel, and a letter of introduction to a well-known Armenian export house. He had packed a small suitcase with toiletries, underwear, two changes of clothes, a large plastic bottle of Ibuprofen tablets, and a warm, kapok-filled jacket.

On the third night, Jake took a taxi thirteen miles north from Ankara's Kızılay Square to Esenboğa International Airport. He arrived just after seven thirty in the evening. After a leisurely dinner at the airport restaurant, he hobbled out to the tarmac where, shortly before nine o'clock, a U.S. Air Force truck stopped adjacent to him.

"Going out on the egg flight?" the driver shouted good-naturedly.

"Uh-huh."

"Girlfriend in Tel Aviv?"

"Something like that."

"Man, I've heard those honeys down there are hot," the driver, a young airman, said when Jake had climbed into the truck and slammed the door shut. "You can't get anything in Turkey, not even the clap," the driver said. "Wish I could afford to go down there for a weekend."

"Maybe you can," Jake said, casually slipping the young man a fifty-dollar bill.

"Hey, thanks, bud. That was completely unnecessary, but I sure appreciate it."

"No problem, Airman," Jake replied. "Just a little something to let you know we appreciate what you guys are doing here, manning the farthest outposts of democracy."

"You wouldn't know it," the young fellow replied. "Enlisted housing's pretty grim. I've only got eight months left. I'll sure be glad to get home."

The truck pulled up to a small, old-fashioned aluminum hangar at the far end of the field. There was a single pole with two sodium lights illuminating the area. A four-engine propeller-driven plane waited quietly under the lights. As Jake alighted from the truck, he was met by a petite young woman wearing an U.S. Air Force flight suit and a flight cap bearing the six-pointed Jewish star of the Israeli Defense Forces.

"Hi, I'm Colleen Miller," the woman said. "Dick Gorman told me you were gonna hop on when I had my back turned." She chuckled. Jake liked her immediately.

"You could say that, Captain. How were you so lucky to get this gig?"

"Connections. Listen, if you'd like, there's a third seat in the cockpit we hardly ever use. You can take your choice, fly cabin class or fly chickenshit class."

"All the way to …?"

"Just about all the way to …" Captain Miller replied. "Fifteen minutes out of Zvartnots, you gotta' get back with the chickens, 'cause we don't know you're aboard."

By late October, Yerevan's early morning winter chill had set in. At four in the morning it was 40 degrees Fahrenheit. Damned cold. Jake, who'd been in the controlled temperature of the hospital for more than three months, could not believe how painful his joints were as he emerged from the aircraft. Only one man, a civilian, met the plane. While that man concentrated on loading a few crates of eggs onto his truck, Jake unobtrusively wandered away from the aircraft, limping stiffly along the perimeter road toward the barely-lit terminal a quarter mile away.

YEREVAN, ARMENIA, LATER THAT DAY

Jake listened in growing frustration as Frank O'Neil told him what little he knew. No one at either of Yerevan's two main airports had seen anyone remotely resembling Aviva. "There's a third airport, Armavir," O'Neil said, "but it's pretty much abandoned, no tower, a short, pockmarked runway, and no one's filed a flight plan into or out of that field for years."

"Could she have gotten out of Armenia by any other means?"

"The only other practical way out would be over the mountains to Georgia. Turkey occupies a huge chunk of Armenia's western border. Armenia's border with Azerbaijan is even larger, but since the Azeris align with the Turks, those borders are never safe."

"But you can't be sure of that?"

"No, Mister Baumueller, I can't. Just because borders exist doesn't mean that thousands of people don't cross the no man's land every year — smugglers, slavers, and opportunists."

"So, the trail turns cold just outside Zvartnots Airport?"

"Uh-huh."

"I thought America was one of two superpowers in the world," Jake said.

"I wouldn't be surprised if within the next year we'll be the *only* superpower left," O'Neil replied. "The one thing you can bet on is that in this part of the world is that Uncle Sam isn't about to capitalize on the mess. You saw what happened in Afghanistan. There are many people more intelligent than me, who say *that's* what's brought the Soviet Socialist paradise crashing down. Thank God the U.S. is too smart to get involved in that rathole. Let the friggin' mullahs have their dry-ass mountains."

"No hope, then?"

"I didn't say that. There's always hope. At least that's what I'm supposed to tell anybody who asks." A middle-aged man stopped at their table.

"Good evening Captain Artakian," O'Neil said.

"Good evening, gentlemen," Artakian replied. "I trust you are enjoying our fair country's hospitality, Mister Baumueller? Or would you rather I call you by your new Canadian name?"

"Whatever, Captain," Jake said. "I heard of the kindness you showed my wife while she was in your custody. I appreciate it."

"But you'd be more appreciative if I had any clues," he said equably. "I'm afraid that officially I can't help much. Armenian jurisdiction extends no farther than our own borders. Times are hard now. We can't even control our own nation. *Unofficially —*"

"Yes?"

"How long would it take you to pack your suitcase?"

"A minute-and-a-half. Why?"

O'Neil piped up. "Gentlemen, perhaps it would be better if I didn't hear this conversation."

"You're probably right, Mister O'Neil," Artakian said. "Not that it would make much difference."

37

THE CAUCASUS MOUNTAINS

The trip through the mountains took the entire night. Jake managed to catch five hours of sleep. The sun had already risen when the driver dropped him off at the thirteenth century Sanain Monastery. "Give this to the priest," the driver said in English, handing Jake a small envelope. With a barely muffled roar and a clashing of gears, the truck took off in a cloud of blue-black smoke, leaving Baumueller in its wake.

The man who greeted Jake wore a light cassock and was pale, with a shaved head. He nodded wordlessly as Jake handed him the envelope. After glancing at the contents, he motioned Jake to follow him into the monastery and down a hall to a large cell. When the priest opened the door, Jake saw two young women, one slight, the other taller and more robust looking.

"Good morning, Mister Baumueller," the priest said in perfect, unaccented English. "My name is Arov Nikssarian. Until my recent incarceration at Yevtushenko penitentiary, I was a doctor in Yerevan State University Hospital, where I had the privilege of treating your wife. She risked her life to try to get my niece, Nadya Vartunian, out of Armenia during the recent troubles." he said, nodding at the smaller of the two women.

"To say my thanks are profound would be an understatement," Jake said. He rubbed his eyes, which were puffy from lack of sleep.

"Would you like some coffee or tea, Mister Baumueller?" Nadya asked.

"Please. Either one is fine." He ground his hands into his thighs, trying to massage feeling back into them. Turning back to Doctor Nikssarian, he said, "Actually, Captain Artakian arranged for me to come here. I didn't know why at the time, and he gave every indication it was best for me not to ask."

"Strange things happen in this part of the world," Nikssarian said. "Friendships that cross borders are precious. My Nadya was in her first year at the university when she met a girl from the Georgian SSR. They stayed in touch, even when Nadya was sent to prison. When Nadya was released, her friend crossed two borders just to be the first to celebrate Nadya's freedom."

"Two borders?" Jake said.

"As far as the Soviet Union is concerned, it's all one country, but Nadya's friend was working at a temporary job in Chechnya, north of Georgia, when she saw something I think will be of interest to you, Mister Baumueller." Jake looked at the taller woman. A spark of hope entered his eyes as he saw her expression. "Mister Baumueller, I'd like you to meet Nadya's friend, Rosa Dudayev."

"It's been a several days since I saw her, Mister Baumueller. I can't promise she's still there."

"How did you — ?"

"Quite by accident. My cousin Arkady and his wife, Anya, have worked at the compound for the past year. They have no love for the rebels, but nowadays jobs are very hard to come by in the northern Caucasus and they need to eat. Anya's mother became ill in September. They told Arkady they could not spare Anya, even for a week. I had ten days' vacation time from my job in Tbilisi and I'd never been to Chechnya, so I agreed to replace Anya. The third day I was there, Count Napolitano appeared. Two days later, Mrs. Baumueller — I recognized her from the television — was there as well."

"Count Napolitano?"

"He tried to get me to go to bed with him the first night he was in the compound. He believes every woman on earth is his next conquest. You're aware that he had — has — designs on your wife?"

"Yes," Jake said, keeping his rising anger in check. "Is she still there?"

"Anya sent word that as of two nights ago she was still there. Fortunately, Count Napolitano was called away to Baghdad and Aleppo the day after your wife arrived. She's under constant guard, but at least he hasn't been there. Anya told me he's due back day after tomorrow."

"How would you know about Count Napolitano's comings-and-goings?" Jake asked.

"Not from the Chechen officers, that's for sure," Rosa responded. "But the janitors, the maids, and many of the lower grade empnloyees have their own underground network. And I can tell you Napolitano has few if any friends among the 'little people.'"

Jake paced the floor of the room nervously. "How far is the compound from here?"

"Seventy kilometers to Tbilisi, and another eighty to Itum-Shale. I understand your wife's an Israeli?"

"Yes, why do you ask, Miss Dudayev?"

"She seemed to be the only one in the camp who did not fear Count Napolitano. No sooner had he left than she asked me many questions. I believe she was planning a way to escape from the compound from the second day after she got there. She mentioned someone named Halide Orhan …"

Doctor Nikssarian interjected, "Chechnya's an Islamic hotbed. Tbilisi used to have more than fifty thousand Jews. It's got half that number today, since the rest emigrated to Israel."

"So," Nadya chimed in, "it's a matter of getting Aviva out of Chechnya." She blushed momentarily when Jake glanced at her. "I feel I know her well enough to call her that," she said, proudly showing Jake the letter Aviva had written for her.

Now that he knew that two days ago Aviva had been within ninety miles of where he was at the moment, Jake was eager to depart for the rebel camp immediately.

"But first you must have a plan," Doctor Nikssarian said. "It would be foolhardy to attack a fortress single-handedly and expect to come out alive, let alone with your wife in tow."

"You're right," Jake answered dejectedly. "I hadn't given it much thought."

"Fortunately," Nikssarian continued, there are some assets your wife can count on. As I said, strange things happen in this part of the world. Friendships that cross borders … You'll excuse me for a few moments, please." The doctor left the room and headed down the hall.

Within five minutes, he'd returned with a burly man of thirty-five who could not have been more than 5'7" tall. Jake immediately noticed that although the man was bulky, there was not an ounce of fat on him. Holding out his right hand and shaking Jake's he said, "Mr. Baumueller, I'm Simcha Bar-Ilan, Third Secretary for cultural affairs at the Israeli consulate in Tbilisi. Dr. Nikssarian told me you could use a little help in dealing with Marco Napolitano's nasty little friends across the border in Chechnya …"

The Monastery, Two Hours Later

"Let's go over the plan again," Simcha continued. "We make a show of trying to kidnap Count Napolitano. When we find he's not there, we try to kidnap your wife. When we get to Aviva's room, she'll be gone. We'll take whoever shows you to Aviva's room at gunpoint, tie him up, and put him in the back of the car, a beat-up old Moskva with Azeri license plates. The bad guys will be sure to follow you as soon as they believe you can't see them anymore. Within two minutes after you leave the rebels' base, you'll see a Soviet State Police cruiser pulled off to the side of the road with its lights flashing. You'll pull over behind the cruiser. A uniformed policeman will order you to get out of the Moskva, leave the prisoner behind, and get into the police car. When your prisoner's associates come to get him, he'll only be able to tell them truthfully that you abandoned the car and drove off with the police."

"Simcha, I can't thank you enough for your help."

"No problem, Mister Baumueller, she's one of our own, even though she is temporarily displaced."

"Where will my wife be when all of this happens?"

"Miss Dudayev told me about a plan Mrs. Baumueller conveyed to her, something a woman named Halide Orhan pulled off more than seventy-five years ago. I believe we should adopt that idea. I'll have

Rosa Dudayev let her know we'll be there to implement it," the Israeli agent said.

"But you haven't answered me question," Jake persisted.

"She'll be fairly close by, safe, and well out of sight. For her own safety, that's all I can tell you." The Israeli operative turned to the Georgian woman. "Rosa, do you still have a key to the building where Aviva's kept?"

"Yes."

"You know what to say?"

"Anya's mother has taken ill again, and I've been sent to replace her for the next few days. Then I'll tell her about your — her — plan."

"Okay, we'll get started within the hour. Jake, you, the ladies, and I will drive up to the staging area. Doctor Nikssarian, a couple of my associates will pick you up here fifteen minutes after we leave."

"What about the police cruiser?" Jake asked.

"God, working through the Israeli consulate, will provide," Simcha responded. "It's always convenient to have friends inside the Georgian State Police Department."

38

ITUM-SHALE REBEL COMPOUND, CHECHNYA

"Darling Rosa," the young sentry said. "I thought you'd been taken from my life forever."

"Today's your lucky day, Gyorgiy," she responded. She'd actually developed a strong liking for the twenty-two-year-old guard, Raskov, who was not Chechnyan, but, like her, a hired Georgian laborer. He seemed so innocent. She knew he was smitten with her. "Anya's mother's ill again."

"I'm sorry to hear that," he said, in a tone that betrayed he wasn't sorry at all. "How long will you be here?"

"Until she gets back. Two or three days."

"Then we'll have time to talk?"

"Perhaps." She winked at him, happily conscious when she saw him blush. "I'm so thankful you stood up to the count when he tried to get fresh with me."

"He is not a gentleman," Gyorgiy remarked acidly.

"Aren't you worried that if he sees the two of us together …?"

"*Nyet*. He'll be in Syria for at least another two days."

"What about the lady from the Turkish television?"

"She's still here, and none too happy either."

"Is she in the same guest rooms?"

"Unfortunately, not," Raskov replied. "Count Napolitano told me she'd be a target for potential kidnappers since her face is so well-known. The Turkish television is very powerful. It beams into all the bordering countries. He's keeping her in his own suite, under the heaviest guard in the camp, until he returns."

"Have they become … lovers?" she asked casually.

"Hardly. He flew off to Baghdad the day after she got here. Although he's left word that she's his woman and if anyone touches a hair on her head they won't live to tell about it, the women in camp have taken her under their wing. Napolitano's wealthy and powerful but I don't think one person in the camp would be sorry to see him gone permanently."

Damn! Rosa thought. *Not only will that make it harder to get to her, but it will be next to impossible to get word to the others in time.* "Gyorgiy," she said warmly. "I'm one of the few people here she trusts. Could I see her for a few minutes, just to say hello?"

"Well …" he said uncertainly. "Count Napolitano left word no one was to see her."

"What harm could there be in my spending a few moments with her? I'd be happy to have you search me …" she saw his eyes light up with interest, "provided there's a woman close by to protect me."

"Rosa!" he said, abashed. "Surely you wouldn't think — ?"

"Of course not, Gyorgiy. I know you're too much of a gentleman — and a Georgian, which means you know how to treat a woman."

"Are you armed?" he asked.

"Of course not. Truly, you can search me if you want," she said, taking his right hand and pressing it to her pants pockets, the area of her stomach, and her shoulders.

"No, no, I trust you."

"You can stay in the room with us the whole time. I just want to say hello to her."

Aviva flushed with pleasure when she saw Rosa. They hugged and spoke inanities. Aviva, who knew she'd have to be cautious, asked if Rosa had heard anything from the outside. Rosa responded there were daily rumors about how poorly things were going in the Soviet Union, but otherwise no really exciting news.

"Have you heard anything about my husband?" Aviva asked.

"Not a word," Rosa replied, but Aviva was quick to catch the other woman's sharply raised eyebrows while Rosa was sure her back was to the guards. Suddenly, Rosa grasped at her stomach. In response to Aviva's questioning look, Rosa said, "It's nothing really. Just a slight bit of indigestion from the journey. Is there a loo I could use?"

"There's a private bathroom in this suite."

"I'll only be a moment."

While she was in the bathroom, Rosa spotted a clothes hamper in a corner of the room. She opened it. Seeing there were only women's underclothes in the basket, she taped the message to the bottom of the container, beneath the clothes. Then, she flushed the toilet, washed her hands, and emerged from the room, her hands wet.

"Mrs. Baumueller, I hate to be a pest, but there was no towel in the restroom and I wasn't about to dry my hands on the soiled underwear in the hamper …"

"Oh, I'm so sorry, Rosa," Aviva said. "Would you mind using a kitchen towel?"

"Of course not."

Aviva found the note less than a minute after Rosa Dudayev had left. The instructions were explicit. "Our friends like your plan. 'Operation Halide' goes into effect tonight." She tore the message into tiny strips and flushed them down the toilet. Just before sunset, she asked the guard outside her door if she might take a short walk along the perimeter of the camp. "It's so stuffy being in the apartment all day. You can have a guard accompany me if you wish."

The guard summoned young Gyorgiy Raskov and directed him to keep watch on "our important guest."

"Would you mind if I brought her friend Rosa along, Sergeant?"

"Suit yourself."

North of the Georgian frontier, the great, wild mountains of the Caucasus gradually descend into foothills, and the land flattens out between the Chechen steppe and the forests of Great Russia. It is a place of small farmholdings and endless large skies. In fall, the land is golden with sheaves of wheat and bales of drying hay. It is a land of few private automobiles. *Kamyons,* huge trucks plying the international highways, rule the larger roads, and one frequently sees more horse-drawn wagons than motor vehicles on the byways.

Just after Aviva, Rosa, and Gyorgiy Raskov had started their walk, a Soviet police cruiser pulled up to the camp's entrance. A loudspeaker blared from the headquarters building, "All guard personnel report to the front gate! We have a report of a potential armed insurrection. I repeat, all guard personnel report to the front gate immediately!"

"Please stay with us Gyorgiy," Rosa said, gripping his arm. "It can't be that important and I need you more than they do."

The young guard paused, uncertain what to do. More than anything, he wanted to impress her with how important she was to him. On the other hand, disobedience of a direct order might have dire consequences. Finally, his sense of duty — and his fear of what could happen if her were found derelict — made his decision for him.

"I give you my word I'll be back in less than thirty minutes," he said.

"Come back sooner," she begged. "I fear for my life without you here to protect me."

As he trudged away morosely, he could not see Rosa wink at Aviva.

✿✿✿

Ten minutes after Raskov left, Aviva and Rosa were sitting uncomfortably in a farm wagon, under a blanket atop which lay a thin veneer of hay covered by a large, odoriferous pile of manure. The short, grizzled farmer driving the wagon who, if truth be known, had an Israeli accent normally unheard-of in these parts and usually went by the name Simcha Bar-Ilan, shouted out the imagined name of some animal every minute or two. His "daughter," a small, slender young Armenian woman whose real name was Nadya Vartunian, wrapped in a shawl and loose clothing, punctuated the farmer's entreaties by occasionally yelling out the same name, oblivious to what was going on at the camp's entrance. A mile up the road, discouraged by their inability to find the lost animal, the "farmer" and his "daughter" turned the horse and wagon onto a rutted path leading to their cottage.

✿✿✿

At the camp's gate, a Soviet State Police officer told the six guards, "We have reports of an Armenian insurgent group in this area. They've taken up arms against the Soviet government. We don't believe Itum-Shale is a target, but this camp has a cache of weapons that could prove useful to them." As he was speaking, a nondescript Moskva pulled up to the gate. Through its badly scratched side window, its driver, a balding man of late middle age, wearing lieutenant's bars on his shoulders and a blue plastic nametag identifying him as "Markov" on his left breast pocket, nodded to the Soviet officer, who continued, "With your permission, Lieutenant Markov from Groszny regional office will examine your headquarters building for electronic devices or anything else unusual. If you experience any problems, let him know and we'll respond immediately. I suggest you remain here and guard the entrance until I return."

The police cruiser pulled into the camp, followed by the Moskva. No sooner were they out of hearing range than the senior guard snarled, "Fucking Soviet bullies. They think they still own the world! Can you imagine they have the balls to think we're on *their* side?"

"It's all right, Captain," his second-in-command replied. "Let them play their little power games as long as they leave us alone. Have you heard anything about insurgents?"

"Of course not. It's just an excuse to rub our nose in the dirt by showing us they can still come in here without an invitation any time they want. I suppose we'll have to stay here until that cruiser comes back. No sense messing with them."

The Moskva followed the police cruiser to the headquarters building, then returned to the main gate. When he was sure no one was looking, "Lieutenant Markov" popped the trunk and two "insurgents," Doctor Nikssarian and Jake Baumueller jumped out.

"It's fortunate we only had to share each other's company for ten minutes," Jake said. "It was getting pretty stuffy."

"Are you sure you know what to say if anyone asks anything?" Nikssarian asked.

"I know enough Russian to muddle through," Jake said. "I just hope they don't look closely enough to see — "

"You don't look that bad," Doctor Nikssarian added. "Unless someone really examines you at close range. Besides, it's the best we could do on such short notice," he continued. "Fortunately, one of Simcha's men retired from *Gosfilm* after thirty years in the makeup department. What's the plan now?"

"Simcha gave me three miniature devices and showed me how to conceal them in the main security office. Since the operation should take less than an hour, camp security probably won't detect them. They've only got a three-mile range, but that's all we need, since I'll be on a side road less than two miles from here."

When he returned to the gate, the Soviet "security officer" said, "There's nothing that looks suspicious, but you should keep your eyes and ears open tonight." He touched the second and third fingers of his right hand to the visor of his service cap and pulled away.

A few minutes later, the Moskva followed in the cruiser's wake. "Captain," Lieutenant Markov said to the head of camp security, "I'm really sorry to have troubled you. I've just received a radio call from Groszny. The insurgents have been surrounded twenty miles north of here, and the danger is past. I regret any inconvenience we've caused."

❧❧❧

"Good evening, Captain." The senior camp security guard was startled as he faced two rifle-bearing men who stood waiting as he entered his office.

"Who are you?" he barked, "And just what the hell do you think you're doing?"

"Now, now, Captain, there's no need to get defensive — *offensive*, actually," one of the armed men said. "*We* know who we are, and that's sufficient for our needs. We also know why we're here. It may or may not concern you."

"Smoke?" the other man said pleasantly. "Ah, I see you're not interested in niceties. Very well then, we'll get to the point. We're not interested in you and we're not interested in the little soldier games you're playing at this camp. We want Napolitano."

"Who — ?"

"Ah, ah, ah," the first man said, coming closer to the guard and shoving the barrel of the rifle into his belly. "We told you that was really none of your business. Where's Napolitano?"

"He's not here," the senior guard answered truthfully.

"We're told he's holding an Israeli woman hostage. Where is she?"

"None of your goddam business," the captain growled.

In response, the second man smacked him across the face, not especially hard, but enough to sting. "Wrong answer, Captain. Want to try again?"

"You think you're frightening me?" the guard snarled. "There are over a hundred men in this compound. You may kill me. You may even kill a few of my forces, but your chances of getting out of this camp alive are nonexistent."

"Look," the first man said calmly. "We told you we're not interested in you or in what goes on here. Be reasonable, man. We've been told your people don't hold Napolitano in high esteem."

For the first time, the guard's look softened somewhat. "Go ahead, I'm listening."

"Napolitano may be here, or he may not, but if he's the mouse, the woman's the cheese. She comes with us. Bait for the trap. How important is she to your mission? I mean really?"

"She means nothing to us, but if he comes back and she's not here —"

"He'll what? Shoot you? You just said there are over a hundred men here. There are two of us. There's one of him. His chances of getting out alive would be half of what ours are."

"You don't understand. The Chechen Independence Movement needs arms and money. Napolitano's the source of that money and he's been the source of most of our semiautomatic weapons."

"He wouldn't have to know you were even aware of Mrs. Baumueller's abduction," the second man said. "Don't look so surprised, Captain, we know her name. If you've watched Turkish television you've probably seen her."

"How could he not know?"

"Detail an expendable man to take us to her room. We'll knock him out and take the lady."

"Do I have a choice?"

The first man, Jake Baumueller, said, "All life is a choice, Captain."

The captain hesitated an instant, then picked up an old-fashioned, heavy black phone on his desk and dialed three numbers. "Lieutenant Grechko, find Gyorgiy Raskov and send him up here. No, it's nothing I can't handle." He grunted. "I know he's not really one of ours, but it's not that important an assignment."

Less than a quarter hour later, the two armed men and the young guard who'd been detailed to go with them returned to the captain's office.

"You lied to us," Nikssarian said. "She's not there."

"What do you mean she's not there?" the captain asked incredulously.

"She's gone, Captain," Raskov answered. "Nothing's missing. Her clothes are all in place."

"What do we do now?" asked the captain. He was seated at his desk, ostensibly writing out a report.

"We wait for Napolitano to return," Niksarian replied.

"That could take two days," the captain said.

"We've got time."

"I think not," the captain said. In a split second he'd reached under his desk, grabbed a service revolver, brought it up and fired into Nikssarian's heart. Within moments, the doctor was dead.

What happened thereafter was a blur. Jake instinctively fired point blank into the captain's face, pulping it in an instant. As the young guard raised his firearm, Jake barked, "I can make it two as easy as one. This man was a doctor who saved more lives than your captain ever killed. Someone's going to pay for this. Do you want to be next?"

"N…n…no, Sir," the young guard stammered. "P…p…please, Sir, I have a mama and daddy in a s…small town near Tbilisi. I d…didn't mean any harm, Sir. I was just, just o… obeying orders," he blubbered. Then he looked down at the floor. "It doesn't matter anyway." He started sobbing. "If you don't kill me, they will."

The two men stood facing each other, each uncertain what to do next. Jake was the first to speak.

"Tbilisi? You're not a Chechen then?"

"No, sir, but jobs are scarce in Georgia and one needs to eat."

"What did you mean, 'If I don't kill you, they will?'"

"I was the last one to see Mrs. Baumueller."

"Explain."

"She wanted to take a walk outside to get a bit of fresh air. A young woman named Rosa Dudayev, who'd worked here in the past, had just come back to work again. Miss Dudayev suggested she accompany Mrs. Baumueller. Rosa — Miss Dudayev — asked me to walk with them to make sure nothing happened. Then I was called back to the gate. It's not my fault …"

"What's not your fault?"

"That Mrs. Baumueller wasn't there when you went looking for her."

"What's your name, guard?"

"Gyorgiy Raskov, Sir," the young guard replied. Somewhat incongruously he added, "Are you going to kill me, Mister … Mister …?"

"Baumueller, Guard Raskov. And the answer is no. It's not your time to meet the Angel of Death. But I think it is time for us to go for a ride."

39

THE FARMHOUSE – TWO HOURS LATER

But for the fact that Jake and Aviva could not stop hugging and nuzzling one another, the reunion at the farmhouse was subdued.

"He was such a good man," Nadya said, sobbing softly. "I could always count on him to stand with me. Now that he's dead, whatever protection I might have had in Armenia is gone."

"What about Captain Artakian?" Aviva asked.

"Artakian's only concern is *Artakian*," Nadya replied. "He was helpful to you because you could be useful to him," she continued. "Now that it's only a matter of months, maybe weeks, before the Union collapses, he's lining up his support wherever he can find it."

"Georgia's friendly, Nadya," Rosa said. "You could stay with my family —"

"I appreciate that," Nadya responded. "But I'd be an imposition. Don't look at me like that, Rosa. You and I are close enough that I know how hard things have been for your family. Georgia's no better off than Armenia."

"What about America or Israel?" Jake interjected. "You could stay with us while the paperwork went through."

"That could take a long time," Nadya said. "I've got no ties to either place. Even if you and Mrs. Baumueller were kind enough to sponsor me, how could you persuade either of those governments to take me in?"

"Political asylum," Jake said. "There's a good case for that."

"The fact that you saved an Israeli citizen's life would not escape consideration," Simcha Bar Ilan interjected. "And we have a strategic alliance with Turkey."

"From everything I've heard, Turkey won't be eager to accept an Armenian girl."

"Have you ever been there, Nadya?" Aviva asked gently.

"No."

"You might consider giving it a chance. Istanbul has a large, thriving Armenian community. While the antagonism between the Turks and the Armenians goes back several hundred years, Turkey's main target for now is the Kurds."

Gyorgiy Raskov, who'd been standing in a corner of the room silently watching the exchange between them, spoke up. "Turkey's never been unfriendly to Georgia. It's easier to hide in Turkey than Armenia, and Turkey's much wealthier than any other country in the area. Who knows? Perhaps Rosa could visit you and —"

"If I did, I would need someone to protect me," Rosa said, looking directly at Raskov. The young man's face reddened. "Do you intend to return to the Chechen compound, Gyorgiy?"

"No, Rosa. As difficult as things are in Tbilisi, I'd rather sweep streets there than return to Chechnya."

"Have either of you considered working for the Jewish Agency in Tbilisi?" Bar-Ilan asked. All eyes in the room focused on him. "I'm serious," he said. "Each of you participated in rescuing a well-known woman who's an Israeli citizen. I believe funds could be made available."

"The New York *World* can certainly use a stringer in a newly emerging republic," Jake Baumueller added.

Simcha Bar-Ilan lit up a pipe and said, "Mister Raskov, how long did you work in the camp?"

"About a year."

"What can you tell us about the operation?"

"For the first five months I was there, it was a training ground for Chechen malcontents, people interested in breaking away from the Soviet Union and forming their own republic, not too much different from Nadya's ideas about an independent Armenia. Then, Count Napolitano appeared on the scene. Things became much better-organized, and there were more sophisticated weapons. There were other differences, too."

"Such as?"

"Although the camp nominally had a Chechen commandant, Count Napolitano brought in his own people to actually run the place, Syrians, Iraqis, even some Palestinians. It became more of a training area for his people, but since Napolitano was paying the bill, no one complained."

"Was there any type of a political agenda?"

"I believe it was more religion-oriented. Muslim. The destruction of Israel was very high on the agenda. There were also plans to keep Turkey's secular government off-balance and try to make Turkey more like Iran."

"I see," Simcha remarked. "Do you have any other information?"

"At any given time, Napolitano would have two hundred of his own people in the compound. They'd stay for about six weeks, then they'd be replaced. I have no idea where they went."

"I've got an idea," Simcha said. "But for now, I think you've provided invaluable assistance for us. We'll watch Itum-Kale much more carefully."

THREE MONTHS LATER – ISTANBUL

By November, 1989, Jake was back at the *World's* Istanbul bureau. Aviva's morning sickness was a thing of the past. The cracks in the formerly impregnable Soviet Union became deep chasms. On a Saturday afternoon two weeks later, Jake answered a telephone call at their flat. "It's for you," he said, holding the receiver out to his wife.

"Who'd want me on a Saturday afternoon?" Aviva asked.

"It's a male voice. Probably some lovestruck admirer," he said playfully.

"In my condition? Hardly," she said, taking the phone from his hand. "Good afternoon, this is Aviva Baumueller," she said into the receiver.

"Aviva? Kâzim Hükümdar here. It's been a while. Sinop, I believe. By the way, congratulations on marrying that fine young Baumueller lad."

"Mister Justice Hükümdar?" she nearly stammered. "To what do I owe this … immense surprise? As far as I know I'm a law-abiding, er, alien."

The Chief Justice chuckled. "And a very famous and charming one, my dear. Nur and I are in Istanbul this week. I wonder if you and your husband could join us for dinner this evening?"

"It's about our son, Zeynep," the Justice said at dinner. "Last month he met an Armenian girl who just moved here from Yerevan, Nadya Vartunian. He seems quite taken with her. She mentioned that you and Jake played a very large part in why she's here. I wonder if you could give me some information about her."

Aviva and Jake took turns relating the story of how they'd met Nadya. When Aviva got to the part about her family coming from a small village west of Diyarbakir, Justice Hükümdar frowned, as though he was concentrating on a critically important point. He steepled the fingers on both hands, resting his chin on his thumbs.

"Please forgive me, but I need to be absolutely certain about this. You say her great grandfather's older brother, Shadran Vartunian, was killed by Turkish troops in 1907?"

"That's correct, Justice Hükümdar," Aviva said. "When the Turks set fire to the village's Armenian church and Shadran tried to help get the people out, a young Turkish boy, Shadran's student, was the only one who tried to help the Armenians?"

The jurist swayed momentarily, as if he were dizzy. His wife reached over and held her husband's arm tightly. "Do you feel all right, darling?"

Almost simultaneously Aviva said, "Did I say something to upset you?"

"I don't think upset is the right word," Hükümdar replied. "Stunned might be a better word. You're sure she told you the boy's name was Turhan?"

"Yes."

"And the slaughter of the man's brother took place when the Turkish boy was about ten?"

"That's true."

"May God and Allah protect us!" Hükümdar said, exhaling. "You know of my relationship with Turhan Türkoğlu?"

"I do," Aviva said. "My grandmother told me …"

Justice Hükümdar's eyes took on a faraway look. "He and your grandmother saved my life," he said.

"So I've heard," Aviva replied quietly.

"Almost seven years ago, I reintroduced myself to Turhan under somewhat strained circumstances. We saw each other a few times after that …

"Turhan was born in 1897 in a village two or three days' walk from Diyarbakir, about a two-hour drive today, so certain pieces of the puzzle fit together. He told me his first teacher was named Shadran. The story he told me about the fire at the Armenian church parallels everything Nadya told you. I wonder …?"

"Turhan's not an unusual name," Nur said to her husband.

"But the facts and the timing are too similar to be coincidental. Do you believe there's a God?" he asked both young people.

"Of course," they said, simultaneously.

"They say that God works in strange ways. I think it's time I met Miss Nadya Vartunian."

As unrest increased in Moscow, conditions in Armenia deteriorated rapidly. A paralyzing strike in neighboring Azerbaijan cut fuel and other supplies which were normally shipped to Yerevan by two-thirds. Deputy Chairman Kodzhamirian claimed that the Armenian Soviet Republic was suffering an economic blockade. Things were at a flash point.

Although six months pregnant, Aviva continued to broadcast the increasingly dramatic news coming into Istanbul from Moscow. "Today, the Presidium of the Supreme Soviet ordered Lithuania, Latvia, and Estonia to comply with the Soviet Constitution."

Two weeks later she reported, "On November 26, Premier Gorbachev affirmed that the Soviet Union must retain a one-party system. He added that the economic crisis facing Russia today is the equal of that faced in the war against the Nazis. The screen switched to a photograph of an exhausted and distraught-looking Premier Gorbachev, the large red birthmark more noticeable than usual.

On November 29, 1989, Aviva led off the six o'clock evening news with an astonishing report. "Good evening. Earlier today the Supreme Soviet of the U.S.S.R. ratified the Law on the Economic Sovereignty of the Baltic States. Under pressure from Azerbaijan and after a series of rallies in Baku, the Soviet Parliament relinquished control over Nagorno-Karabakh. Premier Gorbachev arrived in Rome for three days of talks with his Italian counterpart and said, 'I have arrived here in a very good state of mind.' This is Aviva Baumueller, *2 Kanal* news."

As the year came to an end, the news from Moscow grew steadily more desperate. The Baltics were aflame. It had become increasingly obvious to nations the world over that the only superpower in the world other than the United States of America was about to collapse.

On February 18, 1990, six-pound nine-ounce Edwin Baumueller the Fifth lustily announced his entrance into the world. A month later, Justice and Mrs. Kâzim Hükümdar announced the engagement of their son, Zeynep, to Nadya Vartunian. When General Kenan Evren's term expired, Türgüt Özal was elected President of the Turkish Republic. Little more than a year later, the Soviet Union was nothing more than a memory. Following the defeat of the Motherland Party in the general elections, sixty-seven-year-old Süleyman Demirel returned to politics and formed his *seventh* government since he had first been vested with the title of Prime Minister twenty-six years earlier. The circle had turned and the guard had changed once again.

PART NINE:
THE FOOTSTEPS
OF CHANGE
1993–2002

1

Early in 1993, Yavuz Akdemir was notified of his selection as brigadier general. While waiting for his first star to be pinned on his shoulders, the family settled into a large flat in Çankaya, an exclusive district in the southern hills above Ankara.

Although his eldest son, Nessim, twenty, showed no interest in following the two-century-old Akdemir military line, Yavuz was proud that the boy, now in his last year at Ankara's Middle East Technical University, was an honors graduate in the engineering department. It was not as if the Akdemir military line would be extinguished. His younger son, fourteen-year-old Ibrahim, had played with toy soldiers from the time he was a tot until he had entered the local military academy. Even now, Cadet Akdemir loved to move military pieces around a board battlefield. On more than one occasion he had told his proud parents he wanted to be an officer just like Papa and Uncle Omer.

Yavuz's oldest child, Kari, twenty-two, posed a more complex set of problems. As Colonel Adkemir was only too painfully aware, she possessed the stunning beauty her grandmother Ayşe had shown at that age. She had resisted all attempts by the Akdemirs to find a suitable military mate for her. As a Political Science graduate student at Istanbul University, Yavuz Akdemir's headstrong daughter was very much her own person.

Early in the year, Kari had attached herself to the rising star of Tansu Çiller. "She's intelligent, sophisticated, and beautiful," Kari told her brother, Nessim. "Everything I want to be. She's proof that Turkey's come so far that a woman may be the next Prime Minister."

"What about the rumors?" Nessim had asked.

"Rumors always follow anyone in power. Anyone jealous of her success will try to bring her down, probably because she's a woman."

"I wouldn't be too sure," Nessim had replied.

"Oh, Nessim, you've been reading too many tabloid newspapers."

But lately, Kari had been hearing more rumors. She was mildly troubled about her powerful heroine, who seemed poised to ascend to Turkey's highest political office. Much of Kari's information came from Kemal Araslı, a slender young assistant professor in political science, four years her senior, from whom she'd taken a class a few months back. As rainy April gave way to balmy May sunshine, she found herself more and more attracted to this obviously intelligent, soft-spoken man, who shared his ideas about a wide spectrum of Turkish politicians with her and who seemed interested and respectful about what she had to say. On one of their frequent walks around the campus, Kari pointedly asked Kemal what he thought of Tansu.

"You're asking because you're in awe of her?" he asked mildly.

Kari blushed, and Araslı thought, *what an incredibly beautiful young woman she is.* Out loud, he said, "I'd approach her with extreme caution."

"Why?" Kari asked, a bit more peevishly than she'd intended.

"How much do you know about her?"

"She's a Robert College-trained economist, who's always loved all things American."

"She's an American citizen." In answer to her arched eyebrows, he continued, "She and her husband became U.S. citizens in 1970."

"Why did she come back to Turkey?"

"Kari, I know a quiet café near here, Tea and an afternoon dose of *lokum* sounds good to me about now. How about you?"

"Why not?" Within moments, they were seated in a tiny, four-table hole-in-the wall establishment, enjoying sticky-sweet Turkish delight and two glasses of plain tea.

Araslı continued where they'd left off. "My honest opinion? She's a climber who won't let anyone stand in her way." Kari sipped her tea and looked thoughtfully at Kemal. "I've never asked you, Kari, what do you think about the rise of fundamentalism in this country?"

"I'm from a military family. We've never been religious. My father and my uncle always felt that the state must have nothing to do with religion."

"Have you ever thought Islamlic fundamentalism might be the wave of the future?" She looked at Arslı and saw he was becoming visibly excited. "Did you ever think that after seventy years we might discover we took the wrong path?"

"You sound like some ancient *mullah*," she said, smiling to let him know she did not mean to insult him. "Seriously," she continued, "would you want Turkey to become another Iran?"

"No, Kari, I would not." Kemal said, "But we do have a border with Iran. It wouldn't be that difficult for their brand of Islam to come across the border. Regardless of what our politicians tell you, once you leave Istanbul and the Aegean seacoast, Turkey *is* Islamic. I fear that unless we adopt a more moderate brand of Islamic practice, we could very easily lose Atatürk's dream to a more militant type of fundamentalism."

"I thought we were going to talk about Tansu Ciller."

"We are," he said. "I believe if you hitch yourself to Tansu's apparently rising star, you might be shortsighted. Kari, I believe you're too…too special to let yourself be drawn in."

"I gather you're not her most ardent admirer," Kari remarked.

"Do I admire Tansu Ciller? Yes. Do I trust her? No. I believe she'll promise everyone everything and hope their memories don't last much beyond the election."

Kari knew better than to touch Kemal. By the time they'd returned to the campus quadrangle, Arslı said to her, "If it wouldn't offend you, I'd like you to meet an acquaintance of mine. You might be interested in hearing what he has to say.

UNIVERSITY OF ISTANBUL – A FEW NIGHTS LATER

"Professor Gürgün, I can't tell you how much I appreciate meeting with us," Kemal said deferentially.

The tall, silver-haired man, his tie slightly askew, his silver-framed glasses hanging on a leather thong around his neck, smiled gently. "I must say, meeting with you folks is a bit more exciting than watching the grass grow in my backyard."

Professor Yücel Gürgün, retired Dean of the University of Istanbul law faculty, looked around the 15-by-15 foot wood-paneled room adjacent to the law library. "Quite an assortment of interesting types, if I must say so," he continued. "Recep Tayyip Erdoğan, who's starting to make a name for himself in Istanbul's local politics, Aviva Kohn Baumueller, Israel's gift to Turkish television." He turned to Jake questioningly.

"Mister Aviva Baumueller," Jake said good-naturedly. "For want of something better to do, I help out as a volunteer at *Isharet*," Jacob Baumueller continued.

"Ah, ah, ah," Professor Gürgün shook his right index finger at Jake and grinned knowingly. "Have you ever worked for any other media source, Mister Baumueller?"

"Well, we did meet once when I interviewed you some time ago, Professor," Jake smiled. "Back when I was a stringer for my grandfather's little newspaper."

"That leaves one person I've never met," Gürgün said, turning to Kari. "And you, young lady, are the spitting image of your grandmother, who was one of the loveliest women I've known. Is your father Omer or Yavuz?"

"Yavuz, Professor," Kari replied. "If it's not impertinent, might I ask if you ever met Turhan Türkoğlu? He, Halide Orhan and my grandfather Nadji were such important parts of our family history."

""Briefly, Miss Akdemir. We met during the troubles surrounding the selection of the Turkish Immortals. Before that, I'd read *The Conscience of a Nation* and thoroughly enjoyed it."

After Professor Gürgün's five guests were seated, the erstwhile law school dean began. "Ladies and gentlemen, so that none of you might feel uncomfortable, can we agree in advance — and I respect each of you enough to trust your word — that what we say tonight remains in this room and that this private conversation among friends is completely confidential and totally off the record?"

"Absolutely, Professor Gürgün, Recep Bey," Aviva said without missing a beat. When Aviva smiled, Kari put the back of her hand to her mouth to stifle a gasp. Turkey's most famous television personality was much lovelier in person than on the TV.

Jake added, "Nor will it ever be mentioned in the New York *World*."

"I notice you're wearing a shawl and very modest dress, Mrs. Baumueller," Erdoğan said.

"How much privacy do you think we'd have had, had I come in my television attire?" Erdoğan looked at Aviva with frank appreciation as she continued, "It would take a fool not to see that the average Turk is sick and tired of business as usual and politicians whose main philosophy is 'something for everyone and as much left over for me as I can get my hands on before I'm thrown out of office.'"

"Agreed," said Erdoğan. Seventy years ago, the country looked to Ankara for leadership, but people migrating from the villages chose the old Ottoman capital of Istanbul. Atatürk could never stamp out that Turkey was, and is, a conservative country. Ninety-eight out of every hundred people are Sunni Muslims."

As the evening progressed, Jake asked, "Do you think the National Security Council will allow Erbakan's Welfare Party to take power?"

"They may have no choice," Erdoğan responded. "The poor villager who comes to Istanbul with little more than the shirt on his back, a wife, and four or five children, needs the dignity of work. He needs food he can afford, not charity. He needs hospitals and schools, honest leaders, and most of all he needs to see results."

"Tansu…?" Kari started.

"Do you have any idea of how wealthy she is?" Erdoğan asked.

"N…no." Kari stammered.

"She owns four houses, a boat, an apartment house, land, and cars in the United States."

Professor Gürgün added, not unkindly, "Miss Akdemir, Turkish Islamism is not Middle Eastern Islam. Contrary to anything you may have heard, I believe the Welfare Party or whatever they'll call its successor when it's banned, the *Turkish* Islamists if you will, are the *only* hope of preventing Turkey from becoming another Iran."

"So you think that the only way to guard against a fundamentalist Iranian, Saudi Arabian, or Libyan Turkey is to elect a fundamentalist Islamic *Turkish* party?" Aviva asked,

"Exactly, Mrs. Baumueller. I'm not saying you must agree with what I'm saying. I'm asking you to give us a fair hearing if — when — we prevail, and that you take a wait-and-see attitude before you make harsh judgments. For all you know, we Islamists may be called at some later date, to help you."

2

On April 17, 1993, President Turgut Özal suffered a sudden fatal heart attack. The grand old man of Turkish politics, Süleyman Demirel, succeeded to the presidency. Tansu Çiller reinvented her image once again. She started to wear white for a look of innocence. She assumed a rapid walk to look dynamic and during speeches she put one of her hands on her waist for a look of authority. Her smile charmed even those who were unsure of who she was and what she stood for.

Kari was starting to become disenchanted with her erstwhile heroine. Tansu, who had been so cosmopolitan, had co-opted a substantial segment of the Welfare Party's constituency. She abandoned her urban, liberal image and embraced a nationalist, traditionalist one. Two months after Özal's death, Tansu was elected the first female Prime Minister in Turkish history. European newspapers called her, "the symbol of modern Turkey."

On a chill January afternoon in 1994, Kemal Araslı approached Kari. Both of them wore heavy overcoats and black *karakul* caps from Pakistan. Kemal had trouble seeing clearly, as the steam from his breath fogged his glasses. "If you'd join me for tea in the student cafeteria, I might at least be able to see you better," he said.

Once they were in the cafeteria, Kemal came right to the point. "Erdoğan just announced he's running for mayor of Istanbul. Are you still as crazy about Tansu Çiller as you were last year?"

Kari thought for a few moments. "Not really."

"Would you be willing to help the Erdoğan campaign?"

"If I did, I think my father would disown me."

"But you're an adult and independent."

"Not really. Father jokes that I'll be 'on the payroll' until I have my Master's degree. He's a wonderful man, certainly not the stereotype high-ranking Turkish military officer. I know they say you can choose your friends, not your relatives, but I truly *like* him as well as love him."

"You value his opinion." It was a statement, not a question.

"Absolutely. No matter what his politics, my father has always been scrupulously honest."

"Would you mind if I spoke with him? Where's he stationed?"

"TGS, Ankara."

"Wow!" Araslı whistled. "That's about as high up as you can get."

"He's just been promoted to Brigadier General, which means he gets to serve coffee and run errands for the really big shots."

"Still, no matter what the politicians say, everyone knows that Turkish General Staff runs the country. Is there a chance we could meet somewhere other than TGS headquarters?"

"Sure, Kemal. The only daughter is always welcome at General Akdemir's Çankaya place. In fact, my room's still *my* room."

"Three days later, Yavuz and Gülay greeted their twenty-three-year-old daughter warmly. When she introduced Professor Kemal Arsalı, a quiet, respectful young man, mother and father glanced knowingly at one another. They were totally unprepared for the conversation that followed.

"Father," Kari began, once the younger people were seated on one of the two beige leather living room sofas, facing the senior Akdemirs, "What do you think of *Refah*?"

"The Welfare Party's a dangerous bunch, and one to stay away from if you cherish your freedom in this country," Yavuz replied.

"Why do you say that?" Kari asked.

"I've read that the Islamic fundamentalists want to take Turkey out of Europe and into the orbit of Iran and Libya."

"With respect, General Akdemir," Araslı interjected quietly, "may I ask if you've studied the party's platform or listened to any of its leadership?"

"Truthfully, no, Professor Araslı. My information comes from *Hürriyet, Milliyet,* TGS position papers, and some hearsay. But I've never been close enough to a bear or a snake to have them attack me, either. Are you saying *Hürriyet* and *Milliyet* don't report the truth? You notice I've avoided mentioning the various political party organs."

"I accept your statement, but haven't you often found that the driving force of even those papers is to sell as many copies as they can? Kari told me you knew Turhan Türkoğlu."

"Uncle Turhan…" Yavuz slipped back into private memories. "I certainly did."

"What do you think his reaction would have been to *Refah?*"

"Probably cynical acceptance."

"Or a wait-and-see attitude?"

"Maybe." He glanced over at his wife and his daughter. Kari had been born when the old man had been a youthful, exuberant seventy-four.

"Do you know *Isharet's* position with respect to *Refah?*"

"I do. Frankly, I'm quite surprised by it. They're taking a neutral stance. In fact, they're actually promoting this new fellow who wants to be mayor of Istanbul."

"Recep Tayyip Erdoğan," Kari said.

"Yes, that's the name," Gülay Akdemir said. "Do you know him?"

"I do, mother," she said. "That's the reason we wanted to see you."

"I don't mean to be rude, but is there a reason you brought Professor Araslı with you? Your father and I thought there might be something else afoot."

"At that, both young people blushed. Kemal was the first to recover. "Kari told me she not only loves each of you, but she respects your judgment and will abide by your wishes. I have become involved in Mister Erdoğan's campaign, and I've asked Kari to join me. She said she'd have to speak with you first, so I suggested we come to Ankara."

"But why is there a need for both of you?" Yavuz asked, a hint of impatience in his voice. "Kari's old enough to speak for herself, without the need of a spokesman."

"True, papa, but there may be things about the Welfare Party I don't know. You're military and you *have* to take one position officially. That's why I wanted to meet here, on private ground. Beard the lion in his den."

Yavuz rose from the sofa and paced about the room, his eyes narrowing. Finally he spoke, softly, but with hard conviction, "Kari, you're my daughter, my flesh and blood and my first-born. There's no way I'll disown you, no matter what you do. If you want my consent to do what you propose to do, I cannot stop you. If you want my blessing, I cannot give it, and I may have to publicly disavow what you say. What you propose could destroy my career in its tracks. I am a Brigadier General. My life is the military."

"Gülay Akdemir looked at her husband, her loyalty to the man to whom she'd been married for more than a quarter century wavering with the conflicting emotion of love for her daughter. She knew Yavuz was casting a stone into a pond that might tear apart the fabric of the family. In the end, she remained silent.

"Kari, Professor Araslı, this discussion is at an end." He turned coolly on his heel and walked out of the room. Kari, shocked, stared fixedly as he left.

"I think it's best that I return to Istanbul," Kemal mumbled, finding it difficult to recover from the older man's harsh words. "Perhaps we might discuss this another time."

"Unfortunately, I think not," Gülay Akdemir replied sadly. "My husband is a good man, but although he covers it well, he's been deeply hurt by this turn of events. I must say both of us had expected something entirely different."

Istanbul — February 1994 — Three days later

"Can you believe that cheek of that girl? Yavuz asked.

"Frankly, yes I can, little brother," Omer replied. "What do you think, Sara?"

"Mama Zari, bless her late soul, fought for everything and everybody, particularly the little guy. Lest you forget, Israel's not the most popular player in the Middle East."

"Meaning?"

"Meaning, Yavuz, you'd do best to, as the Americans say, cut her some slack. Whether you like it or not, she's going to do what she's going to do. You'd have done better to thank her for trusting you enough to ask your opinion, and then listen with an open mind to what she had to say."

It had been three days since Kari had disclosed her intentions, three very uncomfortable days for Brigadier General Yavuz Akdemir. Afterward, Yavuz had acceded to Gülay's suggestion that they invite the *other* General Akdemir and his wife over for a serious talk. "You don't understand, Sara," Yavuz said. "This could impact both of our careers, Omer's and mine."

"How?"

"The Welfare Party, the fundamentalists, stand for everything the military does *not* stand for. How would it look if the daughter of a junior brigadier were seen consorting with the enemy?"

"I wouldn't exactly call a Turkish citizen whose views might conflict with yours the enemy. Have you any idea how many officers are sympathetic to the Welfare cause?"

"Precious few, I'm sure."

"Precious few you're sure," the former Israeli colonel chided her brother-in-law. "I ask you for a statement of fact and you cover it with a platitude that tells me you have no idea. You needn't bother blushing, Yavuz, I'm not trying to embarrass you, but unlike your daughter, I can love you without cowering in awe before you. Let me show you something." She walked over to the kitchen counter and opened her large purse. I'm sure TGS knows the exact count. Israeli intelligence gave me a list last month with reasonably accurate figures." She handed him a neatly typed bar graph showing numbers and percentages. "42% of army lieutenant-colonels, 31% of air force light-colonels." Her finger moved farther to the right side of the paper, the part that listed senior officers. "Turkish Air Force: 18% of brigadier generals support *Refah's* platforms, another ten percent undecided. Turkish Navy: six percent of two-star admirals and above in favor, twelve percent undecided. Here's the big one: Turkish Army: 22% percent of major generals and above favor *Refah*. Ten percent undecided."

"How do you know they're accurate, Sara?"

"A week ago, *Isharet's* headline story, written by someone we both know, questioned whether the Welfare Party was the wave of the past or the wave of the future?"

"Aviva?" Yavuz asked.

"Uh-huh."

"Gülay and Omer had listened to the exchange between brother-in-law and sister-in-law with curious interest. Finally, in mock frustration, an obviously relieved Yavuz sighed and said to his brother, "I thought that in Turkey, and particularly in *Islamic* Turkey, the men were supposed to rule over silent, submissive women."

"Oh, yes, silent and submissive women," Omer grinned, tapping first one finger, then another into his palm. Let's see, there was Halide Orhan, Zahavah Kohn-Barak, Ayşe Akdemir, Sara Akdemir, Kari Akdemir, Aviva Baumueller…"

"You've made your point, brother. What do you suggest I do?"

"The first thing I'd suggest, Yavuz, is maybe you should get some direct first-hand knowledge. Go to a *Refah* rally and see what the 'crazies' have to say. That way, you can confront Kari with real information, rather than fearful rumors. Was Kemal Araslı rude or impolite to you in any way?"

"Quite the opposite. Five minutes after I exploded, I felt I'd made a fool of myself. He didn't once raise his voice. Gülay told me he was very courteous, even when he left."

"Why don't you telephone him? Perhaps you could even meet with him outside of Kari's presence, and just listen and learn a little bit."

ISTANBUL – TWO WEEKS LATER

"It was most gracious of you to see me after the way I treated you in January," Yavuz said, addressing Kemal Araslı. Although the general was wearing a casual civilian outfit, tan slacks and an open-necked argyle shirt, it was obvious from his posture and his bearing that he was a member of the Turkish military, and a senior one at that.

"I felt bad for Kari, but I figured you had your reasons." It was an unseasonably warm early-March day. The two men had agreed to meet on the grounds of Dolmabahçe Palace, the gaudy, grandiloquent European monument to pride that had been built midway through the nineteenth century. Today, there were few tourists. Most guides were on their lunch break.

"My brother suggested I listen and learn a little bit about *Refah*. I should have done that four weeks ago, but I was …"

"Defensive?" Araslı suggested.

"That's as good a word as any."

"We can use that as a starting point," Araslı said. "General, do you think that if *Refah* came to power the Israelis would be surrounded by one more enemy in the Middle East?"

"That's a fair assumption."

"Fair, but not necessarily true. You're acquainted with Ottoman history?"

"To some degree."

"Then you'd know the Sultan sent his own ships to rescue the Jews from Spain and Portugal in 1492. If you equate Islamic beliefs with the *political* anti-Semitism of Arab countries, who feel dispossessed by the *state* of Israel, you might be taking a rather black-and-white approach. *Refah* is a *Turkish* party."

"But thousands of Iranians, Iraqis, and Palestinians, are flooding into Istanbul every day."

"Why do you think they're doing that?" Araslı asked.

"Possibly to spread their brand of Islam to a large and powerful neighboring country. To subvert it from the inside."

"You could be right, General. But could you conceive that these foreigners might have come to Istanbul to move up to a better life, to make money, and to make sure their children had a better opportunity than they did?"

Yavuz bent over and retied a nagging shoelace that had come loose. "Wouldn't those Middle Eastern fundamentalists feel most at home with Turkish Islamists?"

"Absolutely, General, which is precisely why it is so critical that *Turks* keep control of Turkish political life."

At that moment, two young boys, who couldn't have been more than five, crossed in front of them, playing a game of tag. Three more children joined the game. Yavuz and Kemal spent the next several minutes watching the young innocents at play.

"Are you hungry, General Akdemir?" Kemal asked.

"Famished."

"I know a little kebab house not too far from here. The *doner's* good and the price is right." As they walked the four blocks to the kebab house, the two men watched a continuous parade of humanity from beggars, porters and truckers to young men in Savile Row suits, women dressed in tight-fitting, revealing outfits, and some young women wearing shawls and conservative attire which covered almost every visible inch of skin.

"A lot of them are *Refah* people," Arası remarked. "Those who came from the villages, poor, uneducated, frightened of the big city. Those who never had a voice. *Refah* is their voice. Ah, here we are, General."

The *lokanta,* a five-table restaurant, was on a side street, near a rank of old *dolmuşes* — shared communal taxis, Although it was early afternoon, the place was packed. In a few moments they were pushed and jostled to the front counter, where they could order. *Döner,* thinly-sliced lamb on pita bread, topped by melted butter and tomato sauce, was the only entrée. A *regular* order cost the equivalent of one U.S. dollar, a double order cost a dollar-fifty, and two-and-a-half orders cost two U.S. dollars and included rice and a soft drink.

"You were right, Kemal. Our bellies will be full for less than ten thousand lira," he said, reaching into his pocket and paying the cashier. "If this food is as good as it is cheap, I'm indebted to you."

It was, and soon they were companionably munching their meal, while seated at one of the rear tables. "It's very cheap for us, but barely affordable for ninety percent of Turkey's population." Arası remarked. "Tansu Çiller takes two trips a year to Argentina, first class of course. Have you any idea how many mouths the cost of a single round trip ticket could feed?"

"Can the Welfare Party really cure that?"

"Yes, and no," Arası said. "Everywhere there's rampant poverty there's an ugly, festering wound that will kill a nation if the government doesn't at least try to effect a cure."

"You sound like a politician yourself, Professor," Yavuz said. "When and where did you say the *Refah* meeting was?"

"Tonight, just after sundown in the university quadrangle."

"Perhaps I should attend. Might I ask you a favor, Professor?"

"Of course."

"For the time being, it's best if Kari doesn't know I'm at the rally. For her safety and —"

"I understand," Kemal said. "A friend of mine has an office that faces onto the quadrangle. I suggest you preserve your anonymity by wearing the same civilian clothes you're wearing now."

3

ISTANBUL – LATER THAT EVENING

Yavuz Akdemir sat by the open window of the darkened third story office. Kemal Araslı had fashioned a prearranged signal, three winks of a flashlight, followed by a sweep of the light that stopped to show Yavuz where Kemal and Kari stood. Yavuz was no more than fifty meters from the speaker's rostrum, which had been set up in a quadrangle adjacent to a nearby street.

At six-thirty, there was an impatient, anticipatory rustling through the crowd. The star of the evening, Recep Tayyip Erdoğan, the man they'd come to hear, was about to speak. Moments later Erdoğan stepped onto the stage. Forty years of age, he looked almost boyish, but in a distinctly Turkish way, not like movie-star handsome Mesut Yilmaz. Tall, erect in his bearing, there was an air of coiled electricity about the man.

"My friends," he began, in a calm, reasonable voice. "I am privileged to be here tonight. Our party leader, Necmettin Erbakan referred to you as 'Young Turks.' Without disrespect, anyone short of sixty-five would qualify as a 'Young' Turk to him." There was appreciative laughter from the audience.

"But does it really matter whether we are twenty or sixty? Once again, Turkey is the 'sick man.' The lira keeps going down in value, real wages go down, savings evaporate, and the General Assembly stumbles around arguing about whose fault it is. It's business as usual in Ankara, while the average Turk wonders how long it will be before the military steps in again.

259

"How many of you think it's an honorable line of work to be a politician?" Very few hands were raised. Yavuz thought, *What he says may be true, but it's what so many other politicians have said. How is he any different?* The answer came in the next few words.

"What the politicians don't tell you is that they are *not* the leaders. *They are nothing more than the hired help*! You vote them into office, and you can vote them *out* of office. Kemal Atatürk saw that the Sultanate represented stagnation. But today, many of his grandsons and granddaughters wallow in that same kind of stagnation. Why? Because in our race toward secularism we've turned our backs on who we are!"

"Hear, hear!" shouted a voice from the midst of the crowd. More than a thousand, took up the chant. "Recep! Recep! Recep!" The speaker waited before he continued.

"Is a woman more enticing because she's dressed like a whore? Is a man braver because he speaks with strength fortified by alcohol? Are we any the less Turks because we're proud of who we are, what we've done and what we stand for?"

"No, no, no!" chanted the crowd.

Erdoğan waited patiently until there was an opening in the rising chant. "You are in power — each one of you is a force unto yourself! And if ten of you think and act together you increase your power not tenfold but a hundredfold!" Now Erdoğan's voice raised appreciably. "Do not tear down the walls of what you have built!" Yavuz noticed that Erdoğan emphasized the word you rather than Atatürk. "Listen to the words of Ziya Gökalp!" Yavuz was shocked. Erdoğan was coming awfully close to the edge of apostasy. The highly religious, Islamic poems were non grata in modern Turkey, and the military proscribed public utterances of his words.

But Erdoğan did not cross the line. "Most of Turkey is poor, but that does not mean that most of Turkey must starve, or that they cannot be paid a fair wage for a fair day's work. It does not mean you must go without medical care simply because you cannot afford it. It does not mean that you are less than any other human being simply because of an accident of birth.

"My friends, there are more than ten million inhabitants of Istanbul. Think what we could do if each of you gave two hours a week to perform volunteer work? Twenty million hours a week! Fifty-two weeks a year. Think of what our great city would be like if each person contributed one hour's wage each week to a fund for the *really* poor?"

Erdoğan knew he had the crowd in the palm of his hand. He finished his speech on a high note. "There once was a writer named Türhan Türkoğlu. I never met Mister Türkoğlu, but I read his book *The Conscience of a Nation*. My friends, I charge each and every one of you to become the conscience of this nation. May Allah protect you and may Allah protect Turkey!"

The man exited the stage as quickly as he had come onto the rostrum. Yavuz Akedmir looked at his watch. The speech had consumed less than half an hour. Not once had Erdoğan announced he was running for public office. Not once had he solicited a vote. Not once had he uttered anything adverse to the Turkish nation, the Turkish people, or Kemal Atatürk. Yavuz concluded that Erdoğan was very much a pragmatist. Would he remain a man of principle or would he become just another politician on the take, as they all seemed to be?

Yavuz's reverie was interrupted by a sudden eruption of shouting and the sound of shots being fired. Instinctively, he riveted his attention on where Professor Araslı and Kari had been standing moments ago. A melee had broken out, and a cadre of police armed with truncheons raced to the center of the quadrangle. While other police officers on the outer perimeters of the field fired their rifles into the air, the inner group of officers swung their bat-like weapons indiscriminately through the crowd.

Suddenly, to Yavuz's horror, one of the police truncheons struck Kari in the head. She collapsed in a heap. It took less than three minutes for Kemal and Yavuz to race down the stairs and out to the field where Kari lay immobile. As Kemal Araslı bent to help her, a policeman kicked him in the ribs and brought a large stick down on his head as well.

"No!" Yavuz shouted. His voice was drowned out by the noise. Yavuz Akdemir was normally a calm man, but his daughter had been assaulted. Within moments, he pushed through the crowd to where Kari was moaning, half-conscious. Two policemen surrounded Araslı, Kari, and half a dozen others, their clubs raised.

Yavuz walked up to the older of the policemen and demanded, "What is this all about?"

"What business is it of yours?" the policeman responded. "These are a bunch of hooligans. If you don't want to get arrested, you'll clear out of this area immediately."

"I think not," Yavuz said, his coolness returning.

"Very well, then, I don't know who you think you are, but you are under arrest for aiding and abetting a treasonous gathering."

"I think not," Yavuz responded again.

"What do you mean *you* think not? Who are you to question the authority of the state?" he said, moving toward Yavuz.

"Officer, I think you'd make a rather large mistake if you tried anything rash," Yavuz said coolly.

The policeman was clearly irked by this unexpected turn of events. He blew a police whistle three times to alert his superior. Within moments, a smaller man wearing lieutenant's bars came over. "What seems to be going on here, Officer?"

"This man is resisting arrest and inciting to riot," the first policeman said.

"Is that so, sir?" the lieutenant addressed Yavuz rspectfully.

"No, Lieutenant," Yavuz answered. "This man illegally assaulted my daughter and Professor Kemal Araslı of the university faculty."

"You expect me to take your word for this over one of my own officers?"

"You may come to any conclusion you wish, Lieutenant. I saw the incident from a third floor office, and I would be willing to so testify."

By this time, the immediate area had become quiet. A crowd of some fifty people watched the exchange, among them Kari, who'd fully returned to consciousness. She was holding a makeshift bandage, made from a portion of fabric torn from her blouse, to her head. The police lieutenant had his orders to break up what he'd been told was a militant riot, but he had not risen to his rank without the intelligence that characterizes senior law enforcement officers everywhere.

"Do you have some sort of identification I might see, Sir?"

"I do." Yavuz pulled put a card case and handed it over to the lieutenant.

The lieutenant looked at the identification. His eyes widened. *Allah!* A brigadier general attached to Turkish General Staff in Ankara. One of the *real* power elite of the country. Despite his orders, he found himself in a deep dilemma. If he did not find a graceful way out of this situation, his next assignment could well be on Turkey's far southeastern hinterland, abutting the Iranian border. "General, perhaps you and I might discuss this in a quieter place."

"We might, but first I want someone in authority to attend to my daughter and her friend, and I would like the names and precinct numbers of those responsible for this atrocity."

Within an hour, eight people were seated around the conference table at the District Police Commissioner's office, the commissioner himself, the lieutenant, Yavuz, Kari, and Kemal. They had been joined by Professor Gürgün, Necmettin Erbakan, and Recep Erdoğan, whom Yavuz had insisted be present.

"Surely we can resolve this without the necessity of a full-fledged report and investigation, General Akdemir?" The man was almost obseqious in his demeanor.

"Perhaps, Commissioner, but only if I get to the bottom of how this was even allowed to happen," Yavuz replied.

The Commissioner cleared his throat. "We received a call from a highly-placed member of ANAP that what had been announced as a peaceful political rally had turned into an uncontrollable mob and that security measures were necessary to keep the peace."

"Who was this ANAP member?" Erbakan interjected.

"I'm not at liberty to disclose that, Mister Erbakan," the Commissioner replied.

"I see. Has Turkey become a closed society where truth is hidden under the cloak of national security?" The Welfare party politician's nostrils flared in anger. "If that's the case, Commissioner, this meeting will come to an end very quickly."

"Please, Mister Erbakan," the Commissioner said, raising his hands, palms out. "Can we at least try to resolve the problem amongst ourselves without creating a political firestorm?"

"You're sure this was an ANAP call?" Erdoğan asked mildly.

The Commissioner deferred to his lieutenant. "The party identified herself … er, himself … as ANAP," the lieutenant said, tripping over the words as if he'd made a slip of the tongue. On the way to the station, Yavuz had spoken at length with the lieutenant and had been impressed with his candor. He believed the "slip" was deliberate, a way of defusing the situation by identifying — and *not* identifying — who was behind the call. Yavuz saw the Commissioner relax. He'd been taken off the hook.

"I see," Erdoğan responded. "You recognized her, umm, his voice?"

"The office from which the call came, yes," the lieutenant said evenly, continuing the game where everyone now knew the answer.

"Did you find a riot going on when you came, or did your men create the riot, lieutenant?"

"Did Allah create man or did man create Allah?" the lieutenant answered.

"Well spoken, Lieutenant," Yavuz said. "By the way, in all the confusion that's gone on, I'm afraid I never got your name. Is that also a state secret?"

"I'm sorry, General. It's Mütlü. We're actually connected indirectly, General Akdemir."

"Oh?"

"Your brother, General Omer Akdemir, is married to an Israeli intelligence officer, I believe?"

"Yes."

"And your brother's wife has a close relative in Istanbul, Mrs. Aviva Baumueller?"

"You've done quite a bit of homework in the space of an hour, Lieutenant," Yavuz said admiringly. "But I don't see the connection?"

"Some years ago, before Mrs. Baumueller married, I was a Detective Sergeant in the district where she lived. There was a fire and — "

"She never mentioned your name, Lieutenant, but I recall the event. Did the police ever catch Count Napolitano?"

"I'm afraid not, General," Mütlü sighed. "When you have access to the money and the connections he has, you can insulate yourself from the law, even from as aggressive an agency as the Istanbul police."

"So, lady, gentlemen," the Commissioner said, "How can we resolve this problem?" After listening to the tape and to General Akdemir's statement, he continued, "I think we can certainly confirm that the political rally was peaceful."

"Would you go so far as to publicly acknowledge your error?" Erbakan pressed.

"Well, now," Mütlü interjected, "That could cause a bit of a problem. ANAP is the party in power. They approve our budget each year. If ANAP sensed what they felt might be disloyalty … As civil servants, we must strike a rather delicate balance, don't you see?"

Despite Necmettin Erbakan's often harsh public utterances, he was a survivor, well aware that concessions had to be made privately, particularly where one's party was not at that moment in power, if they wanted to pass even a portion of their agenda. Over the next half hour, the Welfare Party leaders, aided by the rest of the group assembled in the commissioner's office, crafted an artfully worded press release. Lieutenant Mütlü personally telephoned Aviva Baumueller on a conference call in which Yavuz Akdemir took part. He reminded Aviva that they'd met in a previous life, and that he remained one of her greatest admirers.

That evening, on the eleven o'clock news, Aviva reported the incident at the university, which, of course, had become citywide knowledge. She added, "In an exclusive report to *2 Kanal* news, a highly-placed Istanbul police officer and a brigadier attached to Turkish General Staff," — a reminder to all political parties that the armed forces were still very much *the* controlling power in the country — "advised this reporter that the political rally was entirely peaceful, that Mister Erdoğan had come up with a remarkable new concept of volunteerism to help all Istanbulus, and that the Istanbul Police Department sincerely regretted if anything untoward occurred. Here are some excerpts from Mr. Erdoğan's speech …"

ISTANBUL. LATER THAT WEEK

"Papa?"

"All right, all right,," Yavuz said in mock surrender. "I'll admit, you were right and I was … *less right* …"

"And you don't mind if I help with the Erdoğan campaign?"

"Well, Kari, Professor Araslı," he nodded in the direction of the younger man, noticing, but not calling attention to the fact, that the

Professor and his daughter were openly holding hands, "You both know I can't be seen to be political in any way. Let's just say that I withdraw my objections, provided you do it quietly."

"I can promise you Papa that the Akdemir name will not in any way be used in this campaign." Yavuz noticed that Kemal Araslı was blushing furiously. Kemal and I would like to discuss something personal with you and mama. Would you mind if we came to Ankara next week?"

"Depends on what you want to talk about," Yavuz said, grinning openly. "Are you looking for some other kind of blessing?"

In response, Kari's large, luminous grey-violet eyes looked down, then up at her father again. She winked coyly. "I think we should wait to discuss this until we get to Ankara."

❀

In September, 1994. Yavuz proudly gave the bride away. The groom was still incredulous that the most beautiful woman in the world had accepted him as her husband. He loved and admired his in-laws. To top matters off, Recep Tayyip Erdoğan, the newly-elected Mayor of Istanbul, served as an usher in the wedding party.

4

"Is this your first time in the East?" the senior supervising engineer, Ibrahim Coşur, asked his newest recruit, Nessim Akdemir.

"I was in Diyarbakir a couple of times, but only a few days each time," Nessim replied. My family's been stationed mostly in Ankara or Izmir."

"It's good to have you on board. We need all the good engineers we can get."

"I'll accept that with thanks, Ibrahim Bey," Nessim replied. "When can we expect the blasted heat to stop?"

"October," Nessim's superior said wryly. "Maybe. Then you'll freeze your behind off for the next six months. Pretty brutal out here, but what we're doing will change the face of this country."

"It must be ninety-five degrees Fahrenheit. Can we go inside for a little while?"

"Sure," the chief remarked. "It'll take you a month or two to get used to the heat."

Once inside the air-conditioned office, Nessim's supervisor brought out cups of tea and sweet pastries and conversation became more serious.

"From what I've read, every country to the south is up in arms over the Southeastern Anatolia Project," Nessim said.

"Can't say I blame them," Ibrahim replied. "If I were Syria or Iraq I'd be mighty nervous. They think they hold the world hostage because they've got a lot of oil, but you can't drink oil."

He stood up and pointed to a wall-sized map of the Project. "The Euphrates and the Tigris Rivers both rise in Turkey. When the Project is completed, we could turn 'em both off with a couple of twists of the spigots."

"But that could trigger —?"

"Could, but probably won't," Ibrahim acknowledged. "GAP — that's the popular name for the Project — is as well-protected as anyplace in the world. You think anyone will really try coming over the border and try messing with us?"

"Yes, I do," Nessim said. "The Kurds have been coming across the border from northern Iraq for years. They're particularly upset about the Ilisu Dam. They claim we intend to commit cultural genocide by flooding their ancient city of Hasankeyf."

"*Bohk!* Bullshit!" Ibrahim spat. "GAP will provide three million new jobs and double Turkey's irrigable farmland. Same thing's happening in China where they're building the Three Gorges Dam. Same thing happened in Egypt when they built the Aswan High Dam. When I was growing up, there were two billion people in the world. Now there's triple that. How is the world supposed to feed that many people without projects like ours?"

MID-OCTOBER 1996 – BATMAN

Gyula Ferenc, a young engineer who'd migrated from Hungary to work on the project, had become close friends with Nessim during the latter's three months in the southeastern hellhole that paid so well. At first they talked comparisons between Budapest and Istanbul, and interests common to single men in a remote assignment. As the days and nights grew cooler, they shared confidences with one another.

One evening in the project's cafeteria, Nessim remarked to Gyula, "If the Kurds want to live in Turkey how come they're so against the Project?"

"Old enmities die hard," Ferenc replied. "I lived in Hungary under the Communists until I was fifteen. No matter what they tried, Communism never worked. Stalin said, 'Trying to make Hungary a Communist society is like trying to fit a saddle on an ox.'"

Both men laughed.

"On another subject," Gyula continued, "I saw the way you were looking at Talia Kalkan when we were in Diyarbakir last week. It might pay to be a bit more careful."

"Is it that obvious?"

"Uh-huh."

"Gyula, can you keep a secret?"

"It's not that big a secret, Nessim. People are already talking. My friend, have you ever heard of Romeo and Juliet?" In answer to his questioning stare, the Hungarian said, "This place is much smaller than it looks. The walls have ears. Maybe we should take a little walk."

❧❀❧

"Long story short," Ferenc began, "two powerful Italian families had been feuding for a long, long time. One of those families had a girl, Juliet, the other had a boy, Romeo. They fell in love. Didn't work, couldn't work. Not one of those sappy movie plots, boy meets girl, boy loses girl, boy gets girl. This one had a really bad ending."

"What are you talking about?"

"Nessim Akdemir and Talia Kalkan, my friend."

"I don't understand."

"TGS, PKK. I'll lay it out as simply as I can. Your father and your uncle are Brigadier Generals at Turkish General Staff. You can't get more Establishment than that, Arusha Kalkan is the number four man in the PKK, the Kurdistan Workers Party. You can't get more *anti*-Establishment than that. PKK's the devil s far as the Turkish government is concerned."

"I … never realized —"

"You've never met her parents?"

"No."

"Are you aware she's Kurdish?"

"I'm aware she's human … and beautiful."

"How long have you known her?"

They stopped walking. Nessim looked over the edge of the dam into the water far below. "Four weeks."

"And …"

"We've spoken."

"Touched?"

"Barely."

"Define 'barely.'"

"What business is it of yours?"

"Oh, one moment it's 'Gyula can you keep a secret?' The next it's 'What business is it of yours?'"

"I'm sorry," Nessim said, chastened.

"You're right," Ferenc continued. "It's none of my business, but you're a good guy and a sensitive one. I'm just advising you to be extremely careful."

HARRAN, SOUTHEASTERN TURKEY – A WEEK LATER

The two lovers sat in a declivity in the hills outside of town. After awhile their glum mood gave way to words.

"God, what a mess," Talia cried. "There must be a place we could go and get away from it all. Europe, Canada …"

"They'd find us … " Nessim said.

She was openly weeping.

"Talia, Talia," he repeated her name. "There must be a way."

"What if I become pregnant? What then? 'Papa. I'd like you to meet Nessim Akdemir. Yes, he's General Akdemkir's son. Yes, the same Akdemir who was in Diyarbakir when the troubles broke out.' Can you imagine his reaction?"

"Same with my parents. 'Arusha Kalkan's daughter? Are you out of your mind?'"

"We've got to think this through," she said. "As miserable as we are when we're together, it's so much worse when we're apart."

JANUARY 1997 – ISTANBUL

"Kari, Kemal, I don't know who else to turn to," Nessim said to his sister and brother-in-law. He'd flown back to Istanbul for a week.

Although the city was wet and sullen in January, it was far more clement than Harran. The three of them were seated in Kemal's office at the university.

"If you're going to make a move, now's as good a time as any to do it," Professor Araslı said. "The Welfare Party got 21% of the vote last month. Tansu's out of office and they're all trying to put together a coalition government. They're so involved in infighting they'll ignore the Kurds for a few months."

"But what would father say?"

"I'm sure he'll be upset, just like he was when I told him I wanted to work for Erdoğan, but I think he'll listen," Kari replied. "Besides, she wouldn't be the first Kurd to become family. Muren and Lyuba have been married for almost ten years."

Nessim brightened. "Do you think Uncle Omer and Aunt Sara could help?"

"It's certainly worth a try," Kari said. "What about her parents, though?"

"The Kalkans would be infinitely harder. The PKK's not a political party, they're a terrorist organization."

"And yet, you're in love with the daughter of one of their top leaders," Kemal said. He rested his chin on his wrist and tossed a few paperclips from a small dish on the left side of his desk to the magnetic paperclip holder in the center. "Is there any way Talia could come to Istanbul?"

"What good would that do?" Nessim asked.

"Ankara's not a good place to meet. Perhaps we could get Uncle Omer to come out for the weekend. He's always impressed me as someone who's got his head on straight."

DIYARBAKIR, TURKEY – SEVERAL DAYS LATER

"I'm asking for your help Hüseyin, not for your judgment. You've never even met him."

Hüseyin Kalkan looked at the tear-stained, lovely face of his youngest sister, twelve years his junior, the baby of the family. *His* baby.

She'd adored him heart and soul since she'd been a toddler and she still looked to him for wise counsel. Even though Hüseyin was a Kurd, he was a moderate.

"Akdemir. That's a tall order. The military line goes back forever."

"But Omer put his career on the line for Muren."

"I wouldn't exactly call Muren Kolchuk a loyal Kurdish militant," Hüseyin said. "The Apo sees him as one of his great disappointments. Turned coat and he's lived in Israel for the past decade. Not a good idea to use that name around father."

"Nessim said if I could go to Istanbul just for a weekend…"

"How can you be sure she'll be safe in Istanbul?" Arusha Kalkan asked his son.

"Come on, papa, you're realistic enough not to count spiders where there are no webs. She wants to see the university. How can we ever hope for a Kurdish nation if the world sees us as a bunch of uneducated bumpkins?"

"You're sure there's no hidden agenda, Hüseyin? I've heard rumors …"

"As have I."

"Thank you for being truthful, my son. You're not disturbed?"

"Do you want me to answer like a big brother or like a Kurdish politician?"

"Artfully put. Promise me you'll watch her the whole time?"

"Absolutely."

5

"Not the first time that dogs have cross-bred," Omer said.

"That's a terribly crass way of putting it, General," Kemal replied. "I know a Muslim Turkish general who married a Jewish Israeli. Of course, Israeli women don't seem to be particular about whom they marry. Why I know of a 'Turkish' TV star who even married an American."

"Touché," Omer said, laughing. At forty-nine, he still looked ten years younger than his age. "Have you seen this girl?"

"Only a photograph."

"Pretty?"

"If Nessim says she's beautiful, what does it matter what the rest of the world thinks? You'll get a chance to meet her when she flies in this weekend."

"Oh God, please don't tell me the father's coming."

"He's not. Her older brother is."

"A pre-summit meeting?"

"You could say that, Omer. Each of the main men sends his 'second' to explore the territory."

"Twenty-one and nineteen seem awfully young, Kemal."

"How old were you and Cana when you fell in love?"

"If there's anything I can't stand it's a smart-mouthed in-law."

273

"It's probably not a good idea to talk politics, Hüseyin Bey," Omer said, his tone neutral but not unfriendly. They were seated in an anonymous restaurant on Divan Yolu, halfway between the Blue Mosque and the Covered Bazaar. Omer was enjoying the fiery Adana kebab, while Hüseyin Kalkan munched the much milder şiş köfte, cigar-shaped meatballs wrapped in pita.

"Ethnically, there's no difference, General." Kalkan's tone was equally neutral.

"You know, Hüseyin, the irony of the situation is almost funny. The idea of star-crossed lovers goes back thousands of years. Yet here we are, two grown men whom fate cast on opposite sides of the political spectrum, sitting here talking like old friends about two young relatives who couldn't give a damn about our differences."

Hüseyin raised his tulip glass of tea and sipped thoughtfully. "Do you love your nephew, General?"

"I don't mind if you call me Omer. And yes, he's a good boy and I do love him."

"She's my baby sister and her happiness is a lot more important to me than the rhetoric and the bombings. I'd kill him with my own hands if he ever did anything to make her unhappy."

"I'd think less of you if you said anything different," Omer said, smiling warmly. "May I ask you a personal question? You don't need to answer if it's uncomfortable."

"If you're asking if I'll pay for the lunch, I could probably manage that."

"Seriously, Hüseyin, what do you think of this whole political mess?"

"The Kurds think and act like terrorists because they don't see any other way to get what they feel they're entitled to. If only the government in Ankara would let them participate in the Assembly…"

"My thoughts exactly. Ah, thank you," Omer said, addressing the waiter who'd brought him the check. "Well, Mister Kalkan, I suggest we spend the afternoon browsing through the Grand Bazaar and exploring our options for the young people."

HARRAN, SOUTHEASTERN TURKEY – TWO WEEKS LATER

For the first time since they'd started coming to "their" spot in the hills beyond the town, Nessim and Talia felt the beginnings of optimism.

"Praise Allah my uncle and your brother got along well, darling," Nessim began. "Maybe there's hope after all."

"And if there wasn't?"

"We'd manage somehow. They don't even know the difference between a Turk and a Kurd in Canada."

"Do you know the difference?"

"Of course. I'm a Turk and I'd give my life for the love of a certain Kurdish girl."

❧❀❧

APRIL 14, 1997 — DIYARBAKIR, TURKEY

The British Aerospave 146 turbojet, THY Flight 7142 from the capital to Diyarbakir, circled the military / civilian airport before touching down on runway 34 for a smooth on-time landing. The summit meeting between Arusha Kalkan and Yavuz Akdemir, each accompanied by his second, was to take place at two in the afternoon at a private lounge adjacent to the Demir Hotel's upscale restaurant, a five-minute drive from the airport.

Nessim and Talia could not hide their anxiety about the meeting. They felt their entire future hung on its outcome. An hour before the meeting, they arrived at the hotel. Neither of them was hungry. Nessim ordered two glasses of tea and two plates of baklava.

While they were waiting, a young Kurdish woman furtively entered the restaurant. Talia looked up and said, "I know that girl. She and I went to the gymnasium together. Come, I'll introduce you to her. It will make the time go faster." They rose and approached the woman.

❧❀❧

ISTANBUL – LATER THAT EVENING

Aviva's expression was somber as she read the lead story on the six o'clock news.

"In a tragic incident in Diyarkabir earlier today, nine people including twenty-one-year-old Nessim Akdemir, son of Brigadier General Yavuz Akdemir, and nineteen-year-old Talia Kalkan, daughter of Arusha Kalkan, a high-ranking member of the Kurdistan Workers Party, were killed when a bomb strapped to the waist of a female suicide bomber exploded in the Demir Hotel.

"Government sources condemned the event as an unprovoked and vicious act of terrorism. PKK sources said that the government in Ankara could not expect less and that retribution for Turkish violations of basic civil rights would continue until the legitimate rights of the Kurdish people were recognized.

❈❈❈

During the next two years, the fragmented coalitions ensured only that the government changed hands half a dozen times. The political horizon stagnated, the military threatened to take control once again, and the Turkish people grew increasingly restive. The sole element of stability and success was Istanbul, where Recip Tayyip Erdoğan served as the most popular mayor in recent memory.

Under Erdoğan's administration, the city became cleaner, greener, and less corrupt. The serving of alcoholic beverages in numerous public places was banned and women were encouraged to wear the shawl and headscarf.

Erdoğan was becoming a major force in national politics, a harbinger of things to come — things more fundamentalist and Islamist — and the National Security Council was not pleased. Erdoğan was arrested, tried, and convicted of inciting hatred on religious grounds because he had read an Islamic patriotic poem in public. He was sentenced to ten months in jail, but was freed after four. However, because of his criminal record he was barred under Turkish law from standing for elections or holding political office.

❈❈❈

For the first year after Nessim's death, Yavuz and Gñlay were inconsolable. But life went on, and ever so slowly life returned to a semblance of normalcy. Omer and Yavuz were simultaneously promoted to Major General, and Ibrahim pinned on his lieutenant's bars, the fifth generation of Akdemirs in a long and distinguished line of military officers.

Little more than a year after their eldest son's tragic death, the Akdemirs had cause to celebrate another beginning as Nessim Akdemir Araslı bellowed his arrival into a rapidly changing world.

PART TEN:
THE FOOTSTEPS
OF FOREVER
2002–2005

1

"Mister Baumueller, this is Semra Heper Osman. I hate to interrupt your day, but I have horrid news. Melek suffered a heart attack last night. He passed away an hour ago."

"That's ... I don't know what to say, Semra. Does anyone else know about this?"

"No."

Aviva watched the concern on his face. At forty-seven, Jake — she had now taken to calling him by the more distinguished name of Jacob — was, in her eyes, handsomer and more virile than ever. The scars on his face had all but disappeared, his limp was scarcely noticeable, and he'd regained most of the use of his left arm. The touch of gray at his temples only added to his allure. Jacob wrote on a scratch pad, "Melek Heper died an hour ago. Heart attack." Aviva inhaled sharply.

"I'm so sorry," he said, returning to his telephone conversation. "Thank God Kiral Suvarli, the city editor and assistant publisher, will make sure things will run smoothly for the time being. Have any arrangements been made for the burial?"

"Yes, Mister Baumueller. My husband is attending to that, thank you."

"Semra, I believe you should contact the family lawyer at the earliest moment. Perhaps you, your sister Lâle, Aviva, and I can meet in the next few days. Do you mind if I ask Justice Hükümdar to sit in? He's been a great friend of the family for twenty years."

"I think that's a good idea, Mister Baumueller."

Three days later, the family gathered in attorney Ali Karaca's spacious offices in the Beyoğlu district. Kâzım Hükümdar had graciously joined them. *My God,* Aviva thought, *he was thirteen when Grandma Zari rescued him. Now he's seventy-two and I'm in my forties! How can time possibly pass so quickly?* Out loud, she said, "Thank you so much for coming Justice Hükümdar."

Attorney Karaca was appropriately deferential in the presence of the erstwhile Supreme Court justice. "Your Honor, ladies, and Mister Baumueller, things appear to be very much in order." He turned to the sisters. "When your father Abdullah decided to take Isharet Communications public in 1983, he set up a trust to ensure that the family would maintain voting control of the company. Of Isharet's one hundred million shares of stock, twenty-five million were placed in the trust. His four children were equal remainder beneficiaries. Since your older brother Levent was unmarried at the time he died in 1990, his share went to the three surviving siblings. With Melek's sudden tragic death, the two surviving sisters own twenty-five percent of Isharet's stock. Since the trust provided for only direct lineal descendants, the shares you own are your separate property. None of them belong to your husbands."

The lawyer stood, walked over to a white board, and wrote a series of figures in green. As he continued writing, he said, "Semra and Lâle each own 12,500,000 shares. At the current Istanbul Exchange price of ten U.S. dollars per share, that equates to $125,000,000 each."

The sisters stared fixedly at one another, barely comprehending how incredibly wealthy they were. They and their brothers had always lived simply and frugally. While they knew Isharet Communications had value, they'd had no idea what they were worth.

Advocate Karaca continued. "In the same year your father set up the trust, he wanted to further ensure that a great block of Isharet's stock would be owned by someone he trusted completely. He and Jacob's grandfather had been friends for many years. At that time, Isharet's shares were worth about two U.S. dollars apiece. Old Ed Baumueller's stake in the New York *World* was worth well in excess of two-hundred-fifty million dollars, so a forty-million-dollar investment was not going to break him." The lawyer wrote more figures on the white board.

The Edwin Baumueller, Jr. Family Trust, Edwin Jacob Baumueller IV, Trustee: 20,000,000 shares, 20%. Current price USD $10 per share, value of holdings: USD $200,000,000.

Karaca walked over and sat at the head of his large oak conference table once again. "The people sitting in this room own forty-five percent of *Isharet Communications*. Thus, it looks like the Heper and Baumueller families control the corporation and will continue to control it for the foreseeable future."

"But fifty-five percent of the shares are publicly traded," Aviva said cautiously. "Are there any other substantial shareholders?"

"I assume there are institutional investors in various parts of the world," Karaca said. "But Turkish law affords significant protection. A majority interest in the company must be held by Turkish citizens."

"Does that include Turkish corporations in which shareholders may be of different nationalities?' Jacob asked.

They turned to Justice Hükümdar, who answered. "The way the law presently reads, the answer is yes."

"So theoretically, a foreigner who invests in a Turkish corporation can get over the fifty percent-plus-one-share hurdle?"

"Theoretically, yes," the Justice continued. "Your forty-five percent holdings are a virtual iron-clad guarantee that you control the company."

"I'd feel more comfortable if we had more than a *virtual* iron-clad guarantee," Aviva said.

Switching subjects, Lâle asked ,"How do you like your new position as the morning anchor at *2 Kanal*, Aviva?"

"It's a change having to get up at five every morning, but at least I can be home at a normal hour. Eddie's twelve and Leah's nine. It's good for mom to be there when they get out of school." At forty-two, Aviva still had the same lithe figure she'd had a dozen years before. Her dark hair, cut shorter now, needed some help every few weeks to keep the color she'd been born with, but she was still a striking woman.

"Do you miss the excitement of two full-time jobs?" Lâle continued.

"Oh, I still write articles for *Isharet* from time to time, but nowadays, it's more important to me how the kids are doing in school and who their friends are," Aviva said.

"Would you like me to investigate the complete shareholdings in *Isharet*?" Karaca interjected.

"That might not be a bad idea," Jacob said. "Perhaps we could research it together and get back to one another in a few days."

A few evenings later, after the children had retired to their rooms, Aviva came into the den and noticed that her husband seemed preoccupied. "Something wrong, darling?" she asked.

"I really don't know. That's why I think two heads are better than one."

"What's up?"

"The Istanbul Stock Exchange requires that an 'insider' — anyone who owns more than ten percent of the stock in a publicly-traded company — report their holdings each year. Short of ten percent, nothing is required. During the past fifteen years, *Isharet* stock has been very stable. The *Heper Trust* reported 25% ownership and the *Baumueller Trust* reported 20% ownership. It was almost impossible to find smaller shareholders on the radar, although the big funds like Dreyfus and Fidelity, and major players like George Soros and Warren Buffett always listed their holdings in various companies, even if they owned only a one percent stake. That's because their own investors wanted to know exactly what *they* owned."

"That's easy to follow," she said.

"Just on a hunch, I asked the *World's* financial editor to learn what he could about the owners of *Isharet* stock, to find out if there'd been any unusual trading activity." He tapped a few keystrokes on his computer, then turned to his wife.

"Until 1997, when the Welfare government came to power, *Isharet* shares were thinly traded. On average, no more than fifty thousand shares changed hands on any given day. During the time the Welfare party was in office, trading inched up, seventy, eighty, ninety thousand shares a day. When the National Security Council disbanded the Welfare party, trading slowed to thirty or forty thousand shares a day."

"Why would that concern you, darling?"

"Because *Isharet* has been the biggest newspaper in Turkey for years, and *Isharet* holds a major stake in *2 Kanal*. Just because the National Security Council broke up the Welfare Party does not mean its constituency simply disappeared."

Aviva walked over, read the figures on her husband's computer, then unconsciously pulled at a strand of hair that had fallen loose over her forehead. "Whoever controls the news controls the nation," she said. "People read the left-wing and right-wing tabloids for amusement, semi-naked women, and sports, but only a few people take them seriously. When it comes to serious players you've got *Isharet, Hürriyet, Milliyet*, and then you have 'all the rest.'"

"And *Isharet's* the biggest plum of all," he said.

"Largely because of its tie-in with *2 Kanal*."

"So, it would be the ideal takeover candidate," Jacob said.

"It would be, but you heard Karaca. Between the Heper family and your family, you own forty-five percent of the stock."

"That means fifty-five percent is out there being publicly traded. Karaca's statement that we have *virtual* control made me nervous. I think it's time we did some deeper digging. Do you know someone you could trust to help us investigate? Someone very, very discreet?"

"I do." Aviva remarked.

By week's end, five of them, Ali Karaca, Justice Hükümdar, Jacob, Aviva, and another man, retired Istanbul police captain Ahmet Mütlü, gathered in Karaca's office.

"Do we agree it's best not to say anything to the sisters at this time?" Karaca asked.

"Not to keep them out of the loop, but to make sure we've got all the evidence before we go to them. What have you unearthed so far, Captain?"

"Ilhan Osman, Semra's husband, is an attorney who works primarily for Iranian and Afghani interests," Mütlü began. "Rustem Kemer's an industrialist with strong ties to Libya. The women know only that their husbands work very hard and are respectable. When it comes to their financial dealings, both sisters are kept in the dark."

"From my own investigation, both Kemer and Osman are large, but not ostentatious, contributors to the Justice and Development Party, Erdoğan's replacement for Welfare," Aviva said. "That's not necessarily a bad thing. Recep has often told me that Justice and Development, the AKP, may be an Islamist party, but it's a *Turkish* Islamist party and they don't trust fundamentalists from outside the country."

"You wanted to have this meeting, Mister Baumueller," Karaca added. "What have you found?"

"Nothing that would alert someone unless he or she was interested *only* in the ownership of *Isharet Communications.*" Jacob pulled out a fifteen-page single-spaced document. "It's based not only on my *New York World* sources, but also on investment analysts within the United States and France." For the next forty-five minutes, Jacob Baumueller spoke. The rest listened, occasionally yawning, but becoming visibly disturbed as he carefully made his points.

"There are eighteen Turkish domestic companies, all subsidiaries of Liechtenstein Corporations. Ilhan Osman's law firm represents fifteen of the eighteen. The incorporator and nominal shareholder in each is a Liechtenstein lawyer, Hans-Friedrich Höffer."

"You said '*nominal*' shareholder?" This from Justice Hükümdar.

"Yes, Your Honor. Liechtenstein corporations have one feature no other corporations anywhere else have: bearer stock. No matter whose name is registered as the owner of the shares in the corporation, the real owner is the one who holds the stock certificates. In the case of all eighteen corporations, Höffer is listed as the registered owner of the stock. To further hide the trail, the true owners of the stock in these corporations are trusts, residents of various tax haven states. For example, the stock of one of the corporations, Paradise Fun Park Ventures, is held in various amounts by three trusts located in Namibia, the Cook Islands, and the Cayman Islands."

"Making these entities almost impossible to trace," Hükümdar observed.

"Exactly, Justice Hükümdar," Jacob replied. "That's nothing new. It's been done for years. The most common reason is to avoid taxes and preserve capital, but there are others: to hide the identities of assassins, religious fanatics, and even legitimate interests like the United States Central Intelligence Agency."

"Interesting," Karaca said. He sat back and lit up a meerschaum pipe. "But what does all this have to do with *Isharet Communications?*"

In response, Jacob extracted five copies of a nine-by-seventeen-inch chart and handed them around the table. The names of the eighteen Turkish corporations were listed in columnar order. "Earlier, I told Aviva, and I told you, Captain Mütlü, that *Isharet* was a thinly traded stock. For the past two years, twenty-five thousand shares a day have been traded, making the market thinner and less interesting to traders than ever. As an investment, the growth of the stock was very modest, never less than $9.50 a share, never more than ten dollars a share. Less than a five percent swing in either direction, most times less than one percent. With a one hundred percent per year inflation rate in Turkey, no one in his right mind would think to make money by buying or selling *Isharet* stock.

"So I was surprised that the stock was selling at all. As I dug deeper, I found something very strange. With very few exceptions, the buyers were one of these eighteen companies. To make it less suspicious, each of these companies would *sell* a portion of their holdings from time to time, but curiously, on the day they sold, *another* of the eighteen companies would be the buyer."

Each of the four listeners turned to the chart and read the year-end holdings of the eighteen companies.

CURRENT SHAREHOLDINGS IN *ISHARET*
(In thousands of shares)

Company	Shares	Percentage Ownership
1. Aslan	2,300	2.3%
2. Ay tutulması	2,100	2.1%
3. Bankacı	2,250	2.25%
4. Birleşmiş	2,000	2.0%
5. Cennet	2,200	2.2%
6. Doğuya doğru	2,100	2.1%
7. Ev	1,000	1.0%
8. Fil	1,750	1.75%
9. Ideal	2,500	2.5%
10. Krala ait	1,800	1.8%
11. Meşe ağacı	1,250	1.25%
12. Millete ait	2,700	2.7%
13. Parabol	1,400	1.4%
14. Rektör	1,300	1.3%
15. Seçkin kimseler	2,100	2.1%
16. Tepe	1,800	1.8%
17. Üstün	1,900	1.9%
18. Vefa	2,000	2.0%
TOTAL:	**34,450**	**34.45%**

The group sat stunned, in various states of agitation. "How certain of you of your figures, Mister Baumueller?" Avukat Karaca finally broke the silence.

"Very," Jacob said.

"I can confirm Mister Baumueller's findings," Detective Mütlü said quietly.

"It looks like we've got a raid on our hands," Aviva said. "I think it's time we came to a consensus on how to deal with it."

❀❀❀

"First thing we must do is get the sisters' shares in a voting trust, with a provision that if any members of the trust wish to sell, they'll give the other members the right of first refusal to buy at the fair market value," Aviva said. "That will lock up the sisters' twenty-five percent and insulate it from the any hostile takeover attempt,"

"That might not be so easy to do," Jake replied. "They'd certainly ask their husbands' advice. At least one of them, Ilhan Osman, is legal counsel to fifteen of the eighteen outsider companies. For all we know, he may be counsel to the others as well."

"I know of a way we might convince them, but let's hold that in abeyance for right now," Aviva said. She wrote some figures on a legal pad. "If the raiders had almost thirty-five percent at the end of last month, I bet they've acquired another five percent this month. With the national elections coming up in October, they'll make their move as quickly as possible. My guess is, they'll put a lot of money into AKP's campaign."

Aviva continued punching in figures on a pocket calculator. "We've got forty-five million shares, they've got thirty-four million, four hundred fifty thousand shares. That leaves twenty million, five hundred fifty thousand shares up for grabs. We need only five million and one share to control the majority. If we were to start buying as many shares as we could tomorrow …"

"Maybe, but if we bought too fast, that would alert them and they'd try to outbid us or get to the market first," Jacob added. "The moment there was even a mild spike in sales, the war would be out in the open. Picture a scenario where the bidding goes higher and higher each day. People who own shares would hold them and wait for the price to go to astronomical heights."

"What if we did an exposé about foreign elements trying to take over a Turkish communications conglomerate?" Aviva said.

Jacob cupped his chin in his left hand and thought for a moment. "Great idea, but the timing would have to be right. They'd fight back with allegations that every one of the eighteen companies is a *Turkish* company, and twenty-percent of *Isharet Communications,* my twenty percent, was already in American hands. Add to that that one of *Isharet's* star journalists is an American citizen by marriage, and a Jewish Israeli. That could have very negative connotations, and we'd be in a bloody smear campaign."

"Two quick questions, Jacob. How much do you trust me, and how much money can we raise over the short term?"

"The first one's easy. Thirteen years ago I entrusted my whole life to you, and I trust you more than ever now. Is there any reason you need to know how much money we can raise?"

"I'm an Israeli citizen by birth and an American citizen by marriage, but five years ago I became a Turkish citizen as well. I was 'grandmothered in,' since Grandma Zari never renounced her citizenship. If you were to transfer all your shares from the Baumueller Trust to me as my separate property, and I put those shares in a Turkish trust in my name, the claim that our shares were not owned by a Turkish national would have no legitimacy."

"Shrewd," he said. "*Isharet Communications* closed at $10.50 U.S. this afternoon. Once the war for control of *Isharet* starts, there's no telling how high the bidding will go. The stock might double, even triple in price, but those last shares could command one hundred dollars a share or more. We might need a war chest of half a billion dollars."

She whistled. "That's an impossible sum! Half a billion dollars for a five percent stake in a company where one hundred prcent of the shares have a book value less than a tenth of that."

"Yes, but that five percent could be the tail that wags the dog. It'd be a squeeze, but if I pledged my interest in the *World*, we could make it. Of course, you might have to go back to working two full-time jobs."

"You know," she said, "I'd give a lot, to find out who's behind this whole thing."

2

"Gentlemen, one thing I truly love about Dubai," Count Napolitano expounded, blowing smoke circles from his Gurkha Black Dragon cigar. "Politics, religion, morality and all that extraneous garbage are trumped by the simple, well-cultivated greed for power."

"Well said, Marco," the oldest of his three associates replied. They were sitting on the veranda facing the outdoor pool. It was two o'clock in the afternoon. Because it was still mid-February, the temperature was a tolerable eighty-four degrees Fahrenheit. Two months from now, the electronically configured summer tent would enclose the entire area, and the temperature would return to an even balmier seventy-six degrees. "Praise Allah for fundamentalists who like to forget about Islamic orthodoxy when they come here. How much did we take in last year?"

"Ten billion from the hotels, another ten from the gambling," another of his associates replied. "Plus a rather lucrative take from the black trade. Marco, why are you so anxious to take control of the Turkish media company?"

"Frankly, Your Highness, because in the next ten years or so, we'll need to expand our operations to the next world powerhouse."

"Explain," the Iranian confederate, a man of early middle age, said.

"Certainly." He handed a printout to each of his confreres. I've chosen well, he thought. Not one of these men is known outside the closest circles of power. Yet each of them commands respect and fear. The oldest man was one of Osama Bin Ladin's closest confidants. The

288

youngest was a Saudi Arabian prince, one of hundreds, not very high up in the line of succession, but a prince nonetheless. The third, the middle-aged man, was personal advisor and second in command to Mahmoud Ahmadinejad, a hard-line fundamentalist politician who, at present, wielded no real power in Iran, but who was said to be a particularly vicious, charismatic rabble rouser, who was close to the Ayatullah Khamenei. The printed list read as follows:

Country	Population	Square Miles	Gross domestic product
UA Emrates	2,560,000	32,000	USD $63.7 billion
Syria	18,448,752	71,498	USD $60.4 billion
Afghanistan	30,000,000	250,000	USD $21.5 billion
Israel	6,275,000	8,019	USD $129 billion
Saudi Arabia	26,417,599	756,985	USD $310.2 billion
Iran	68,000,000	636,296	USD $ 500 billion
Turkey	70,000,000	301,384	USD $ 515 billion

"Gentleman," Marco, Count Napolitano continued, "the importance of Turkey cannot be overstressed." The count had aged gracefully. His hair, now snow white, was still thick, luxuriant, and immaculately coiffed, and his mustache was stylish. "Turkey has a standing army larger than that of Great Britain and Germany *combined*, well over half a million troops. It produces ninety percent — *ninety percent* — of the world's legally-grown opium. It grows more food and cotton than the other six countries on this list combined. But all that is meaningless without the biggest treasure of all. Today, large wars are fought to gain control of oil. Fifteen years from now, the wars will be fought for *water*. You can't drink petroleum, you can't use it to grow crops, and once the multinational corporations that hold the rest of the world hostage lose out to those who are building technologies that are not oil-dependent, the oil-producing countries will go back to where they were in the early Twentieth Century."

The Iranian was the first to speak. "So, Turkey's the Queen in the international chess game."

"Eloquently put, Halabi."

"But Turkey's a secular state," the Saudi remarked. "and the National Security Council has a vested interest in making sure it stays that way."

"Yes. Oh, thank you, I will have another dry Rob Roy. Gentlemen?" Each of the other three ordered a non-alcoholic beverage. "Where were we? Oh, yes. The secular state. My friends, there are four very important reasons why that whole charade is at risk. First," he said, raising his index finger, "the National Security Council insists on its irrevocable friendship with Israel. They ignore the fact that more than fifty percent of the population would just as soon have Israel and the damned rude and arrogant Israelis fall into the sea.

"Second," he said, raising his next finger, "the Turkish fundamentalist Islamic movement has grown larger each year, and every one of those people vote. Third, the Americans are starting to get on the Turks' nerves. If the war in Iraq gets off the ground, the Kurds will suck up to the Americans so they can get an independent state *right on the Turkish border*. If you think that won't drive the Turks mad …"

The Al Qaeda leader smiled. "And the fourth reason, Count Napolitano?"

"The most dangerous and unpredictable reason of all. The Turks want desperately to get into the European Union. They've lusted over that dream like a man salivates over being the first to deflower a virgin. EU, on the other hand, wants the Turks in the Union about as much as a man wants a fat, warty old whore. So the European Union raises almost impossible barriers the Turks will never overcome. The Europeans make it sound so reasonable. 'Honor your human rights obligations.' Translation, 'Stop letting the military run the country. Stop the secret trials and the human rights abuses. *Get rid of the NSC and let the true democracy of civilian rule really take over.*'

"The NSC can't do that because they'll lose control. The NSC can't *not* do that because they'll lose EU. But they're acting as stupid and naïve as the Europeans want them to act, because, deep down, to the Europeans the Turks are no more than stupid, dirty Muslims, whose only redeeming grace is that they work eighteen hours a day cleaning shit out of the sewers of Germany, sleeping ten or twelve to a room in Denmark, and never bathing. Gentlemen, let's call a spade a 'shit shovel,' shall we? The Turks are to Europe like the Palestinians are to us. Someone to look down on."

"How does that help our cause, Marco?" bin Ladin's lieutenant asked.

"Eventually, Turkey will get tired of being slapped in the face. Turkey will realize it has much more to offer the world than the Europeans think. Europe will drive Turkey to the welcoming arms of its Muslim brothers, and we'll be in the forefront of the 'Welcoming Committee.'"

"No more Israel," the Iranian emissary said with glee.

"The American devil will be a clawless, toothless tiger," Al Qaeda agreed.

"But why *Isharet*?"

"Your Highness, no one knows better than you that control of the media is everything. Control their hearts and minds, you control the rest of the body. Control the media, you control the politicians."

"Please answer me one question, Count. So far, we've spent more than three hundred forty-five million dollars for a minority interest in a company that has one newspaper and a stake in a partly government-owned television station. For less than a tenth of that amount, we could have started a dozen newspapers and applied for a national television license of our own. Why *Isharet*?"

"Because we'd have to build those dozen newspapers. We have no guarantee that the television station would successfully compete against *2 Kanal*. And," he added quietly to himself, "*because I have an important personal score to settle, eh Carrissima?*"

MARCH 2002 – HAMILTON, BERMUDA

Napolitano's yacht berthed at Kings Harbor in Hamilton, Bermuda overnight. Early the following morning, two men in their sixties came aboard, where they were greeted by a tall, willowy woman of early middle age. As they entered the yacht's large stateroom, they were met by Count Napolitano. Even though it was early morning, each of the men was formally attired. Their host directed them to the elegant breakfast buffet. As they sat at a round table, Napolitano addressed the attorney. "Mister Höffer, do you think it's time we shuffled some of the stock to different companies?"

"It's your decision," the Liechtensteiner said noncommittally. "None of the Turkish companies owns more than a minuscule percentage of

Isharet stock, not enough for us to have to report to the stock exchange commission."

"What are the combined shareholdings today?"

"Thirty-nine percent," the woman said. If there was a perfect foil for the operation, it was Lisa Lumet Erdbacher. Forty-three, the tall, attractive American woman had been raised in Groton, Connecticut, with all the rights and privileges accorded the only daughter of wealth and breeding. Originally an editor at Doubleday, she had passed the New York bar six years before. Count Marco Napolitano was the only one aware of the real reason she had become involved.

After she'd been jilted by her fiancé, she'd fallen into the willing arms of the genteel and consummately charming Napolitano, who'd been waiting opportunistically to pick up the pieces.

Napolitano frowned. "That means that on average each of the companies owns a little more than two percent. If anyone were to try to track the companies, which I'm sure they haven't, they'd see each of the companies' holdings edging up slightly over the past few years. Ilhan, are there any established Turkish companies we can pick up cheaply?"

Ilhan Osman fidgeted nervously. He was torn between loyalty to his wife's family, the Hepers, and the phenomenal amount of money waiting for him if — and it was a big *if* — Napolitano's coup was successful. "How many more companies do you think we'd need?"

"We need just over another eleven percent to control *Isharet*. I'd like to see our eighteen companies start to divest themselves of some of their holdings to avoid any hint of suspicion. Also, I'd want to make very sure that our new acquisitions would be well-aged, established Turkish companies in good standing."

"Shells." Höffer interjected.

"Absolutely," Napolitano replied. The practice of having new companies purchase shell companies was known all over the world, and had been completely legal for over a hundred years. Napolitano had engaged in the practice more than fifty times. The same thing happened in nature when a hermit crab crawled into and took over the empty shell of a deceased shellfish.

What occurred was simple. As time went on, old but respectable publicly traded companies failed. They didn't need to file bankruptcy, since there were no assets to pay debts or distribute to shareholders.

It cost only a nominal amount each year to keep the failed company currently registered on the stock exchange. This trifling sum was normally advanced by sales agents. Since there was no market for the shares, the shareholders willingly signed their holdings over, in trust, to the agent, in the hopes that the shell corporation would be purchased and they might see *some* money, since some return, no matter how small, was better than none.

Enter the buying company, usually a startup concern, looking for a shell to give it instant respectability. There were two immensely valuable benefits to the buyer: first, it would acquire the name and the assets of an old, established heritage company, and second, the shell company normally came with a huge tax loss carryover, that could be applied against any profits made by the new company.

"How much would they cost, Ilhan?" Napolitano asked.

"You could have your pick for fifty thousand U.S. dollars per company."

"Including all transfer fees?"

"Yes," the Turkish lawyer replied.

"Do it. Lisa, give the man six hundred thousand dollars, plus his finder's fee."

"Which account, Marco?"

"Spread them."

Within three weeks, a series of new Liechtenstein corporations had purchased and reactivated twelve shell companies. The following week, each of the eighteen Turkish companies holding stakes in *Isharet Communications* began to divest a portion of their holdings.

3

APRIL 2002 – ISTANBUL – THE BAUMUELLER HOME

Spring had come to the City with a vengeance. Jacob, Aviva and the children had just finished a delicious dinner of broiled salmon, rice, and shepherd's salad, a wonderful blend of chopped onion, tomatoes, red peppers, cucumber, and parsley in lemon juice on their balcony overlooking the Bosphorus. The kids had gone back into the house, while their parents remained outside, sipping Villla Doluca Red Klasik wine and enjoying a picture-perfect sunset over the Golden Horn.

"Alright, Jacob," Aviva said, taking his hand in hers. "I can tell from the way you've been picking at your food that something's amiss. Out with it, husband."

"Something funny's going on," Jacob said. "Each of the eighteen companies has been selling off its holdings at market rate, but we haven't been able to get in fast enough to buy any of the shares they're selling."

"Shall I call our stock analyst?" Aviva asked.

"I think that's a good idea."

Metin Ülker, a vice president of the Exchange who'd been a close acquaintance of the Baumuellers for ten years, reported back to them within twenty-four hours. "Every share being sold by the eighteen companies, and whatever other shares openly being traded on the market, have been snapped up by twelve companies, each more than thirty years old, which, until two weeks ago, had been dormant."

"Shells?" Jacob asked.

"Yes."

"So, the beast is mutating?"

"It seems that way, Jacob."

"How many shares do we control?"

"We've been able to add three percent to your holdings by bidding them up to fifteen dollars a share."

"And the raiders?"

"Including the recently activated shell companies, the thirty companies between them own forty-three percent."

"The game's getting close," he said, turning to Aviva. "I think it's time Captain Mütlü, you and I met with Semra Osman and Lâle Kemer."

❈❈❈

A week later, Jacob, Aviva, Captain Mütlü, the two Heper sisters, Lâle's husband, Rustem Kemer, and Justice Kâzım Hükümdar met in Isharet's conference room. Semra turned white as Captain Mütlü went over the unassailable fruits of his investigation. He presented evidence he'd received from the Süreté, the Istanbul Stock Exchange, and numerous connections from around the world.

"I … I can't believe my husband would be involved in such a thing. This amounts to stealing *Isharet* from my family, *his* family, since it was Heper money and the lucrative *Isharet* legal retainer that got him started."

"Unfortunately, Semra, money is a powerfully addictive narcotic," said Aviva.

Lâle turned to her husband, who'd been invited to the gathering after Mütlü had confirmed that although Kemer Construction had been dealing with conservative fundamentalist Middle Eastern operations, Rustem Kemer had no involvement in what was going on. Rustem shook his head in disbelief.

"You're sure of your facts, Captain?"

"I am, Rustem Bey. If you'd like to spend the necessary time —?"

"No, I trust what you say. The problem will be having my sister-in-law confront her husband. Is there anything criminal in what he's been doing?"

"No. He is staying on this side of the line, but barely," Jacob said. "That's why what I suggested will avoid the confrontation, and it will be perfectly legitimate. Do you want to consult a lawyer, Semra?"

"No," she said. "What Justice Hükümdar has written is so simple even a lawyer's wife could understand it."

"Lâle, Rustem?"

"It's my wife's property, not mine," Kemer responded. "But it's certainly appropriate to protect the family."

"Very well, I'll be the first to sign," Aviva said. She passed the single sheet of paper around the table. In the world of lengthy legal documents, this was an anomaly. The document read simply that each signator irrevocably assigned all of the voting rights in their stock to the *Trustees of the Isharet Communications Voting Trust*, to wit Semra Heper Osman, Lâle Heper Kemer, and Aviva Baumueller.

Forty-eight percent.

JUNE 2002 – ISTANBUL

"I still think we should publish the exposé before it's too late, Jacob," she said.

"It could have the opposite effect. There's a strong Islamic tradition in Turkey, and they'll surely fight back with their own campaign."

"Perhaps Justice Hükümdar could speak with President Sezer? They were colleagues on the constitutional court. Sezer's a staunch secularist," Aviva persisted.

"The elections are coming up four months from now. The Justice and Welfare Party could make very strong inroads. What about your friend Erdoğan? He'd be the first to admit you've been extraordinarily fair to him, both in *Isharet* and on *2 Kanal*."

"What are the current holdings, darling?"

"Forty-nine percent for us, forty-eight for them."

"Are shares still being bought and sold?

"Less than fifteen hundred a day. The price has jumped to fifty-five dollars a share, and no one wants to sell."

"I think it's time for that exposé. But first, we've got to find if there's a single bad guy behind it all. Someone at whom we could point a finger. … "I have an idea," Aviva said. "It's not entirely legal, but …"

Several days later – Istanbul

"Good afternoon, Ilhan Bey. Might I speak with you for a few moments?" It was shortly after five o'clock in the afternoon. Osman's secretary and staff had already left for the day.

"I'm sorry, but do you have an appointment, Mister —?"

"I don't, Ilhan Effendim, but I assure you it will just take fifteen minutes at most. I can pay …"

The attorney raised his hands, palms out. "I suppose if it will only take fifteen minutes." He glanced at his watch. "My wife and I have tickets for the concert tonight."

Mütlü opened his card case and displayed the card identifying him as a Captain of the Istanbul Police Department. He hoped Osman wouldn't look too carefully lest he notice the card had expired a year ago. He need not have worried. By the shift in the lawyer's eyes, Mütlü knew the man was caught off balance. "May I bring in my partner, Lieutenant Oncalı, to speak with us?

"Of course," Osman said. "Would you like some tea, Captain?"

"Please."

After Osman handed the men two cups of tea, they sat in the clients' chairs and nodded when the lawyer sat in his own executive chair. "This talk is totally off the record, Avukat Osman," Mütlü began. "We're investigating matters concerning *Isharet Communications*. We understand there may have been a violation of the Law of Turkish Ownership of the Media. Specifically, I understand that the Baumueller Trust, which legally owned twenty percent of the company under the earlier law, transferred its holdings to an individual, Aviva Kohn Baumueller, Jacob Baumueller's wife."

At this disclosure, Ilhan Osman's eyebrows raised. What a wonderful bit of luck! he thought. If there's been an illegal transfer, Baumueller's entire twenty percent stake in Isharet would no longer be a threat. That meant there'd be a decided shift in power, even without majority interest. Semra and his sister-in-law, Lâle owned twenty-five percent of the company between them. His client's interests owned forty-eight percent. He was sure he could convince Semra it would be in the best interests of the company to vote with the new majority.

"I'm sure the Baumuellers have excellent counsel and they would not have done anything illegal," he said.

"I understand you've provided legal counsel to *Isharet*, Mister Osman. Did they ever ask you about the legality of the transfer?"

"No, Captain, they didn't, but that's not surprising. The *New York World* maintains its own law firm in Istanbul, and they must have cleared it through that firm." He rose, lit a cigarette, walked to the window, and looked out. The sun was at a beautiful angle in the west, and the Golden Horn truly became *golden* at this time of the day.

"Would you mind if I asked you, Ilhan Effendim, what are the legalities of transferring interests under the law?"

"Any Turkish citizen can legally own equity in a Turkish media communications company. A foreigner cannot. It's pretty simple."

"So, a Turkish corporation would qualify as a Turkish citizen?"

"As long as it pays taxes, yes."

"Let's suppose the Baumueller Trust transferred its holdings to a Turkish corporation. Would that be going afoul of the law?"

"No. You see, the corporation, which is Turkish, would own the shares of the company."

"But what if the owners of the corporation were not Turkish citizens?" Mütlü persisted. "Wouldn't that be circumventing the law?" He thought he saw a momentary clouding over of the lawyer's eyes. It was only for a split second, then Osman regained his composure.

"It could be, yes. I've never really researched the question."

Mütlü paused. "Would you mind if I used the restroom facilities for a moment, Avukat Effendim. I'm afraid at my age it becomes rather important to be close to a toilet."

"Of course."

When he returned, Mütlü recommenced his questions in an innocuous tone. "I don't mean to change subjects, Mister Osman, but if — and I'm saying *if* — someone like, say, Jacob or Aviva Baumueller helped one another to circumvent the law, would they be culpable of aiding and abetting?"

The lawyer relaxed and smiled. "Now you're going into something where I must plead ignorance. That's an entirely criminal matter and I handle civil transactional law. If you're asking for a totally off-the-record opinion, and one I couldn't be quoted on, I'd say your assumption would be correct."

Mütlü sat silent for several seconds. Lawyer Osman began to fidget. When thirty seconds had gone by, the lawyer started to stand up. "I'm sorry, it really is getting on to five-thirty and I must be going, Captain Mütlü. If you've nothing else to say …"

"Only one or two more questions, Ilhan Effendim."

"Go ahead."

Mütlü opened a small, thin, zippered attaché case and laid several sheets of paper on Osman's desk. Osman's eyes widened perceptibly as he read the names on the top of each document. Aslan Holdings, Ay Tutulması Enterprises, Bankacı Investments; Birleşmiş Security Funds. There were twenty-four more packets. "I believe you're familiar with all of these, aren't you Mister Osman?"

"Umm, that is…"

"Attorney-client privilege? Is that what you were going to say, Mr. Osman?"

"That's preposterous!" the lawyer thundered.

"Is it, Avukat Osman?" Mütlü extracted copies of fifty checks, all drawn on foreign banks, all made payable to cash. He shoved the copies in front of the stunned lawyer, then placed what appeared to be the reverse side of the fifty checks, showing they had been endorsed over to an account in the name of Ilhan Osman Investments in the Thun branch of the Union Bank of Switzerland.

The lawyer went red, then white. His breathing became harsh and shallow. "What do you want?" he croaked, his voice hoarse with fear.

"I want one thing and one thing only, and for that I'll trade you these papers and your freedom."

"That's blackmail!"

"That it certainly is," Mütlü said calmly. "Or a private plea bargain, if you'd prefer to call it that."

After what seemed like an eternity, but was probably not more than a few moments, Osman choked out, "What's your deal?"

"I want the name of the person or persons behind all this, and I want those names before I leave this evening."

"I can't do that. It's a violation of the attorney-client privilege. It's… it's…"

"Outrageous," Mütlü continued softly. "And now you have to decide whose skin is more important, yours or your client's."

"There are a lot of clients."

"There are a lot of *corporations*, Avukat Osman. I don't want the names of a lot of corporations. I already have all I need. The evidence of your involvement in the purchase of those shell corporations is so tight it would fit as perfectly as a noose around your neck."

The lawyer stood up, then sat down in his chair, crushed.

"The name or names…?"

"They'd kill me if they knew I —"

"Yes, they probably would. But how would they know unless you told them?"

"I'll think about it."

"No, Mister Osman, there's no time for you to think about it. It's them or the State Prosecutor, your decision."

Osman tore off a piece of yellow paper from his legal pad and printed five names in a trembling hand. Mütlü nodded, took the paper from the desk, and looked at it fixedly.

"The last name on the list, is he the leader of the entire operation?"

"Yes." The voice was barely a whisper.

"Thank you for your time, Avukat Effendin," Mütlü said, bowing deferentially. The lieutenant rose with him. Mütlü looked at his own watch. "My goodness, five thirty-five. I've overstayed my welcome by five minutes. Pity. Enjoy the concert Effendim."

4

"Marco Napolitano!" she exclaimed angrily. "That b—" Aviva stopped in the mid-word. "Evil incarnate, that's what he is, and his associates don't sound much better." She was as furious as Jacob had ever seen her, and he knew better than to try to calm her. "He's got to take me down, does he?" She looked over at Jacob and suddenly burst out laughing.

"What is it?"

"Oh, you men! I'm sure a man made up the saying, 'Hell hath no fury like a woman scorned.'"

"Shakespeare?"

"Well, he was a man. I've never seen a fury to match Napolitano's, though. Burning down the apartment house, kidnapping me to Chechnya, and all because —"

"I've got to admit, you're certainly worth it."

He pushed her onto the bed, and, giggling uncontrollably, they wrestled with one another.

"Ssshh!" The children —"

"You're right," he said quietly. He tiptoed over to the bedroom door, locked it, and came back to the bed. He saw the look in her eyes. "Different kind of wrestling in mind?"

"The annual shareholders' meeting is scheduled for October 1, one month from today," Jacob told his inner circle. "I'm sure we can expect an interesting meeting, coming as it does just before the national elections. What are shareholdings as of last night?"

"Forty-nine million, eight-hundred fifty thousand shares for the Trust, forty-nine million, eight-hundred thousand shares for the opposition," Karaca replied. "One-hundred forty-thousand shares have given their proxies to current management. So, if the vote were held today, it would 49,990,000 to 49,800,000."

"I can recite every one of the by-laws in my sleep," Jacob commented. "If it's deadlocked, the Court of Cassation in Ankara puts one provisional director from each side in office while it decides the issue. Who we get as judge is up to an impartial drawing,"

"With forty-nine point eight percent, wouldn't they be able to put a strong minority on the board anyway?" Aviva asked.

"No," Jacob replied. "*Isharet's* by-laws provide for all or nothing. Fifty percent plus one share elects the entire board. Anything less than fifty percent plus one share, the loser walks out with a lot of shares worth less than a dollar."

"The corporate elections are next Tuesday, four days from now," Count Napolitano addressed his companions. "It would have been nice had we gotten an absolute majority, but we've got what we need to paralyze the present management. Current management bought up the proxy shares for one-hundred dollars a share, and they got another ten-thousand shares just ahead of us on the open market."

"How much did we pay for the last two-hundred thousand shares, Marco?" the prince asked.

"Thirty million dollars. One-hundred fifty dollars a share, but that's nothing compared to what we'll gain, even by the deadlock. When the Islamists come in, as I'm sure they will, they'll start appointing judges to the Court of Cassation, and odds are we'll get a very friendly judge."

"One-hundred million shares outstanding," Jacob said, as they got ready for bed that night. "Fifty million for them, fifty million for us. Yet you seem so cool about it, Aviva. Do you know something I don't know?"

She shrugged noncommittally.

❧❁❧

At five minutes to ten on the morning of October 1, 2002, Count Marco Napolitano, Lisa Lumet Erdbacher, and their associates from Iran, Saudi Arabia, and Afghanistan walked through the boardroom door, accompanied by Hans-Friedrich Höffer, who'd flown in from Frankfurt the night before. Ilhan Osman did not attend the meeting. Four of the current directors of *Isharet Communications*, Aviva Baumueller, Semra Heper Osman, Lâle Heper Kemer, and Ali Karaca were already seated. There was one empty chair. Jacob Baumueller and several members of the press corps were seated in the visitors' gallery. Napolitano glared haughtily at Aviva, who looked particularly fetching in a white blouse, dark skirt, and demure shawl. She ignored him.

Jacob Baumueller looked shocked as he recognized the tall, slender woman who accompanied Napolitano.

Promptly at ten o'clock, Aviva banged the gavel. "Good morning, ladies and gentlemen. My name is Aviva Baumueller. The Board of Directors requested that I fill the term of the late Melek Heper. In the temporary absence of the Vice Chair, it is my pleasure to welcome all of you to the annual meeting of shareholders. The first matter is the reading of the minutes of the last meeting, followed by the treasurer's report."

"Madame Acting Chair," Marco Napolitano raised his hand. "I move we dispense with the reading of the minutes and the treasurer's report and proceed with the business at hand."

"Sir, I believe you are out of order," Aviva said, her voice equable. "We will go ahead with the agenda as noted."

"Perhaps you don't understand, Madame Acting Chair," Napolitano said, as if lecturing a child. "I said I *move* we dispense with the reading of the minutes and the treasurer's report."

"Very well sir," Aviva replied, deliberately not recognizing Napolitano by name. "Is there a second to the motion?"

"Second," replied the Saudi prince.

"Discussion?" As Aviva glanced at her watch and looked toward the door, she noticed no one had said a word.

"Call for the question," Lisa Erdbacher said.

"The question has been called for," Aviva intoned. "All in favor of dispensing with the reading of the minutes and the reading of the treasurer's report, please write your vote on the paper I am circulating. Include the number of shares you are voting." After the vote was taken, she announced, "Fifty million votes for, fifty million votes against. The motion falls to carry a majority. We will proceed with the reading of the minutes and the treasurer's report."

The reading consumed fifteen minutes. A few moments before the treasurer's report concluded, Justice Hükümdar entered the room and quietly sat in the empty director's chair. When the treasurer's report was finished, Aviva Baumueller announced, "Ladies and gentlemen, the next item on the agenda is the nomination and election of officers. As you know, several years ago, the shareholders voted to extend the directors' terms to three years. Management has placed in nomination the names of Kiral Suvarli, Semra Heper Osman, Lâle Heper Kemer, Aviva Kohn Baumueller, and Kâzim Hükümdar to serve for the coming three-year term as directors. Are there any nominations from the floor?"

"Yes, Madame Acting Chair," Höffer said, smoothly. "I put forth the names of Marco, Count Napolitano, Lisa Lumet Erdbacher, and…" he named Napolitano's other three associates.

Clever bastard, Jacob thought. The *shareholders* must be Turkish citizens, and technically the thirty Turkish corporations were Turkish citizens, but the officers and directors could be from anywhere.

"Thank you, Sir," Aviva said. "Are there any other names to be placed in nomination?" There were none. "Very well, I will read Section Seventeen point zero-two point three of the by-laws, so there is no misunderstanding. 'This corporation does not recognize cumulative voting. A simple majority is necessary to conduct any business, including the election of officers and directors. In the event of a deadlock, each of the competing sides will name a provisional director to serve on the Board of Directors. The Court of Cassation in Istanbul will appoint a third provisional director, and will supervise the conduct of the corporation's business until the next election."

The voting took place by writing. After considering the ballots, Aviva started to say, "Ladies and gentlemen, it looks like we have —"

"Excuse me a moment, Madame Chair." Justice Hükümdar spoke in calm, measured tones. "Before you make the announcement you were contemplating, may I say a few words?"

"Of course, Your Honor."

"It appears that the shareholder register of the corporation is slightly out of order."

"What do you mean, Justice Hükümdar?"

"The register provides for one-hundred million shares of stock. How far does the register go back, Mrs. Baumueller?"

"Ten years."

"Is there an earlier registry?"

"I don't know, Your Honor."

"I do, Madame Chair," Justice Hükümdar said mildly. He reached into his briefcase and extracted a creased, yellowing piece of paper. He handed photocopies of the document around the room. Although the ink was faded, the handwriting of Abdullah Heper was clearly recognizable, as were the words on the document:

Received this first day of December, 1983 the sum of 100 TL from
Turhan Türkoğlu
In full payment of Share Certificate Number 1 for
One (1) Share of Isharet Communications Common Stock
s/Abdullah Heper, President and Chairman of the Board.

A collective gasp erupted around the room.

Lisa Erdbacher, who'd been jilted several years before by Jacob Baumueller, glared daggers at him. She turned pale, knowing exactly what Justice Hükümdar was about to say.

The elderly jurist removed two more documents from his briefcase. The first was the actual share certificate, signed by Abdullah Heper as president and by the original secretary of the corporation. The corporate seal was clearly embossed on the document.

The second document was a notarized assignment by Turhan Türkoğlu of his one share of stock in trust to "The People of the Republic of Turkey, by and through The Honorable Kâzim Hükümdar as Trustee and attorney-in-fact for the duration of his life, and thereafter to such Trustee as he in his sole discretion shall name."

The reporters were already on their feet and heading to the door to call in their dispatches when a sharp bang from Aviva Baumueller's gavel stopped them in their tracks. "Order! Order!" Aviva barked. "Is there something further you wish to say, Your Honor?"

"Yes, there is, Madame Chair. On behalf of the People of the Republic of Turkey, and as Trustee of those people, I exercise my right by voting the People's one share for the incumbent board's slate of directors."

"This is a fraud! It's illegal! It's blasphemous! You'll never get away with this cheap charade!" Napolitano shouted as he stormed toward the door, his entourage in tow.

He had just opened the door when he was met by six men barring his exit. Retired Police Captain Mütlü, accompanied by Ilhan Osman, stood to the side, while the apparent leader of the group addressed Marco Napolitano.

"Mister Napolitano, my name is Carlo Bianchini. I am with the Italian unit of Interpol. If I might have a few words with you, I think we have much to talk about…"

"What nonsense is this?" Napolitano blustered.

"Miss Erdbacher," a large, blocklike man said, "I believe you are an American citizen, traveling on an American passport. Permit me to introduce myself," he said, opening a card case. "I'm Special Agent Ivan Field, Federal Bureau of Investigation —"

In the firestorm of television cameras and flash photographs that followed, the newly re-elected board quietly elected the officers for the coming year. There being no further business, the meeting adjourned.

5

NOVEMBER 4, 2002 – ISTANBUL

Isharet's headline on November 2, 2002 said it all:

EXTRA! JUSTICE AND DEVELOPMENT PARTY SWEEP ELECTIONS!
FIRST MAJORITY NON-COALITION GOVERNMENT IN 20 YEARS!

"Günaydin," Aviva began her *Bugün — Türkiye* morning program on *2 Kanal*. "In what is nothing less than a democratic revolution, the AKP, Justice and Development Party, headed by Islamists Abdullah Gül and Recep Tayyip Erdoğan, captured 34.27 percent of the national vote, sending 360 members to the 550 member Turkish Parliament, the first time since the days of Türgüt Özal that one party has held an absolute majority. In an even more stunning development, all but one of the remaining nine political parties that sent representatives to the last parliament are now without a single member in the Turkish legislature! Süleyman Demirel, who retired in 2000 after his term of President ended is out. Bülent Ecevit, out! Tansu Çiller, out! Mesut Yilmaz, out! The camera focused on a large, colorful chart:

Part	57th Government	Today
MHP (National Movement Party)	124	0
DSP (Democratic Left Party)	58	0
ANAP (Motherland Party)	71	0
DYP (True Path Party)	81	0
YTP (New Turkey Party)	58	0
SP (Felicity Party)	46	0
AKP (Justice and Development Party)	59	360
CHP (Republican Peoples' Party)	3	190
TOTAL in Turkish Grand National Assembly:	550	

"This morning, President Sezer expressed disappointment at yesterday's election results, but said he had no choice but to ask Mister Gül to form the 58th government," Aviva continued. "It is virtually certain that in the days to come, the new Grand National Assembly will vote to terminate the ban on Recep Tayyip Erdoğan holding any public office, and that thereafter, Mr. Gül will step down in favor of Mister Erdoğan. The National Security Council had no comment."

Three days later, on November 7, Aviva Baumueller hosted one of the most highly-rated television shows in Turkish history because she'd managed to land the former mayor of Istanbul, the man destined to become the next Turkish prime minister. Her interview gave the future Turkish leader free rein to express his views.

"Mister Erdoğan," she began. "Are you the scary Islamic ogre, the next Ayatollah Khomeini, that many people fear you to be?"

"Hardly, Aviva," the man said easily. "If you're asking whether I'm sincere in my beliefs, the answer yes. Does my wife wear a shawl? Yes, but that's her decision, not mine. Turkish women have the same rights as men, and in my family, maybe even more rights than the man." He smiled. Aviva was charmed by the man, who usually looked so dour in his photographs.

"Are you an Islamist?" she asked pointedly.

"That depends on your definition of Islamist," he said, chuckling. "I'm not trying to give you political doubletalk. I'm just trying to define who *I* am and what *I* stand for. Did I publicly chant the poem I was convicted of reciting? Yes, guilty as charged. I spent four months in jail for reading that poem. Pretty silly, if you ask me, but it taught me a lesson about Turkish power politics. Do I consider the Justice and Development Party that Abdullah Gül and I founded to be a warmed-over reincarnation of *Refah*? No, and I believe Mister Erbakan and his Virtue Party would be the first to say we're not *Refah*."

"Does AKP have an agenda, Mr. Erdoğan? And if so, what is that agenda?"

"Do you want me to answer that all in one breath, Aviva?"

"If you would."

"Very well. AKP rejects the 'Islamist' label. We are a pro-Western mainstream party with a conservative social agenda, but also with a firm commitment to liberal market economy and European Union membership."

"Can we really expect it will be business as usual in Turkey if and when you are asked to form a government?"

"That depends on your definition of 'business as usual,' Aviva. If business as usual means graft and corruption, I don't expect that to occur. If business as usual means an attempt to curb inflation and entice foreign investment, then yes, that will happen during my administration. If people choose to dress in a more conservative fashion that is their decision, not mine. I'll certainly continue to promote a lifestyle more attuned to what I feel to be appropriate behavior."

"President Sezer has publicly expressed antipathy for your program and for you, personally. Do you think the two of you can work together?"

"We'll never know 'til we try, will we? We're both grown men, and it's up to us to try to accommodate one another."

"And the National Security Council?"

"Well, all of us have to walk a careful line, don't we?"

ISTANBUL – FEBRUARY 2003

"What do you think about our future Prime Minister?" Jacob asked his wife.

"I don't think he's changed much. He was a good man when I first met him, he was a great mayor, and I think he'll do better as prime minister than a lot of people think," Aviva said. "Frankly, I don't mind what his religion and political beliefs are, as long as he's willing to respect mine."

"Speaking of which, it's nine months until Eddie's *Bar Mitzvah*. Have you got any idea of how many people you'd like to invite?"

"A lot."

"Define 'a lot,' Mrs. Baumueller."

"We're going to have to struggle to determine who we can get away with *not* inviting," she said. "It'll be a real test of diplomacy."

Three weeks later, the AKP-dominated parliament voted to amend the constitution to allow Recep Tayyip Erdoğan to be elected to parliament, and thus become prime minister. Abdullah Gül stepped down in favor of Erdoğan and assumed the position as foreign minister. As spring started to creep up the Bosphorus, Jacob Baumueller telephoned his wife with the disappointing news. "Would you believe it, they've already double-booked the *Neve Shalom* for the fifteenth? They said we could get on a waiting list, but they couldn't promise anything."

"Not even for us?" she asked.

"Not even for *you*,' he replied. "The Chief Rabbi of Turkey, told me to tell you he's a great fan of yours, and if you could put the *Bar Mitzvah* off three weeks…"

"It may not be that big of a deal for him, but it is for us. Eddie had his thirteenth birthday on February eighteenth, so he's already going to be late for his *Bar Mitzvah*. Where do you suggest we celebrate his coming into manhood?"

"I'd vote against New York. The Society Jewish scene really rubs me the wrong way. I read last week where some big New York actor rented a *ship* and held the celebration in New York harbor, just off Ellis Island. He bragged that it cost him over two hundred thousand dollars. Do you know how many starving children that could feed for a month? That's not the kind of values I want to instill in our son."

"That leaves Jerusalem."

"Can you think of a better place? They've been doing it there for a long, long time."

"Do you think it's safe, Jacob? The suicide bombings —?"

"Nowadays, no place in the world is entirely safe, darling. New York was attacked in September, 2001. Who'd have thought anyone would ever attack the United States?"

"Maybe we could put Eddie's *Bar Mitzvah* off a few weeks. Turkey really would be the safest place to have it."

"Are you telling me you're afraid to go home? What would your grandmother Zari have thought?"

"All right, Jerusalem it is. It's just that so many kids from the United States, Europe, and South Africa are celebrating their *Bar* and *Bat Mitzvahs* at the Western Wall."

"And you have no idea why?" he said, hugging her to him.

❈❈❈

August of 2003 was particularly warm and humid in Istanbul. For the first time in the memory of most living Istanbulus, the parliament had actually taken control by voting to make the National Security Council an *advisory* body, *and* there were more civilians than generals on the Council. While the Turkish General Staff chafed, no one for a moment believed the military had given up its place as the true power in Turkey.

During the first week of August, the Chief Rabbi had telephoned Aviva at *2 Kanal* and let her know that one of the *Bar Mitzvahs* scheduled for November fifteenth had asked to be pushed back to December. If they were still interested in celebrating Edwin Baumueller's *Bar Mitzvah* at *Neve Shalom*, the large synagogue was available.

"I think we should ask Eddie his opinion," Jacob said.

Their thirteen-year-old son, already five feet four inches tall, considered the options seriously — as seriously as a thirteen-year-old can — and finally said, "Mom, Dad, I think we should keep the celebration in Israel. Somehow it seems more meaningful, don't you think?"

"Absolutely," Aviva replied. "But we thought we'd give you the chance to voice your own opinion."

"Besides," the youngest male Baumueller said, "We've never really been involved with the Istanbul *shul*, except that they referred Elijah Bronstein to us." Elijah was an American Jew studying at Bosphorus University, and he'd jumped at the chance to earn some extra money teaching young Baumueller his *Torah* and *Haftarah* passages.

"Spoken like a sage," Jacob said. "Israel it will be. How many replies have we gotten back, Aviva?"

"One hundred-fifteen out of one hundred-fifty have responded yes. Twenty maybe's and fifteen 'Sorry, we can't make it.'"

"With only a month to go, that's pretty final. What about my dad and mom?"

"We've booked them into the King David Hotel, where the four 'p's' have always stayed since it first opened in 1931."

"The four 'p's?" Jacob asked, raising his eyebrows.

"Pashas, potentates, presidents and pretenders."

NOVEMBER 2003 – JERUSALEM

November fifteenth finally arrived, a balmy, beautiful fall day in the Holy City. From their stateroom in the King David Hotel, the Baumuellers had a perfect view over the Old City to the dry hills beyond. By nine o'clock, the entire *Bar Mitzvah* entourage, including 125 guests, was walking down King David Street, through the Jaffa Gate and into the Old City. From there, the party continued into the Jewish Quarter, where King David Street became the Street of the Chain. A slight jog to the right brought them within sight of the great square abutting the Western Wall.

Young Eddie had been to the Wall once before, three years ago. "It's much smaller than I remember it. Was this really the wall of the Great Temple?"

"No, Ed," his mother remarked. "It's a small segment of the outer retaining wall that was built around Mount Moriah twenty-five hundred years ago, to guard the entrance to the Second Temple. It's the only part that survived the Roman destruction of the Temple."

"What are all those people doing touching the wall and sticking things into the crevices?" Deborah, their nine-year-old asked.

"It's become a tradition for everyone visiting the wall to write a small prayer on a tiny piece of paper and stuff the prayer into the wall," Jacob responded.

"Does it really work?" the little girl persisted.

"They say it does, darling. It's between the person who stuffs the prayer into the wall and God to know whether it works or not."

The ceremony at the wall was brief, no more than half an hour. Each member of the Baumueller family felt spiritually moved. Each believed, in their own way, that one doesn't need the trappings of a large and impressive synagogue to make communion with the Almighty. Young Edwin Baumueller V recited his portions in a strong voice, which, if truth be known, adolescently broke in a few places. Afterward, he dutifully wrote his prayer on a piece of paper, and stuffed it in a hole as high above his head as he could reach. "So my prayer will be closer to God and a little easier for Him to read," the boy said.

As the large group walked back toward the King David Hotel, Jacob remarked, "I wonder what all those military vehicles are doing cruising up and down King David Street at this hour. Seems a strange time to be engaging in defense exercises in Jerusalem."

When they arrived back at their hotel in anticipation of the large party to follow, Aviva's antennae picked up that something was amiss. As they fought through the crowd inside the huge lobby, Aviva looked up and saw a black-bordered television screen.

"We repeat," the newscaster's voice said, "within the past hour, a car bomb exploded outside the *Neve Shalom* Synagogue in Istanbul, Turkey. Preliminary reports say at least twenty people were killed and more than two hundred-fifty were injured. In Ankara, the government expressed outrage at this senseless atrocity. Stay tuned for further news as it develops."

6

"I'm really glad we decided to stay in Israel another month," Eddie said to his parents one week after the Bar Mitzvah. "Don't worry, mom," he quickly added. "I got all my school assignments before I left, and I even get extra credit for doing a report on the Holy Land."

"Just as long as you know it's not holiday time all the time," Aviva said.

"All work and no play... Would you mind if I tagged along with you to visit Aunt Lyuba and Uncle Muren?"

"Fine with me," she said. "Your sister can come, too."

Jacob entered the living room of the apartment they'd rented for the month. His limp had become more noticeable, and one could tell that his arm was not comfortable since the winter chill had come to Jerusalem, but his good disposition remained intact. "Ahem," he interrupted, clearing his throat and looking directly at his son, "If I had to wager, I'd say Uncle Muren and Aunt Lyuba are not the reason you want to go with your mother, young man, and since Yossi's back on active duty, that leaves only one other member of the family."

"Ummmm, yes," Eddie said, a flush rising from his neck to his cheeks.

"Eddie's got a girlfriend! Eddie's got a girlfriend!" Debbie sang out. Eddie glared at his little sister stonily.

"Am I mistaken, or do I recall seeing you actually dancing almost every dance with the same young lady the entire evening?" Jacob asked.

"Mmm…" Ed Baumueller mumbled in a monotone.

Jacob smiled knowingly at Aviva and winked at his two children left the living room and disappeared down the hall.

"Well, Leah's his own age. She's Jewish, she's a pretty little thing, and she's almost family," Aviva said. "Hey, Ed, Debbie!" she called. "I'm leaving in five minutes. If you guys want to tag along, you'd better get moving."

❈❂❈

"So, he knows all about his kidnap?" Aviva said. She and Lyuba were shopping in a supermarket not far from Beit Knesset.

"Oh, yes, we've told him over and over and over, and of course I told him about Muren's role in getting him back safely." Lyuba tore four bananas off a larger bunch, and placed them in her shopping cart.

"Does he show any anger toward the Palestinaians?"

Lyuba shrugged her shoulders. At forty-three, Lyuba Kolchuck's striking blonde hair had a few gray streaks, and she'd succumbed to the middle-age spread which seemed to be common in Russian women, but she still had a lovely face and large wide-set eyes. "Who knows? He doesn't talk much about them. He's too interested in other things."

"A girlfriend? Here, let me help you bag all this stuff."

"Thanks, 'Viv. Uh-huh, a young woman in his unit. A sergeant, no less."

"An older woman?"

"She is. Twenty," Lyuba said, unlocking the door to the year-old blue Toyota Highlander.

"*He's* twenty."

"Yes, but he's twenty and *two* months. She's twenty and *five* months."

"Big deal."

"That's what I said. Would you believe, he had the nerve to say his mother married a younger man and she was pretty darned happy?" She laughed, the same musical laugh that had enchanted Muren twenty years ago. Then she turned more serious. "He's a good boy, Aviva. Sometimes, I'm afraid for him, but if my life's any example, I trust God will make everything come out all right."

They drove in silence for a few minutes, then turned northwest into the hills toward one of fifty new housing developments on the western edge of the city. Jewish Jerusalem. As the SUV approached the driveway, the two women saw that Eddie and five other boys were involved in an informal basketball game in the park at the end of the cul-de-sac, while a like number of girls, including Debbie and Leah, watched. Eddie scored a three-pointer from twenty feet out. Leah applauded delightedly, seemingly oblivious to the frankly admiring stares from the boys on the court. She was wearing white shorts and a white cutaway blouse that concealed just enough.

"I remember when I had a body like that," Lyuba sighed.

"Me too," Aviva rejoined. "Time is the greatest thief of all, and gravity takes its toll. Would you trade places with her?"

"Hard question," Lyuba replied, turning off the ignition and alighting from the Toyota. Each of them carried two bags of groceries toward the house. "Life seemed so much simpler and safer back when we were growing up, but I suppose every generation says that."

"Your life wasn't at all that easy, my friend. Don't forget, I was there."

"How could I ever forget? I guess as you get older, the bad old memories fade and you remember the good times."

LATER THAT NIGHT. RAMALLAH

Yossi had guard duty at the community nursery every Thursday, from nine in the evening 'til four the next morning. Natan Goldstein, Hirsch Isaacs, and Dov Blaufeld shared duty with him. They were good guys, all three near his own age. It was amazing how, from a distance, they all looked alike. Each had close-cut hair, each ranged in age from nineteen to twenty-one, and all were of similar height and lanky build. Natan and Hirsch carried regulation army rifles, Dov had a shotgun, and Yossi was armed with an Uzi semiautomatic. Each treated their weapons like treasured lovers. They'd *better* treat them like treasures. Lose a weapon, leave a weapon anywhere unattended, and you faced a court-martial. Hours and hours of boredom, punctuated by brief moments of stark terror. Such was life for the Israeli Defense Forces, both men and women.

Like young men everywhere, their conversation while on guard duty did not center around Shakespeare or literary or artistic pursuits. It was an unspoken rule that one did not talk *that* way about one's serious love interest, but each of them talked about their alleged adventures and their self-invented sexual prowess, most of which were firm products of their overactive hormones and their overinventive imaginations.

"Man, I was home on leave for the weekend, and I've gotta' tell you guys, Netanya rocks. Two college girls at the same time, a blonde and a redhead, and let me tell you, they were hot to trot."

"Wet and wild?"

"You betcha'!"

"D'ja get their names?"

"Nawww. One of 'em was an American, U.C.L.A., but that's *all* the talking she did. She was better at other kind of noises. A real screamer."

"You were pretty noisy yourself when you got back Sunday. You kept me up most of the night with your snoring."

"Well, it took a little time for me to rest up from all that action. Hey, guys, Ssshhh," Hirsch said. "What's that?"

"Where?"

"I think it came from the nursery. Sounded like a door being pushed open."

"I hear voices," Yossi whispered nervously. "There's no way to tell how many."

"I'll sneak around the building and look through the windows. Cover me, Brother."

Moments later he returned, "Five of them," he whispered. "Looks like they may each be kidnapping a baby." Yossi froze in his tracks. "Something wrong, Yossi?"

"I…I just need to sit for a moment." Yossi said, his head swimming with terrible thoughts, indistinct memories.

"You do that, my friend. I'll get the others. That would even the odds.

As if to underscore his words, a scream coming from the nursery rent the air. It was followed by the harsh sound of a hard object striking a softer one with great force. By that time, Hirsch and Natan had arrived, their rifles at the ready. On the count of three, the four soldiers kicked open the front door of the nursery.

A shotgun blast and Natan went down, moaning incoherently. Instinctively, Dov and Hirsch fired their own weapons in the direction of the discharge that had downed Natan. They heard the sound of something crumpling to the floor, followed by a high, keening wail of pain.

By now, Yossi had recovered from his shock, and moved around to the rear entrance to the nursery. A well-placed kick from his heavy Brogan shoes, and the door collapsed around its lock. Unwilling to rush in like the others, he proceeded cautiously, his semiautomatic raised and pointed in the direction he was walking.

"Natan? Hirsch? Dov?" he shouted. "I'm in the back of the building! Two down!" He continued, striding purposefully over to the two fallen men. One was reaching for a revolver, when Yossi, with a swift kick, smashed the man's hand and wrist. The other man was grabbing at his groin and moaning.

"Natan's down! We don't know how bad!" A shout came from the other part of the building. "We've got one of 'em, D.O.A.! Wait a minute! The other two have just come out with their hands up."

"I've got two infants and two guys with me! I need cover! Can you get over here?"

"Don't think so!" a voice from the front responded. Yossi could tell it was Dov. "We've got two covered. A dead nurse and three more babies. Looks like we may have a standoff."

"My God, there's only two of 'em our age. The other three look like kids," Yossi gasped.

The three Israeli soldiers seemed to have the upper hand, but the four invaders were sullen and unrepentant. The mood in the room was heavy.

"How old are you?" Dov prodded one of the two uninjured attackers with his gun.

"F—f—fourteen, sir," the boy answered. He was visibly trembling and looked as if he'd break down in tears in any moment.

"And you?" he barked at the second man.

"Twenty, Israeli pig!"

Hirsch raised the butt of his gun, but Yossi signaled with his right hand that he should put the weapon down and maintain his cool.

"You seem like an intelligent man," Yossi said calmly. "Did you volunteer for this duty?"

"What business is it of yours?" the young prisoner asked bitterly. "You Israelis don't give a damn if we live or die."

"Maybe you're right, maybe not. What's your name?"

"Fuckhead."

"I don't think so. What's your real name?"

"What difference does it make? I'm a dead man if I go back empty-handed. I'll be killed in an Israeli prison if I stay."

"Cigarette?" Yossi asked, thrusting a pack toward him. Yossi had decided he was probably the leader of the failed kidnap attempt.

"Why not?" the young man said, extracting an Israeli cigarette. "It's the only thing I've ever gotten from an Israeli."

"You're a Palestinian?"

"What do you think, asshole?"

"I think if we're going to communicate at all, we might at least try to be civil to one another."

"Why? You don't give a rat's ass what I think or who I am."

"How do you know what I think?"

"You Israelis are all the same. Keep us down any way you can."

Everyone in the room had fallen silent, as if a spotlight were shining on the two of them.

"I see," he said. "And you know my background?"

"What do I care about your background?"

"You might be interested to know that for a short while I was known as Yassir Beir."

"You think I believe that for a moment? A blue-eyed Israeli with a Palestinian name. I suppose you're going to tell me you're the Jewish Messiah."

"Twenty years ago, I was kidnapped from an Israeli nursery similar to the one you invaded. I was five days old." Yossi looked around the room and saw the shock in his compatriots' eyes. Facing the young Palestinian, he tried a daring gambit. "Maybe you and I could speak more candidly if it was just the two of us."

❖

"You think I set out to kill you, or hold you down, as you put it?" Yossi asked.

"If not you, who?"

"Whoever sent you across the border. You've got a mother, don't you?"

The young Palestinian mumbled something indistinct.

"Brothers? Sisters?"

Silence.

"Sometimes silence speaks louder than words," Yossi said calmly. "Would it hurt you to tell me who sent you across the border?"

"It's not anyone's border," the other replied. "It's all part of greater Palestine."

"All right then. Another cigarette?" He held the pack out again. "You may as well take the whole pack. I don't smoke."

"So, what are you doing with a pack of smokes?"

"Army benefits," Yossi said. "As if that would make it easier for us."

"Easier for *you*?" the Palestinian sneered. "You Israelis think you own the whole fucking world. We've got nothing. Not even the hope of a decent job unless we sneak across what you call the border and get work here."

"You think we're that much different? Suppose it had been me that took the bullet instead of your friends? Do you think I'd have bled any less? Or that I wouldn't have died?"

The Palestinian looked directly at Yossi for the first time. "Amir," he said.

"Yossi."

There was intense silence in the room for what seemed an eternity, but was probably only a few seconds. Yossi walked closer to where the young Palestinian sat, and held out his hand.

It took the longest moments of their lives, but slowly, slowly, Amir held out his hand and grasped Yossi's hand in his.

"All right, the two of us have done the most unimaginable thing we could — we spoke and we held out the symbol of peace and friendship." Yossi said. He looked up and saw tears in the other's eyes.

"Why do you care about me, Israeli?"

"Because we happen to suffer from the same disease. We're both human."

The room to which they'd adjourned was small, perhaps twelve feet by twelve feet. Amir rose from the straight-backed wooden chair and walked to the single entrance door. He returned to the chair and stood behind it. "I meant what I said, Yossi. If I go back to Palestine without a baby, they'll kill me. They may kill my parents, or they may not, but my family will be disgraced to the tenth generation."

"You really believe that?"

"Yes, I do. You don't understand. You *couldn't* understand. I've heard that every day since I was four years old. We're trained to die for the destruction of the Jewish state. We're trained to take one of your live children each time we lose one warrior in the *intifada*."

Now it was Yossi's turn to sit down opposite where Amir was standing. "So it's a war of attrition. One replaces one until there's only one left standing in either country, and that one is the winner. That sounds like a story I heard once: in the country of the blind, the one-eyed man is king. But that story didn't make sense to me. Wouldn't it be the reverse? If the one-eyed man described what he saw to those who could never see, they would call him a liar and destroy him."

Amir used his dying cigarette to light another one. "It really doesn't make sense. If only there was some hope for us. Something positive that could replace the killing." He sat down in the wooden chair again. "But there is nothing. No land, no money, no work. Nothing but hopelessness and the refugee camps."

"But Israel has said it would give up land. Rabin and Barak were willing to give ninety-five percent of what Palestine was demanding. Why wasn't that enough?"

"Oh, Yossi, can't you see? Are you the one-eyed man? When Israel wanted to *give* us what *the Iraelis* were willing to give, we saw it as nothing more than the Israelis rubbing our noses in the dirt once again. 'Here you are, little brown brothers. We will generously give you the rocks and the clay in the desert and the shit-land *we* don't want, so long as *we* get to make the final decision on what that land is.' We would have taken less had we Palestinians been able to choose the land we wanted."

"And all we can see is that Palestine wants Israel to have all the land it wants, provided that land is under the Mediterranean Sea. Arafat vowed to destroy us and that's never changed."

"Do you really believe that's the way the majority of Palestinians feel? Let me tell you something, Yossi. Israel is going to be very, very surprised one day when *Hamas* takes over the country."

"The terrorists?"

"Call them what you will. Terrorists, freedom fighters, it all depends on who's calling them what. We call it education, you call it propaganda. Whatever. They're the ones that build what few hospitals we have, that give us what few jobs we have so we can earn a little bit of self-respect. *Fatah* talks a good game, but they're in it for themselves and for their own leaders. The world sees them as our leaders, but we know better. They put on a good show for the Western world, even for the Israelis, who say they can deal with Abu Mazen. But they're not our leaders."

"Were you sent by *Hamas*?

"*Hamas, Fatah*, who knows? Those in command tell us exactly what we *will* do. We're never asked. The little people never are."

"Isn't that the truth?" Yossi replied. "So what do we do, now? We can't just let you walk out the door. We'd be court-martialed and do a long time in an Israeli prison."

"Shoot us then," Amir said bitterly. "At least you have the choice — and the weapons. Either way we lose. You might as well give us the mercy and the dignity of dying quickly."

Yossi felt a huge lump in his throat. *Was this all there really was to life?*

7

Yossi was the first to speak when they returned to the larger room. He addressed all the young men, Israelis and Palestinians alike.

"What I have to say may offend some of you, maybe all of you, but I feel it has to be said. Just before Amir and I went into the other room to talk privately, I told you I had been kidnapped by Palestinians when I was five days old. Truthfully, I have no recollection of how long I spent in a refugee camp in Gaza. I was less than a year old when Israeli agents and one other person retrieved me and returned me to Israel. So, if anyone has a right to feel angry or offended at the fact that your small group tried to repeat my history, it's me.

"Something I've never told anyone, but it's family history, so I'll tell it now. My real father, a Russian, was killed in a Palestinian suicide bomber attack. My stepfather, one of the men who rescued me, was a Kurdish freedom fighter, who planted a bomb in a Turkish military jet, killing an innocent man no older than we are. He was just obeying orders, but he had no real choice in the matter. He had the courage to admit this to a Turkish colonel and begged forgiveness.

"In the Jewish liturgy, and I'm sure in Islam as well, they say whoever destroys a life, it is as though he has destroyed the whole world, but whoever saves a life, it is as though he has saved the whole world.

"My stepfather was sent into Gaza to atone for what he had done. I was his atonement, and after he brought me back, he met and fell in love with my mother. From the worst of circumstances can come the greatest of miracles. Is he any the less a Turk, a Kurd, or an Israeli because of an accident of birth over which he had no control?

323

"I've asked myself this question over and over again: Must I blame you for something over which you had no control? You were told what to do. Amir was honest enough to tell me that none of you had any choice in the matter. You were told we are wicked and evil, just as we've been led to believe you are wicked and evil.

"That's been going on since 1948. Neither you nor we created the State of Israel nor the present situation. The State of Israel was created by the British and approved by the U.N. Did we have a vote? No. Did you have a vote? No. That was the start of the war that has gone on to this day."

Amir raised his hand, as if volunteering to give an answer in school. "Have any of us ever wondered why it's the *young* people who get sent to fight the war, but it's the old, fat, comfortable people who do the *sending*? I don't know about you guys, but frankly I'd rather watch beautiful women on TV or ..."

"Wait a minute," Dov interjected. "Muslims all wear chadors and are covered head to toe with yards and yards of clothing. How can you see *anything*?"

"Come off it, Israeli," Amir growled, but not viciously. "That's a stereotype. Have you been to Gaza lately?"

"Well, no."

"Have you been to your *Mea Shearim* lately?"

"That's different."

"How different? There are fundamentalist Muslims and there are fundamentalist Jews. Or do you believe young men don't think the same thoughts everywhere?"

"Point taken," Yossi rejoined. "Amir's right. It's the old men who direct the wars, while they sit safely on the sidelines. If there's ever going to be peace, it's going to have to start with people our age, while we're young enough to build the future. We Israelis can do it from within. Heck, there are so many splinter groups in our perfect democracy, it's a miracle we can get *anything* done. But Amir told me if he returns to Gaza without what he came for, he won't live to see the next sunrise. And we all know that if we turn him and the rest of you, in, you'll be left to the charitable mercy of *our* old men."

For the first time, the tension in the room started to abate. These were young men, some of them still boys, and they shared the camaraderie of young men in every culture, in every civilization, and in every generation. "Make love, not war," one of the young Palestinians said quietly.

An Israeli soldier pointed to a sign on a wall above them. "If many little people from many different lands all come together and join hands, there's no end to what can be done."

"What do you suggest, Yossi?" Hirsch asked, deferring to Yossi's apparent leadership.

Yossi thought a moment, then glanced over at Amir, who nodded.

"We heard a noise coming from the nursery. When we came in, we heard the night nurse scream. A shot rang out and she was killed. A Palestinian gunman seriously injured Corporal Goldstein, who, thank God, was able to dispatch the invader and save the child. We thought there might be a second gunman, but when we searched the nursery, we didn't find anyone else."

"Yeah," Natan joined in. "That's exactly how it happened."

"We can get Natan fixed up at the army hospital. What about the Palestinians?"

Yossi shrugged. "I imagine if there was a second man, he probably went to Doctor Ismail Jamal in the Old City." He wrote a name and address on a piece of paper and handed it to Amir. "But then again, we'll never know, and we'll never tell."

✿❁✿

As the Palestinians were leaving the building, Amir turned and looked at Yossi. "I don't know what to say," he remarked.

"Yeah. Sometimes I feel the same way. They say when you do a good deed for someone, it comes back in a different way, maybe not even to you, but to someone else. Same goes for a bad deed, I suppose."

"If there's ever a way …?"

"I don't think we need to address that issue right now. It's been … different." He handed Amir another piece of paper. Amir nodded and the four Palestinians left the area.

It was only when Amir was safely in Doctor Jamal's office that he took the paper out of his pocket and read, "Yossi Vonets-Kolchuk. One week from Thursday afternoon, 2:00 p.m. The souk, near the Roman ruins."

✿❁✿

A week later, Yossi, Amir, and a middle-aged man with a noticeable limp headed down a side street togther when Yossi addressed the Palestinian boy. "You thought he was an Israeli cop? Why would I have let you go free only to turn you over to one of the old guys? What made you decide to trust me?"

"He didn't walk like an Israeli," Amir replied, nodding at the older man.

"Have you seen that many Americans?" Jacob Baumueller asked.

"Some. You have such a different 'We own the world' walk."

"If you'd like, I suppose I could hunch over and let you buy me some tea."

Amir looked momentarily shamefaced. "Well …"

"From what my nephew told me, it would probably be better if I paid for the tea. It took both of you a lot of courage to do what you did. Why don't we stop at a tea house close by and we can talk for awhile?"

Once there, the two young men ate ravenously of the pastries offered. Jacob waited patiently until they'd slowed down.

"I understand you're kind of a stateless person," he said, addressing Amir. "You can't go back to Palestine and there's no future for you in Israel."

"Uh-huh."

"And, I trust, you've got no money to go anywhere?"

"Uh-huh."

"It would be nice if you could start all over again. A place where no one knew you?"

Amir looked down at the floor. This man seemed to be reading his every thought. Amir had not known what to expect of this meeting. Still, he'd come. What other choice did he have?

As if continuing to read his mind, Jacob continued. "Yossi and I spoke about you for several hours the last week. He made a very wise comment for someone his age."

"Revolutions start when one has only hopelessness for company every night," Yossi said.

"Hopelessness can mean no place to go and no future that one can see." This from Jacob.

"I've lived that way ever since I can remember," Amir said miserably.

"How old are you, Amir?"

"Twenty."

"Education?"

"I graduated the Gymnasium and did one year at Gaza University, before …"

"Languages?"

"Arabic, of course. A little Hebrew, some English."

"I'll have more tea, please," Jacob said to a passing waiter. "Yossi? Amir?" They each nodded affirmatively.

"You know, we've been talking and talking and talking —"

"No, uncle, *you've* been talking and talking and talking," Yossi said.

"Old people get that way. I apologize that I haven't even introduced myself. I'm Yossi's uncle, Jake … Jacob Baumueller. I own an interest in a small newspaper in Istanbul, Turkey. I was just thinking … we can always use two intelligent young workers at the newspaper. Many, many years ago, long before I was born, the founder of our little newspaper offered a job to a boy about your age. He was also a young man from a nameless village in Turkey. A lad with no future. His name was Turhan Türkoğlu …"

The End of Volume Four.

HUGO N. GERSTL COLLECTION

See below some of Pangæa Publishing Group's bestsellers by the same author:

Do not miss them on your shelf!

For Hugo N. Gerstl's complete novels list and descriptions,
go to www.HugoGerstl.com

Printed in Great Britain
by Amazon

64413828R00190